BreakupBabe

BreakupBabe

A NOVEL

Rebecca Agiewich

BALLANTINE BOOKS   NEW YORK

A Ballantine Books Trade Paperback Original

Copyright © 2006 by Rebecca Agiewich

Published in the United States by Ballantine Books, an imprint of The Random House Publishing Group, a division of Random House, Inc., New York.

BALLANTINE and colophon are registered trademarks of Random House, Inc.

ISBN 0-345-48400-2

Printed in the United States of America

www.ballantinebooks.com

1 2 3 4 5 6 7 8 9

Book design by Susan Turner

When I began this book, more than three years ago, the plan was to write a memoir. It was going to be about the disastrous breakup that launched my blog, Breakup Babe, and the ways in which Breakup Babe aided and abetted my dating life and renewed my confidence as a writer. The framework of this story, then, is based on real events.

As I was writing this story, however, I decided it needed a little more oomph. More drama! More excitement! More conflict! So I turned it into a novel and let my imagination recast characters and take the story to new places.

For example, the blog as it's portrayed in the novel is much more detailed and revelatory than was the real-life Breakup Babe. Perhaps this is part of the reason Rachel gets in a whole lot of trouble that, I, personally, never experienced, including heat from her employers. The antagonists who spur Rachel on are also much meaner than anyone I ever encountered in my own life.

I'll give this to Rachel, though: While she may be more impulsive and hot tempered than I, she also learned her lessons a lot faster than I ever did. But that's the beauty of fiction, isn't it? As a novelist, you get to take people and events from your own life and reinvent them to become bigger, brighter, badder, crazier, uglier, more daring, and much more fun to read about than they might have been otherwise. Or you can just totally make stuff up. I've done both in this book. The end result is a work of *fiction* that should in no way be confused with the real events or people in my life.

For Mom and Dad

Acknowledgments

Thank you to Erica Agiewich, Karen Baker, and Leslie Duss for reading my drafts and so much more (listening, comforting, advising, loving); Brooke Chapman for being the perfect writing partner; Byron Ricks for encouraging me to write way back when I was a lowly sheepskin slipper salesperson; Nick O'Connell for coaching me through the first chapters of this book; my managers for their flexibility (I swear I don't slack off as much in real life as the protagonist does in this book); and the readers of my blog, who made it come alive with their wildly entertaining comments and who heaped so much love on me that I was suddenly confident enough to write a book.

Thanks also to the Boyd-Woods family for feeding and sheltering me in times of need (which was always), and to Fredd Luongo and Gary Moore for all the adventures (on the town and out of it) when I wanted to have fun (which was always).

Finally, thanks to my agent, Elisabeth Weed, who made it all happen, and to my editor, Allison Dickens, who never once failed to answer questions, offer guidance, or reassure me when I needed it (which was always).

BreakupBabe

Chapter One

Sunday, August 11, 2002
12:58 PM Breakup Babe

Hello, my name is Breakup Babe. Tomorrow I get to go to my new job at a large Seattle software company, where my office is right down the hall from the man I thought I was going to marry, who just lied to me, cheated on me, and then dumped me on my f*cking a*s.

That was the paragraph that started it all. I had no idea that starting a free weblog called Breakup Babe would change my life. It was just something to do to keep me sane. But what I've learned in the last year is that things never turn out how you envision them. When your life cracks open, like mine did, you're messed up at first, and because of that, you do stupid things, but you also grow and change in ways you couldn't before. Then, suddenly, you're a lot closer to "happiness" than you were—even though "happiness" looks different now than it did when some creepy-crawly bastard broke your heart.

But let's start at the beginning, shall we?

When The Great Unpleasantness (as we shall henceforth call it) struck in June 2002, one of the first thoughts that hit me was *I want to start a blog about this*. A few friends of mine were bloggers, and articles predicting a "blogging revolution" had just begun to appear in places such as *Newsweek*. But I didn't want to revolutionize anything. I just wanted a place to vent.

Why I chose the Internet rather than writing in the diaries I'd been sighing and moaning in since age thirteen, I'm not sure. I'd been writing in semi-obscurity for years, being paid to write bland freelance pieces and slaving away on a book that sucked, though I could not yet pinpoint the reason for its suckiness. So I think I was just ready to be heard in my own voice—to write something that was not a fluffy newspaper travel article or a trying-too-hard book that I was afraid to show people anyway.

It was a hot August day when I sat down to type the first entry in the upstairs bedroom of my friends Jane and Henry's town house. I'd been "sleeping" there for the last month (if you could call my tortured, nightly horizontal sessions sleeping), ever since my once-so-devoted boyfriend had kicked me—begging and pleading for mercy—out of his waterfront home ("Lake Washington lapping at your backyard!" the listing had said) onto the streets of Seattle.

A month before that unceremonious event, when The Great Unpleasantness actually began, I'd set up a site on Blogger.com and toyed with blog names like "Relationship Hell" or "Breakup Girl." Eventually I'd settled on "Breakup Babe." But, amid the emotional turmoil of The Great Unpleasantness, I couldn't write about the actual breakup. I was too busy clinging to hope, even though my once-glorious relationship was pointing nose down into the water like the *Titanic*. So the blog remained empty. Now that the relationship had irrevocably sunk, however, writing seemed like my only means of survival. It was the life raft that would carry me away as grief tried to drown me.

But, as I sat down on that too-sunny Sunday, a dangerous wave of self-pity swept over me. If only Jane and Henry hadn't had to be their adventuresome selves and fly off to Iceland that very morning with their two toddlers in tow! I thought it would be comforting to be at their town house, even without them, but the place felt deserted. The room was stifling, as usual, and smelled of baby and detergent. Their stuff was scattered everywhere—baby clothes, outdoor gear, toys—but without the four of them, the place was even lonelier than my new apartment with its unpacked boxes.

I stared at the computer screen, willing myself not to collapse on the hard futon next to it, where I'd spent the last month weeping. Maybe, just maybe, once I started writing, the loneliness that was stalking me, that was poised to put its sweaty hands around my neck and throttle me, would slink back to its hole.

That was my state of mind as I wrote my debut entry for Breakup Babe. I was unaware of the momentous occasion at hand. All I wanted was to get through the day, and putting words on the screen was a way to pass the time at least. That first entry went on forever. All my pent-up emotions spewed forth without a thought for the attention span of my poor audience—whoever that might end up being (though they got into the action soon enough).

So a month ago I started my new job, at a company we shall call "Empire Corporation," in a godforsaken suburb of Seattle filled with strip malls and loathsome chain restaurants.

I had to admit, the bennies rocked. I might be giving up my identity as a free-spirited *artiste*, but look what I got in return. Money. And lots of it.

Before I left her office on the day I accepted the job, the perky blond human resources person, "Wendii," handed me an orange and green folder with the words "Welcome to Success!" splashed across the front. It described all my benefits and contained everything I needed to know to "succeed" at working for The Man (thirty-two-year-old Rodney Rolands, CEO and international playboy) and his great company. Except, of course, the truth. There should have been one more benefit entitled:

Build Your Character
Your adoring boyfriend of two years, whose group you just signed your life away to work in, will brutally dump you within one month of the time you start your job. You will therefore have the opportunity to work down the hall from the man who lied to you, cheated on you, and broke your heart. Look forward to being challenged both personally and careerwise in ways you never dreamed possible!

Even if it had been in the brochure, and Wendii had pointed it out to me, tapping on important words for emphasis with her pearly pink nails—"dump," "cheated," "challenged"—

I wouldn't have believed that retarded sorority-girl clone anyway. Who did she think she was? That was my man she was talking about, my almost-fiancé, my one true love! The one who told me, when we first started dating, that I brought "order to the universe"!

When I looked up from the screen and saw the time, I was shocked to see that forty-five minutes had passed. What a change from these last two months when every minute that passed threatened to crush me. I was writing, really writing, for the first time in months, and time was almost slipping away.

So, on my first day on the job, into Empire Corporation I marched, proud employee, to the office right down the hall from my beloved boyfriend's (let's call him Loser), who'd sworn to me that we would never part.

And what reason did I have to suspect him? We'd just returned from a stunning sojourn to Thailand. We'd spent two blissful weeks traveling together. After that, I'd spent two weeks traveling alone, resting easy in the knowledge that he would be waiting oh-so-devotedly for me at home.

Because Loser was, after all, devoted. Any of my friends could have told you that. His steady presence had even helped me to settle down and focus on my true life's work, my raison d'être, writing the next *Bridget Jones's Diary*. The book I'd been struggling with for three years would make me the darling of the publishing world, if I could ever get it finished. Now that I was swapping my unpredictable contractor's lifestyle for a steady paycheck, now that I would have both a stable domestic *and* work life, I would finally be able to write something of quality.

When I returned from Thailand, he showered me with love. Attention. Flowers at the airport. Though always attentive, he became over-the-top adoring. I was in Deluded Girlfriend Heaven.

While sunning ourselves on the Thai beaches or trekking through the hill towns, I would make idle chitchat with Loser. "Is it really such a good idea that I took a job in your group? What if we break up?" But it was just a formality. I knew what his answer would be. "Baby," he'd say in a sweet but slightly condescending tone, as if I were a five-year-old, "we're *not* going to break up."

Of course not, I would think smugly. WE are going to get MARRIED. Not that we were engaged. But we'd talked about marriage from the beginning. He was the One. Handsome. Jewish. Smart. (Loaded, too, but that was merely a pleasant perk.) We conversed about everything, laughed about lots of things, and best of all, he adored me. It was true that maybe we fought a bit too much, but conflict was a part of all relationships, right? He'd even broken up with his live-in girlfriend for me! And, God damn it, I was thirty-four years old! If we broke up . . . Hell, we weren't going to break up and that was that.

So imagine my surprise when one sunny June day, a month after I'd started my new job, life as I knew it ended in an instant.

When I next stopped typing and read what I'd written, my euphoria slipped away. All I could think was *God, how self-indulgent*. This stuff wasn't badly written. But wasn't it incredibly narcissistic for me to put it online and think anyone else would want to read it?

I was dripping sweat now, despite my tank top and shorts. (Air-conditioning does not exist in Seattle, because 95 percent of the time, we're wrapped in a 52-degree shroud of gray. But we *do* pay for it, when the hell fires burn, as they did this summer. My God, it was hot and sunny and all I wanted to do was crawl back into the cave of winter!) As I stared at the black words dancing on the white background, I felt the bottom start to slip out of the day again. Who was I kidding? I couldn't write worth shit. And why had I ever thought writing about Loser might make me feel *better*? But I had momentum, so I plunged back in, praying for this exorcism to work.

Besides, just because I was writing this crap didn't mean I had to post it. And what else was I going to do in that quiet, quiet town house on a summer day when the rest of Seattle was living out a sun-drenched Coke ad and I was a miserable, brokenhearted wretch?

We were out jogging around the well-manicured Empire grounds when it happened. We'd been jogging together since the early days of our friendship, when I was an Empire temp, he worked in the office across from me, and he was living with that psycho redheaded Scorpio I shall dub Astrology Chick.

We fell in love on those runs, and one May day, after I confessed my feelings to him, he broke up with Astrology Chick almost immediately ("F*cking Venus retrograde!" she'd cried out to the sky, before calling him every bad name she could think of and throwing his best pair of Kenneth Cole loafers in the hot tub).

"I can't turn down this opportunity to be with you," he'd said, looking at me over soggy pizza in the Building E23 cafeteria, his hazel eyes brimming with adoration. And instead of the big warning sign that should have been flashing in my head—"Danger! Danger! Don't Trust Men Who Leave Their Girlfriends in a Snap!"—there were only the words *"Destiny, destiny, destiny!"* blinking like a neon sign at some roadside dive.

And here we were, two years later, more in love than ever. Or so I thought. Until he said, on this sunny June day, while we were jogging on Rolands Drive, "I can't do this anymore."

"Okay, we can slow down," I said. We still had a mile left to go, and I didn't want to cut my workout short. (My figure had gotten away from me a bit during the last two years of domestic bliss.) Underneath us, the cars on Highway 520—also known as Highway to Hell by Empire's worker bees—were rushing east and west, not yet jammed together for the night.

"I want to break up." He stopped jogging.

The world warped for just a second. The trees got taller. The squat office buildings along Rolands Drive stretched out, and I was acutely aware of sweat pouring down my back. Then things snapped back to normal. He could not mean it.

"Are you serious?" My voice sounded high and quavery. Loser stared intently at the ground for what was probably five seconds, but seemed like an hour. I had stopped running now too, and watched him with a sense of detached terror, as if I were about to see the heroine in a thriller get pulled underwater by an enormous squidlike monster. Finally, he turned to look at me.

"Yes," he said. His hazel eyes looked wet. His sandy brown hair, normally moussed to a frothy peak above his forehead, lay flat and sweaty on his head. On his left cheek, a tiny scar glistened, the result of a freak childhood accident with his mother's curling iron. "I'm sorry."

I heard the cars rush by on 520, felt the sun on my back, and saw the Cascades gleaming in the distance. It was a beautiful summer day on the Puget Sound. There was no giant squid monster here. He was my beautiful boyfriend, the one I was going to marry. He couldn't take that away from me. Could he?

He could take it away and he did. But it was nothing like the quick, merciful death the bikini-clad heroine would have had in the jaws of the squid monster. If only I had agreed, right there, on Rolands Drive, to make my exit, it could have been almost graceful. But how was I to know, when I asked him if there was another woman, that he was lying when he said no? And so I did what any self-respecting woman would do. I groveled.

Something unexpected happened when I wrote this line. I laughed.

I looked around the empty room in embarrassment. Had I really just laughed? About being dumped in this incredibly painful way? Now *that* was a novelty. I turned my eyes back to the screen before I could lose momentum.

I spent a month crying, repenting, trying to atone for my "sins." Promising I could change, writing him anguished letters, giving him gifts, and hanging on each (increasingly rare) gesture of affection. He put me through hell, and all because HE was guilty.

For a month, I begged him to change his mind, and for a month he changed it on a daily basis. One day he'd be loving and kind, telling me how much he wanted to be with me. The next he'd be cold and distant, turning away from me at night and snubbing me at work functions.

I moved out of his house, where we'd lived together for a year, to give him "space." As he dangled the promise of togetherness before me, I scrambled for a couch to sleep on and spent my evenings writing him lovesick notes. If only I could make my prose eloquent enough, I thought, scribbling away at 2 A.M., maybe he would take me back.

When my friends pointed out that my once-loving Loser had been transformed into a hideous squid monster, I couldn't see it. I went from being a confident woman who stood up for herself in every situation to a sniveling, cringing wreck who would do anything to make her boyfriend want her again. I was making a stunning debut in the role of Doormat.

Then I found out the truth. Just like in the REO Speedwagon song, I heard it from a friend who heard it from a friend: Loser had cheated on me while I was in Thailand. Then the doormat was replaced by a raging bitch. At midnight on a Tuesday, I stormed unannounced into our home—his home—and demanded to know: Who was she?

One thing that I didn't write about here was my vague suspicion—completely paranoid, of course—that perhaps the *she* had been my boss (his boss too)! My boss's boss's boss to be exact. Theresa of the supermodel smile and supersize thighs, the deputy vice president of our unit. At age twenty-five!

I could tell Loser had a thing for her, even though he'd denied it. Who wouldn't? Besides being young and rich, she was the only other semi-attractive woman in the vicinity of our building besides me. Everyone else was a fat, balding, ponytailed developer in a bad tie-dye. Thank God she had a boyfriend (an underwear model, so it was rumored), a colossal butt, and no fashion sense. Because even if Loser did have a crush on her, she was taken. She'd even paraded her boyfriend around the halls just a month before, making sure all we girls had plenty of time to get an eyeful of his hot bod. This fact didn't stop me from feeling like roadkill under Loser and Theresa's tires.

Even if I did want to exorcise the thought by writing about it, I knew better than to make such accusations on the Internet (even though my audience was, currently, zero). Plus, it simply wasn't a possibility. What would a wealthy executive with an underwear-model boyfriend want with a less-wealthy tighty-whitey-wearing nobody like Loser?

Who? I screamed. *Who was it?! Who did you cheat on me with while I was gone?*

A friend of a friend! (But he had no friends!) *She was no one! Just a fling!*

Are you still seeing her?! Have you been cheating on me these last two months?

No! It was a fling!

Why would you ever do such a thing to me?!

I—I wanted out but I didn't know how to tell you.

Finally I saw it. Loser was a squid monster after all. He'd twisted his slimy tentacles of guilt and deception around my neck, all because he wasn't strong enough to break up with me like a man. After I'd hurled a few choice epithets at him, degraded his character in a voice loud enough for all the neighbors to hear, and almost broken down and hugged him because he looked so pathetic, I half stumbled, half ran out of the condo into the warm July night.

And just like that, it was over.

The courtyard was quiet when I at last looked up from the computer screen. The light outside had turned flat and gray. A bird chirped in the tree right outside the bedroom window, a single, lonely chirp that filled the air briefly and was met with silence.

I slumped on the desk, the wood cool against my forehead. I felt emptied out. I lay there for a minute, enjoying the complete lack of emotion. No loneliness. No anxiety. Nothing except relief. I had done it! I had beaten back the demons. For the afternoon anyway.

I lay there, trying in vain to hold on to my feeling of Zen calmness. Because now I had to decide what to do with this sprawling confessional. Post it? Delete it? Save the decision for later?

"When are you going to start your blog?" Lucy—soon to be known by her screen name, "GalPal #2"—had been asking me lately. "You'd be great at writing a blog!"

I played Lucy's words over in my mind for encouragement as I raised my head and fiddled with the settings on Blogger. What template to use? I tried several. How to make it so my name didn't appear? Enable comments? Sure, why not? After a half hour of experimentation, all that was left to do was click the "Publish" button. Then Breakup Babe would be live on the Web. First, however, I had to beat back the voices in my head.

This stuff is crap! And those friends of yours who know you as a "writer" but who've never actually read your stuff? They'll now be able to see what a phony you really are. No one is gonna read this.

That wasn't true, though! Lucy would read it! And Sylvia! Oh-so-loyal Sylvia (soon to be known as GalPal #1) who—while we were both in grad school at the University of Washington—had written an outraged letter to the editor of *U.W. Daily* when they terminated my year-old humor column, admonishing them: "Rachel Cooper is the best writer the *Daily* has EVER had!"

Fine. I would just do it. Then I would send the link to Sylvia and Lucy and that was it. Oh, and maybe my sister, Sarah, and Jane, too (soon to be known as Li'l Sis and GalPal #3, respectively). Before my upswing of courage could fail me, I stared at the "Publish" button and took a deep breath. It was like all those times I'd dialed the first six digits of a cute boy's phone number, and then let my finger hover, trembling, over the seventh.

Press it!

I'm scared!

Just do it.

I can't—

DO. IT.

So I pressed the button. And five seconds later, Breakup Babe was born. The site was pink and purple. And, like any baby, small, unformed, and poised to change my life forever.

But all I could think was *Oh my God, what have I done?*

What I had done, in fact, was set the recovery process in motion. On that August afternoon, however, all I cared about was that posting my first Breakup Babe entry had successfully eaten up three hours of my day. Three hours in which I had not cried or felt as if I were about to go insane with fear and loneliness.

The next day, I got my first inkling of things to come. Because there, in the Comments section, were two entries:

POST A COMMENT

Hey, back when we were kids, I got in trouble for reading your journal! Are you sure you won't try to hit me with the Wiffle bat now? Good entry!

Sarah

•   •   •   •   •

See, I told you you'd be great at writing a blog! Keep it up! It will give me something to read at work when I'm bored.

Lucy

These comments, innocuous as they were, elated me. Even when I'd written for major newspapers and glossy magazines, never had I gotten responses that quickly, that directly. I could only imagine the kind of thrill it would be to get comments from readers who weren't close friends and family members. It made me want to write more, just to keep them entertained. To keep the comments coming!

So began my addiction to blogging.

This addiction had its drawbacks. But it was only later, over the course of weeks, months, a year, during which I dropped twenty pounds, popped countless prescription drugs, and drowned my sorrows in men, men, and more men, that I realized just how liberating—and how risky—blogging could be.

Chapter Two

My new job is one that requires concentration, something I do not possess right now. My title is Technical Editor and my job is to edit "documentation" for programmers, scintillating prose along the lines of:

> The **ReadyCallBack** function supplies event notifications to the DirectoryServices container browser dialog box. A pointer to this function is sent to the container browser dialog box in the **regCallback** member of the SLPBROWSEINFO structure when the SearchForContainer function is called.

Do I understand programming? No. Do I care about programming? No? Did I lie about my "commitment to technology" in my job interview? Yes. But it's a job, it pays a lot of money, and the economy sucks. And I have finally admitted to myself that even an *artiste* needs to eat.

It wouldn't be so bad if I could just lock myself in my window-less office and pretend to understand what I'm doing. But now, as a full-time employee (as opposed to the carefree temp I once was), I have meetings every day. Team meetings, project meetings, face time, and morale boosters, which only serve to make my morale worse because I might see Loser there.

Two weeks after my first Breakup Babe entry, my addiction to blogging had taken root. I'd given the URL to several select girlfriends and to Peter (aka GuyPal #1), an honorary girl who swore that he would not give the location away to any males of his acquaintance, lest I one day want to date them. A "spiritual" type, as well as a would-be *artiste* himself, I figured GuyPal #1 would find the blog shallow and boring. But apparently not.

"You, my dear," he e-mailed me one day, in that pseudo-profound manner he was fond of, "are a Writer."

"I wish you would write every day!" said Lucy (aka GalPal #2).

"I check it first thing when I get into work!" said Sylvia (aka GalPal #1).

And so, because I was now feeling more like a Writer, and because my small but ardent audience encouraged me, I wrote. But their praise made me greedy. After all, there was a potential audience of millions out there! Theoretically, anyone with an Internet connection could read my blog—if they knew where it was, that is.

Each time I posted something new, the link showed up for a minute on the front page of Blogger, on its list of **Ten Most Recently Published Blogs**. But how likely was it that even one person would find it that way? Although I didn't want *certain* people to find it—Loser for one and my cowork-ers for another—I had enough confidence now that I wanted an audience that consisted of more than just my five best friends. What I really wanted was for Blogger to put it on its list of "Blogs of Note." Then people would find it for sure—because that link stayed up on the front page of Blogger for a couple weeks.

While I wondered how to make that happen, the good feedback from my friends cheered me up and motivated me to keep writing. My unfinished book lurked in the back of my mind. Maybe I should be working on that, instead of pouring all this creative energy into the blog. Five agents had expressed interest in my proposal for *Temporary Insanity*, a humorous look at the myriad jobs I'd had since college. Of course that was two years ago now.

After receiving my submission all those years ago, Georgina Owens, assistant to Vicky Roberts at the renowned Hedley Literistic, said, "We would love to see several sample chapters as soon as possible." They'd been so excited that they'd actually phoned me, so as to beat potential competitors to the punch. (Had I accidentally suggested somehow, in my proposal, that any part of my book was actually *written*? Oops.)

I'd *tried* to write the book. Thanks, in part, to the stability of my life with Loser, I became focused and disciplined. I wrote on a schedule. I beat down the voices that told me, "You suck; you can't write; why are you trying?" But two years and hundreds of thousands of words later, I didn't have a single good chapter I could send those deluded agents—no doubt still waiting with bated breath for my masterpiece.

I wanted to finish it. Turn it into a best seller. Realize the potential that all those agents saw in it. But *Temporary Insanity* would have to wait. Venting about my broken heart online, knowing I had an audience (however small), was too cathartic.

Today I started out the day feeling almost like a normal human being. I was about to go to our editors' meeting. I hadn't cried in two whole days. I was also wearing several new purchases to show off my ever-dwindling body (ten pounds bulldozed so far by the Heartbreak Diet!) including a slinky purple shirt from Anthropologie ($70) and a pair of form-fitting Banana Republic jeans ($75).

With a cup of coffee in hand, I rose from my desk in preparation to leave my office. Maybe I would even participate in our meeting today, instead of sitting in zombified silence like an escapee from *Night of the Living Dead*.

Then I made the big mistake. I opened my office door. And there he was, walking down the hall with a coworker, laughing. Laughing! Wearing an outfit I'd seen hundreds of times before on his lanky frame: black jeans and that tight white T-shirt that showed off to advantage those perfectly muscled arms—a product of regular workouts (or rather suck-up sessions) with his boss. Loser was a developer, but he longed to be an executive, and lost no opportunities to hobnob with higher-ups. His brown hair was moussed to within an inch of its life and he wore his usual pair of tiny wire-rimmed glasses (that I thought were pretentious before I fell in love with him, but that I now thought were the sexiest thing in the world).

He started to say something. All I heard were the words "Hey, don't you—" before I reeled backward into my office. The familiar yet now unfamiliar sound of his voice struck me like a hammer. I'd heard that voice say so many things. "You look so cute today!" "Would you do the dishes?" "I love you so much." Whining, in the most insincere tone I'd ever heard, "I'm sorry; I just wasn't getting what I needed from you."

I slammed the door. I teetered for a moment in my new strappy Nordstrom's sandals ($85), wondering what to do. Maybe I could still make it to my meeting? But now the thought of sitting in a windowless conference room debating parameter descriptions with a bunch of Empire-logowear-clad made my despair complete. And, suddenly, I could barely stand.

I dragged myself over to my desk and crawled underneath it. I sobbed under my desk for a full hour, certain that I would never make it to another meeting again. Certain that Security would find

me there and cart me off to the asylum, where I would live out the
rest of my life medicated to oblivion wearing only one of those butt-
less gowns. But at least I wouldn't have to run into Loser laughing in
the halls.

E-mail Breakup Babe | Comments 1

POST A COMMENT
I'm sorry, but Loser *is* pretentious. We never told you this, but M.
and I used to call him "Dieter" behind his back—remember the Mike
Myers character from *Saturday Night Live* who wore all black and
talked in a fake German accent? That's who he reminded us of. You
can do so much better—and you will!
Li'l Sis

This particular under-the-desk episode occurred before
my antidepressants truly kicked in. In a preemptive strike, I'd
gone to see my drug-dispensing shrink, Dr. Melville (not to be
confused with my therapist, Jade, she of the pink office and
the tie-dyed mumus), the day after the running episode, to get
a prescription should Loser and I break up. I hoped I wouldn't
need them, of course, but I'd learned my lesson five years ago,
when my father died.

Back then I was so scared of taking antidepressants (oh,
sweet, innocent, young me!) that it wasn't until I'd become an
obsessive-compulsive insomniac who couldn't leave my apartment until the items on every surface were precisely "cen-
tered" that I finally took the advice of my mental health team:
drugs. I became an instant convert. Hail Celexa, the holy pink
pill!

This time I needed no convincing to hop on the little pink
pill bandwagon. I'd gone off Celexa when Loser and I started
dating. I filled my newest prescription the day after the Con-
frontation in the Condo. And though I could hardly believe it
would help me face the void that had suddenly opened up
around me, it did. Slowly but surely.

Sunday, August 25, 2002

1:37 PM Breakup Babe

Lest you think all I do is moan and sob, I will tell you that I went on my first date since the breakup last night. Yes! I had a great time at a big, sensational party. Unfortunately, I went to this party with Bad-News Boy. I KNOW! I swore up and down I wouldn't do it, and really I didn't do anything except let myself be hugged and touched and made to feel generally desirable.

BadNews Boy is an ex-fling of mine. A blast from the past of my carefree temp days. During those first heady years of the tech boom, while Empire poured its plentiful cash into multimedia ventures and staffed them with artsy young temps, I interspersed temp jobs at Empire with more glamorous jobs (like writing for adventure travel webzines). I had cash in my pocket for the first time ever. I morphed from a sensible grad school drone into a short-skirt-and-chunky-heels-wearing flirt. To complete my image, I slept with cute temp boys left and right. Including BadNews Boy. Who burned me in the end—as they all did—because I always fell for them and they always ran away.

It was a hungover Sunday morning when I dragged my laptop to my favorite Capitol Hill coffee shop to write this entry. When I'd been jettisoned from Loser's lakeside bunga-low, away from his lily-white executive neighbors, I'd landed on upper Capitol Hill, on an elegant street lined with 1920s apartment buildings. The Hill was filled with gays, artists, grunge-era holdovers, and a healthy dose of hipster yuppies like me. There were even (gasp!) a few people of color (at least where I lived, which bordered the more southerly Central District, Seattle's squeaky-clean version of a slum).

I'd jumped out of bed that morning as fast as my swollen head would allow. Mornings were the worst. When I slept I could forget (except when the nightmares came). When I woke up I had to remember all over again, and the knowledge rolled like a boulder onto my chest. *He's gone.* If I didn't get up right away, the boulder would crush me.

Just after the breakup, I'd been waking early, 4:30, 5. The boulder would fall into place and I'd lie there, pinned to my bed, surveying the yawning chasm of the day. How would I fill all those hours? If only I could sleep till noon—or later! "Early waking," muttered Dr. Melville, as he'd written up my prescription for Celexa. "That will go away when the drugs kick in." How I loved Dr. Melville.

Today I'd slept until the insanely late hour of 8:30. Then again, I'd been up until 4:00. When I woke up, the sun was streaming in through the blinds, making the hardwood floor glow. But I was in no mood to appreciate the "old-world charm" of my new apartment, so different from Loser's sleek new house. I had to get out. *Immediately.*

Now here I was at Victrola, the coffeehouse with the best people watching in Seattle. It was filled, as usual, with dyed hair. Hipster band T-shirts. Funky glasses. The 80-year-old piano player who banged out tunes on Sunday afternoons in magenta knickers and a feathered cap. The fiftysomething guy with lank, gray hair to his shoulders, always reading some obscure poetry book and looking not-so-furtively around at all the hot, tattooed chicks with streaked hair and fashionable shoes.

I was slugging down a double Americano, feeling the boulder roll slowly off me the more caffeine I imbibed and the more I wrote. Safely away from my bed, I also felt a kind of hungover dreaminess about the night before. *I'd been on a date!* I tried, however, to write about it in the most cynical way possible. After all, this was BadNews Boy, and this certainly wasn't going anywhere. (Was it?)

But recently BadNews Boy started temping at Empire again and I asked him to lunch. After all, six years was a long time ago. I was over it. All I wanted was some cute male companionship as my relationship exploded in a burst of slow-motion fireworks.

Soon the lunches became more frequent and soon BadNews Boy was hinting around at more dangerous activities. "Doing anything fun this weekend?" he'd say in that languorous, blasé tone of his, with just a hint of eagerness beneath the smoke-tinged surface.

"Resist," said Sensible Girl one Friday afternoon, startling me. I had no idea she was still around. It had been two years since her voice had popped into my head. Two years since I'd wanted to do anything not sensible, at least in the realm of men—so I figured she'd gone off to torture someone else. I hadn't presented her with much of a challenge lately. "Resist," she said, pushing her big, unfashionable glasses up on her nose. "He's no good."

And so I did. For about three weeks.

And then one sultry Friday, as BadNews Boy and I sprawled on the grass in front of one of Empire's many cafeterias, I invited him out to a party with me and GalPal #2 that weekend. Sensible Girl piped up immediately.

"Why are you doing this to yourself? You're going to get hurt!"

Then came another voice I never even knew existed. It was high-pitched and excitable. "Leave her alone!" said Needy Girl. "They're just friends! Besides, doesn't she deserve a little fun?"

Wearing a hot pink minidress with thigh-high white go-go boots that must have been murder in the heat, Needy Girl put her hands on her hips and glared at Sensible Girl. Sensible Girl, who had on a baggy T-shirt and unflattering khaki shorts, must have been intimidated by the newcomer's outfit, because she glared back but didn't say another thing.

Oblivious to the battle of wills occurring right before him, Bad-News Boy accepted my invitation. His long, lean body snaked along the ground, dangerously close to mine. I'd forgotten how sexy his smile was. "Sounds like fun."

I reread what I'd written, wondering where in the world Sensible Girl and Needy Girl had come from. The unexpected depths of my imagination, apparently! It had been so long since I'd let my imagination just go to town.

A year ago, when I'd begun to realize that even stability with Loser didn't seem to be helping my book-writing skills, I decided to take a new tack. I put *Temporary Insanity* on hiatus. I would try to hit it big in the travel writing world. After all, I was already a "travel writer." I'd published numerous travel articles for the *Seattle Post-Intelligencer*. I'd been the editor for a once-glamorous, now-defunct travel webzine called *The Outpost*. I'd written cover stories for *Horizon Air Magazine*!

So, six months before my trip to Thailand with Loser, I'd cranked out query letter after formulaic query letter. "Spa vacations in Phuket!" "Stay Alive Eating Street Food in Bangkok!" To *Outside* magazine. *National Geographic Adventure. Travel and Leisure.* I didn't get anywhere, of course, except to a place of complete creative bankruptcy. I devolved into a writer who could write only unsuccessful query letters.

So as I sat there in Victrola, with characters popping unbidden out of my head, I felt as if I'd gotten something back again. *My creativity.*

Suddenly I remembered the whale dream. A week before Loser and I broke up, I dreamt that we were having one of our tortured pre-breakup discussions in a dinghy in the middle of the ocean. He was telling me yet again—in that new, cold tone of his—that he wanted to break up with me. That he didn't "see how it could work" anymore. Just as I was about to accept that Loser was dumping me for good, a whale surfaced near us, about ten times bigger than life-size. I was so thrilled and terrified at the same time, I practically fell into the water. I woke up balancing on the boat, watching the whale slide beneath the waves.

And after a profound $90 discussion with my therapist, Jade, I determined it meant this: Something creative was going to come out of this breakup. It *had* to. Otherwise, this pain was going to sit on my chest and crush me.

I hadn't thought about that dream in a while. In all the ensuing turmoil, I'd forgotten it. Now that I remembered it, a flicker of excitement stirred in my stomach. A shadow of the same thrill I'd felt in the dream. It felt—just a little—like this blog could be the start of that "something." I sipped my coffee and got back to it.

It was fun, all right. At 3 A.M., we spilled out of the party into the August night with a crowd of laughing, drunken people. My ears were ringing with DJ Krush. My head was spinning with the electric blue punch I'd been drinking for three hours straight, and I felt like I'd rejoined the human race.

But when BadNews Boy—who'd been touching and flirting with me all night long—draped his arm around me, put his stubbly cheek against mine, and said, in my by now half-deaf ear, "Can I walk you home?" my whole body tensed like that of a dog that's just heard a set of unfamiliar footsteps approaching the door.

Sensible Girl appeared immediately, her hair flying this way and that. She was wearing an ankle-length cotton nightgown covered with pink flowers. "Watch it," she barked at me.

"Jesus Christ, give the girl a break, would you?" Needy Girl tottered up to us in spike-heeled sandals, her little gold cocktail number swishing midthigh. From the looks of her, she'd been drinking too. "He's just putting his arm around her. What's the harm in that?"

I melted instinctively into BadNews Boy's embrace. So what if the feeling of "love" and "protection" it offered was a sham? I was like a scarlet tulip bursting into bloom after months of subterranean dwelling and saying, "Let's partay!" I wanted nothing more than to stay glued to BadNews Boy's body for the rest of the night. The rest of my life.

"Damn it!" Sensible Girl was furious now. She'd stalked up to Needy Girl and yelled in her face. "You know he wants to sleep with her! And that if she lets him walk her home, she's going to invite him in!" Needy Girl looked startled but held her ground. "And, yeah, it might feel good tonight, but how's she going to feel tomorrow if she sleeps with him? Any little crumbs of self-esteem she's managed to gather together in the last month will get instantly blown away!"

As I paused in my typing and let my eyes wander over Victrola's other patrons—the woman with a hot pink shawl and a fluffy white dog, the gorgeous olive-skinned dad with his angelic daughter—I felt a tinge of apprehension about what I'd just written. Should I really cross this line—I took a quick, embarrassed gulp of my coffee, as if Hottie Dad could read my thoughts—into *sex*?

I'd never written about my sex life for public consumption before! Hell, *Temporary Insanity* didn't even have a make-out scene in it!

Heartbreak was a safer topic. No one could judge me for getting my heart broken.

Then again, I thought, downing the last of my coffee, which was sugary and cold by now—who was going to judge me? It was mainly my best girlfriends reading this and they knew all about what had happened anyway. Why not write it up for their entertainment? In all likelihood, no one else would ever read it. Plus, you couldn't exactly call what happened last night "sex."

"Hey, we're going to IHOP, wanna come?" said GalPal #2, holding the hand of her husband, B., who towered over her five-foot two-inch pixielike frame. Her short blond hair was tousled, her voice animated from a rare night of drinking. GalPal #2 wore a maroon tube top that we'd shopped for together the other day at Banana Republic. Despite her hemp-clothed girlhood on an organic farm in Eugene, Oregon—or maybe because of it—GalPal #2 tolerated the occasional indulgence in corporate consumerism, though not without beating herself up afterward. ("I'm going to make all my own clothes after this!" she'd say. And she would. For about a month.)

BadNews Boy paused and looked unsure. Sensible Girl and Needy Girl glared at each other. For a moment, the night was still, with only the sounds of distant I-5 in the background. Then a burst of drunken female laughter pierced the air. It must have startled Needy Girl, because one of her stilettos buckled and she nearly fell to the ground.

"Yeah!" I said to GalPal #2, almost hugging her in gratitude. I was half hoping BadNews Boy would come along, half hoping he would decline and leave before I lost any shred of willpower I might possess.

Needy Girl scrambled back up, her face red, watching BadNews Boy intently. Sensible Girl closed her eyes and grimaced.

"I think I'll pass on that," said BadNews Boy, though the cloud that passed over his face indicated that he was going through his own tug-of-war. His arm was still around me. He smelled of cigarettes and alcohol, a delicious and dangerous nighttime smell. I breathed it in deeply, and then breathed it out, trying to expel it from my body.

A few blocks later we went our separate ways. "Okay," I said as I turned to hug him, "I'll see you later." I felt the hardness of his chest against mine. The way his six-foot frame felt so strong as he embraced me and kissed me on the cheek. I hadn't felt a male body against mine in two months. Needy Girl let out a little moan.

"Bye, R.," he said. And he turned left to go up Madison, while I turned right. GalPal #2 and B. were walking ahead, still holding hands. I breathed in the warm night air, and Sensible Girl sighed in relief.

"Good job," she whispered in a ragged voice that wasn't quite relaxed. As if she knew this was only the beginning of a stint of hard labor, perhaps the hardest she'd ever faced.

As we walked toward IHOP, I was breathing fast and hard. Just three years ago, I would have let BadNews Boy—or someone like him—walk me home. I would have invited him in. Slept with him and then regretted it, because, of course, I would have ended up getting hurt.

As I gazed off into the distance, trying to decide how to end the entry, someone tapped me on the shoulder. I was so startled, I nearly jumped out of my seat. My first thought was "It's BadNews Boy!" who lived, inconveniently, in the neighborhood. "What if he sees this?!" In the world's most unsubtle move, I lowered the screen of my laptop so that Breakup Babe was not so glaringly visible, and looked up.

But in fact, it was only Victrola's cutest barista, the black-haired one with the orange-framed glasses. Had he just come in? I hadn't noticed him earlier. He was smiling at me and pointing to my plate, which had sandwich crumbs on it.

"Are you done with this?"

"Oh—yeah," I said, my heart pounding so hard from my initial fright that I could hardly hear myself speak. "Great," he said, taking my plate away, then smiling at me again before he walked to the next table.

Jesus, what was I so damn jumpy about? It wasn't even like I'd said anything that *bad* about BadNews Boy, or anything that embarrassing about my feelings for him.

Heart still pounding in my ears, I scanned the café for him. Loser. Anyone. But all I saw was the regular yet ever-changing crowd of hipsters, couples, and intellectuals. When I finally returned to my computer, my fingers were trembling slightly as I typed.

I watched GalPal #2 and B. ahead of me and thought about what I had just done. Maybe, just maybe, I was stronger than I had been before. At least on this one particular affection-starved Saturday night. But if BadNews Boy had come along to IHOP? And then walked me home?

The door to the restaurant swung open, and I was engulfed in the aroma of maple syrup. I took a deep breath. I didn't need to worry about that. Who knew what might happen with BadNews Boy in the future? All that mattered was that I was safe for the moment.

E-mail Breakup Babe | Comments 1

POST A COMMENT
Who is this BadNews Boy? Have we met him? I knew we should never have let you move out.

Worried About You | 8/25/02—2:17 P.M.

Chapter Three

I'd been at work for a full thirty seconds on Monday before I knew it was going to be one of those days. For the most part, life at work had gotten better thanks to the holy pink pill. Fewer crying fits. Fewer urges to run to Loser's office and beg him to take me back, tearing my clothes off for extra added encouragement. But there were always the days that grief blindsided me, and this, apparently, was one of them.

No sooner had I turned on my computer than I felt the slimy tentacles of despair reaching up my back. Going for my neck, where they would paralyze me. Making me unable to work, yet unable to go home and face my utter aloneness. I knew that within an hour, when my morning caffeine high had worn off, I'd be on the phone with GalPal #1 or #2, blubbering "I c-c-can't work down the hall from h-h-him anymore!" Sob, gulp, cough.

As if that weren't enough, I was now in the disagreeable

position of waiting to hear from BadNews Boy. Ye Olde Unreliable. Who, in the old days, had ignored my calls and e-mails until he was good and ready to answer them (i.e., when he was horny). Not that I *wanted* to have lunch with him. Or sleep with him! No! I would *not* get myself into a "situation" with him again! It's just, I wanted . . . oh God. I just wanted him to want me. To keep making me feel good the way he had on Saturday night, without any ramifications. *Ha.*

Grimly I turned my computer on. One minute of my workday down, 479 to go. Before entering my office, I'd caught a glimpse of my colleague Thomas next door, typing away. He appeared to be working on one of the novel-length e-mails that he was famous for. In each one, he went into dazzling detail about minute stylistic inconsistencies in our documentation and proposed sensible solutions, that were then ignored because no one could ever read that far. I knew, from our brief weeklong stint as officemates, that he arrived every day at precisely 9 A.M. and left at 5:30 P.M. He took a half hour lunch at his desk at 12:30, eating a peanut butter sandwich on oat bran bread, an apple, and a rice cake. His life seemed so predictable. So free of *drama.* Typing away with that solid gold band on his left hand to anchor him down. Oh, how I wanted that life right now!

When my computer came to life, I clicked over to my blog. It was now the first thing that I did every morning. More than my e-mail, it was likely to yield satisfying personal results. Today, I knew, I would scan my e-mail for a message from BadNews Boy, and there would be none. Instead there would be a backlog of e-mails with subject lines like: **Schema Changes: Parameters now render as italics.** I could put that inevitable disappointment off for a few minutes. At least on Breakup Babe, Jane could usually be counted on to leave a witty comment.

There, indeed, was a comment from Jane, and:

You need time to recover from the breakup. I recommend taking time just for yourself—to regroup and figure out what you want and need in the future. I sent you an e-mail about this; check your account.
Juliana | Homepage | 8/25/02—5:02 P.M.

Juliana? Who in the world was Juliana? I raised my head, which I'd been resting in my hands, barely able to support the weight of it. A second ago, all I'd wanted to do was lay it down on my desk and close my eyes. But suddenly I was completely alert. As Juliana instructed in her message, I checked my Breakup Babe e-mail account, which so far had received a grand total of three messages—from GalPals #1, #2, and #3—in the month since its inception. I had set up the e-mail account when I started my blog, just because it seemed like the thing to do. All the other bloggers I'd read had e-mail accounts to go with their blogs, so what the hell. I never expected people to actually send mail to it!

From: *Juliana Stamford*
To: *Breakup Babe*
Date: *August 25, 2002*
Subject: *You Are Me*

Hi, Breakup Babe,

When I was in my twenties, I was just like you.
Though it was fun at times, I would never go back there!
I think you should do what I did. Go ahead and date, but make sure you keep a list. List the red flags you find, and when you get to five, dump him. Because if there are five things that concern you within a short period of time, there's a lot more where they came from.
Within a year of when I started keeping track this way, I met my

husband. Because I stopped depending on the potential of a man and started to look at reality.

I have linked to you from my blog, Big Bad Swede.

Juliana
http://bigbadswede.blogspot.com

"Oh my God!" I mouthed, staring at the screen. "Oh my God!" I had a fan! My mind reeled. *How had she found my site?* The only possible way was through the front page of Blogger. Every time you updated your blog, the name appeared for about a minute on the front page. She would have had to click on it at exactly the right time.

I got up from my chair and did a little jig around the office. My troubles were, for the moment, completely gone. *I had spoken to someone out there in the big, wide world. My writing spoke to someone.*

I didn't think much right then about the advice that Juliana had given me, or about the odd fact that this complete stranger had given me advice at all. All I could think was *she liked me*! Even if it was just one person, her e-mail made me feel completely justified for baring myself online. Someone enjoyed it! Someone related to it! I was a writer!

Monday, August 26, 2002
3:14 PM Breakup Babe

Today was a big day here in Breakup Babe Land, thanks to Juliana. Her e-mail was the first thing that helped me survive this Monday, which promised to be A Very Bad Day.

I woke up this morning drenched in sadness. Last night I dreamt that Loser was caught in the crossfire of a gunfight downtown. As he lay there bleeding to death on Pike Street, I threw myself over his body (ruining an $80 Anthropologie blouse in the process) and screamed, "No! No!" But of course he died anyway, the bastard, without any parting words for me other than a death rattle.

Plus, any ridiculous illusions I may have had about Saturday night are gone. GONE, do you hear me? Believe me, I've fantasized repeatedly about those two shimmering, innocent hours at the party when BadNews Boy made me feel like a human being for the first time in two months. Now if only it could *stay* like that. If only he and I could go out occasionally and flirt and fondle while the lights flash and the music plays, and I could feel good and warm and forgetful; then we could go our separate ways and the night would just vaporize into pleasant memories.

But that's not reality, see? If I see him again, I will sleep with him, and he will screw me literally and figuratively, and we'll be even worse off than we are now, which is hard to imagine, but possible. Believe me.

So thank you to Juliana for helping me avoid another under-the-desk crying jag today! Juliana is an outspoken and happily married blonde of Swedish descent who wrote to give me her hard-won advice about dating. She is also the first reader of my blog to whom I did not give the URL. After writing back to her, I discovered that she'd found my site through the front page of Blogger, when it appeared for a whole sixty seconds after I'd refreshed it yesterday.

Not only did Juliana take the time to send me good, practical advice, she also posted a link to my blog on hers. So I did the same. Because I discovered, after a day exploring blogs (instead of doing the ridiculously boring work I was actually *supposed* to be doing), that that is what you *do* in the blogosphere. You link to your friends, and they link to you, and everyone becomes like one big happy family.

Meanwhile, no e-mail from BadNews Boy today. Are we surprised? No, we are not. Do we care? No, we do . . . NOT.

No, not at all. Really.

E-mail Breakup Babe | Comments 1

POST A COMMENT

You're welcome! It's always exciting to discover a blog as well written as yours. And stay away from BadNews Boy if you can. Remember, you are starting with a clean slate now. Try to go forward instead of back.

Juliana | Homepage | 8/28/05—9:45 A.M.

Chapter Four

Friday, August 30, 2002

9:03 AM Breakup Babe

My little sister is getting married this weekend in San Francisco. Everyone in my family, naturally, is worried about how I'm going to handle it. My mom keeps warning me: "I'm going to be stressed out; I'm going to miss your father and I need you to be there for me." Subtext: Don't have a breakdown, young lady, or you will forever cement your reputation as the unreliable, self-centered one of the family.

I performed poorly at the wedding shower. Not that I could be expected to do otherwise. By law, dumpees in their mid-thirties should not have to attend wedding showers. But the principle rule of my family is guilt. Do this for us or you will forever be branded The Bad Sister or The Bad Daughter. I'm already The Flake, The Airhead, The Bad Driver, The One Who Couldn't Deal with Dad Being Sick, so I can't afford to falter.

Thus, one and a half months after breaking up with Loser, I had flown down to the Bay Area suburbs to participate in that torture ritual known as the bridal shower.

First of all, what kind of a party can you have without men? Especially for those in attendance who are horny, desperate, or recently dumped, what kind of fun is it to have the concept of wedded bliss shoved in your face?

Please, at least allow (or hire!) a few good-looking males to come and circulate so we don't have to die of boredom from all the cutesy stories about marriage and watching the bride-to-be open gift after gift of expensive lingerie. Hell, *she's* not the one who needs all that booty; it's us, the ones who are actually out there on the front lines fighting one another for the ever-dwindling pool of hot, emotionally available, gainfully employed men! And besides, Bridey has two salaries to draw from—let her buy her own f*cking lingerie!

So, not only should there be attractive men circulating, they should be showering us single girls with lacy Victoria's Secret outfits, and offers to help us take them off later. Then, while the rest of the gals are playing games like "Bridal Bingo" or "How Well Do You Know the Bride?" (just two of the "kah-razy" competitions at Li'l Sis's shower), all to win some girly prize like a lavender sachet for your underwear drawer that will lose its scent in exactly one week, the single girls will be off in the back f*cking the hot guys, being made to feel like warrior princesses rather than loser old maids. Everyone wins!

My sister's shower, needless to say, did not follow this format. There was much sitting around, much playing of stupid games, much tittering about lingerie, much inane chatter, and absolutely no men. After about an hour and a half of displaying a fake smile, I disappeared into my old room, where I lay immobile in the dark for the next several hours, unable to cry, unable to do much of anything except lie there in a vegetative state.

I was, however, able to unleash a well-timed torrent of tears for my mother's entrance into the room.

"Well, that was a great performance!" she said, storming in with her hands on her hips. I inherited my mom's flashing smile, her big brown eyes, and her fair skin, now lined but still youthful for her age. Hopefully I will not inherit her middle-aged penchant for flowing red-and-gold tunics of the kind she had on now.

Unbidden, the tears came to my eyes. I realized, suddenly, how hard I'd been working these last two months to keep things together. I'd had to go to work every single day and perform in a new job—with Loser right down the hall! I'd had to move, always one of life's most stressful events even when you *wanted* to do it! I'd been functioning at such a high level when all I wanted to do was break down. Or lie down. In a place that was not surrounded by memories of him. Like home. Where no one would betray me, no matter what.

"I'm sorry, but I th-thought home was the one p-p-lace I could just let myself go!" I cried, erupting into sobs. Our dog, Barney, nosed his way into the room, and put his big, blond head down heavily on my chest and gazed at me with liquid brown eyes, his eyebrows twitching in the way of golden retrievers, as though they're puzzling to understand something. This made me cry harder.

My mother, ultimately, forgave me. So did Li'l Sis, who even came to lie on the bed with me as she did when we were little and scared of something in the night. Back then, we looked almost identical except for the wavy golden brown locks that flowed, like Farrah Fawcett's, down her back in contrast to my straight black pigtails. She later shot past me in height to become tall and statuesque, and she was casually yet fashionably attired in a way that befits a Silicon Valley success story. (The start-up she worked at had recently been bought by Yahoo! for loads of cash—a fact that usually inspired more pride in me than jealousy.) When she lay down next to me, she confessed that she had a headache and was glad the shower was over. "If I give you some of that lingerie, will it make you feel better?" she asked.

The wedding, however, is to be a different story; I need to be on: charming and friendly, supportive and helpful, and—most important—happy. I have serious doubts whether this is possible.

I'd gotten so addicted to writing my blog that I'd lugged my laptop to Sea-Tac Airport with me so I could use the free wireless access and write while waiting for my flight. (Writing while in the air was out of the question since one moment's inattention on my part would cause the plane to plummet to earth. Perhaps the laptop would survive me if the plane crashed somewhere over the Cascades. They'd find my last Breakup Babe entry—the one that I never got to post—and publish it posthumously. Perhaps my blog would gain a cult following after my death!)

After the startling e-mail from Juliana, I started to wonder how many people might be reading my blog. I knew I had at least a small following because I'd installed a "hit counter," a little tool that told me how many readers per day I had (twenty!), and which website had "referred" them (meaning where they'd found a link to Breakup Babe). And I couldn't help checking the damn hit counter at least three times a day. *Have my numbers gone up yet?*

They were going up, but oh, so slowly. It was all thanks to Juliana, too. Regular readers of Juliana's site clicked on her link to Breakup Babe. Then they put links to Breakup Babe on *their* sites. Now there were links to my site on at least five other blogs, including Suburban Sex Kitten, Knut's Corner, and Tales of a Two-Bit Housewife. I dutifully linked back.

Delilah, aka the Suburban Sex Kitten, had the most interesting blog, since she wrote about her numerous torrid affairs with biker dudes and other bad boys. She'd written me an e-mail when she discovered my blog:

Dear Breakup Babe,

   We are like the yin and the yang. The sense of heartbroken longing in your blog is refreshing in a strange way. Like what my blog would be like if I hadn't hardened my heart a long time ago.

Anyway, keep writing—your blog reminds me of the innocent soul
that's buried inside me somewhere. . . .

—Delilah

It was, of course, a thrill to get this e-mail—only my second from a Breakup Babe fan—and I wrote back promptly, telling Delilah how much I "enjoyed" her blog as well. It was true, at least, that her enthusiastic, if unpoetic descriptions of sexual acts ("I'd been staring at the bulge in his pants all night long, wondering if it could possibly be as big as it seemed, and when he finally pulled it out—oh my fucking God!") helped free my own inhibitions. If not quite yet, then down the road, when the boudoir began to figure more prominently in Breakup Babe.

I knew I could garner more hits by leaving more comments on other people's blogs with a link to Breakup Babe. I was too impatient for that, though, mostly because the majority of blogs I came across were boring as hell. I wasn't even inspired enough to read a whole entry, much less leave a comment just so someone would check out my site. Besides, I really needed to curb my growing addiction to hits. I'd been reading an essay in a book called *Blogger Nation* that advised bloggers to ignore the number of hits they got. "There will always be people who get exponentially more traffic to their site, for whatever reason—deserved or not," said the essay. Another essay in the book confirmed this by informing me of the presence of "A-list bloggers." A-list?! I didn't like to think of what that made *me*. The A-listers got thousands of hits per day, and if they happened to link to you—thus anointing you with their A-list holy water—you, too, would get thousands of hits a day and join the Inner Circle.

Hmmph.

I'd checked out one such blog: Sean O'Reilly, one of the

founders of JournalLand (a competitor to Blogger) had an A-list blog. But it was boring! Yes, I could concede his celebrity, of course. JournalLand founder, mover and shaker in the high-tech world. If anyone's blog deserved lots of hits, it was his (not that he'd *invented* blogs, but he had helped make blogging available to the masses). He didn't write about his personal life, but instead about the high-tech world, with bits of high-tech news and links to other sites on the Web. Snooze. Yet he got upwards of 10,000 hits a day!

But *Blogger Nation* was right. I just couldn't worry about the popularity of other people's blogs, or I would regress to a high schoolesque state of insecurity. I needed to do what made me feel best, and that was write.

On the highly dubious assumption that I survive my soon-departing flight to San Francisco, there are a few things working in my favor for this wedding.

One, the drugs. The drugs perform. Some days at work, with my door closed, I can almost forget that the man who lied to me, cheated on me, and broke my heart is working only a few feet away. And for each workday that I manage to get through without a nervous collapse, I offer up a prayer of thanks: *Thank you, Lord, for inventing Celexa!*

Two, the dress. After the first round of dress shopping, wherein everything I tried on made me look like Mrs. Potato Head, I found a clingy black silk dress adorned with a fringe of hot pink appliqué roses and finished off with a flamenco dancer's hem. This dress looks like it was made for my body. And post-breakup, I have magically become a size 6. *Size 6!* I want to tell people. To point at myself! *Did you know I'm a size 6 now?*

Finally, a date.

A date, you say? You have a date for the wedding?? Is it Bad-News Boy?!

WHO? Oh, *that guy*. The one who showed up two hours late for our second outing, where he then proceeded to flirt with GalPal #2's cute cousin for the rest of the evening? Since he wasn't even horny enough to exert the minimal effort required to get me into bed, that would be a big NO.

We are talking, instead, about my on-again, off-again, friend and lover Longtime Lover Boy (LTLB). He got a crush on me when we were fifteen and cooking partners in Home Ec, sweating over Beef Stroganoff (we got a B+ on it, cheated out of an "A" by a faulty salt shaker). Back then, I thought he was too "nerdy" (as if I were any paragon of high school hip myself)! But now he's a gourmet chef, gorgeous actor, and talented comedian, and I would be his girl-friend in an instant if he asked. Hell, I would marry him.

"Welcome to Flight 1203, with nonstop service from Seat-tle to San Francisco. We're about to begin preboarding . . ."

Shit. Why, oh, why did I have to fly so much? Why couldn't my stupid family just move up to Seattle? They were going to drown in guilt for forcing me to come to this wedding when my plane went nose down into Mount Rainier!

I grabbed my backpack from under my seat. It rattled loudly, filled as it was with my meds. Time for a Xanax. Xanax was the third musketeer in my triumvirate of Happy Pills. Celexa kept me sane, Trazodone helped me sleep, and the Xanax was reserved for when I really was fucking freaked out. The toddler seated two seats away from me looked over in interest at my rattling backpack. I gave him an apologetic smile. *No, baby, it's not a toy for you! This is* survival gear. I turned my attention back to my laptop; five more minutes to complete Breakup Babe's final masterpiece.

We hooked up for the first time right after college; I got my hopes up, then he pulled away. It happened again. Then, yet again. The first couple of times it pissed me off. Then I tried to stop wanting more from him and accepted things for what they were: Friends Plus.

Besides, he lives in Los Angeles and has no desire to move. I would never live in L.A. either, except under pain of death and maybe not even then, since it would be equivalent to death but with traffic jams. LTLB, though, is perennially single and usually good for a little romance when I most need it.

Ever since the breakup, I've been fantasizing about him, hoping he would come to the wedding with me, hoping this would be one of our on-again times, because, Lord knows, I need some action.

And can I help it if maybe I want a little more, too? Is there a possibility—even a remote one—that LTLB will come to his senses and decide to try this relationship thing? Swayed, perhaps, by the romance of my sister's wedding? We could have a long-distance marriage; I know it would work!

Because, you know, it would be really nice to just get this all over with. To not have to go through the whole dating routine again. The roller coaster! The wondering, waiting, worrying—will he call, should I have s*x with him, where is this going, what does this mean? Oh my God, the thought makes me so *tired*.

"We will now begin general boarding of Flight 1203, with nonstop service from Seattle to San Francisco . . ."

Now I'm off to board my flight. My only consolation, since I know, of course, that my plane will crash, is that, if it does, Loser will probably feel *horrible*. In fact, it might be his undoing! And that's something we can *all* get behind.

E-mail Breakup Babe | Comments 2

POST A COMMENT

I hope your plane doesn't crash, but if it does, can I have that new red couch of yours from the Bon Marche?
Tired of My Furniture | 8/30/02—11:04 A.M.

•   •   •   •   •

Hope you get the Friends Plus action! Try to make sure your ex "accidentally" finds out about it too.
Delilah | Homepage | 8/30/02—5:02 P.M.

Chapter Five

Wednesday, September 4, 2002
9:41 AM Breakup Babe
Shit, I thought. *Why didn't I take a Xanax?*

The wedding day was sunny and perfect—too perfect almost, as if we'd jumped into a wedding from *Brides* magazine. As I teetered in my spike heels toward the gazebo where Li'l Sis was about to get married, I cursed myself for not realizing that the ceremony itself might be an occasion for total breakdown. We'd been so busy with preparations in the last two days, there had been no time to panic.

But now that I was alone for a few moments in the rose-scented sunshine at the Mirassou Winery, with the murmur of guests nearby and the drone of an airplane above, anxiety coiled like a snake in my gut. My heart was pounding like a jackhammer. *Could I really do this?*

As I entered the gazebo, the world suddenly felt skewed and surreal. Li'l Sis about to get married. Me, 34 and alone. Dumped.

The anxiety demon saw his chance. He jumped out from behind a rosebush and grabbed me with clammy hands. He wore an ill-fitting sports jacket with a hideous purple tie. "Hey, R.," he yelped. "This is weird! You are going crazy! Run! Hide!"

When I saw LTLB sitting down in the front left row, I was reassured just a little. And the Celexa, even without the reinforcement of Xanax, was in there fighting a tough battle. "It's okay. Just keep walking!" yelled General Celexa as he pounced on Anxiety and tore him off my back. "If you wanna freak out, do it later. Like after the wedding, when everyone has seen you in your dress. I am not going to let you mess this up for Li'l Sis!"

With one burly arm around the demon's scrawny neck, General C. raised the binoculars to his eyes and looked meaningfully off into the distance. I didn't move. "Now, get going!" he barked, keeping the binoculars glued to his eyes.

Postwedding, I was back at Victrola on a bright, sunny morning before work. I'd dragged myself here at 8:30 A.M. with my laptop to write about the wedding in all its bittersweet glory. A few of the early-morning regulars were there— like the five-foot-tall guy with a shaved head and a lightning bolt tattooed on his scalp, who eyed me over the top of his *Wall Street Journal* as I walked in.

I gave him a disdainful look (*"Don't try to flirt with someone before they've had their morning coffee, midget!"*), then got in the line, which, as usual, was almost out the door. I'd gotten back to Seattle the night before last, and had just started to get back to "normal"—not that I really knew what that was anymore.

I missed LTLB desperately, but that was better than missing Loser. At least with LTLB there was a teeny-*tiny* possibility that we could someday be together. Not that we'd discussed that this time around. I'd been too shy to bring it up, too afraid of getting shot down in my already vulnerable state. LTLB, of course, had not come forth with any marriage proposals.

I missed my mom, too, and Barney. The morning before I left, he'd jumped into the bed with me and lay down within licking distance of my cheek. He had to be removed bodily by my mother when it was time for me to get up, because he'd pinned the comforter on top of me and blocked all movement.

I roused myself enough to give my coffee order to the excitable and flamboyantly gay barista at the register. Today, when I arrived at the register, he looked at me slyly and said, "Do you know what band this is that's playing? QUICK!"

"Aztec Camera?" My voice was hoarse, this being the first time I'd spoken today. I was not normally an expert on music trivia, but for some reason I'd purchased this relatively obscure album back in tenth grade.

"YES!" he yelled, his small body wriggling with excitement. Then he high-fived me. "Good job!"

Jolted awake by that minor success, I was now realizing— not for the first time—how the best moments of my day happened when (1) I was halfway through my first cup of coffee, and (2) I was writing. Today was no exception. General C. (along with Sensible Girl and Needy Girl) was, apparently, the product of just the right amount of caffeine. Enough for my brain to be awake but not overstimulated.

I was worried, though, about how much detail I was going into about the wedding. Did my readers really want to know all this? How the flowers smelled? How the music sounded? I wasn't writing a novel, after all. Wouldn't my readers enjoy it more if I was just funny and snappy, giving ironic commentary on everything rather than plunging into the particulars?

Then I remembered something that Wes, a former writing teacher of mine, used to say. "You are building a world for your reader, one that is made up of very specific sights, smells, sounds, and sensations. The more concrete the details, the more the reader will be submerged in your world." Wes taught creative writing for the University of Washington Extension program, where I'd taken classes several years back. He was a great teacher—so much better than the famous Roger Garth, who'd condescended to teach undergraduate creative writing at U.C. Berkeley.

After reading my first story aloud in class, Garth announced, "I have nothing, really, to say about this story." Then, all jowls and world-weary green eyes, he looked at the rest of the class and waited for some poor soul to jump into the void and say something, *anything*, nice about my beginner's attempt at fiction. Garth helped destroy what little confidence I had in my creative writing abilities by my sophomore year in college.

So it wasn't until age twenty-seven, my self-worth boosted by my minor success in the journalism world, that I dared to attempt fiction again in my class at the University of Washington.

I was hoping, when I signed up for Wes's class at U.W., that fourth grade would not forever remain the pinnacle of my creative career. Back then, encouraged by my fourth-grade teacher, Mrs. Bloomstedt, I had produced an entire book of short stories, hand-printed on colored index cards and bound together with brass tacks. Mrs. Bloomstedt read one of these stories—"The Man Who Paid Only in Change"—out loud one rainy November day, and I remember the pride I felt as my ten-year-old classmates listened in stunned silence (or was it abject boredom?) to the tragic ending of the tale, the part where the protagonist collapses fatally on the street due to the immense weight of all the change in his pocket.

After finishing the story, Mrs. Bloomstedt lowered the book with a rhapsodic sigh and said, "I do think Rachel is going to be a famous writer one day, don't you, class?" She was not the most *nonpartisan* of teachers (while my talents were always expounded on, for example, Davy Nystrom was often dragged around the classroom by his ear), but her adoration did wonders for my self-confidence. I decided right then that yes, I probably would become a famous writer, thank you very much. That is, if I decided not to become a rock-and-roll singer or a movie star—two of the other options I was considering.

Over the years, though, after countless professors tearing my writing to shreds, I was no longer so sure of my calling. So I was thrilled to discover in Wes's class, seventeen confidence-busting years later, that my imagination was still alive. That I could, in fact, finish a fictional story (something I'd failed to do since my Roger Garth days), and that my writing teacher, as well as my fellow students, had good things to say about my efforts.

"Your stories always have great details," one of my fellow students had commented. "They really bring me into the scene."

Ah, what the heck. If my blog readers didn't like the details, they would tell me, right?

When I sat down next to LTLB, tripping on the hem of my dress, he looked at me and said, "Wow, you look great."

"Thanks." I tried to sound calm. The sight of LTLB momentarily replaced my anxiety with lust. To think—this glossy-haired, high-cheekboned, well-built man was my date! Due to our frenzied make-out session in the car last night, I knew this was one of our on-again times. I was praying that we'd be on again at least one more time after the wedding.

The sound of a saxophone startled me. I looked over to see my uncle Simon, professional musician and debonair bachelor-by-choice, puffing away. The song he and my sister had agreed upon was Debussy's "Claire De Lune." The sweet and slightly melancholy tune brought tears to my eyes even before Li'l Sis appeared with my mom at the back of the gazebo.

"Tears are okay," whispered General C., his gruff voice surprisingly gentle. "But try to hold off just a little bit before you start with the waterworks." He sounded a bit choked up himself. "You're doing good, kid. Count down twenty-five minutes and then you can get shit faced. Now, make me proud!"

I grabbed LTLB's hand and he held on to it in return. His hand was warm and steady, in contrast to mine, which was clammy and trembling. My sister looked tan and sensational in her sparkling champagne dress. She was also smiling what looked like a real smile—not just her normal nervous facsimile of one—and was turning this way and that to make eye contact with people as she walked down the aisle. Li'l Sis, unlike me, did not like to be the center of attention, and so her poise impressed me. My mom, dressed in an olive and silver concoction, was also smiling broadly (she didn't mind the spotlight), and I was glad to see that she was not bawling yet.

I looked over at Super Brother-in-Law, waiting for my sister. If Li'l Sis looked calm, SBL looked positively serene. For a few seconds, I couldn't look away from him—the way his green eyes shone as he watched Li'l Sis advance toward him, at the way he looked so *sure* of things. What the hell was *he* on anyway?

And I realized, with a start, how much harder this would have been for me if Loser were here. Whenever Loser and I were around Li'l Sis and SBL, the tension in our relationship stood out in stark contrast to the ease and peace in theirs. It never helped that they could barely hide their dislike for him. I hadn't felt sure of Loser the way Li'l Sis and SBL felt sure of each other, and I understood now that there had been good reason for that.

As I watched my little sister—former archenemy and closest playmate combined—marry this man who totally adored her, I cried for both of us. I cried a little bit because I was unlucky, but mostly because she was so lucky. And when I stood up to clap with everyone else, I was clapping not just for her but for myself, because I knew, at least for the moment, that my loss was not nearly as big as her gain.

Seven hours, four glasses of champagne, two glasses of Merlot, and three pieces of wedding cake later, I was lying next to LTLB in bed, waiting for him to go to sleep. I'd been giddy ever since I'd chugged my first glass of champagne. I'd given a witty yet sniffle-inducing toast. I'd charmed friends and relatives alike. I'd danced for hours with a variety of small children, nearly throwing my back out to lift them up and twirl them around. I'd posed for an endless number of pictures, looking like a flamenco dancing queen. I'd honestly felt nothing but selfless joy and happiness and proved to my family that I could be strong when it counted. Best of all, I'd managed to slip over to spend the night at LTLB's parents' house (they were conveniently out of town) without upsetting my mother.

But now I was paying for it. The sadness and anxiety that had unsuccessfully tried to worm their way in all evening had breached the champagne- and Celexa-fortified gates. General C. seemed to have gone AWOL after his hard night. (When he'd promised me earlier that I could get "shit faced," he'd directly contradicted Dr. Melville's warning to "drink alcohol with moderation while on Celexa.") Even sex with LTLB had distracted me only briefly. Or maybe even made things worse. I was now headed full speed toward a complete crash.

I'd been so excited to come over here and take up where we'd left off during our last on-again time. I knew it wouldn't go anywhere, but it would feel good, I knew that. And it would help me forget Loser.

Ha.

As soon as I heard LTLB's gentle snoring, I rolled into a fetal position and started to cry. I cried quietly, so as not to wake him. He already felt insecure enough. Ever since we'd climbed into bed, he'd been asking questions like "What do you want me to do?" and "Did that feel good?"

The truth was it felt fine—great, even—but immediately afterward the downward spiral began. Instead of making me forget Loser as I thought it would—instead of *liberating* me—having sex with LTLB only made me miss the lying, cheating weasel.

> Besides, LTLB and I were never going to be together. Why had I made myself emotionally vulnerable by sleeping with him when I was already so messed up?
>
> My tears dripped onto the soft flannel sheets, which were white with little blue sheep on them. Against my will, I could smell Loser's green-apple shampoo. I could feel his soft lips on mine, the weight of his thick chestnut hair in my hands. I remembered how he used to kiss me so much, before, during, and after s*x. How we knew each other so well in bed. I was remembering how, every time it was over, he'd wrap his long, thin body around mine, and whisper in my ear, "I love you."

I stopped typing. Swiped at my eyes. *Damn it.* I was not going to cry here in Victrola. This was the happy place, the place where I wrote my troubles away and got high on caffeine. I grabbed my Americano and took a slug, then put it down too hard on the shaky table, where it splattered slightly. I looked around, embarrassed. Then, out of the corner of my eye, I saw him.

The cute barista. He'd somehow slipped in unnoticed again, and was now behind the counter in a sky blue T-shirt that flattered his fair complexion. He was also—no. That couldn't be. Was he looking at me? When I met his eyes, he gave me a quick, shy smile and looked away.

Oh God. He'd seen me crying, hadn't he? But maybe he hadn't even been looking at me. I glanced around furtively to see if there was someone else he might have been smiling at. There was a girl with her back to me at the table just in front of me. She had long blond hair streaked with expensive-looking copper highlights. She wore a mauve sweater with a black feather boa at the neck and a black beret. Maybe it was her he'd been smiling at. In fact, hadn't I noticed her talking with him recently?

Yes. I had. I recognized the beret. She'd been chatting him up the other day as she bought her double-tall-nonfat-no-sugar-vanilla-soy latte. And she looked like a fucking model. I, on the other hand, had rushed out of the house today without a shower and stuck my hair up in a high ponytail that had strange bumps in it and lots of hair falling out of the rubber band. I also hadn't been able to find any usable eyeliner. Things were still in disarray after my move. And, of course, I hadn't unpacked anything from my trip to California, either.

Of course he was looking at her. Not me.

Whatever.

This interlude, however, at least had the effect of drying my tears. Funny how heartbreak could disappear in an instant in the face of possibility, no matter how remote! Casting an annoyed glance at the long, graceful neck of Beret Chick (how pretentious to wear a fucking beret!), I reread what I'd just written. Then laughed to myself when I realized I'd written a whole paragraph about sex. Or, rather, s*x. (I'd learned from other bloggers about the judicious use of asterisks in any sex-related words so as to cut down on hits from porn seekers who might leave rude comments. People seeking online gratification were much more likely to Google the word "sex" than "s*x" or "fuck" than "f*ck.") And to think, just a couple weeks ago, I'd hesitated to even *hint* at sex.

Hmm. Well, for now, I would leave it in. It was integral to the story I was telling, after all. If it hadn't been for the sex, I might not have gotten so depressed, right? I could only hope LTLB would never find the blog and read about how our sexual escapades had thrown me into despair.

I pulled my knees closer into my chest and worked harder to stifle my sobs. After about ten minutes, the sheets were wet beneath my face. I opened my eyes and saw that all the blue sheep in my immediate vicinity were stained cobalt blue with tears.

I really wanted to wake LTLB because I did not want to be alone with this grief. But that's what it means to be single, doesn't it? You go through the scariest sh*t in life without anyone to hold you.

There's no for better and worse, in sickness and in health. There's just you, crying alone in strange beds, counting out the days until you die alone, like Eleanor f*cking Rigby.

Then a chill went through my body. The feverish memories disappeared. And for the first time all night, for the first time through all the jittery prewedding preparations, the beautiful ceremony, the champagne-dazzled reception, I was jealous of my sister.

She got to marry the man she loved. She would have babies before she was too old. She would never have to deal with sleazy, noncommittal men again. If she became incontinent, there would be someone to change her diapers. I, on the other hand, was equally deserving of a husband, if not more so. *I'd had more boyfriends! I was older! Thinner! More glamorous! Wasn't I?* But when I became ready for Depends, she and SBL would put me in a nursing home and forget about me, leaving me to the mercy of sadistic half-wits in white coats.

So why her and not me? Maybe, I thought, feeling the heat from LTLB's body—so close and yet so far away—I'd been too busy chasing Mr. Wrongs down deserted back alleys. All that time, Mr. Right had probably been waiting in the wings and I'd missed my chance.

Suddenly, LTLB rolled over onto his side and draped his arm across me. I held my breath, willing the tears to stop, hoping he wouldn't say anything to me. A few seconds later, he started to snore again. As I listened to him, and moved my head so that my face was resting against warm, dry flannel, I started to calm down. I let my breath out. A couple more halfhearted sobs escaped.

I was cold now, so I moved in closer to LTLB. His body radiated heat. It was bigger than Loser's. Stronger, bulkier, more muscular. But it was familiar, too, in its own way. And after a little while, I fell asleep, my arms intertwined with his.

E-mail Breakup Babe | Comments 2

I checked my watch. *Shit.* 10:30! Time always flew when I was writing. I packed up my laptop quickly. At least no one at work cared if I got in at 11—as long as I had no meetings to go to and got my work done.

As usual after writing my blog, I felt cleansed. High. I would probably crash when I got to my pile of boring work and my dark little office, but at least for the twenty-minute drive there I could crank up the radio and enjoy the creativity and caffeine buzz.

When I strode out of Victrola, I tried not to look at the cute barista. *Play it cool. You look like crap anyway.* But I couldn't help it. He was right there at the counter. I glanced his way and—he looked up at me. His brown eyes locked onto mine. Then he smiled. Yes!

I practically did a little jig when I got outside, where the September sunshine put a honeyed sheen on everything. I breathed in the warm air, with just a hint of fall on its edges, and thought, *I still got it.*

POST A COMMENT

Glad you got some, anyway. Things have been a bit slow around here.
Delilah | Homepage | 9/4/02—3:13 P.M.

•   •   •   •   •

OMG, I recently had to go to my best friend's wedding after being dumped by the guy I thought I was going to marry. The only way to get through it was with loads of alcohol and flirting with every single guy there (of which there were about two). I can totally relate to everything you went through, only I didn't get as lucky afterward.
nukie | Homepage | 9/4/02—9:37 P.M.

Chapter Six

Sunday, September 15, 2002
10:03 AM Breakup Babe

The phrase "up and down" fails to do justice to my emotional state about as much as the word "hot" does to Benicio del Toro.

Just last night, I was sprawled on my velvety red couch from the Bon Marche ($750) sobbing yet again. I was alone, except for Mr. Pickle, a gray stuffed elephant my mom had bought me in the midst of The Great Unpleasantness. My housewarming party had just ended. The last of my friends had tumbled cheerfully down the stairway, all chatting and laughing, loud and half drunk.

Half an hour after that, I was on top of the world again after making a date with the hottest man west of the Mississippi (save Benicio del Toro), who we will dub "Sexy Boy" (SB).

Let me explain.

SB has been an acquaintance of mine for some time now. I've always thought he was cute, but when he walked into my housewarming party that night, I saw him in a whole different way. *God, he was sexy! That soft, tousled brown hair! Those green eyes! That strong yet comforting-looking body.*

Maybe it was the big shot of tequila I'd just tossed back, but still—the feeling was so novel, yet also so familiar. That *pow* feeling I got in the pit of my stomach, the high that took over when hormones mixed with hope. I took one look at him and he went into soft focus. My legs became weak and I felt sparkly little stars shooting out of my eyes à la Davy Jones of the Monkees (for whom, at age six, I'd declared my true love).

But now, after an evening of intense flirting, during which SB had asked for my phone number and suggested, casually, that we "hang out," he was about to disappear into the night. Who knew if he'd actually call? I remembered GuyPal #1, SB's best friend, saying once, "SB is a nice guy, but he can be a flake when it comes to women."

Flake or not, SB was the only one to notice my downcast expression during the farewells. "Are you okay?" he asked, after hugging me good-bye in the doorway, his strong arms around me. He smelled of a clean, citrusy aftershave that made it hard to pull away. "You look kind of sad."

I suddenly felt self-conscious. I had no good reason to be sad. My housewarming party had been a smashing success. Amidst my sparse furniture and a few cheesy decorations—fish lights strung across the fireplace and a disco ball hanging from the ceiling— coworkers and former coworkers had mingled with friends and former roommates, getting cozier the more liquor and cheap red wine they drank.

I'd felt so popular and lubricated by tequila that nary a thought of Loser had entered my mind except those of the "Fuck you, I'm so cool and you're such a pathetic weenie" variety. But, with the departure of my thirty or so guests, the alcohol-induced giddiness was quickly morphing into self-pity.

"Oh yeah, I'm fine," I said to SB, not sounding fine at all. All the oomph had gone out of me. I didn't even have the energy to pretend I was the sparkling hostess of half an hour ago. Besides, if I sounded lonely enough, pathetic enough, who knew what SB might do to comfort me? "Just tired." I looked down at his black loafers shining against the scuffed hardwood floor.

"All right." He hesitated. He was standing only inches away from me, this six-foot-tall man with broad shoulders and a sculpted torso, who piloted planes through stormy Alaskan skies. I looked up into his eyes: big, lazy, watchful, seductive eyes. I held my breath.

"Ask him to stay!" Needy Girl whispered suddenly in my ear, her alcohol-tinged breath hot against my cheek.

"Jesus God, no." Sensible Girl gripped my shoulder, startling me. Her nails looked so neatly trimmed compared to Needy Girl's, whose were long and ragged and bore the scarlet traces of a months-old manicure. "You don't need that kind of complication right now. Take things slow."

Needy Girl was whispering to him. "Offer to stay. Offer to stay." But he didn't hear her. "Well then, Miss R.," he said, and the false cheer in his voice made my heart drop to my stomach. "I will call you soon."

I closed the door behind him, and stared at it for a few seconds. Then I grabbed Mr. Pickle from the bedroom and stumbled back to the couch—the only piece of furniture in the living room. Mr. Pickle had a pouch in his stomach that had come with a little piece of paper inside it. This piece of paper had said "Write your wish here and dream upon it!"

And I had. Like some deluded six-year-old, I'd scrawled, "I wish that things with me and L. would work out." Then I stuffed the piece of paper back into Mr. Pickle's pouch, hoping no one would ever see it. Or hoping maybe, that one day, Loser and I could joke about it together. When I checked the pouch a week later, though, the piece of paper was gone. It had fallen out God knows where, and was now floating aimlessly around Seattle for strangers to laugh at.

As I sobbed facedown on the couch, I realized I didn't know exactly what I was crying about in the early hours of a warm September morning in my sparsely furnished living room lit by two red Ikea lamps ($5 apiece).

Then my phone rang.

My heart leapt. Froze. Hammered in my chest.

Could it . . . ? Was it . . . *Loser*?

"R., it's J."

"Oh." Sniffle. *"Hi."*

"I just called to make sure you were okay."

And I knew, suddenly, what I'd been crying about.

For the first time, I knew that I was going to get over Loser, that I was going to leave him behind, that, in fact I was *already* starting to leave him behind.

And this knowledge made me both intensely happy and intensely sad. That is why the tears continued to slide down my face even as I talked on the phone with SB. As I tried to hide my sobs, he asked me out for a date—my first *real* post-Loser date—on Thursday night.

E-mail Breakup Babe | Comments 3

POST A COMMENT

Are you sure you're ready to start dating again? This all smacks of "rebound" to me.

The Frenchman | Homepage | 9/15/02—3:18 P.M.

•   •   •   •   •

Rebound schmebound, just let the girl have fun!

nukie | Homepage | 9/16/02—12:10 A.M.

•   •   •   •   •

When I was a kid, I used to kiss the TV when Davy Jones came on. Then I'd feel all trembly inside. Later I learned that the trembly feeling was just static.

CandyCane | Homepage | 9/16/02—9:53 P.M.

Chapter Seven

The Monday after my housewarming party, my boss shocked me in our "1:1" by telling me that he was getting "good feedback" about me from all my coworkers.

"What?!" I wanted to shout. "Are you people blind?" Lyle was, quite possibly, blind. He had the worst fashion sense of anyone I'd ever met, except for the hordes of Empire logowear-wearing developers who swarmed the cafeterias, their French fry–fed paunches busting out of their extra-large T-shirts announcing product releases, "launch parties," and various inside jokes. One popular T-shirt featured a line drawing of Rodney Rolands as God, brandishing a tequila bottle at his earthly workers and yelling down, "What about *zero* bug count don't you understand?"

At least Lyle didn't wear Birkenstocks or tie-dye or have a beard down to his crotch. He favored polo shirts in colors such as lime green and royal blue (with a few too many gray-ish chest hairs poking out), tucked into black jeans about a size and a half too small and finished off with a pair of bright white Reeboks.

Instead I nodded knowingly. Modestly. "That's good to know," I said. *Good to know no one has noticed I'm only working five hours a day, half of which I spend crying on the phone!*

"And all the writers seem to enjoy working with you."

Aha. That was the key. All the technical writers were men. Nerdy men, married men, Xbox-playing men. Many of them had worked at Empire for years and had 10,000-square-foot houses in the suburbs, multiple BMWs, Cessnas, and dowdy yet appreciative wives.

Most of them could have retired on their stock options, but they liked their geeky jobs too much. Nerds or not, married or not, I enjoyed their company because they were, after all, *men*. They clearly enjoyed me as well, and who could blame them? I was looking better than ever, and the old charm was apparently still alive and kicking. And thank God, because I needed this job. I needed it to pay for my cool apartment, my new furniture, and my exponentially growing size 6 wardrobe. The recession got worse every day and I hated to think about what would have happened to me had I still been a temp when The Great Unpleasantness unfolded.

On this particular Monday, I'd been editing for two hours straight. Usually, each time I tried to buckle down and edit a piece of documentation, it felt like putting a straitjacket on. I would struggle against it at first—the strange language, the words I didn't understand, the bad grammar. Then eventually I would stop resisting, concentrate, and realize that this was just language after all. I took a deep breath and looked at the words in front of me.

In the following illustration, the **serviceBusiness** class represents the business service information type. The **serviceBusiness** class con-

tains the class attributes **servicePin, serviceCode, name,** and **properties.** It also contains a class attribute called **bindingGrids,** which
contains one or more **bindingGrids** class instances.

As I added commas here, fixed tenses there, I imagined—
for the hundredth time—my upcoming date with Sexy Boy. I
imagined how, when he picked me up for dinner, we would
embrace. The embrace would be long, significant. A recognition. Perhaps he would whisper, "Thanks for meeting me tonight, Rachel." His breath would be hot in my ear. The vibe
would be so intense, we'd almost start to kiss right away. But
after the first heated brush of our lips, I'd pull away and say
in my most sultry voice, "Why don't we save that for dessert?"

I was feeling so cheerful about my prospects with Sexy
Boy that I actually had my office door cracked open. I was getting sick of being a blinds-drawn, door-shut mole, walled off
against any memory, any hint of Loser.

The problem was that I'd been shoved into a windowless
office. Once upon a time, all the full-time employees got their
own window offices, while it was the temps who got shoe-
horned into the windowless offices two or three at a time or,
worse yet, into old test labs, cold as meat lockers, where several others worked in perpetual icy twilight. Now, though, just
like the stock options that made you rich, window offices for
all employees were a thing of the past.

One day, after years of loyal service to "The Rod" (as Rodney Rolands was also known), I'd work in the light. But for
now I was destined to dwell in this airless hole. Though the
cafeterias and hallways at Empire were cheerful and decorated with a rotating multimillion-dollar art collection, these
windowless offices—though preferable to the meat lockers—
were still akin to Purgatory. So I'd started keeping the door
open for short periods of time each day. Fifteen minutes. An
hour. Today it had been open for two whole hours.

There hadn't been any Loser sightings in about two weeks.

He was perhaps the farthest thing from my mind when a shadow suddenly darkened my doorway that Monday afternoon.

I didn't look up at first. Instead, I tried to concentrate on the paragraph in front of me:

> Over time, as a growing number of objects become registered in the **PSID server,** it becomes difficult to maintain a register of the allocated unique identifiers. Use the **GetRegisteredKeys** class to get the unique identifying keys for the entities you have registered.

Something about the familiar sound of those footsteps gave me an uneasy feeling.

Don't look up.

The Dixie Chicks blasted through my headphones. "ToNIGHT, the heartache's on ME . . ."

The shadow swept by. And though I knew I shouldn't, I did it. I looked up. In time to see him looking at me over his shoulder, attempting an expression of nonchalance. When our eyes met, we both looked away.

Still, I saw the dark circles under his eyes. The unnatural pallor of his normally tan skin. His hair looked greasy.

The Dixie Chicks continued to wail in my ears. "Let's drink a toast to the FOOL who never SEES . . ."

I tore my headphones off. Then I jumped up from my seat and slammed my office door. Falling back into my chair, I faced the computer screen again and stared at it, my entire body trembling. The words blurred together on the screen. I waited for the tears to come.

But they didn't. Instead, something unexpected happened. My stomach and face got hot, and I felt like something was about to explode inside me. I grabbed a sheaf of papers on my desk and hurled them into the air as hard as I could.

God damn it, what a fucking asshole.

The papers fluttered to the floor in an unsatisfying manner. Suddenly I was high on anger. I wanted to get on one of the tables in the B40 cafeteria in my new black cocktail dress from the J. Crew sale rack ($55) and belt out that Gloria Gaynor karaoke classic "I Will Survive" to the delight and amazement of three hundred horny men. Loser would be there too, of course, cowering in the crowd with his piece of pizza, wanting to run, but unable to tear himself away from the sight of me, rising like a sexy size 6 phoenix from the ashes.

Instead, I looked around for something else to throw. Something that would hit the wall. Hard. My dictionary? The ceramic bowl that Loser had bought me at a craft market in Thailand? I raised an eyebrow.

I reached for the bowl and then stopped myself. *You're at work, remember? You need this job.*

But the adrenaline pumping through my body got the better of me. I flung my door open and marched to the kitchen, almost knocking over a pimply developer in a tank top and flip-flops (no doubt a millionaire). I grabbed a drink from the cooler, rattling all the cans inside when I slammed the door closed.

I felt like I could run ten miles. Maybe that's what I should do, I thought, as I stalked back to my office, clenching the can of Talking Rain in my hand so hard that my skin turned white.

But after I got back to my office and slammed the door, I thought of one other thing I could do that might make me feel better. More and more now I turned to the blog when I felt down, just as in the past I'd always turned to my journals. Softbound journals. Hardbound journals. Flowered journals, striped journals. Boxes of journals that I'd been keeping since age thirteen, all about boys, boys, and more boys.

Though I'd never blogged at work before, I logged on to Breakup Babe and wrote without stopping for forty-five minutes. I was so furious that I almost forgot to worry about what might happen to me for blogging at work or, worse yet, for blogging about a coworker. Trouble was, in my first innocent blush of blogging, I didn't consider Loser a "coworker." He was a villain first of all.

Monday, September 16, 2002
3:34 PM Breakup Babe
Welcome to Loserville

Well, today I saw Loser in the hall and it just made me MAD.

He encouraged me to take this job in his group, and then promptly CHEATED on me and DUMPED me—me, the best thing that has ever happened to him in his whole, pathetic life—and now he has the nerve to walk down MY hallway as if he is man enough to be within ten feet of me.

Do you know what this man used to do with his weekends before he met me? Play video games. I would come to work on Mondays and relate my own tales of outdoor adventure, and he would always tell me that he'd played video games and cleaned his house. But he was envious, and would tell me, "I'd love to do that kind of stuff."

But of course his loser girlfriend at the time had no interest in the great outdoors; all she did was read her horoscope and pop painkillers. Before her, his loser ex-wife considered it exercise to drive to the beauty salon for another bad bleached blond perm.

When we started dating, though, he began *using* that fancy bike that he owned but never rode; he began socializing with MY friends (having none of his own); began traveling to exciting destinations near and far; and began to see that the world was not just work and loser women. And then, after our grandest adventure of all, during which he seemed (SEEMED) to blossom into a bold and inquisitive human being, trekking through jungles and snorkeling with sea lions, all the while telling me how lucky he was, how much he loved me, he came home (while I was still away) and, high on a wave of confidence, decided he no longer needed me.

But the story doesn't end there, of course. It's one thing to decide you don't need someone anymore. It happens all the time. It's also one thing to cheat on someone. That happens all the time too. But it's another thing entirely to cheat on someone, lie to them, and then for the next two months punish them by telling them they are selfish, unfeeling, and that the relationship has been all about THEM for the last two years.

You know all about how I groveled. How I cried and begged and demeaned myself until I found out the truth from outside sources. And when I confronted him with it, he cowered—a small, weak animal caught in a deadly trap. And I almost felt sorry for him. In that moment when my rage took over, when I finally stopped cowering myself, he knew what the truth was. He knew that what he'd done was horrible. But all he could manage to say was "I'm sorry" in the smallest, most insincere voice I've ever heard, "I wasn't getting what I needed."

Now this man dares to walk down my hallway, right past my door. Maybe he wants to see me. Maybe he knows what he's lost and wants a glimpse of it, shimmering in the fog. Or maybe he's just a f*cking idiot. All I know is next time I'm not going to avert my eyes. Next time I'm going to look him in his sad, pathetic face as he walks by, and watch him as he can't meet my gaze.

Loser.

E-mail Breakup Babe | Comments 2

I was filled with righteous anger and it fueled me after I wrote that entry. Next time I saw Loser, he would melt under my withering stare! I went back to my editing and when that straitjacket became too much to bear, I comforted myself with a combination of caffeine and rock and roll blasting through my headphones. I was determined that getting over this breakup would be a piece of cake. Hell, it had only been three months, and I was halfway over it already.

Besides, SB and I were going out in a few days. No doubt we'd get liquored up and fall into each other's arms with unbridled passion, and . . . Well, I couldn't imagine much past that. It would be something along the lines of fall madly in love, live happily ever after, and forget about Loser.

POST A COMMENT

Ooh, sister, the RAGE! I didn't know you had it in you! Keep it coming—that's how you're going to get over it!

Juliana | Homepage | 9/16/02—10:46 P.M.

•   •   •   •   •

You know what they say: The best way to get over someone is to get under someone else. Or else take a gun and mow the f*cker down.

Knut | Homepage | 9/17/02—8:33 A.M.

Chapter Eight

It was Sunday afternoon, 3:34 P.M. Sexy Boy hadn't called. I was writing at Victrola. I kept turning my cell phone on and off, checking for messages. On the one hand, I didn't want it to be on while I was writing, because I would keep waiting for it to ring and it would distract me. On the other hand, I was distracted anyway and kept turning it on every thirty minutes to see if he'd called.

After our date, he'd said, "I'll give you a holler this week-end." And with those seven little words, my heart had leapt up into the air and done a little victory dance. But now it was Sunday and he still hadn't called. Technically it was still the weekend, of course. Maybe he meant he'd call me today to make a plan for next week. I knew, though, that he had just flaked. My heart had been on a sinking trajectory ever since Saturday afternoon. Going lower and lower. Waiting for that call. "He can be a primo flake when it comes to women," Guy-

Pal #1 had said during that one, distant conversation. "He always wants what he can't get, and what he can get doesn't interest him."

It didn't help that couples swarmed all over Victrola today. The sleazy male singles who usually populated the place were gone, and in their place were couples. Middle-aged couples with matching salt-and-pepper hair reading *The New York Times*. Teenage couples wearing headphones and doing homework. Married couples with toddlers in tow. There, in fact, was Hottie Dad, with a woman who appeared to be Hottie Mom, sleek and exotic looking in designer clothes, gazing with adoration at her beautiful child asleep in her stroller.

Gag.

Once upon a time, I had been part of a Happy Couple who frequented Victrola. Loser was the one who'd taken me here for the first time. We used to come here on Sundays together, full from brunch in Coastal Kitchen next door. I'd write, he'd read, and we'd hold hands or play footsies under the table. Happy to be together. Or at least I was. Who knew how long he'd been unhappy before he decided to fuck some other girl, lie to me about it, and dump me?

Stop it. Just focus on writing. It'll make you feel better.

I logged on to Blogger, praying that blogging would have its usual therapeutic effect. Today, I was going to write about my date with Sexy Boy. I knew it was dangerous, seeing that GuyPal #1 was SB's best friend, but he had promised, *promised* not to give away the URL or say a word about what I'd written. I didn't trust him completely, though. Who knew what he might give away to Sexy Boy under the influence of some substance or other? But my readers, up to twenty-five a day now, were demanding to know how the date had gone. I couldn't exactly let them down. Several more comments had appeared on my previous entry about SB, asking for details PLEASE.

POST A COMMENT

Your date was Thursday, now it's Saturday, are you going to tell us what happened or WHAT?

Delilah | Homepage | 9/21/02—12:33 P.M.

•   •   •   •   •

Yeah, come on, I need my Breakup Babe fix! We want to know what happened—don't leave us hanging!

Little Princess | Homepage | 9/21/02—9:02 P.M.

"Little Princess," I discovered, from reviewing the referral page on my hit counter, was a blogger from Ohio who'd put a link to my site on hers. She was an especially atrocious writer, who wrote about the very mundane details of her mundane life as a dental hygienist, but her comment delighted me no end. It was one thing for my friends to say they liked Breakup Babe—who knew if they were telling the truth, after all?—but another thing for strangers in cyberspace to beg for their fix.

Twelve years ago, as an unpaid editorial intern at *Alaska Airlines Magazine*, writing filler pieces like "Alaska's History Comes Alive at New Museum" or "Portland Entrepreneur Puts the Fun Back into Office Supplies," my editor and future writing mentor, Noah, had told me, "You have a distinctive voice. Keep at it."

I didn't know exactly how he could discern my "distinctive voice" amid the fluff, but I tried to believe him anyway. The confidence Mrs. Bloomstedt had instilled in me when I was ten had not completely disappeared, after all. It had only gone underground during college and the brutal, recession-plagued postcollege years, when I'd been forced to take jobs like receptionist in a chilly basement, receptionist in a gleaming high-rise, receptionist in a desolate industrial park.

That all changed when I fled California for Seattle and got a job selling sheepskin slippers at Pike Place Market. Sure, it was an unlikely choice for a *magna cum laude* graduate of U.C. Berkeley, with a degree in comparative literature, but it beat being a receptionist. At least I got to be in the thick of things, hanging out on the waterfront with artists and actors and musicians who treasured the flexibility that working at Seattle's biggest tourist attraction gave them. I, too, benefited from this flexibility, because now that I wasn't working 8–5 in some prison of an office, I had time to do the internship at *Alaska Airlines Magazine*. I didn't know it then, of course, but that internship would launch my writing career. All I knew was that it was great to be writing—even if I wasn't paid, and even if I had to hawk slippers to make it happen.

Now—finally—more evidence that I had a distinctive voice! Because, even though I'd published plenty since the internship days, this was the first time I'd put my real self out there on the page for people to see. And they liked it! They *liked* me! Hell, maybe my scintillating articles in the airline magazine had garnered reader adoration too, but in the stodgy world of periodicals, there was no way for them to immediately broadcast their feelings to me. All hail the Internet!

So, good little attention whore that I was, I wrote a thank-you e-mail to "Little Princess" and put her on my own, growing, **Nice Peeps Who Link to Me** list. And now, ignoring the fawning couples who drooled all around me, I delivered the latest fix to my addicts.

Sunday, September 22, 2002
4:40 PM Breakup Babe

When we arrived at his rambling rental in upper Queen Anne after a long dinner, Sexy Boy's roommate Ganja King greeted us in the "music room." "Hey kids!"

"The group housing situation is temporary," SB had told me, anticipating that I might look askance at a man in his thirties who still lived with roommates in a dwelling straight out of *Animal House*. "Since I'm out of town so often, it doesn't really make sense for me to have my own place. That way I can save my money to travel. I'll have my own place soon, though."

All the lights were on and Ganja King and his girlfriend, Ganja Queen, were wide awake, hanging out as if it were eight o'clock on a weekend, not midnight on a weeknight. Miles Davis blasted from the stereo. The room, full of keyboards and amps, reeked of pot.

We'd just returned from dinner at Marco's Supper Club, where I'd been so thrilled by SB's presence, I could barely breathe. With his bangs in his face, wearing a cream-colored fisherman's sweater, he looked equal parts rugged and cuddly. Throughout the fried sage leaves with a medley of dipping sauces and the first vodka tonics, he hefted compliments my way. *You look very beautiful tonight. I've always wanted to get to know you better. How did you get such shiny hair?*

At one point, he complimented the necklace I was wearing (Something Silver, $18), and reached across the table to touch it, brushing his fingers across my neck as he did so. I practically fainted. Sensible Girl, clad in baggy overalls and sipping on herbal tea, guffawed.

"Could he be any more obvious?"

"Shut up!" said Needy Girl, rousing herself from her swoon and looking longingly over at SB, her mouth hanging open ever so slightly. "I haven't been this attracted to anyone in a LONG time." She was wearing a tartan miniskirt that looked suspiciously like the $150 one I'd coveted at Kenneth Cole's the other day, along with a too-tight black cashmere sweater.

"Yeah, WHATEVER." Sensible Girl rolled her eyes, crossed her arms, and settled in for a long night. She was clearly conserving her resources.

Now, back at the ranch, as he called it, SB seated himself in a beanbag chair. I stood there in my coat, clutching my purse, and tried to look nonchalant, as if I were perfectly sure of myself and Sensible Girl and Needy Girl were not at this very moment putting on their gloves and preparing for another violent round in the ring.

"Hey, R.," SB said, sensing my uncertainty, "would you like to go hang out in my room?" He looked up at me with those deadly green weapons and my knees started to buckle.

"No!" Sensible Girl got in the first jab. "You've got to work tomorrow! And look at this house—it's a den of drug addicts! Go home now!"

"Oh, for crying out loud!" Needy Girl's high-pitched voice carried over the music. "After all she's been through? You would DENY her this?!"

I looked into SB's seductive eyes, which stayed fixed on mine. They promised all kinds of debauchery. My stomach fluttered. Yet, I hesitated.

At dinner, he'd made one comment that I wasn't quite sure how to interpret. "R.," he'd said, after we'd both had two cocktails and he'd talked a blue streak about his job piloting rich executives to and from resorts in Alaska, nearly forgetting to ask me questions about myself in the process, "that breakup hit you pretty hard, didn't it?" He paused, took a sip of his drink, then looked at me with an expression that was part concern, part something else I couldn't decipher.

I looked down at my dinner. Felt my cheeks flush. Why was he bringing this up anyway? "Yeah, I guess." I moved some food around my plate with my fork.

"Well," he said. I looked up. He leaned toward me. Around us, candlelight flickered and contented yuppies murmured. I wanted to reach over and touch the bangs that fell across his eyes. To run my finger across his cheek, which revealed just a trace of stubble. To touch his full, soft lips with mine. "It takes a while to get over that kind of thing."

I swallowed. Nodded. What the hell was he talking about? I didn't need time to get over it. I was over it!

He reached across the table and laid his hand on my arm. I could feel the warmth of his hand through the flimsy material of my revealing purple blouse (Nordstrom's, $53). The warmth not only penetrated the sleeve of my blouse, it shot its way down my arm and through my torso to the crotch of my Victoria's Secret underwear ($7), where it burst into flame. I started to sweat.

"This is a good time for you to just go out and have fun, then, isn't it?" he said, giving me a smile that was so devilish, so alluring, that it threatened to turn the flame into a towering inferno. Quickly I took a drink of water.

"Yeah," I said. But it came out hoarsely, barely a word at all.

Now, as I felt his silken web tighten around me, I rolled that "fun" comment around in my mind. Was he trying to tell me that I shouldn't get too serious about anybody, much less him? Or was he trying to tell me that he would help me forget about Loser? And what kind of "fun," exactly, was he talking about? Because if I have any dating rules in this post-Loser world it's that I'm not going to sleep with someone until I have a f*cking rock on my finger!

Kissing, however, is a different matter. SB had definitely passed clearance for that, even though GalPal #1 had warned me to hold off as long as possible. "It can't hurt to wait," she had said. "Even just to kiss him. That way you won't jump in without knowing what his intentions are." (She herself had first kissed her boyfriend within ten minutes of meeting him at a party.)

Was it possible for me to wait? Could I look at those magnetic green orbs and tell SB I had to go home? *SB always wants what he can't get,* GuyPal #1 had said.

I looked at Sensible Girl. She made a cutting motion across her throat with her finger, then mouthed a single word. *Wait.* Her eyes pleaded with me.

Then I looked over at Needy Girl, who was staring at SB with a starved expression on her face, like one of those malnourished African children you see on TV. Pity overcame me. I would pledge half my salary to this starving child to help her get out of poverty and into Harvard! Look at those wide, imploring, innocent eyes! She was a victim; she needed me!

"Okay," I said to SB. "Sure. For just a little while."

"Yes!!" shrieked Needy Girl, pumping her arms and twirling around in her pointy black cowboy boots. Instantly, the starving-child image was gone, replaced by an obnoxious *Sex and the City* wannabe.

"First, R.," said Ganja King, who was tall and skinny, with a gaunt face and big hair à la Keith Richards, "would you like a little *refreshment*?"

I turned around from putting my coat in the corner to see Ganja King holding out the biggest bong I'd ever seen. It looked like a brass hookah, with a wide, intricately carved base, a narrow valve about a foot long, and a bowl at the top with a little lid. From the side curled a snakelike tube, one end of which—I guessed—you were supposed to put in your mouth.

"Um, no thanks," I said, after recovering from the sight of the giant apparatus. I did not want to give Sensible Girl the opportunity to beat me over the head with it. Besides, if I took one hit off that thing, I would ingest enough to make me high for the next year.

SB, however, apparently had no such qualms. He took the bong from Ganja King, settled back in the beanbag, and inhaled. Deeply. He suddenly looked like the fat, lazy caterpillar from *Alice in Wonderland*, sitting on his big leaf and sucking on his hookah. Grotesque and lethargic, his eyes half closed as he inhaled.

Still holding his breath, SB passed the bong to Ganja Queen and the caterpillar image disappeared. When all three of them exhaled, one right after the other, the room was so thick with smoke I could barely see. I held my breath so I wouldn't get a contact high, and tried not to pass judgment. Who *didn't* smoke pot these days, after all?

"Not everyone does, missy, and you know it," said Sensible Girl, who sensed an opening now that Needy Girl had inhaled some of the secondhand smoke and was lolling on the floor, head nodding in intense concentration to Miles Davis's *Bitches Brew*.

"Aren't you just a little old for this kind of thing now?" she asked, looking around the room with a sneer at the three adults with dilated pupils and dreamy smiles. It was true I'd dated several stoners in the not-so-distant past. Right before Loser, in fact, I'd dated a minuscule rock-climbing pothead, who could turn any type of fruit into a bong. I was more discriminating than that now. Or so I hoped.

But then SB said, "Shall we dance, madam?" All intelligent

thought fled my brain, and next thing I knew I was sitting on a mattress on a white(ish) carpet that had seen better days. Soccer balls, tennis balls, baseballs, and other assorted balls filled the room, accompanied by a cornucopia of white(ish) socks scattered freely about. Despite the preponderance of socks, the room smelled surprisingly nice, of lavender, perhaps.

SB went directly over to the stereo, the most expensive item in the place. The speakers were nearly as tall as me. A few seconds later, to my surprise, Beethoven came blasting out of them.

"At least your father would have approved of his taste in music," muttered Sensible Girl. Then she fled into the night, all hope abandoned. Needy Girl, on the other hand, sat on the edge of the mattress, her eyes wide, her expression trancelike, whether from drugs or anticipation I didn't know.

I could barely believe what was about to happen. Finally my feverish kissing fantasies would come true! As SB fiddled with the stereo, I quickly ran my tongue over my teeth to eradicate any stray lipstick. Why hadn't I brought any mints?

I took a deep breath as SB sat down close to me. He sat there for a moment, looking at me suggestively through dilated eyes. As he leaned toward me, smelling of Drakkar Noir and pot, I felt his soft lips on mine before they even touched me.

He never actually kissed me, though. Instead, as he leaned toward me and opened that soft-looking mouth of his, he started to talk. And he talked—nonstop—for an hour.

About how he didn't like his job. About how he needed to move into his own place. About the ex-girlfriend (Summer) who had cheated on him numerous times and who he was still obsessed with. About how he was going to stop being obsessed with her any day now. About how he knew he smoked too much pot, but that soon he was going to stop and turn his life around. I listened, nodding vigorously (and then less vigorously, and then hardly at all), interjecting supportive comments, and all the while looking with an ache in my chest at his eyes, his lips, willing him to shut the hell up and just kiss me.

At 1:30 A.M., when I finally realized that kissing was not on the agenda, I claimed tiredness and excused myself. As SB walked me to my car, I struggled to find just the right stance between hope and despair. And then, with one little statement from him, a malignant tumor known as Hope-a-noma took over and erased any doubts I might have had about him. He said, "I'll give you a holler this weekend." And with that quaint little phrase, hope-a-noma took over. Stoner, so? Self-obsessed, so? Stuck in his life? Who cared? He would call me. Love would conquer all! La-de-da-de-da!

E-mail Breakup Babe | Comments 2

After I hit the "Publish" button, I felt lighthearted. Free! I'd outed Sexy Boy for the big, fat flake that he was and laughed at myself in the process. Clearly, I could now care less about the bastard! Feeling giddy, I looked out of Victrola's plate glass window at the scene on 15th Avenue. It was a mix of funky and generic. Safeway and Walgreen's mixed with consignment shops and used bookstores. Sun had given way to drizzle, and half the people strolling around outside wore summer clothes and smiles that said they hoped it would stay summer awhile longer. The other half wore Gore-Tex shells and had guarded, winter expressions on their faces.

My euphoria lasted for all of a minute before the urge to check my cell phone gripped me again. Was it possible he'd called?

My mood plummeted.

No! I would not check my messages. So what if he'd called? I should go for a run. Work out. Do something else that would make me feel powerful. Build on this good feeling that writing had just given me. I stared out at the rain and imagined myself at the gym, feeling sweaty and strong, not checking my messages until later.

But what if he wanted to make a plan for tomorrow? Or even TONIGHT?

There was a reason I hadn't told my readers about his failure to call. I was still hoping, of course, deluded idiot that I was. Unable to control myself, I turned my cell phone on. Stared at it. Yes! The little envelope floated onto the display! There was a message!

"You have one new message," said the fembot. "To hear your new messages—" I pressed "1" without listening to her stupid spiel. I held my breath. Waited to hear his voice.

"Hello," said my mother's cheerful phone voice. "It's your mother." (Why, why WHY did she always say that? As if I didn't recognize my own mother's voice after thirty-four years, the mother who inevitably called and left messages at just such times, when the last thing I needed was for her to identify herself.) "Just calling to see how you're doing. Give me a call back when you get a chance."

Fuck.

All my energy drained out of me. Three cups of coffee, gone. Good feelings inspired by creativity, gone. Otherwise pleasant weekend spent with friends, gone. I looked in vain for the cute barista, but he had not deigned to appear today. The couples surrounded and overwhelmed me. Next time I would go to a different coffee shop.

Out on the street, it had started to rain harder. Of course I didn't have an umbrella with me. As usual, my laptop case was stuffed with too many things—books, copy of the *Seattle Weekly*, glasses, wallet—to wedge one in. I wanted to sit on the sidewalk and weep. At least, I thought, getting wetter and more bedraggled by the second, this weather suited my emotional state. An Everly Brothers song popped into my head, "Crying in the Rain." My mom and I always sang it in the car when no one else was there.

Hell, I was nothing but a rock-and-roll cliché. A manic-depressive one at that: one minute the table-dancing heroine of a Gloria Gaynor song, the next a down-and-out weather-dependent crybaby. But at least being a cliché meant I wasn't the only person ever to have felt this rotten.

It started to pour. I put the *Seattle Weekly* over my head, but it was instantly soaked. So I walked the rest of the way home in the storm bareheaded, trying to make the best of it. *This storm is going to wash away all my hopes for Sexy Boy,* I told myself. Meanwhile, I tried not to care that the hair which I'd so painstakingly blow-dried that morning was now plastered to my head.

POST A COMMENT

Aw, BB, things will get better, don't worry! If it's any comfort, you're one of my very favorite reads.

CandyCane | Homepage | 9/23/02—11:02 A.M.

•   •   •   •   •

Perhaps you should consider getting involved with some charity organization, do some volunteer work, or try a new hobby (besides boys)—to get yourself out of your apartment and take your mind off yourself!

Anonymous | 9/23/02—3:00 P.M.

Chapter Nine

I spent the next few days dragging my ass around the office in a stupor of self-pity. Without a crush, I had no Hope, and without Hope, it was exponentially harder to be an editor of programming documentation. So instead of working, I checked my e-mail, wrote my blog, and worked myself into a paranoid frenzy about Loser and Theresa—the deputy vice president of our unit.

When I walked past Theresa in the hall on Monday morning, she looked distinctly nervous. Attired in a typically tasteless outfit (visible bra lines, white tights, tassled suede boots), she looked down with great interest at the pen in her hand. Her springy red ringlets, reminiscent of Little Orphan Annie, covered her eyes. She said "Hi" to my kneecaps, and then squirmed over to the other side of the hallway, though her colossal ass took up much of the room between us.

Not that she owed me much of a greeting; I was a mere underling, after all, but she did know who I was, and—up

until this particular Monday—had always given me her dazzling trademark grin, the one that said "I'm young and rich.
How about *you*?" Her demeanor on this grim Monday morning, therefore, disturbed me deeply.

Since the breakup, I'd made a conscious effort not to
think about the two of them. I had no doubt Loser wanted to
fuck her. Just before we'd broken up, I'd seen them flirting at
the morale boosters. Standing in a corner together while he
cracked his stupid jokes and she flashed that self-satisfied
grin. I tried to tell myself that he was just sucking up. After
all, she *was* his boss's boss. It behooved him to kiss her ass.
Still, my heart cracked a little more with each second they
spent together. I knew this man too well to miss the signs: that
dopey smile, the googly eyes, the overanimated demeanor
that had once been the symptoms of his early infatuation
with me.

Just because he wanted her, though, didn't mean he was
going to get her. Still, I couldn't help but be paranoid. And I
couldn't blog about it, which only made things worse. While
I lacked the foresight not to blog about Loser, I had the single
ounce of common sense needed not to blog about ridiculous
fantasies of my ex seducing my V.P. (his V.P. too!) away from
her six-packed, buns-of-steel boyfriend.

"It's NOT going to happen!" said my coworker Arthur,
when I'd confessed my fears about Loser and Theresa to him
two weeks ago. "Just take a deep breath and let that idea GO,"
he'd said, extending his arms in front of him in a meditation
pose. Arthur was a fifty-five-year-old gay former Deadhead
who lived in a "co-housing" project in Snohomish (where, he
hinted, people shared more than just the chores and cooking).
Despite our differences, he was my one friend in the group
because he was actually sociable. My first day on the job, he
was the only person who introduced himself and asked me
to lunch. When The Great Unpleasantness struck, I told him
about it because I so desperately needed a confidant at work.

He was a good listener and easily interruptable. His door was always open, the music of the Grateful Dead wafting out.

Arthur taught yoga and meditation classes at the commune, but at this stage in his life, except for the Grateful Dead T-shirts he often wore, he was very clean-cut, with short graying hair and John Lennon glasses. His eyes were very blue as he looked at me from behind those glasses, his arms still extended. "You're just being paranoid."

That had been my mantra ever since. "I'm just being paranoid. I'm just being paranoid." It had worked just fine, up until Monday, when, for the first time, Theresa did her squirrelly act. By Wednesday afternoon, I'd gotten almost nothing done at work. I was obsessively checking and rechecking all my e-mail accounts for personal messages, and instant messaging with GalPal #3, who spent several hours each afternoon at a University of Washington lab, tabulating results for an important study on E. coli that was on the verge of making her famous and saving a bunch of lives. Despite (or maybe because of) her high-pressure work, Jane was always up for mindless messaging:

> *Rachel says: I have to write my "status report" today. What am I supposed to say? Here's what I've achieved this week: (1) went on a date with the man of my dreams, (2) plunged into a fit of despair because he never called, (3) had paranoid fantasies about my ex fucking my vice president, and (4) realized that I will die old and alone in a nursing home.*
>
> *Jane says: That's a pretty impressive list.*
>
> *Rachel says: You think?*
>
> *Jane says: Well, it's a lot to achieve in one week!*

But apparently my brain chemistry was now wired such that I could not mope around for more than forty-eight hours without taking *ACTION.*

Wednesday, September 25, 2002

4:56 PM Breakup Babe

This has not been one of my finest weeks. Not only have I been rejected by my one and only hope for the future, Sexy Boy, but there are some other *unmentionable* things going on around here that are probably just a result of my fevered imagination. I wish I could tell you about them *anyway,* but I *#!@$ can't! Just take my word for it; they're not *good.*

Up until yesterday, then, I was naught but a useless blob. Attempting, but failing, to do my tedious job, reverting to post-breakup weepy behavior. I was slumped over my desk in the afternoon, pointlessly checking my e-mail yet again for something, *anything* that might offer Hope, when General Celexa put in an appearance.

"Get your ass up!" he barked. "What is this crap?" He poked me with the butt of the machine gun he wore slung around his neck. "I can't do my job if you don't!" He looked around my office. At the walls where I'd hung one colorful poster when I first moved in but otherwise hadn't touched. At the coffee stains on my desk, and the unwashed cup with the crust of two-day-old hot chocolate in it. At the stack of as yet unedited documents on my desk that were supposed to be done by Thursday.

"Why don't you get that lazy ass of yours up and go for a run? You used to be a triathlete! A mountain climber! What are you now? A SISSY, that's what! Three miles. NOW!"

General C.'s bossiness had paid off. Exercise cleared my mind and, by the next day, I was halfway out of my SB-induced slump. Not only that, I had a plan of action! Last night, fueled by cheap Merlot, I'd spent two hours posting an online personal ad on Nervy.com. When I went to bed, it was with the drunken certainty that I'd wake up in the morning to responses piled like Christmas presents in my in-box.

But, when I did wake up, I felt hungover and weary. As my computer booted up, I gazed out my living room window at 17th Avenue, a tree-lined oasis between hip Capitol Hill and the seedier Central District. On the southern horizon, Mount Rainier was bright and clear, but a giant cloud hovered directly over the summit. I remembered lonely nights in GalPal #3's spare bedroom, perusing the online personals until after midnight, feeling a rush of excitement with every promising-looking photo, then a wave of nausea as I realized, *"He's not Loser."* Was I really ready for this?

"Maybe," said Sensible Girl, her voice calm, clear, authoritative, "you need to take some time to be alone." I turned to look at her, not at all startled by her sudden intrusion this time. She leaned in the doorway between the kitchen and the living room, a cup of coffee in hand. She looked wide awake and was dressed surprisingly well for fall in an all-Gap outfit of cream-colored turtleneck and olive corduroy pants.

So, as I stood there by the window, I tried to envision "taking time to be alone." Solitary walks on the Olympic Peninsula, working late into the night on a book that would launch me to literary superstardom, forgoing s*x for yoga.

Then Needy Girl's voice shattered my reverie. "Oh, come on," she said. "This is no big deal. You're just doing this for fun! To mix things up a little." I looked over at her, standing by the computer in a short black negligee, last night's makeup smeared under her eyes. I could smell her rose perfume. "Come on, just see what's up there!" she wheedled. She gestured at the monitor with her head. "Don't you want an attractive man to hang out with this weekend? Don't you want someone to KISS? Don't you at least want some prospects?"

I thought about the upcoming weekend and how I had no cute boys to hang out with. About how SB hadn't called and probably never would. About how I had hadn't kissed anyone in a month, and had no hope of anyone to kiss, much less get married to and have children with. I had to do *something,* didn't I? So I did it. I walked over to my computer, and without even sitting down, I logged on to Nervy.com, clicked My Messages, and—

What?

Even Needy Girl was stunned into silence.

Well.

I certainly hadn't expected that kind of response. In front of me on the screen were zero messages.

Zero.

Not a single male out there had been desperate enough to contact *me,* the unlovable. The untouchable. The controlling bitch who drove men away.

I leaned down and pressed the power button on my computer for the requisite eight seconds until it shuddered off. Then it was just me, alone again in my apartment, with the sound of children's shouts—children that I would never have—filtering in from the school down the street.

Alone, that is, except for my demons Loneliness and Boredom flanking me on either side. Often, the two of them threatened and mocked me, but today they were eerily silent. Each one had a clammy hand pressed down on my shoulder, as if daring me to get up and push them aside.

I did push them aside, though, or rather General C. did. He charged into the apartment in his camouflage, knocked Loneliness and Boredom over, and then dragged me out of there before the two of them could chain me permanently to my bed. He allowed me to throw on clothes, then pushed me down the stairs, onto the street, and into my '87 Honda Civic with these parting words: "You have a job to do. Now, do it. I'll take care of those candy asses."

So I did it. I drove to work, hustled into my office, and slammed the door behind me. Mentally, I prepared for another day *sans* hope. Once I caught my breath, once the caffeine from my soon-to-be-imbibed first cup of coffee wore off, I would be in for it. Not even General C. would be able to keep those two at bay today.

He made a valiant effort. For a few hours, I managed to stay upright and dry-eyed, though unable to do any actual work. Instead, I reorganized all my e-mail folders, banishing any remaining e-mails from Loser to a deeply buried folder called "Other," along with e-mail from the stupid guys I'd spent time with since The Great Unpleasantness began. Maybe I'd mine these for material someday, when I finally wrote my masterpiece, in which every single guy who'd ever dumped me over the years would be eviscerated by my deadly wit.

But even that thought didn't cheer me up. It just made me feel more like the bitter, vengeful spinster I was. I couldn't even turn to GalPal #1 in this crisis, because I was too mortified to tell her about my devastating unpopularity.

By three o'clock, despite a double nonfat split-shot mocha (no whip) and a trip to Empire's cushy gym, The Sports Club, I was ready to go fetal under the desk. It did cross my mind once or twice, as I pumped my leaden limbs on the elliptical trainer, that maybe my expectations had been a bit high. After all, the guys I knew who did the online personals went weeks without ever getting responses from women. But I quickly dismissed this thought. I was a *girl*. Girls got flooded with responses! That's what everyone said!

Every girl, that is, except me.

When I returned from the gym feeling more hopeless than I had before, I knew I was doomed. Even the dark clouds that now threatened to dump down rain did nothing to improve my mood. Tears dribbled out of my eyes as I sat down at my desk. Loneliness and Boredom, looking nearly identical, stood in the doorway.

I started to slither down toward the floor even before they reached me. Like a drowning man taking one last, pointless, reflexive breath, I checked my e-mail before disappearing under the desk.

And there, like a bright orange life preserver tossed to me on a stormy sea, was a message from Sexy Boy, asking me to go flying with him on Saturday!

E-mail Breakup Babe | Comments 4

Though I'd made it a practice not to blog at work, I nonetheless felt compelled to blog about the most recent developments five minutes after they occurred. The general unspoken rule at Empire was "Do a good job, get your work done, and we don't care how much you fuck around."

Of course, there were the ultraparanoid people like Arthur—made so, perhaps, by too much pot smoking in his former life—who made a point of never sending a single personal e-mail from work or, God forbid, visiting a nonwork-related Web site. Most of us, however, reaped the benefits of this relaxed corporate culture. I often arrived after ten. A few coworkers regularly came in at noon or later.

The Rod himself was known for keeping strange hours. It was rumored that he sometimes came to work after hitting the bars (GuyPal #1 had once spotted him at the meat market to end all meat markets, Axis), and was often found the next day sleeping on the couch in his giant office with its picture window facing the Cascades.

Therefore, after breaking my own rule earlier in the week by blogging at work, I didn't feel quite so bad when I did it again. I had to entertain myself one way or another in between sessions in the editing straitjacket. As long as I didn't divulge company secrets or write nasty things about my coworkers, I figured I was okay.

Besides, I was starting to feel as if, when I didn't blog about something that happened in my romantic life, it hadn't really happened. A codependent relationship had blossomed between my readers and me. I compulsively checked the comments on my blog several times a day, feeling a thrill of anticipation with every new comment and a wave of emptiness if there were none. My hits were creeping up, too. I was up to thirty a day now.

After posting the latest on my blog, I decided the day was a wash and spent the rest of Thursday afternoon using Empire resources to engage in detailed e-mail and Instant Messaging analysis with my friends about the meaning of Sexy Boy's "turnaround" and an exhaustive survey of my wardrobe.

Forward to: *Sylvia Bern*
From: *Rachel*
Date: *9/26/2002*
Subject: *What do you think of this?*

S.

   I got this email from Sexy Boy yesterday. What do you think about his "cold" excuse? And is this a date or what? (Also, is it a very bad idea to go flying with a stoner?)

Dear Miss Rachel,

   What are you doing Saturday? I'm planning a fun little flight to San Juan Island for the day. Would you like to go? (Sorry I didn't get in touch this weekend; I was laid up with a pretty bad cold.)

J.

To: *Rachel*
From: *Sylvia Bern*
Date: *9/26/2002*
Subject: *What do you think of this?*

   HMM. It's hard to tell what his intentions are. I think the "cold" excuse is lame, frankly, but you'll have to see if it happens again. Just be careful of him! I like him, but I don't think he knows what he wants. The pot smoking concerns me too.

   As for the flying part, you're on your own. I, personally, would never get in one of those little planes, and I can't believe you would either with your fear of flying! If he's a professional pilot, I'm sure he's safe enough, though.

Rachel says: What does one wear for a date in a small plane?

Lucy says: How about those striped, bell-bottom cords you just bought from Anthropologie and a tight black turtleneck?

Rachel says: That's an idea. I guess a miniskirt is out—very little skin protection should the plane crash.

Lucy says: Hey, Brian has a sheepskin aviator's cap—you know, from the forties—you should wear that too!

Rachel says: What, and make my hair go completely flat? I think not. Besides, it's not an open-cockpit plane! I HOPE.

By Thursday evening, Loneliness and Boredom had long since been banished from my office by the recurrence of Hope-a-noma. I hadn't gotten any editing done, of course, but at least I'd been in my office typing away when my boss, Lyle, stopped in for a quick chat that evening. As we discussed a minor editing issue, I was quite perky, radiating enthusiasm from every pore. Today I even appreciated the reverse fashion sense it took for him to wear a thigh-length white shirt that looked like a lab coat, with "Empire Blast-Off 2001" sewn onto the back in rainbow-colored script. Ah yes, work was so much easier when I had Hope!

I'd become so hopeful, in fact, that I forgot about my pathetic personal ad for three whole hours. It wasn't until I was packing up for the day, and was about to turn off my computer, that I remembered.

I sat frozen at my desk for a minute. Should I check? Not check? Pretend like I'd never placed a personal ad, since Sexy Boy and I were obviously destined to fall into each other's arms with an all-consuming passion that would last the next sixty years of our life? What if that didn't happen? Shouldn't I keep my options open?

Then, affecting a breeziness I didn't really feel, I muttered, "Fuck it," and logged on to Nervy.com. Who cared if those losers had responded to me or not? I had a date with SB this weekend after all! No one could take that away from me. It would therefore not hurt me to just take a peek—a little teeny peek—at Nervy.com before I went home for the night.

When I logged on, heart pounding a little harder than it should have, I found this message at the top of the page: **"Nervy has been experiencing technical difficulties for the last twenty-four hours, and we apologize for any delays you may have encountered in sending and receiving your messages"** followed by . . .

I blinked. Once. Twice.

That couldn't be right, could it?

POST A COMMENT

I don't think I approve of this. You can't go flying with a stoner!

Li'l Sis | 9/25/02—9:18 P.M.

•   •   •   •   •

Remember, keep track of the red flags!

Juliana | Homepage | 9/26/02—10:34 A.M.

•   •   •   •   •

So many men these days seem to suffer from a tragic passivity. I can't speak definitively for this guy, but habitual pot smoking is definitely a sign of that. (Take it from someone who used to do it.) His hot-and-cold behavior would also seem to indicate a deep-rooted indecisiveness. You deserve better than that.

El Politico | Homepage | 9/26/02—6:56 P.M.

•   •   •   •   •

Flying? You're gonna go flying with him? Oh, I bet I'm gonna get that red couch now.

Ambulance Chaser | 9/26/02—7:34 P.M.

Chapter Ten

Sunday, September 29, 2002
11:48 AM Breakup Babe

"So," Sexy Boy was saying as we stood out on the tarmac of Wings Aloft, the wind whipping my hair around so that I could barely hear, "we'll all be wearing the headsets, and that's how we talk to each other."

I glanced over at GuyPal #1, whose long black hair was contained in its habitual ponytail, and who, oddly, was wearing sports goggles instead of his usual black-rimmed glasses. He looked like he could barely contain his excitement. Next to him stood a surprise guest, whom we will dub "Jenny," who was gazing at SB in either fear or adoration, I couldn't tell. I'd been none too thrilled to find Jenny in the front seat of SB's truck and GuyPal #1 in the back that morning when he picked me up.

Not that I didn't like having GuyPal #1 around, but wasn't this supposed to be a date? And who was this Jenny person, with her strawberry blond bob and tight Calvin Klein jeans? (Following GalPal

#2's advice, I'd opted for the striped cords, which were fashionable but not exactly *tight*. They were, perhaps, a size or two too big, because I could never buy pants without worrying that at any moment I would gain back those twenty pounds I'd lost.)

SB had introduced her, simply, as "Jenny." As if, like Prince or Cher, I should know who the f*ck she was and why she was sitting in the front seat of SB's truck while I was banished to the back with GuyPal #1, who wasn't even supposed to be there in the first place.

During the ride to Boeing Field, I'd formulated numerous excuses as to why I'd have to bail out of the flight at the last minute. Truthfully, I was just plain terrified. And now that I knew I didn't have a day of romance on San Juan Island lying ahead of me—SB and I frolicking on the shore! SB and I spotting whales with our binoculars! SB and I holding hands as we window-shopped in Friday Harbor!—I was much less inclined to squelch my terror.

These fantasies had danced in my brain the night before *despite* the running list of red flags I was now so sensibly keeping. Stoner. Flaky. Lived in a repulsive group house in a room littered with dirty socks. That was three right there!

Hope-a-noma had such a hold on me, in fact, that I hadn't even responded to any of my Nervy supplicants, of which there were now about thirty. When I'd logged on Thursday night, prepared for more stony silence, I'd found, along with Nervy's apology for their "technical difficulties," thirty-two responses.

After fifteen minutes of clicking through them, though, my excitement turned to overload. How was I supposed to keep track of all these handles: Air_and_Water, Duke_of_Gville, HotelNeutral? And how was I, SeattleSweetie, supposed to make any kind of informed choice? What if Mr. Right looked just the least bit wrong in his photograph so I didn't choose him?

So I responded by not responding. Instead I let the messages pile up in my in-box, checked them when I needed an ego boost, and spent most of my energy daydreaming about this moment with SB.

But now, as the sun played hide-and-seek and little drops of rain beat against my Windbreaker, I couldn't see a single reason to risk my life for such a red flag–ridden man—if you could even call someone who lived in a group house at his age a "man."

Unless . . .

Maybe Jenny was GuyPal #1's date?

"The flight will probably take forty-five minutes," said SB. "The weather is supposed to be pretty good, but—" He looked up at the darkening sky. "Well, I think it will be fine. The forecast was good. Each one of you has your own parachute in the plane, just in case."

WHAT? No f*cking way. PARACHUTES? I was not going on this plane.

"Hey—" I started to say.

"Just kidding," said SB. GuyPal #1 laughed. Jenny smiled. She turned to GuyPal #1 and giggled. Maybe she *was* his date.

"Yes, Miss R.?" said SB, looking over at me, smiling a dazzling grin that contained the sunshine of an entire Seattle summer in it.

"I—uh—" *I have terrible motion sickness. I'm just not feeling well. I'm terrified of flying.*

"I'm—um—just wondering which airport we're going to, you know, since there are two on San Juan Island?"

"Roche Harbor," he said. "Does that meet with your approval, madam?" He winked at me, and I knew, right then, that I would do anything for the attentions of this man, including climbing aboard this four-person death trap and flying into the Bermuda Triangle.

"Yes," I said. It came out just above a whisper.

Thirty minutes later, we were two-thirds of the way toward San Juan Island. For the first fifteen minutes, I'd gripped the arms of my seat in sheer terror, and could not join in the seemingly unconcerned banter of the other three as the plane bounced through the sky and the cheerful blue blanket of Puget Sound spread below us.

After half an hour, the Xanax I'd taken was having its calming effect, I'd gotten used to the bouncing, and with only fifteen minutes left, what could happen? I was irrationally reassured, too, by how light the plane felt: as if you could crash in it, and not do much more than bounce once or twice, dust yourself off, and walk away.

Then the radio went out.

One minute there was a reassuring crackle of voices through my headphones, then there was silence.

"Shit," said SB. "I forgot to—"

The plane jolted suddenly upward, my stomach down. And I realized I had made the worst mistake of my entire life getting on this plane.

"Well y'all, our radio seems to have gone out, but it's nothing to worry about," said SB, suddenly taking on a soothing Chuck Yeageresque southern drawl that—I remembered from reading *The Right Stuff*—had probably been drilled into him at flight school.

I turned for a glimpse of how GuyPal #1 and Jenny were taking this. Jenny, right next to me, had gone completely pale. GuyPal #1 had a half smile frozen on his normally beaming face, as if he were trying to decide exactly how to react: scream, or go on pretending everything was fine?

The plane swung to the left, as if punched. We entered a thick veil of gray. "That's just a little bit of turbulence," said SB. "Also nothing to worry about. It looks like we've hit a bit of a cloud cover, but I expect that once we get through it, it will be clear"—*sharp downward jolt*—"sailing again."

Oh, how I wished I'd called my mother back last night when she'd left me a message. I'd often say to her, when flying to or from Seattle to California, "My plane's not gonna crash, right?"

"Right," she'd say. "Your plane is not going to crash."

"Do you promise?" I'd say.

"I promise."

And for some silly reason, I always believed her. Now, however, it was clear that we were going to crash. All because I hadn't asked her. I stared out the window, but all I could see was gray. I whimpered under my breath. *Mommy.*

"Hey P.," SB was saying, his voice sounding more tense now, "there's a switch right over there. Can you—"

WAP! WAP WAP WAP! The plane bounced—once, twice, three times, and seemed to skid.

"Jesus," muttered SB. Something icy touched my hand and I

jumped. It was Jenny, reaching to put her hand in mine. I took it, clutching it hard.

"What?" said GuyPal #1, his voice much too high. "What did you want me to do?"

"Never mind, brother," said SB, clearly trying to keep his tone light, which only made me more terrified. "I got it." He reached across the control panel and flipped a switch, in the process briefly letting go of the steering yoke. Like a toddler freed from its parent's grasp, the plane skittered off to the left, then jumped upward, as if for joy.

I was going to throw up. I put my hand over my mouth and tried to stare out at the horizon. But there was no horizon. There were only layers of gray—some light and gauzy, some thick and ominous. I had never seen so many shades of gray.

So this was it. This was how I was going to die. A strange calm descended over me. My nausea disappeared.

"We just have to ride out this chop, guys," said SB, over the headset. "It's kinda fun, isn't it?" None of us answered. "The radio should come back on soon. I forgot to turn the alternator on earlier, but it's on now so the radio should come back and if it doesn't, well, no biggie."

No biggie? NO BIGGIE? For a moment, fury destroyed my preternatural calm. Then we hit another bump and the fury fell away. I didn't have time for such emotions now. I had to prepare. I had to be optimistic yet ready for the worst. I had to review my life and give thanks for what I'd had. Determine what I'd do differently if I got another chance. Which would include never, EVER getting in a small plane with a womanizing flake again.

All of a sudden, a loud noise hissed in my ears. I jumped. A male voice started up. "—and turbulence right over Shaw Island . . ."

The radio!

"Whoo!" said SB, sounding noticeably relieved. "That was quick. Now the landing should be a snap, once I get down through this—"

The plane shook violently from side to side. Jenny gripped my hand even tighter. A dry bag fell from its storage place somewhere above us and landed with a loud thump, right next to one of Jenny's rather tackily shod feet. "Oh my God," she whimpered.

Then, as if the cloud had never happened, we were back in the sunshine. Blue all around us, the whitecaps of Puget Sound winking below. I continued to grip my armrest with one hand and Jenny's clammy hand with the other, staring hard at the landscape I loved—islands, water, mountains—not daring to believe that we might actually survive this flight.

But the turbulence stopped, and in a few minutes SB was on the radio to announce his landing.

Jenny withdrew her hand from mine and gave me a strained smile. With a burst of euphoria, I thought maybe we'd be best friends forever now, bonded by our near-death experience, but then suddenly I remembered. *Shit, who IS she?* If she was Guypal #1's date, shouldn't he be the one in the back holding her hand?

I was taking the f*cking ferry back, I swear to God.

E-mail Breakup Babe | Comments 3

Chapter Eleven

Monday, October 7, 2002
9:18 AM Breakup Babe

So on Friday night, I met a baby stud whom we shall dub the Li'l Rockclimbing Spy. The LRS (a private investigator by trade) is, I regret to inform you, a mere twenty-four years old. Ten years younger than me! But I have such a weakness for climbing boys. And this one was nice. And cute. And had big muscles. So—surprise!—I gave him my card, though I'm old enough to be his grandmother.

Now, I know what you're thinking (besides "that perverted cradle robber!"). You're thinking that after the Sexy Boy debacle, I'd take time to regroup. Recharge. Reconsider. Hell, perhaps even *retreat* from the dating scene for a while until I get my head out of my a*s, where it was so firmly entrenched through the month of September.

But you'd be wrong. Because two nights after I met the Li'l Rockclimbing Spy, I found myself on my red couch, dangerously close to having sex with him. He wore a baggy black T-shirt that I'd

been dying to tear off for a better look at his abs. So far I'd restrained myself, because I feared what might happen to me if I actually saw them.

Bleary-eyed, I paused in my latest entry to take a sip of my
double-tall-split-shot-no-foam-vanilla latte (extra hot) and
glance at the uninspiring scene around me. This morning I'd
decided to take a break from Drooly Couple Land (aka Victrola) and try Vivace, another Capitol Hill coffee shop. People
raved about the coffee here. *Their beans are the best*, they'd
say, in hushed tones. *It's a secret brand imported from Italy!*

So here I was, and the coffee *was* good—much better than
Victrola's—but the people watching sucked. First off, there
were no cute male baristas to flirt with, only one bitchy female
whose role model in life was Courtney Love (pre-Hollywood
transformation), complete with bleached blond hair and gobs
of smeared black eyeliner. Immediately after I purchased my
coffee, she disappeared into a back room. Oddly, there was no
one else in the place except for a homeless-looking guy slumped
over his fancy Italian coffee in the corner. Devo played a little
too loudly over the sound system.

At least I was inspired by my subject today. I was still tired
from my late night with the Li'l Rockclimbing Spy—but it was
a good kind of tired. Not an "I-stayed-up-all-night-and-didn't-
even-get-a-stupid-kiss" kind of tired, but an "I-stayed-up-all-
night-and-it-was-worth-every-second" kind of tired. I knew my
readers were going to be titillated by the juicy details I planned
to provide, but, judging from the newest comments on my last
entry, I needed to wrap up the Sexy Boy fiasco first.

POST A COMMENT

Glad you survived! But what happened on the island? An orgy,
maybe? Details, puhleeze!

Delilah | Homepage | 10/02/02—8:38 P.M.

•   •   •   •   •

As a pilot myself, I can say that forgetting to turn the alternator on is not such a big deal. You can fly without a radio too, if there are no clouds. Sounds like your flight was just fine; planes can handle a lot more turbulence than you can, so I hope you don't break up with him over that.

Pilot Bob | 10/03/02—11:56 P.M.

•   •   •   •   •

Okay, how many red flags are we up to now?

Juliana | Homepage | 10/04/02—8:57 A.M.

•   •   •   •   •

Oh, I would say about 500!

Breakup Babe | 10/05/02—3:48 P.M.

The problem was now that Sexy Boy was off the romantic radar, I'd lost interest in writing about him. The whole thing still hurt, after all. I would much rather write about something new and promising than dwell on that misguided adventure. But my readers were right. I couldn't exactly start a story without finishing it.

> But wait! Before we go down that tantalizing road, I owe you an ending, don't I? I guess we gotta get Sexy Boy out of our system before we move on, so here's how it all played out.

For a moment, thanks to Delilah's comment, I thought about finishing it all off with an orgy. A vodka-soaked foursome in a Friday Harbor hotel room. I could steer my blog into the realm of fiction right now and never look back. Think of all the hot men I could conjure up for myself, the steamy nights, the exotic locales! Hell, if I wanted to, I could tell my readers that I was a best-selling author and fabricate tales about life among the glittering literati! Free from the shackles of Empire and the ghost of Loser, Breakup Babe could roam the world with her laptop, soaking up adoration and cranking out best sellers. My increasingly far-flung readers would never be the wiser!

But no. I was too truthful for that. And maybe I knew, somewhere deep down, that my real life was about to get plenty interesting. I took one last, lackluster glance around Vivace, and set forth to chronicle the dreary end of my "relationship" with Sexy Boy.

As soon as we landed on San Juan Island, the weather turned worse. Sexy Boy, GuyPal #1, and Jenny voted to wait out the storm by getting drunk in a bar in Friday Harbor. For me, however, drinking heavily in my current emotional state—which had morphed from terror to euphoria to depression all within a half an hour—would be a fatal mistake. I'd probably end up weeping on the barroom floor or getting into a fistfight with Jenny.

So I excused myself after one drink to go to the whale museum down the street. There I drowned my sorrows in the deep blue waters of the whale photos, and in reading about the whales' endurance.

Each year humpbacks migrate from the South Pacific Ocean to their northern breeding grounds. It's a huge trip—about 7,500 miles. During this migration they don't feed at all, yet they have enough energy to calve and mate and to swim over 1,000 miles per month.

If a whale can go six months without food, I thought, trying to hold back the tears, I can go a few damn months without having a boyfriend. Why in the world had I allowed my hopes to balloon out of control like this?

But the tears did start falling, so I went into one of the dark audio booths where you could listen to whale sounds on a headset. For half an hour, I listened to orcas talking to each other in the Strait of Juan de Fuca. As their soulful calls echoed through the water, I cried.

I cried because I'd seen Sexy Boy touch Jenny on the back

when we walked into the bar. I cried for my father, who would have known from the beginning that Sexy Boy was an utter waste of time. I cried for my cat, Spider, who'd died three years ago, and for my dead golden retriever, Samantha, who'd played hide-and-seek with me when I was ten. I cried for Loser, and for anyone who once loved me and no longer did.

What made me cry the hardest was that the whale sounds reminded me of the Judy Collins record, *Whales and Nightingales*, that my mom used to play in the seventies. When I'd been five, the whales' eerie songs spoke to me of mystery and possibility. Now, though, they seemed all about loss.

Finally, after three times through the *Orca's Greatest Hits*, I walked out of the booth dry-eyed and determined.

I'd decided three important things: (1) I was never dating a stoner again, (2) I was never dating again, and (3) I was taking the ferry back to Anacortes. How I would get to Seattle after that, I didn't know. I'd take a bus or a f*cking taxi if I had to. I probably had just enough in my life savings to cover the fare. One thing was certain, however. I was not getting back in a plane with Captain Sexy Boy and copilot Jenny.

As I was halfway through my latte and just hitting my authorial stride, two shaggy-looking guys walked into the place, sat down at the table right next to mine (hello, the place was empty!), and started talking loudly. The surly barista was nowhere to be seen, so they hadn't been able to order coffee. But they didn't seem to mind.

"The sound was really off last night, man." Wannabe Rock Star #1 wore a tight-fitting wool hat, a three-day growth of beard, and an Army-Navy surplus jacket of the same type I'd worn when I was sixteen.

"Shit, I can't even remember, I'm so fucking hungover. I didn't think it was bad." WBRS #2 had on a red flannel shirt and khaki shorts over waffle-weave long underwear.

"No, that sound dude had his head up his ass."

I thought about telling them to talk more quietly. There was an *artiste* at work who had important things to tell her fans (ahem!), but then I reconsidered. I didn't feel like making enemies this early in the day. Even if they were just wannabe rock stars who didn't realize that it was 2002, not 1992. Trying to ignore them, I went back to the blog.

So, using motion sickness as an excuse, I didn't get back in that plane. And one ferry ride, one taxi ride, two bus rides, and eight hours later, I was home safe while rain continued to lash the Sound.

The three of them, of course, made it home just fine after the storm subsided late that night. Oh, I was happy that GuyPal #1 was safe, but I wouldn't have minded seeing Sexy Boy and Jenny take a little dip in the Sound.

Because now that Sexy Boy had successfully piloted his plane back to Seattle (damn him!), there was an unpleasant task I had to complete. I had to *confess*. Only after I confessed would I be purged, and only after I was purged could I move on.

I wrote Sexy Boy a heartbroken e-mail confessing my crush on him, and telling him how much he'd confused and hurt me. He'd written back, apologized, and then made me a strange and surprising "offer."

I enjoy spending time around you, R., but I make it a rule not to date people on the rebound, which I think you are. However, I would be happy to oblige if you are looking for a casual romantic encounter, etc.

I did a double take when I first saw this e-mail. I'd expected either a flat-out rejection or a confession on his part (admittedly, a much less likely possibility: *"But I DO love you! That Jenny person— she's no one!"*). I hadn't expected Sexy Boy to take this kind of messed-up middle ground.

After exchanging multiple e-mails on the subject with various

GalPals, it made much more sense. Sexy Boy, in a word, was *lame*. All along his position toward me had defined "messed-up middle ground." So, in fact, his "offer" made perfect sense. The most out-spoken advice came from a long-lost GalPal—now living in the 'burbs with three children—who still loved to experience the dating life vicariously:

From: *Long-lost GalPal*
To: *R.*

Tell Sexy Boy if he wants a "casual romantic encounter" he should have one with himself. Meanwhile, as he's jerking off to thoughts of his ex-girlfriend, you'll be out looking for a real man.

The GalPals were right, of course. But I responded to him by suggesting that we meet to discuss his proposition over cocktails. I knew, on the one hand, that it was ridiculous. I certainly had better things to do with my time than dillydally with men who were offering me casual sex. On the other hand, it seemed apropos—glamorous, even—that in my new incarnation as Breakup Babe, I should be meeting sexy stoners to discuss meaningless flings in pseudoseedy bars.

I planned, of course, to tell him that I just wanted to be friends. But could I help it if I wanted to drag it out a little bit?

We met at Hattie's Hat, the most happening bar in Ballard. As we seated ourselves in the vinyl booth, surrounded by boys in band T-shirts and girls in tattoo-baring tank tops (embarrassingly similar to my own tattoo-baring tank top), it required an act of will not to throw myself at him and say, "Take me, whatever the cost!" My hands trembled as I held my drink. After twenty minutes' worth of small talk, I said "This is what I think." I looked up at Sexy Boy through a smoky haze. He had on a soft-looking brown sweater with a white stripe across the middle. I wanted to reach out and touch it.

> "I think," I said, talking as slowly as I could, trying to ignore the ache in my chest, "that we should just be friends."
>
> The smile fell off his face. He raised his eyebrows. It took him only an instant to regain his composure. Then he leaned back in his chair, nodded, and said, with a wise expression, as if it were his own idea, "It's probably best if we were just friends."

I looked away from the computer, remembering this moment. It had been so bittersweet to see that disappointed look on Sexy Boy's face. Gratifying and heartbreaking at the same time. Just then, the chick from the cash register materialized, interrupting my reverie. She minced over to the table next to me. How she moved in the skintight jeans she was wearing, I wasn't sure.

"I heard you guys were awwessomme last night," she said, beaming. The dark purple lipstick she'd applied far outreached the bounds of her suspiciously voluptuous lips. "Did you read the review in *The Times* today?"

The Times? I whipped my head around. Oh, shit. Was that—??

God, I was obvious. What a celebrity whore! I whipped back to face my computer. My mind worked rapidly. Was it . . . could it be . . . the guys from Nirvana, now the Foo Fighters? I desperately wanted to turn around again. If it *was* the Foo Fighters, was it possible that it was Courtney Love at the counter? But what would Courtney Love be doing working in a coffee shop? Maybe she'd been shooting up in the back. But didn't she have a Hollywood career? And wasn't she embroiled in legal troubles with the rest of Nirvana?

Aargh. When people had raved about the beans at Vivace, they'd said nothing about it being a haunt of loud and hard-to-recognize rock stars. With half an ear cocked to their conversation, I plowed ahead.

So Sexy Boy and I made a toast to friendship, Hope-a-noma was surgically removed from my chest, and we walked next door to the Tractor Tavern—Seattle's temple of alt-country music—for a rendezvous with GuyPal #1.

And that, my friends, is where I met the Li'l Rockclimbing Spy. (Yes, I *know* I said I wasn't going to date anymore. But we all knew that wasn't true to start with, didn't we?)

The LRS was chatting with GuyPal #1 when we arrived. At first I was so distracted by Sexy Boy's presence, I didn't take much notice of the lanky kid with the bleached blond mop of hair. But when Sexy Boy floated over to the bar, the LRS and I started chatting. Then I found out, in short order, that he knew my old flame, Ziggy—the crazy, sexy rock climber I'd dated just before Loser—and that he himself was a rock climber.

That was all the aphrodisiac I needed. I henceforth took a keen interest in the apparently well-developed biceps that lurked under the T-shirt and the charming way he used words like "epic" (as in "that's epic, dude") and "amped" (as in "I was really amped to come to this show tonight!").

Ever since I'd experienced the defining love of my life, at age twenty-two, with a long-haired, guitar-playing, poetry-spouting rock climber named Josh (nicknamed "the Feather" by my father) who discovered god—lowercase g—on a climbing trip and then dumped me, I'd not very sensibly developed a thing for climbers. Before I knew it, the Li'l Rockclimbing Spy asked for my number and I gave it to him. But not without asking, to my credit, thank you very much, "So do you smoke as much pot as Ziggy does?"

Not exactly the most subtle question in the world, but I had my standards to adhere to now. I tried to ask it with a tolerant-looking smile, so that if he was a gigantic pothead he wouldn't be afraid to tell me.

"No," he snorted. "That guy smoked sick amounts of weed." He shifted from one foot to the other, took a sip of his beer, and looked around the bar.

I waited, hoping he would provide a little more information so I wouldn't have to come right out and say, "So how many times a day do YOU get high?" (For Ziggy, it had been at least three. For Sexy Boy, who knew?) Out of the corner of my eye I saw Sexy Boy and GuyPal #1 walking in the front door of the Tractor. They'd probably gone outside for a toke.

"I hardly smoke at all," he said, giving a dismissive little shrug.

Test passed! And now, after just one dinner and half a movie, here we were on the Red Couch o' Love. I hadn't expected things to move so fast, but I also hadn't expected to feel so comfortable with him.

"So," said the Li'l Rockclimbing Spy as he slipped his hand under my shirt, "should we go in the other room?" I let it stay there, even though I knew I shouldn't. It felt hot against my breast. I looked into his gray eyes, which were now staring at me intently. He had a pierced eyebrow, which at first I thought was ridiculous but now found quite alluring.

"I don't know," I said. It felt *so good* to have a male body pressed up against me, to feel, if not loved, then wanted, desired.

"I—um . . ." Before I could answer him, the LRS started kissing me, kneading my breasts gently with his strong hands. My resistance weakened another notch.

"Tell him you have to go to bed!" Sensible Girl's voice was high-pitched, full of alarm. She sat on the end of the couch, watching us with wide-eyed terror, as if the Li'l Rockclimbing Spy were a hockey-masked psycho. "You can date him," she barked, "that's fine! BUT DON'T SLEEP WITH HIM TONIGHT!"

"Oh, for Christ's sake, stop worrying so much." Needy Girl was perched on the sofa's other arm, wearing a pink-and-orange psychedelic halter top. She had a Mojito in hand, and bright blue eyeshadow sparkled on her eyelids. She crossed her legs. "This guy is just a kid! If anyone is going to get hurt here, it's him! Why should she stop herself from having fun? She could die tomorrow!"

"You're really hot," the Li'l Rockclimbing Spy whispered, his voice resonating deep in my groin. Then he slid his hand downward and under the waistband of my jeans. His hand was rough and cal-loused from years of climbing. Somehow I found the willpower to reach down and gently remove it. Undeterred, he slid it back up to my breasts and started gently licking my earlobes. I held my breath. Closed my eyes. His breath in my ear was so . . .

"Don't let yourself go there!" yelped Sensible Girl.

My eyes flew open. I looked up at the ceiling, where the Li'l Rockclimbing Spy and I cast huge shadows that moved jerkily, as if in a silent movie. His shadow looked like that of a monster devour-ing its prey.

When I spoke, my voice was husky. "I really have to get to bed," I said. It came out a half croak.

"Why?" the Li'l Rockclimbing Spy took a breath and then started kissing my neck.

"I have to get up early and . . . and . . . write."

"Oh yeah?" said the Li'l Rockclimbing Spy. He stopped kissing me, and there was interest in his voice. I could feel his warm breath on my cheek, his body resting on top of mine. He peered down at me. "What are you writing?"

"Um . . . a. . . ." I almost said "blog," but then I said, "A book."

"Really?" He sat up and looked at me curiously. His hair was sticking up in different directions, making me melt into even more of a puddle. "What about?"

"It's . . ." Why did I always have to open my big mouth about being a writer? People inevitably wanted to know what you were writing, and at this point, my credibility was questionable. "It's, well . . ." What a liar I was. *It's a book about how I've always wanted to write a book but have failed miserably.*

"How about I tell you next time?" I said, before realizing that up until this second, we had not talked about any "next time." My heart started to pound loudly, right after which he laid his head down on my chest with his ear right up against it. *Great.* My stupid heart al-ways gave itself away.

I waited for him to comment about the loud pounding, or to reject my coded request for another date, but all he said was, "All right." He reached his hand under my shirt again, but this time just caressed my stomach. He sounded completely unfazed that I had just proposed a second date.

"Well, when do you want to get together again?" he asked. I let out a sigh of relief. Then I thought quickly. I was going on a date Thursday night with some Seattle-dwelling friend of Longtime Lover Boy's. (LTLB and I were so practiced at the on-again, off-again thing, that when we were "off" we could do things like set each other up on blind dates.) A Jewish doctor, apparently, who'd gone to Harvard with Longtime Lover Boy. I hadn't seen a picture of him, so I was suspicious, but my mother would never forgive me if I turned down a date with a Harvard-educated Jewish doctor.

"Maybe Saturday night?" I couldn't believe this was really me, staid, devoted girlfriend for two years, now making dates with two different guys in the same week. Then again, I remembered that pre-Loser, GalPal #3 had once referred to me as a "dating machine."

At least, I thought, running my fingers through the Li'l Rock-climbing Spy's soft blond hair, my body humming with desire, I'd learned *something* since then. In ye olden days, I'd sleep with cute boys on a first date only to have things end with a sickening thud three weeks later. This time, I wasn't going to get too close to *anyone* unless I really trusted him.

"All right," the Li'l Rockclimbing Spy said again, sounding relaxed and comfortable. He lay back down on top of me, but the urgency was gone. We lay there for a few minutes not saying anything, our bodies entwined. It was warm in my apartment, and he smelled like clean sweat. It excited me to be this close to someone I barely knew at all. Excited and frightened me at the same time. Maybe because, as much as I seemed to be leaping into beginnings these days, I was also preoccupied with endings.

Now that this has started, I wondered as we lay there together, our heartbeats slowing down, *how is it going to end?*

E-mail Breakup Babe | Comments 4

Back at Vivace, Courtney Love was still sucking up to the Foo Fighters. They were dropping names left and right, but I didn't recognize any of them because they were on a first name basis with the celebs. They talked about a "Pete" (Pete Buck from R.E.M?), a "Dave" (Dave Matthews?), and an "Angie" (Angelina Jolie?), but I didn't have time to sit around and decipher their stoned-sounding babble.

As I packed up my laptop, none of them, of course, even shot me a glance. Why would they, I guess, when they partied with the likes of Angie? They might be a little more impressed if they knew I was a purveyor of soft-core porn! After pressing the "Publish" button to make my blog entry go live on the Web, I couldn't quite believe I'd written phrases like his hand felt "hot against my breast." I giggled at the thought.

I hoped, as I headed for the door, that I wasn't writing about sex just to keep people entertained. Suddenly I remembered Mrs. Bloomstedt proudly telling my fourth-grade class that I would be a famous writer someday. When she said that, she probably hadn't thought I'd be writing things like "his voice resonating deep in my groin."

Embarrassment engulfed me as I hurried out of Vivace into a chilly, gray October morning. Who did I think I was? Danielle Steele? "Sorry," I said under my breath, to whom I wasn't exactly sure. Mrs. Bloomstedt? My younger, more innocent self? I rushed toward the bus stop, late as usual, and waited for a thunderbolt to smite me on the head.

POST A COMMENT

Ah, that's more like it. You're a girl after my own heart!

Delilah | Homepage | 10/07/02—1:02 P.M.

• • • • •

There are people with children reading this thing, you know. Think of the children!

Mother of Two | 10/07/02—4:00 P.M.

• • • • •

Have you ever thought of writing a Romance Novel? I bet you'd be good at it.

Jeannie | 10/07/02—10:38 P.M.

•   •   •   •   •

Good thing Mom hasn't found your blog yet.

Li'l Sis | 10/08/02—8:41 A.M.

Chapter Twelve

Friday, October 11, 2002

9:47 AM Breakup Babe

Last night, I went on my first blind date since becoming a swinging single. On paper, this guy would give my mom a major orgasm with these three little words: Jewish. Doctor. Harvard.

In person, well, let's just say it was a blind date. And you know how blind dates usually are. Lots of nervous anticipation thudding into dull disappointment. Plenty of alcohol to lubricate the conversation in the face of creeping boredom.

This was not one of those dates.

When I walked into Pasta Bella, however, I did not have high hopes. Longtime Lover Boy had failed to provide any details about The Doctor's looks—even when pressed—which I took to be an ominous sign. The Doctor himself had said, over e-mail, that he would be "the tall, dirty blond, dorky-looking guy."

Great.

Not that looks are the most important thing, of course! Even if he were fat and bald with bizarre growths protruding from his face, I would give him a chance. One day I'd probably look that way myself! It would just be easier to give him a chance, if he were, of course, hot.

I determined he wasn't there yet (no solo, dirty-blond, dorky-looking guys to be seen), so I got a seat and immediately ordered a glass of Merlot. I wasn't nervous, exactly. Just apprehensive. This was the first blind date I'd been on in years. And familial expectations were running high. He was an Ivy League doctor, after all, the kind of guy I'd been programmed since birth to marry!

The whole family had been thrilled, at first, when I started dating Loser—my first real Jewish boyfriend. We weren't a religious family, but we nonetheless had the inborn snobbery of the Chosen People. "Jewish men make the best husbands, you know," my mom (who'd never even been bat mitzvahed) had told me I don't know how many times in the last ten years.

About six months into my relationship with Loser, though, she stopped saying it. Occasionally I'd say, "Hey, Mom, isn't it great I'm finally dating someone Jewish? That means we'll definitely have a Jewish wedding!" But she would just look off into the middle distance when I asked this question and say "uh-huh" in a distracted way that precluded all further conversation.

Little did I know then, that she, like everyone else except me, saw Loser for the loser he was. She, like everyone else, was just too polite to say it.

But when I'd told her about my upcoming date with The Doctor, she'd gone into a swoon on the other end of the phone, emitting a sound that was part sigh, part moan, and which signaled to me that all her hopes for a good match were instantly revived. She pictured chuppas and challahs. She pictured kippahs and ketubahs! Dark-haired grandchildren and doctors in the family! "Oh," she'd said. *"Wow!"*

The stakes, in other words, were high. At least for my mother. And for The Doctor, who, tonight, single-handedly had the opportunity to redeem all Jewish men for Loser's sins.

As I waited for my wine, I looked around the restaurant. Pasta Bella was annually voted one of the "most romantic" restaurants in Seattle, but it was "romantic" in a very Seattle way, which is to say it was boring. Yes, it had candlelight, scarlet walls, and green glass lamps that bathed each group of diners in a pool of sea green light, but there was so little energy, so little *sexiness* amid the sea of plaid and Timberland boots, it was hard to feel romantic. At least in this particular "romantic" establishment.

There were several couples of the early middle-aged Seattle variety swimming in the sea green pools. One couple looked nearly identical with their metal-framed glasses, gray-streaked dark hair, and matching REI fleece jackets. If there was one thing that disturbed me about Seattle, it was that fleece was the uniform of choice. Fleece at fancy restaurants. Fleece at the theater. Fleece at the opera! It was a citywide illness, REI the ever-breeding host! I myself owned at least six fleece jackets and tops in different colors, styles, and weights (as well as a pair of fleece pants), but I had the sense to know they were for outdoor activities and outdoor activities *only*. No doubt, when I went to New York City in a week to visit old friends, I would not have to put up with people wearing fleece in fine dining establishments.

As Chet Baker played in the background, I looked at my watch. Eight minutes after eight. Where was The Doctor? Was it possible I was being stood up? I was starting to feel self-conscious, sitting alone. I took a sip of wine that was really more of a gulp. Then I remembered. I had a book with me. Aha. The perfect thing to keep me looking cool and composed. I pulled *Blogger Nation* out of my purse and started to read.

A minute later, I heard the door to the restaurant open. A gust of cool air blew in. I looked up. An incredibly handsome man had just walked in. Tall, with closely cropped hair. Beautiful olive complexion. Big brown eyes. Could it be? But why would a man like that need a blind date?

No. It couldn't. I looked back down at my book, but the words swam in front of my eyes. And even on the off chance that he WAS my date, I could pretend to be totally absorbed in my book, completely indifferent to the fact that he was ten minutes late.

"R.?" I looked up. The beautiful man was standing at my table.

"Are you D.?" I said. Duh.

"Yep, that's me." He put out his hand and we shook. His handshake was firm, his hands strong yet graceful, the kind of hands you could imagine performing delicate surgery or cradling a beautiful olive-skinned baby destined for Yale. Under a fashionably cracked leather jacket (no fleece to be seen!), he wore a white oxford shirt that set off his lovely complexion. A ridiculous thought flashed through my head. *This man is my destiny.*

My destiny apologized for being late and sat down, smiling at me a little stupidly, as if he couldn't quite believe what he was seeing either. The waiter approached.

"Can I get you something to drink while you're deciding?"

Without taking his eyes off me, The Doctor said, "I'll have what she's having." And the starting gun went off.

The morning after my date with the doctor, I was back at Victrola, having decided that Drooly Couples were better than Distracting Rock Stars. Besides, Drooly Couples made their appearances mostly on weekends, and this was a weekday morning. Which also meant—bingo!—the cute barista was here, which only added to my sparkly mood.

Though he wasn't working the register when I walked in, he was farther down the counter making espresso. And just as I could immediately sense his presence when I walked in, he sensed mine. I tried not to look over, but I saw, out of the corner of my eye, the way he looked up as soon as I entered Victrola. The way his eyes stayed on me as he continued making espresso. So, after half a beat, I looked up at him, and Oh. My. God. I had never seen him looking so fine. He'd recently cut his dark hair so that he now had a very clean-cut look, but those funky orange glasses gave him just the right touch of hip. I was such a sucker for a guy in glasses.

He smiled at me, but this time his smile was different. It was more confident than it had been in the past, like, *Hey, I know you like me; I like you too!* The brightness of his smile surprised me—he had been so furtive before—but it thrilled me too. I smiled back, one of my bigger smiles—a seven out of ten on the Dazzle-O-Meter. I had to save some weaponry for later.

Now, half an hour later as I came up for a gulp of air from the blog, I would not let myself look at him again. Not yet. I may have been someone's deluded girlfriend for a long time, but I still knew how to play this game. Besides, suddenly I had more than enough men to keep me occupied. Thank God. The more men I had to distract myself with, the less I dwelled on Loser. Still, I would restrain myself from flirting with the cute barista again until I left the premises. Instead, I watched the excitable gay barista high-five a customer at the register. Then I took a sip of my double-tall-split-shot-caramel macchiato and kept writing.

Forty-five minutes later, however, Destiny was getting the hell on my nerves. So far I'd plied The Doctor with the usual questions— Where are you from? What do you do for fun? How do you like Seattle—to which he'd responded at great length, articulately, wittily. But after each response, instead of asking me a question about my life, he would look at me eagerly, waiting for the next chance to tell me all about his life—again. I felt a sense of déjà vu.

Is there a man in Seattle who knows how to talk about someone or something besides himself? I wondered, watching The Doctor as he dug with gusto into his *Linguine Con Salsa Di Carne Di Vitello*.

The Doctor droned on. I noticed that he had a little lock of hair in the front that curled upward. It made him look a little bit like . . . *Who did it remind me of?* As I focused on that lock of hair, wondering if he could have possibly styled it like that on purpose, my thoughts drifted to the Li'l Rockclimbing Spy. I hadn't told him about this date. Maybe if I got home by ten, I could give him a call.

Ironic, I thought, watching The Doctor's lock of hair bob up and down as he ate, how I'd gone from imagining our darling Yale-bound baby asleep in its Pottery Barn crib to a late-night booty call to the Li'l Rockclimbing Spy. A prick of despair flared in my gut. Or maybe it was indigestion. My *Manicotti Al Forro* was a bit on the heavy side.

"And so," The Doctor was wrapping up another grandiose statement about his career as an orthopedic surgeon who operated on victims of horrifying accidents, "it's all about saving lives. For me."

I looked up at him. Searched his exquisite face for a trace of irony. There were times during our conversation that I thought I detected a tone of self-mockery, a flicker of a smile, as if he knew how egotistical he was being. Then it would quickly disappear. This was one of those moments.

Then it hit me. The lock of hair. Tintin—that's who it reminded me of! The beloved Belgian cartoon character!

I'd started on my second glass of wine by now. My date was a lost cause anyway, so why not have a little fun here while I could?

"Really?" I said, in a mock-enthusiastic voice. "Well," I continued, holding my Merlot aloft, "it's all about selling software. For ME." I took a swig of my drink then set it down just a little too hard on the table, where it sloshed onto the funky pink and green tablecloth.

Then I looked at him and smiled. Oh, how my cynical, cutting father would have been proud. I was channeling him at that very moment.

Tintin stared at me. I wondered if he might just get up and walk out. Instead, after two seconds that seemed to go on forever, a grin started to spread across his face. One of the widest, most dazzling grins I had ever seen. His straight, white teeth gleamed in the lamplight, a product, no doubt like mine, of expensive orthodontics from age eleven to fourteen.

He nodded his head slightly in approval, his stare now an affectionate gaze, the grin still on his face. Then he hoisted his own glass of wine and held it toward me.

"Eggggsxelent," he said. "Now tell me more about this—this

selling software business." And with the way he kept looking at me, that inhumanly sexy grin on his face, those mocha brown eyes boring into mine, the excitement stirred—dangerously—in my stomach again. The Tintin image disappeared.

I held out my glass of wine to his for a toast, then proceeded to talk—at length—about myself.

The Doctor listened, too, and with every passing second, the combination of alcohol, jazz, and candlelight worked its magic on me. (Fleece aside, Pasta Bella *was* a romantic restaurant after all!) By the end, I was almost convinced he was my destiny again. After dinner, he walked me to my car, kissed me on the cheek, and said, "Let's do that again soon, shall we?"

Then he waltzed off into the night, forelock flapping, leaving me excited yet uncertain, lustful yet leery.

Because this match would be so insanely perfect on the surface—the kind of match both sets of parents would have arranged if they could—it's too good to be true. I will probably end up with some pot-smoking, rock-climbing, construction-working psycho who doesn't read books and who I won't even be able to *introduce* to my family, but at least he'll be good in bed!

E-mail Breakup Babe | Comments 3

I chuckled at my own wittiness. Oh Lord, I was funny. I was also high on caffeine and the attention of three different men. How could I have ever thought being the girlfriend of a wet blanket like Loser was "fun"? *This* was fun!

As I packed up my laptop and prepared myself for a final flirtatious look at the cute barista, I felt a twinge of worry. The "pot-smoking, rock-climbing, construction-working psycho" reference had been to Ziggy, the hellion I'd dated right before Loser, who was partial to setting himself on fire and climbing forbidden municipal structures like bridges, radio towers, and baseball stadiums. I knew Ziggy and I didn't have a future, but I'd been carried along by our steamy sex and outdoor adventures.

Now, of course, I wanted to think of myself as more "serious" and "mature." But here I was dating a rock climber again, one who was ten years younger than me and who commuted by *skateboard*! For someone my age, who, theoretically, wanted to "settle down," shouldn't I be out there trolling for better prospects? Maybe I should dump the Li'l Rockclimbing Spy right now. Focus on reeling in the doctor.

Then again, I'd dumped the "inappropriate" Ziggy for the "oh-so-appropriate" Loser and look where it had gotten me! Well down the road to spinsterdom!

Whatever. I didn't have time to think about it right now. It was 10:35 and I had a meeting at 11. I had to get to Empire in twenty minutes. If there was no traffic going over Lake Washington, it would be just doable. I fluffed my hair then turned toward the counter, prepared to flash a smile that was an eight on the Dazzle-O-Meter.

And there he was talking animatedly to Beret Chick. Who was, of course, wearing a beret, because clearly she had a pointy, misshapen head that could at no cost be revealed lest her deluded love slaves realize that she was an alien from the planet Bitch. Unfortunately, the rest of her was quite stunning in a Gwyneth Paltrowesque inbred aristocrat sort of way—complete with silky blond tresses, a lithe body, and expensive clothes that emphasized her petite yet perky breasts and narrow hips.

The smile fell off my face, dropping from an eight to a minus two on the Dazzle-O-Meter in less than a second. Suddenly I felt like an oaf. A chunky brunette of peasant stock, one of the commoners who picked potatoes in Poland, while Miss Paltrow over there ruled Latvia from a bejeweled throne. I tore my eyes away, but not before I saw her hand him something small and white. A piece of paper? Her number? Her *card*?!

I hurried out, eyes firmly on the ground. As I swept past her, a delicious-smelling floral perfume enveloped me. A few scattered words fell on my ears unbidden. "Call, yes! Tomorrow, later!"

I rushed toward the safety of my car. I was *not* coming back to Victrola next time, or maybe EVER.

POST A COMMENT

The doctor sounds like most of the women I date. Narcissism is not restricted to gender I guess . . . But isn't it funny how we get as involved watching their reflection in the water as they do?
Sigh.
El Politico | Homepage | 10/11/02—2:19 P.M.

• • • • •

This doctor person sounds obnoxious. I say dump him before you get in trouble.
Concerned | 10/11/02—5:03 P.M.

• • • • •

I bet there's even more fleece down here in Portland than up in Seattle. If you went on a blind date with a guy and he was wearing fleece, would you walk out then and there?
Jake | 10/12/02—1:41 A.M.

Chapter Thirteen

A week later, I was bored with all the other coffee shops in Capitol Hill, and ready to hit Victrola again—this time as a Frosty Ice Princess Who Flirteth Not With the Help. Mr. Cute Barista would have to pay for his treachery before he got another dazzling smile from the likes of me!

I'd yet to hear from the doctor since our date. But that was fine. Two could play at the playing-it-cool game. I'd gotten a whole lot better at playing it cool after Sexy Boy. Meanwhile, things with the Li'l Rockclimbing Spy were plenty hot. We'd "hung out" several times, meaning we'd had several marathon make-out sessions on the Red Couch o' Love. I'd hung on to my chastity so far, but it was getting harder every day, the more time we spent rolling around on my bed, doing everything *but*. It was so exciting to be with someone new, someone young, someone with so much energy and such hard . . . muscles!

Outside the bedroom, we didn't exactly have much to talk

about. This made it especially hard to delude myself that we had a future. Theoretically we had a lot in common; we were both into music, writing, and the outdoors. But a definite conversational void yawned between us. On the other hand, he made me feel like a sex goddess. And after The Great Unpleasantness, that sex goddess feeling was just too gratifying. I had to hold on to it for a while.

At least I had plenty of other options. Just to reassure myself of this fact, on a mind-numbingly boring Tuesday afternoon at Empire, I perused my Nervy in-box, discovering overly clever tripe such as the following:

"So, how do you want the world to end? If you saw some variety of Transcendent White Light beckoning to you while you were getting your appendix out, what would keep you from joining it?" (SuperTasticGuy)

And tantalizing promises such as the following, which just made me laugh:

"I will massage you from your head to your feet all nite long." (OysterMan)

Out of work-induced boredom, I toyed with answering some of my suitors. I had yet to reply to a single one. But maybe it was time. Who knew if the doctor would ever come through for me? I reviewed my options. SuperTasticGuy was trying a bit too hard, but on the other hand he was a journalist with good taste in books and music. OysterMan was definitely out. Motorcyle_Man looked pretty hot, but how long would he last with his "chopper fetish" before he became just another organ donor? Then again, I wasn't limited to just responding to the people who'd written to me. I could go out there and troll, too. There were thousands of men with ads posted on Nervy!

Just as I started to browse all the men of Seattle, ages thirty to forty, my anxiety growing with each click-through (Was he the right one? Or him?! What about that one?!!), Jane IMed me.

Jane says: Whatchya doin'?

Rachel says: Looking for a husband online.

Jane says: Now why would you go and do a thing like that?

Rachel says: I guess so I can have kids before I'm seventy-five.

Jane says: Well, last night one of my kids threw up all over the new couch, then kept me up till 2 A.M. with a fever. The other kid woke me up at 4:30 A.M. and I never went back to sleep. How much sleep did YOU get last night?

Rachel says: Ten hours.

Jane says: Now, back away from the personal ads with your hands where I can see them!

Since IMing with Jane provided more comic relief than the personals, I did as she instructed. Besides, I didn't need an online date. YET. So, for the next couple hours I edited documentation and intermittently IMed with Jane, who was poring over the results of a study on a protein called CD48.

Rachel says: Okay, I closed the site down. Are you happy now?

Jane says: Thank God! You know I rely on you to have a life for me, right? My life is diapers, Dora the Explorer, *and CD48. So you're not allowed to get married and have kids.*

Rachel says: Fine! I'll just keep dating twenty-four-year-olds then.

At about six, I started to wrap up for the day. I felt good about how productive I'd been. Each day, the fog of sadness lifted a little more. Because of that, I could actually focus on my job. I found that I now could make helpful suggestions about the stuff I was editing rather than just moving commas around. I no longer had a heart attack every time a technical writer popped in to ask me a question, thinking, *"He's going to find out how ignorant I really am!"*

Best of all, I often forgot to dwell on Loser's presence right down the hall. It was true that after our recent close encounter, I'd gone back to keeping my door closed. Yeah, I'd bragged in my blog about how I was going to look him in the eye, but that had been a burst of false bravado. I had no desire to see him. It was amazing, actually, how much protection that door seemed to offer me. With it as a barrier between me and my memories, I could now actually do my spectacularly dull but fabulously high-paying job. I'd invested it with magical powers. *As long as you are closed, O Door, I shall not be visited by ye olde ghost of Loser!*

Now that I was feeling better, I wanted to work harder, and in order to do that, I needed to clear off my desk, both literally and figuratively. So all week, I'd been setting up files and organizing bookshelves. Ordering office supplies that I should have gotten a long time ago. Before I left tonight, I was going to clean the top two drawers of my desk and put some posters up. The office would look so much better with a little color in it.

But I didn't get very far on my organizational spree because I had a desk drawer that, unlike my door, was *not* secure. I oh-so-innocently went to open it, preparing to get rid of any unnecessary crap that might be lurking. And what should happen? Memories poured out of it like a horde of English soccer hooligans, yelling obscenities, brandishing beer bottles, and hell-bent on trampling me.

Wednesday, October 16, 2002
10:57 PM Breakup Babe

It was about 6:00 tonight when I found the card. When I pulled it out of the back of my drawer, I looked at it for a second, confused. "To R.," it said on the front. I didn't even recognize the handwriting at first. Then, when I did, my heart started to pound. I had an irrational thought. Was it a letter from Loser that I somehow hadn't seen? A letter expressing regret? Asking if we could get back together?

No, it couldn't be. Not if I had already stuffed it into my drawer. Could it? When I pulled it out of the envelope with trembling fingers, I saw it was the birthday card that went along with the necklace he'd given me. Written in late May. After he'd cheated on me, but before he'd dumped me. During his ultranice lover-boy phase.

Dear R.,

Happy birthday to my beautiful darling. I love you very much.

L.

Christ. I started to cry immediately, spontaneously. Sometimes it took me a while to work up to it, but this time the memories cut like a scalpel—deep, clean, and to the bone. I stumbled over to the door and closed it. *Damn it.* I thought I was done with these office breakdowns!

I sat down at my desk and stared at the card. Tears fell onto it. I thought back to my birthday, how happy I'd felt. Everything was going my way. New job. Happy relationship. I remembered how Loser and I had gone into the cafeteria and he'd given me my gift because he couldn't wait until that night, when we were going out to celebrate. He'd been so sweet and affectionate. "You look so cute today!" he'd told me. He told me that almost every day, but I never got sick of it.

"Tear it up and throw it away," said Sensible Girl firmly, marching into my office. Even in my grief, I was shocked to see that she was wearing a T-shirt that said "Feel the excitement—Empire!" Had she dug it out of my Goodwill bag? "Come on!" she wheedled, her tone a little more urgent now. She looked around my office apprehensively. "What do you need that thing sitting around for? It was all a lie! The message in there—a LIE."

I picked it up. Prepared to tear it up.

"Wait!" Needy Girl burst into the office, tripping over a pair of pink, high-heeled Mary Janes that she was wearing with a short, flouncy black skirt (hadn't I seen Drew Barrymore wearing the same outfit in a recent issue of *Cosmo*?). "It wasn't ALL a lie! He DID love you. You know that! And now you're just going to obliterate all traces of him?" She pushed Sensible Girl out of the way and came to a halt in front of my desk, panting.

Sensible Girl did not take kindly to being shoved. With a fury that had clearly been building in her for months now, she strode up to Needy Girl, grabbed her by the shoulders, and whirled her around so they were face-to-face. "YOU," she said, "are a menace!" Needy Girl put her hand to her own throat in surprise. She whimpered something unintelligible.

"Why should she keep that card around? Just to torture herself? She needs to move on and that is THAT!"

I could tell Sensible Girl wanted to slap Needy Girl, but she settled for gripping her shoulders and glaring at her. "Furthermore, the way for her to move on is NOT to date a hundred million guys but to face her own fears about being alone and get just a little bit grounded." Needy Girl started to shake. "So I wish you would just CHILL OUT!" She released Needy Girl, who stumbled backward to the wall, then slid down it.

"Look who needs to chill out," said Needy Girl, but there was no bite to her words. She started to sob. Big, heavy, wet sobs, her head on her knees.

"Crap," muttered Sensible Girl. She knew that once Needy Girl started crying, it was all over. She looked at me, forehead creased with worry, then over at Needy Girl. Sensible Girl looked close to breaking down herself.

My own tears abated briefly during the showdown, but now

they came back full force. What a pathetic trio we made! I stuffed the card back into the drawer from whence it had come. Then, all organizational urges destroyed, I gathered my stuff together and prepared to leave the office as fast as I could.

I knew, without a doubt, that Loser was down the hall at this very minute. He never left earlier than seven. There was no possible way I could stay another second, knowing he was so close, yet so f*cking far away. For that matter, I wondered, how the hell could I even work here another day?

When I left, I slammed my office door as hard as I could. The sound rang through the hallways like a shot.

E-mail Breakup Babe | Comments 3

POST A COMMENT

Oh, how miserable! I have also made the mistake of dating at work and then breaking up. Just walking down the hall became a nightmare. I ended up quitting that job. You are a stronger woman than me!
CandyCane | Homepage | 10/17/02 | 9:05 A.M.

•   •   •   •   •

I say go to the spa! It will help you feel better—at least temporarily. My problem is that I can't seem to be happy with or without a guy. If I'm alone I want to find someone. If I'm dating someone, there's always some drama involved. Is it too much to ask that I could just be happy on my own without having to worry about men?
Little Princess | Homepage | 10/17/02 | 4:59 P.M.

•   •   •   •   •

You should definitely throw it away, and sooner rather than later. I've made the mistake of keeping things around like that. They stop you from moving on even if you don't realize it.
Jake | 10/18/02 | 12:34 A.M.

Chapter Fourteen

Thursday, October 17, 2002

1:39 PM Breakup Babe

General Celexa paid me a visit this morning. I woke up after a night of bad Loser-related dreams wondering if I could even make it in to work today. It's just so f*cking unfair that I have to work down the hall from him! How can I be expected to do it?! How *have* I been doing it?

As I lay in bed, trying to summon the energy to call in sick, I wondered if perhaps my boss would let me work at home on a semi-permanent basis. It seemed all my coworkers "worked at home" half the time anyway, which, I was sure, meant working two hours out of the day and then doing whatever it was people who lived on the east side of Lake Washington did the rest of the time. Cleaned their toilets? F*cked the gardener?

But, all of a sudden, there was General C., looking frighteningly awake in his fatigues and combat gear. "Snap out of it!" he said. "Haven't we been through this before?"

I pulled the covers over my head. He pulled them off.

"Sit up. NOW! And look me in the eye!"

Like a sulky five-year-old, I did as I was told, embarrassed to be caught sleeping in an extralarge U.C. Berkeley sweatshirt, ratty pajama bottoms, and wool socks. Not that General C. was any beacon of style himself. But still.

His voice boomed through my apartment. "You are not going to sit around and wallow, repeat NOT. You are going to go to work and suck it up. So what if that worm works down the hall! I hate to remind you of this, but you need this job, sister. Big-time! What are you gonna do if you lose it; go live at home with your mommy?"

I hung my head. The thought *had* crossed my mind just last night. Bereft of a boyfriend and a job, I'd move back to my childhood home in suburban, upscale Palo Alto. Sleep under the *Little Orphan Annie* comforter my mother had forced upon me when I was eleven. Surrounded by high school yearbooks filled with pictures of me with an '80s-style mullet, I would have no social life and probably no s*x. I would not be able to produce creatively because of my agonizing boredom. Consequently I would end up living with my mother for the rest of my life and dying an old maid with the *Little Orphan Annie* comforter as my shroud.

"No," I said, barely enunciating the word.

"Say it again: I am not going to live at home with my mommy! Louder this time!"

"I am not going to—"

"LOUDER!"

"I am not going to live at home with my mommy!"

"That's better!"

Now, half a day later, with the help of several Americanos, support from you, my gentle readers, and General C.'s pep talk, I'm back in the office with most of my old gumption.

Not only that, thanks to the advice of reader Jake, I ripped up that Loser birthday card today—the one in which he called me his beautiful f*cking darling, the one he wrote *after* he cheated on me—and threw it away.

And it felt . . . sad.

I immediately wondered *What have I done?* and wanted to gather up those tiny pieces and tape them back together. I hope they emptied my trash at work last night so I don't have to sit there with those fragments haunting me.

Funny how the thought of that now bothers me more than the thought that Loser is a mere twenty feet away all day long, day in, day out (thank *you*, General C.!). Mostly now I think about spilling coffee on him—by ACCIDENT of course—next time we pass each other in the hall. I haven't had a sighting in three weeks now—praise be!—but Judgment Day is coming.

I was blogging at work again. I figured I deserved it. For one, I'd been to work by the nearly unheard of hour of 9:30 A.M., after thinking that I wasn't going to make it in—today or ever. Second, I'd torn up that stupid birthday card immediately upon arrival. Third, I'd attended an editorial meeting that morning, during which the following comment had come out of my mouth:

"But if it's a Boolean property, doesn't that mean that the return value has to be either 'true' or 'false,' and that 'true' or 'false' has to be tagged as a constant or keyword depending on which programming language it's in?"

The editors, en masse, had turned and looked at me with something resembling shock. I was a bit shocked, too, if truth be told. I'd been sitting in meetings for four months now, barely saying a word, or if I did, commenting mainly on safe topics like grammar. Now it was as if I was toddler and these were my first words. Except instead of saying "Mama!" I'd said something like, "Mom, what do you think of the idea that if there is no normative or unitary concept of 'woman,' feminism can't exist as a movement?"

I could have justified not doing any more work all day after that little comment, but, in fact, immediately after that meeting, I'd strapped myself into the straitjacket with only a modicum of struggle and plodded my way through at least twenty pages of technical mumbo jumbo.

It was time for a little break. One in which I could disembowel Loser to my heart's delight.

> Every time I roam the halls (more freely now, less furtively), I try to have a hot beverage in hand so that when the moment comes that he rounds the corner, and I round the corner, then OOPS, it goes all over his tighty-whitey-sheathed crotch, ideally causing permanent damage.
>
> *"SORRY!!"* I'll say, smiling and barely breaking stride, as coworkers look on and he yelps over the coffee-stained mess that is his manhood (a strong word for what he's packin').

I chuckled, yet again, at my own wit. How many times had I read through my old journals, skimming through the boring boy-related drivel, only to stumble upon comic gems and think, "Damn, I wish I could publish this paragraph somewhere!" Thanks to Blogger, my dream had come true—to a certain degree. Now if only someone other than *me* would publish my witticisms.

Meanwhile, I felt just the teensiest bit guilty for gratuitously insulting Loser this way. It was true that he didn't have the largest member in the history of mankind, but it had satisfied me just fine when we were together. So this wasn't exactly fair, was it? He was probably never going to read this, but what if he did?

Well, if he did, maybe he would think twice next time about fucking someone over, especially a writer. *Ha.*

> And now, for the latest *Boy!* *Boy!* *Boy!* updates . . .
>
> Now that things have gotten hot 'n' heavy with the Li'l Rock-climbing Spy—who possesses an irresistible combination of nice muscles, soft lips, and macho swagger—my chastity is being put to the test.

In this libertine age, there seems to be such an arbitrary line between going all the way and going part way. I have told myself many times in the past that I was not going to have sex with so-and-so, only to have sex with so-and-so because it seemed silly not to—after all, weren't we practically doing it anyway?

But that's a load of crap and I've always known it.

So, in keeping with my newly evolved personality, I've shown remarkable restraint with LRS. But it ain't easy. Because after all, *I'm only human*. I have my needs, you know. And it's been more than three months since I've gotten it nice and reg'lar. That's too *$@#$! long!

Meanwhile, he's making his debut to my friends this weekend when we attend a party together. Now, it's true we've only known each other for two weeks. HOWEVER, I have sworn to myself that I will now solicit opinions from my loved ones much earlier in a relationship (oops, did I just call this a relationship?), and not only that, I will *listen* to these opinions.

Because, if history is any indication, the Li'l Rockclimbing Spy could have a giant horn growing out of his head and I would not see it. A shocking number of people came forth after The Great Unpleasantness to confess what (a) a drip, (b) a self-centered misfit, and (c) an uninteresting asshole they thought Loser was. Qualities, alas, that I, the blindly adoring girlfriend, had never once seen in him myself!

So, the sooner I get this over with, the better. And if they don't like him, fine. I don't want to get serious anyway! Because, as Sexy Boy pointed out, I'm still "on the rebound." (Whatever that means. I guess it means I'm dating twenty-four-year-olds?)

And besides, behind Door #2, there is—da na NAH—The Doctor! The one whom it is hardwired into my genes to fall in love with, mate with, and produce perfect little dark-haired Jewish children who will go to an Ivy League school. Of course there's a *petite* fly in the ointment, which is that he hasn't called me yet.

Mere details, my friends.

He's just playing it cool so I don't realize how MADLY IN LOVE

WITH ME he is. And when I go off to New York next week and my plane crashes (because, of course, it will!), then he will rue the day he failed to make his love known to me. He will be so consumed with regret, in fact, that he will never be able to love another woman again!

Poor guy.

E-mail Breakup Babe | Comments 4

POST A COMMENT

Boys are stupid, remember that, Breakup Babe. I just found your site via Li'l Princess and I've added a link to you.

Chloe | 10/17/02—6:17 P.M.

•   •   •   •   •

I would beg to differ with that previous comment, but I'm afraid Chloe's right—for 95 percent of the male of the species. Present company not always excluded. Good job tearing up the birthday card.

Jake | 10/17/02—10:47 P.M.

•   •   •   •   •

Wow, are you dating two guys at once? Good job, B.B.! I want the details—length, width, circumference, everything. Once you get them, of course. No rush.

Delilah | Homepage | 10/18/02—11:31 A.M.

•   •   •   •   •

Didn't you point out once that being a boy magnet had its drawbacks? For example, you always end up dating the wrong guy? I say ditch The Doctor and the guy in Pampers too, and wait for someone really good to come along.

Still Concerned | 10/18/02—9:01 A.M.

Chapter Fifteen

I jerked awake at about 4 A.M. *Turbulence.* If I did manage to fall asleep on a plane, it was never a very deep sleep because I had to be braced at all times for disaster. Most flights I stared out the window, headphones clamped over my ears, fingers of my left hand crossed. For someone who hated to fly, I sure ended up on a lot of planes.

I gripped my armrests, pressed my nose to the frigid glass, and waited for the next jolt. I knew that flying to New York was a bad idea. I knew it! Even though I'd flown a few times since September 11, this was the first time I'd flown to New York since then, and I couldn't help but feel uneasy. Remembering all the passengers, who, just like me, might have been afraid to fly, but tried to reassure themselves that it was safe. *Flying was really safe.*

It was pitch-black outside, of course, and no lights were visible on the ground. There were some stars in the sky, though, and that was comforting. Suddenly my slumbering seat neighbor, who weighed in the vicinity of 250 pounds, shifted, jolting both our seats. Then I realized the plane was gliding smoothly through the air. It was just my overweight seatmate causing the "turbulence."

I relaxed my grip on the armrests and focused on the trip ahead: a week of pure fun and entertainment in New York City, where I was going to stay with my college friend Richard and his wife. Richard, I was sure, would show me a good time despite his stodgy tendencies. (In college, he was the only guy I knew who listened solely to classical music and drove boatlike American cars.) We would eat well, at least, since Richard—who, like me, had gone to graduate school in Seattle—had declared over the phone with characteristic arrogance, "There are more good restaurants on my *block* in New York than there are in all of Seattle."

Though I tried to imagine the culinary delights that awaited me on Richard's block (where people would hopefully be dining *sans* fleece), my head was still stuck on the Li'l Rockclimbing Spy. Thank God I'd left town when I did. My friends had liked the LRS just fine, but in my opinion, his behavior on Saturday night had been less than stellar.

Monday, October 21, 2002
10:30 PM Breakup Babe

About an hour into Saturday night's party, I was sitting next to Gal-Pal #1 and her boyfriend, The Professor, on a saggy green couch in GuyPal #1's cousin's living room, sipping a frighteningly strong vodka tonic from a red plastic cup.

Across the room, the Li'l Rockclimbing Spy was professionally chatting up a tall blonde in a corner of the room. So far, he'd spent about twenty minutes dancing with me, and the rest of the time flitting around the room, talking to every single girl in sight BUT me. I was—unsuccessfully—trying not to let it get to me.

"Hey," I said to GalPal #1, "don't you think he's flirting with other girls kind of a lot?"

My heart was beating hard when I asked this, fearing she would say, "Yes, he is; he's a horrible flirt. He really shouldn't be treating you this way. Dump him immediately!" in which case I would have to listen to her. A Libra and a lawyer, GalPal #1 always sees both sides of every issue and never rushes to judgment. When she *does* make a judgment, however, it's always right.

She thought for a few seconds. "Oh, I don't know," she said loudly. GalPal #1 says everything loudly. She's tall, whippet thin, and beautiful—with wavy chestnut hair that she can never completely control. Saturday night she wore a shimmery short skirt that The Professor—an intense, bespectacled blond who teaches German literature at the University of Washington and loves phrases like "poststructural deconstructionism" and "phallocentric paradigm shifts" (but who still likes his ladies to look sexy)—had obviously picked out. Left to her own devices, GalPal #1 would have worn sweatpants. "Seems to me," she continued, "he's the kind of guy who just talks to everyone."

"Really?" It was true that I'd teased the Li'l Rockclimbing Spy before about being the "mayor of Seattle." Whenever we ventured out, he ran into people he knew and exchanged numbers with them. "Maybe I'm just being paranoid," I said. "He *is* a really friendly guy."

He had, in fact, gone outside with Sexy Boy and GuyPal #1 about a half an hour ago to get high. (I was none too happy about this, but at least, I rationalized, it was *their* drugs, not his.) After the three of them returned to the party, sucking on breath mints, Sexy Boy sidled up to me in the kitchen and said, "Seems like a nice enough young man. Kind of young, though, isn't he?"

I avoided looking in Sexy Boy's dilated green eyes. I caught a faint whiff of Drakkar Noir mingled with Altoid. I had to be careful around him lest Hope-a-noma recur.

"You only *wish* you could date someone as young, don't you?" I took a swig of my newly replenished and overly strong vodka tonic, trying to sound more nonchalant than I felt. Having Sexy Boy in close proximity still unnerved me a little, even if he was stoned to high heaven.

"Oh," he said, affecting the faux-philosophical tone he was fond of, "the youngsters are good filler, I guess. Until the real thing comes along."

Before I could think of a sarcastic retort, GuyPal #1 strode up to us, black hair in its regular ponytail, eyeglasses in place of sports goggles. Apparently both he and Jenny (who, thank God, was nowhere to be seen) had been completely drunk for the flight back to Seattle from San Juan Island. Sexy Boy, GuyPal #1 said, had been merely "relaxed."

"We like your boy toy!" GuyPal #1 said. He was full of good spirits, as usual, and tonight they were bolstered by drugs and alcohol. Then he glanced at Sexy Boy and they both smirked.

"You do?" I looked at them suspiciously.

"No, seriously," he said, then immediately got a serious look on his face, which caused Sexy Boy to burst out laughing. Then GuyPal #1 started to laugh too, and then they were both laughing uncontrollably.

"Oh, they're just jealous," GalPal #1 said to me after I'd stalked off and thrown myself down next to her on the couch to complain. Her hair was piled on top of her head, falling in fetching tendrils around her face. How I envied hair like that, for which flatness was never an issue. "I'm sure Sexy Boy probably still has a little thing for you, and GuyPal #1 is just being silly. Actually, he told me he thought the Li'l Rocklimbing Spy was a cool guy."

I felt momentarily reassured. GalPal #1 herself had been quite enthusiastic about the Li'l Rocklimbing Spy. "He's really cute!" she'd said, as soon as we were alone together.

"You think so?"

"Oh YEAH," she said, practically blowing my eardrums out, then looking around to make sure The Professor couldn't hear. "Those shoulders! Those muscles! That is *my* kinda guy!" She then took a sip from a red plastic cup reeking of tequila. It appeared that GalPal #1, usually not much of a drinker, was living it up tonight.

Now, an hour later, the Li'l Rocklimbing Spy detached himself from the tall blonde in the corner, though not, I noticed, without giving her his card. *Calm,* I told myself, *stay calm.* He's the mayor of Seattle, remember? He gives everyone his number!

Just as he got to the couch, though, and was about to sit down, GalPal #1's friend, whom we shall dub Marketing Chick, walked up to GalPal #1. I'd noticed the Li'l Rockclimbing Spy flirting with MC earlier in the evening but had attempted to ignore it. I wanted to like MC for GalPal #1's sake, but her expensive clothing and perfect body annoyed me. So I was none too happy to see her just as I was about to get the Li'l Rockclimbing Spy to myself again.

And then imagine my shock when I saw the Li'l Rockclimbing Spy, as he was sitting down, grab MC's arm and pull her down on the couch next to him.

Huh?

MC bounced right back up, annoyed. Her hip-hugging Donna Karan jeans bared a tantalizing slice of toned midriff. "Hey," she said, smiling, but in a pissed-off kind of way, "stop it." She shot a sideways glance at me, and I noted—not for the first time—how beady her eyes were. Clearly she was embarrassed that my date was hitting on her right in front of me, but her chagrin didn't make me feel any better.

I looked over at GalPal #1 and The Professor to see how they were reacting to the situation, but The Professor was whispering in GalPal #1's ear and they were looking over at someone or something on the other side of the room.

My stomach burned. I didn't want to act too pissed off or upset, so I said to the Li'l Rockclimbing Spy and MC with a little fake smile on my face, "Hey, guys, I'll be right back."

The airplane shuddered. I gripped the armrests and stared even harder out into the night. My breath frosted the window, thoughts of the Li'l Rockclimbing Spy instantly gone. *The plane was going down!* But then it slipped back into its groove. And slowly I relaxed again. My thoughts floated back to the party.

Then I pushed myself off the sofa, went to the bathroom, and sat down on the edge of the bathtub. The bathroom featured typical party decor: three lit candles that emitted a vanilla scent. It was meticulously clean. I put my head in my hands and tried to breathe while Needy Girl and Sensible Girl went at it.

"Dump this guy right now, would you? I'd really like to get a good night's sleep for once in my life." For the colder weather, Sensible Girl had donned navy blue flannel pajamas and beige wool socks. She stood by the bathroom door, arms crossed over her chest.

Needy Girl sat on the edge of the bathtub. She wasn't at her most put-together tonight. Her hair was flat on one side, poufy on the other, and her red lipstick was clownlike in its brightness. When she spoke, her voice was tired. "Oh, come on, now, give the guy a break. He's only twenty-four. He's just full of . . . youthful exuberance." She herself sounded anything but exuberant.

Sensible Girl took a deep breath then expelled it. Then she said slowly, deliberately, "Exactly. He's only twenty-four. She's obviously not going to marry this guy anyway, so now that he's proved how immature he really is, it would be a fine time, an excellent time, in fact, for her to end this ill-advised experiment." She looked at us both sternly, her hands now on her hips.

The bathroom doorknob rattled. All three of us jumped.

"Just a minute!" I sat for another few seconds on the edge of the bathtub, and waited for Sensible Girl to say something else, but she remained silent. Needy Girl looked at me from the edge of the bathtub, a hopeful smile on her face. Her black-lined eyes looked sad.

When I walked back out into the party, I saw the Li'l Rockclimbing Spy sitting alone on the couch. GalPal #1, The Professor, and Marketing Chick had all gone off somewhere else. He smiled when he saw me, or, rather, his upper lip curled into a sneer of greeting. He motioned to me from across the room, patting the couch next to him.

I felt I should run in the other direction. Or sidle up to a nearby guy and start flirting madly with him. I felt like I should be doing anything, in fact, but walking obediently toward this boy who'd spent the entire evening blowing me off.

Instead I kept plodding across the room toward him. Sensible Girl had abandoned me and even Needy Girl had disappeared. But I could feel my demons, Loneliness and Boredom, pushing me forward. As Counting Crows filled the living room with their asinine lyrics about love and forever, I felt as if lead weights were attached to my feet. But still I kept walking.

My seatmate let out a loud snore that penetrated my headphones. I jumped. *Something is wrong with the engine!* Then I realized my mistake and turned up the volume on my CD player. Lucinda Williams was moaning for a departed lover, as if in mortal pain, "I envy the wind, I envy the stars ..." I stopped the CD and fumbled around in my backpack for another one. I needed something more upbeat, even if it was four in the morning. I popped in my old airplane standby, *Dookie*, by Green Day. That album had gotten me through numerous bouts of turbulence. Once again, as my pulse slowed, my thoughts spiraled earthward.

"So," I'd said to the Li'l Rockclimbing Spy after we left the party and were back at my apartment. "It seemed to me like you were flirting a lot at that party." I started putting some dishes away as I talked, in an attempt to keep the conversation "light."

"What?!" the Li'l Rockclimbing Spy said in mock horror. He came up behind me, wrapped his arms around me, and started kissing my neck. "I wasn't flirting with anyone! Except you!"

I thought about just letting it go at that. About surrendering to him and his muscles right then. Lightening up. It always felt like such a loving gesture when someone wrapped his arms around me that way.

Instead, I turned to him, kissed him on the lips, and said, in as carefree a tone as I could, which wasn't very, "Come on, I saw you give your card to at least three girls there."

"Dude!" He backed away from me and sat down hard at the kitchen table. "Yeah, I gave out my card, but it was all for music stuff! If you noticed, I gave it to a few guys, too." Private investigation was just his day job. The Li'l Rockclimbing Spy was also a drummer who wanted to start his own record label.

I turned back to the dish rack, heart pounding. I grabbed a couple of plates and put them in the cabinet. They rattled.

"Well," I said, staring into the cabinet, which had been lined years ago with dinosaur-patterned paper, "whatever it was, it would have been nice if you'd spent just a little more time talking to me. I mean, I know you're not my boyfriend"—how strange it felt to be saying that to someone—"and you can do whatever you want when we're not together, but when you're with me, it would be nice if you could pay just a little more attention to me."

God, I sounded pathetic.

His voice got cold. "Don't you think you're being just a little controlling?"

Controlling! I wanted to whirl around and yell. *I am being so fucking mellow right now! You think THIS is controlling?*

Instead I took a deep breath. Then I turned around slowly to face him, the Li'l Rockclimbing Spy sprawled in the chair, legs stuck out way in front. He was chewing on his front lip, jaw tense.

"Yes," I said. "It's possible I'm being controlling." I forced a smile. Of course I didn't think I was being controlling at all, but I'd read enough self-help books during The Great Unpleasantness to learn a few things about arguing.

"Try, if you can, to see the other person's point of view. To really hear what they're saying, instead of reacting defensively, which is a natural impulse" (Amos White, *Relationships for Dummies*).

The Li'l Rockclimbing Spy sat up straighter. Then he ran his hand through his floppy blond hair, watching me. Waiting. I felt encouraged by his expression. He was waiting to hear what I had to say. To hear my side now that I'd conceded his point.

"Many successful couples resolve their disagreements by injecting humor into them, thus defusing tension" (Dr. L. Sega, Ph.D., *He Says, She Says*).

"Is it possible," I asked, "that I might be a little controlling, but that maybe you were also flirting at that party? Just a little?" I injected a teasing tone into my voice.

"NO, it's not!" he said. "I was NOT flirting!" His tone was exasperated. Almost angry, but not quite.

"All right," I said, walking slowly toward him. Half of me was disappointed that my doctor-recommended arguing techniques hadn't worked; half of me wanted to believe him. *Maybe he wasn't flirting. Maybe I was overreacting.*

Then I'd eased myself onto his lap, put my arms around him, and said, in as light a tone as I possibly could, "Okay, let's agree to disagree about this, then, shall we?"

The next day I congratulated myself on handling the issue so well. I hadn't flung accusations. I hadn't yelled. I'd learned a few lessons from The Great Unpleasantness, and one of them was that I had often been too confrontational with Loser. Not that it excused him from being a cheating, lying, low-down bastard, but still—I could have been less of a bitch.

Li'l Sis, however, put a damper on my self-congratulatory mood.

"Why are you even bothering?" she'd asked in a weary tone, after I'd described The Flirting Incident to her over the phone. Li'l Sis had spent her early twenties gallivanting around Eastern Europe on a Fulbright scholarship, having ill-fated affairs with Marines and Romanian Mafioso, but now that she is happily married, her moral superiority complex has gotten a tad worse.

"I'm . . . just having fun?" I said, sounding entirely unconvinced.

Then there was silence on her end. A silence in which, I knew, Li'l Sis was composing herself to sound less judgmental than she really felt. Then she said, "So, seeing him flirt with tons of other girls in front of you was *fun*?"

"No," I mumbled. "Anyway, I'll probably break up with him

when I get back from New York." Then I changed the topic. That was the first I'd talked about breaking up with him, but it seemed like the right thing to say. And after I got off the phone, it even felt like the right thing to do. I'd go to New York, get over him, and tell him when I got back that we shouldn't see each other anymore. First, though, I'd let him drive me to the airport.

But then I couldn't get in touch with him for two days. Had the Li'l Rockclimbing Spy preemptively dumped *moi*? But then he'd resurfaced in time to drive me to Sea-Tac for my red-eye tonight, claiming he'd been "busy" with an "epic" work assignment doing surveillance on "some dude in Woodinville" who was suspected of insurance fraud.

The surveillance process (or so he said) had involved him climbing a tree, hiding in shrubbery, and scaling a ten-foot-high brick wall. Had this excuse come from anyone else, I wouldn't have believed it. But he was an investigator, after all, one who had been hired in part because of his physical agility. Plus, he sounded particularly "amped" about the whole thing and had a scratch on his face from hiding in the bushes.

My resolve to dump the Li'l Rockclimbing Spy melted somewhat during that drive. He looked so cute and manly with that scratch on his face. And he *is* rather accomplished for a twenty-four-year-old, after all. He's already traveled all over the world, climbed myriad spires and Seattle landmarks, and played drums for some of Seattle's loudest punk bands!

It's a lot more than I can say for Loser, whose biggest aspiration was to make sure his toilet was clean and his car expensive enough to impress his millionaire coworkers. Then again my therapist told me that dating someone just because he's different from Loser is a stupid idea.

So, *whatever,* I'm lost on this issue. For the moment. But soon it won't matter because I'm about on my way to New York. In a plane. And we all know what that means. At least I got my kicks while I could!

E-mail Breakup Babe | Comments 4

Well, I could say this much for myself, I thought as I inflated my travel pillow; it had been two whole weeks and I still hadn't had sex with the guy! I made a thumbs-up sign in the window, leaning back a little so I could encourage my own reflection. In the dark window, which hid imperfections, my hair looked sleek and glossy, my brown eyes liquid. I smiled, and my teeth gleamed back at me. "Way to go," I mouthed to my better-groomed twin.

It was also a good thing that I'd kept my options open by meeting the doctor. True, he still hadn't called, but he was busy saving lives, no doubt! Potential faults not withstanding, he was a fine specimen of manhood if ever there was one. "Arm candy" as GalPal #3's husband, Henry (who was always trying to come up with clever phrases in the hopes of getting quoted in my blog), would call him.

I put the travel pillow around my neck. Closed my eyes, and deliberately tried to steer my mind away from the Li'l Rockclimbing Spy. I pretended that I was flying to New York on business. That I was going out to meet my agent. Tomorrow we'd be meeting for lunch at a hip Greenwich Village eatery, and then she'd take me "on the rounds" to meet some editors who were interested in my book. Whatever book that might be. In the evening we'd attend a literary gathering where other up-and-coming young writers would be gathered.

When I got back, the doctor would call me, and we would go someplace quiet yet hip for dinner. Then we'd hit a lively nightspot where we could toss back a few. Heat things up a little. During dinner, I would tell him about my literary adventures in New York. He would look at me in awe and admiration as I talked about the editors I'd met, my agent, the other writers . . .

The next time I jerked awake, it was because of a voice over the loudspeaker. "As you can tell, we've started our descent into JFK airport."

Thank God. I pressed my nose to the window again. Below,

in crystalline sunshine, New York was spread out like the sumptuous centerpiece of a children's storybook. The Hudson River snaked shimmering alongside the city. Speeding through the sky at five hundred miles an hour, destination in sight, I felt like I'd left all my ghosts behind in the night over North Dakota. Sexy Boy. The Li'l Rockclimbing Spy. Loser.

When I got back to Seattle, I would be a different person. A stronger person. One who wasn't scared to stand alone on her own two feet. So maybe I was in my midthirties and didn't have my "whole life" ahead of me anymore. Maybe my biological clock was ticking and the alarm was about to go off. But I wasn't going to jump willy-nilly into relationships just because I was scared. No, sir!

"We've started our final descent into JFK," said the captain, whose voice was unreassuringly high-pitched and fey. Nothing like Sexy Boy's down-home manly drawl. "Flight attendants, please prepare for landing."

I was irrationally unafraid of landing. This close to our destination, I figured, we couldn't crash. As we bumped down through wispy clouds, the plane banked to such a degree that I felt like I was looking at New York from a glass-bottomed boat. As I peered down at the vast metropolis, the theaters, the skyscrapers, the restaurants, the throngs, which doubtlessly contained thousands of men who were just right for me, I knew, without a doubt, that the best in my life was yet to come.

POST A COMMENT

I don't have a moral superiority complex. I'm just always right.

Li'l Sis | 10/21/02—8:13 A.M.

•　•　•　•　•

You can't dump him until you find out the size of his manhood. If it's big and you still want to dump him, give him my number!

Delilah | Homepage | 10/21/02—1:40 P.M.

•　•　•　•　•

Though I hate to ally myself with a stoner, I have to agree with Sexy Boy when he says that youngsters are good "filler." My last girlfriend was more than eight years younger than me. She was a great person with lots of "potential," but at our age, there's not much time for potential, I'm afraid. It's hard to date someone who doesn't really know who they are in the world yet.

El Politico | 10/21/02—8:10 P.M.

•   •   •   •   •

Your plane is not going to crash, but if it does, I get the red couch, right?

Still Tired of My Furniture | 10/22/02—9:53 A.M.

Chapter Sixteen

Crap.

The rain poured in sheets off the windows of Perkatory, a coffee shop right down the street from my apartment. I stared out at Union Street, laptop on the table in front of me. I'd typed three whole words, then stopped. I felt too awful to even blog. What was the point when I couldn't tell my readers what was really going on? I so badly wanted to spill it all. Tell my readers everything so they could comfort and advise me, so they could share my sense of outrage and betrayal.

Well, I *could* tell them. It would just mean putting my job in jeopardy. But maybe I didn't want my damn job anyway, I thought, watching pedestrians hurry down the street with newspapers over their heads. What was so great about my fucking job (aside from the high salary, excellent benefits, and flexible work hours)? Especially after what I'd just discovered.

I watched the rain lash the trees outside. Normally I loved the rain, but I worried it would wash the leaves away before they got to put on their fall display. I'd been waiting for fall ever since the parched, heartbroken days of July. Even if the Northwest autumn couldn't compare to the obscene fall pageants hosted by snooty states like Vermont, the fall here was still more spectacular than anything I'd seen growing up in California. And now that the oranges and reds had just started to splash the trees, I prayed this storm would not take us directly from the desert of summer to the gray prison of winter.

I turned my gaze from the window to my empty coffee cup. Perkatory did have good coffee, I had to admit that much. But otherwise it failed to meet my stringent coffeehouse standards. They had uncomfortable chairs, and people watching even worse than Vivace, which at least had obnoxious rock stars to offer. I'd come here only because I didn't have the energy to drag myself anywhere farther away. I thought about getting a refill, but now even the ten-foot walk to the counter seemed too far. All the life had been sucked out of me yesterday afternoon. Starting with the knock on my office door.

"Come in!" I sighed and took my headphones off. The Go-Go's were belting out "We Got the Beat" in a failed attempt to motivate me. Productivity would be delayed at least another twenty minutes now.

Twelve hours after my return from New York, I hadn't readjusted to life as a tech-editor drone. The euphoric feeling that gripped me on the descent into JFK infused my entire trip. Even though I spent much of the time alone while my friends worked, I hadn't felt lonely. Instead, as I strolled around in the honeyed October sunshine, I felt like a hip, independent woman on the verge of a new life. As much as my existence had felt desolate and devoid of hope three months before, New York (with just a dash of Celexa) made it feel full of promise. Every teeming bookstore, every vertiginous sky-scraper, all the hot Jewish guys (couldn't some of them move to Seattle?), made me feel like an adventuress, a writer, a person in the world again.

Not surprisingly, then, it had been a shock to return to this windowless hole. My life shrank back down from a vast metropolis to tedious black lines on a white page. At least I'd resisted calling the Li'l Rockclimbing Spy so far. I was determined to just let the whole thing go. The passive-aggressive approach wasn't the most mature, but I wasn't quite ready to tell him I was ending it. Yet.

The door opened and my coworker Arthur walked in. Today he had on a painfully bright tie-dyed T-shirt with the words "Forever Grateful, Forever Dead" on it. Arthur wore at least one Dead T-shirt a week. He had 103 of them, he'd told me proudly, when I first met him. The red in this particular shirt coordinated nicely with the red socks he wore under his Birkenstocks.

"Hello," he said, walking in and closing the door. Arthur always wore either a very serious look or a very happy look on his face, and today it was the former. It must be Conspiracy Theory Day. Half the time he came to talk to me, it was about a conspiracy that he thought was being conducted against him by the group. On these days, I was sworn to secrecy on average twice per visit: once when he walked in, and once before he left. I wondered if this paranoia had something to do with the copious amounts of hallucinogenics that a Deadhead might have ingested over his lifetime.

"I have to talk to you about something," he said, his tone grave. I nodded, trying to look equally grave, wondering what evil doings he would reveal this time. I enjoyed Arthur's company; he was, after all, the only real friend I had at work, but still, his conspiracy theories got old sometimes. He looked around the office suspiciously, searching, I could only suppose, for hidden security cameras.

Then he looked at me intently, his eyes big and blue behind his John Lennon glasses. "I know you've been worried about what might be going on with"—he gestured with his head in the direction of Loser's office—"and I don't want to stress you out unnecessarily. Because what I have to tell you might mean nothing at all." Arthur was one of the few people on the team who knew Loser and I had been a couple. I hadn't confided to anyone else about the breakup.

My heart lurched. I took my headphones from around my neck and placed them on the desk. Across the hall, an obnoxious program manager was yelling into his speakerphone, broadcasting his conversation about "bits" and header files for the entire hallway to hear. I looked at Arthur, not nodding, not saying anything. I felt myself grow strangely calm. My computer whirred in the background. I was like a patient waiting for the doctor's diagnosis, when I already knew what he was going to say. *Malignant.*

He paused. Took a breath. Then said, "I saw Loser and Theresa running together." The first thought that struck me on hearing this was *She runs?* Theresa seemed like the non-athletic type. Oh, I could see her daintily walking the treadmill at the gym, wearing a pair of tacky pink five-hundred-dollar sweats, but running outside? Where dirt or bugs might get on her?

Then a strangled laugh escaped me. Of course. Running! Had Loser not seduced me that way, with all our runs around the Empire grounds? Had he not then disposed of me that way too? He was like a serial killer. Jack the Jogger. I could only hope he would destroy and dispose of her in an equally brutal manner.

Arthur raised his eyebrows. Then he continued. "I just thought you should know about this because you said Theresa had been acting strangely toward you, and"—he looked around my empty office again and lowered his voice almost to a whisper—"I'm worried that this could affect your review."

"Right," I said. After my first inappropriate reaction, I now felt nothing. Numb. I flashed back to a time just before I'd gotten my job in this group. Loser was describing a managers' lunch he'd been to, where he'd been seated next to Theresa (whom, at that point, I had never met). "She's such a bitch," he'd told me. "Not to mention, she's an incompetent manager. I don't know how she got to be a vice president." He'd paused here. Dug around in his memory for more dirt. "Did you know she's only twenty-eight and has been married twice? The first one lasted a year, and the second one lasted six months. She got divorced only a few months ago!"

I should have seen his snotty gossip for what it was. Lust. Back then, though, I never would have suspected my adoring boyfriend of actively coveting another woman. After all, hadn't he told me many times that I was the "most beautiful woman he'd ever known"?

Then I felt them. The tears. All of a sudden they were pushing at the back of my eyes, desperate to get out. Humiliation washed over me. I wanted Arthur out of my office. Immediately.

"Are you all right?" asked Arthur.

"No," I wanted to say. "NO, I AM NOT ALL RIGHT! HOW COULD THIS POSSIBLY BE ALL RIGHT?"

Instead I said, in a tight voice, "What do you think I should do? Should I talk to Lyle?" I tried to sound icy. To feel icy. But the tears were jostling one another at the starting line.

"No, don't do that," Arthur said quickly. He distrusted anyone in management, especially our manager, Lyle. Lyle, he had previously informed me (after swearing me to secrecy), was nothing but a "corporate toadie."

Arthur continued. "You need to get a clear head first before you do anything." The decisiveness in his voice irritated me. "Besides, they were just running together. It doesn't necessarily *mean* anything."

If he told me to meditate on it, I was going to kick him.

"Maybe you should—"

"Oh my God," I said, looking down at my watch, my voice high and false. "I have to go to a meeting right now!" Suddenly, I needed, more than anything, to be out of this seething den of deception and lust.

He looked at me with concern. "Are you sure you're going to be okay?"

"Oh yeah," I said. "Fine. Great! Never better!" The kind tone in his voice made me want to weep. I stood up abruptly. He stood too.

"I'll see you later," I said, my voice shaking. Then I grabbed my coat and cell phone and stumbled down the hall, where I half hoped to run into Loser or Theresa so I could tell them exactly what I thought of them. Who cared about my stupid review? My life was ruined anyway. But neither of them appeared, and in thirty seconds, I was outside in the buttery fall sunshine—a perfect October day in Seattle.

I had nowhere to go and no plan, but at least I was out of that office. For a moment, I was disoriented. I turned in three different directions with tears cascading down my face. Empire was so vast, so sprawling. With perfect landscaping, complete with waterfalls, winding paths, and flowers that never died, but were whisked away in the night to be replaced by other flowers in full bloom by a phalanx of Central American gardeners.

A breeze gusted, blowing red leaves into the parking lot of Building B40. My head cleared. I was facing east, toward the Rolands Human Resources building, home of Wendii and her fellow human resources clones. They'd probably like to hear this story, wouldn't they? Their little ears would perk up, their perfectly manicured nails would tap nervously on their photo-covered desks (smiling Aryan fiancés and cherubic toddlers) as I told my story without emotion, just the facts:

My boss is fucking my ex-boyfriend, you motherfuckers. Not only that, she's HIS boss too! Now DO something about it!

I walked, fast, and then faster, before breaking into a jog—as if it were possible to outrun all the images now spinning in my brain.

A crack of thunder rattled the windows in Perkatory. Someone gasped. The three patrons in the place looked at one another. Smiled in a goofy and embarrassed way to acknowledge their weather wimpiness. The screen on my laptop flickered off, then on again. I lost the blog entry I'd been writing, but since there were only three words, it didn't matter much. I looked back out the window, where the rain pelted the glass like bullets. Such different weather from yesterday, when the sunshine had mocked me in my misery!

In the end, I hadn't gone to HR. Instead, I'd paused for breath in a basketball court set in a small grove of trees and called my mother, who'd advised me to get a grip on myself.

"Yes, this situation sucks, but you do NOT want to put your job in danger," she said. My whole family had been thrilled when I'd finally "settled down" with a full-time job at Empire. My father, had he been alive, would have been cautiously happy about it, although worried about what would happen to my creative side. "Don't ever become a technical editor," he'd warned me once. "It's too boring." (He himself had been a technical editor.) My father was always torn between his desire for me to have a safe, stable life and his desire for me to climb the highest mountains and suffer for my Art.

"It's not fair," I sobbed on the phone. "HR should know about this! It's a conflict of interest!"

"I know," she said, trying to sound soothing. Her words, however, did not soothe me. My poor mother was usually the first on the firing line when a crisis occurred. I'd call her in tears, begging for advice, then immediately shoot her ideas down in a fit of anger. "But they have way more seniority than you."

"FUCK seniority!" I sobbed even harder. As the firstborn, I had a very well-developed sense of self-righteousness and justice. *Don't touch that, it's mine! Don't mess with me. I'll tell!* I'd never learned to fly under the radar like my sister. To exact my revenge in subtle ways.

But I knew my mother was right. And that "fair" was a meaningless term. Had it been fair that my father had gotten his first heart attack at age thirty-three, and a heart transplant at forty-three? Was it fair that my mom had to become his caretaker and watch his health slowly fail for the last five years of his life, when they should have been traveling and doing all the things they loved together? THAT wasn't fair. This, in comparison, was peanuts. But I couldn't let it go. Not yet. Not right now.

On the other end, my mother was silent. I was sitting on a bench facing the empty basketball court. Sunlight filtered in through the surrounding trees and a few birds chirped their happiness about this little bit of Empire-sponsored paradise. I'd sought out this bench before because of its secluded location, but the basketball court had often been occupied during the summer. If Empire was *really* thinking of its employees, they would offer a little area just for people who needed to throw themselves on the ground and weep.

"At least think it over," said my mother, finally. "Don't do anything right now. Okay? Sleep on it and see how you feel tomorrow."

I looked longingly over in the direction of the HR building. It was not in my nature to wait. When I was angry about something, I liked to vent immediately. Then the anger passed and I didn't hold a grudge. This, I'd realized in the midst of The Great Unpleasantness, had been a major issue between Loser and me. He'd been too thin-skinned to handle my angry venting, and, unlike me, he held grudges. By the time I understood this dynamic, his massive two-year-old grudge had already caused him to cheat on me and throw our relationship out the window. Now, apparently, it had caused him to start fucking my vice president. His VP too! Man, if it was all true, I really had some dirt on them.

"Okay," I said, sniffling. I wasn't sure I meant it. Then again, I didn't think I could move from this bench much less go all the way to the HR building. It felt like there was a void all around me, and if I took one single step I would fall into it and never climb out. How the hell was I going to get through this day? Then it hit me. *Xanax!*

"Mom," I said, sounding noticeably more perky, "I gotta go."

A dab of Xanax got me through the panicky stage, but now it was tomorrow and I felt no clarity about what to do. All I knew was that I felt like crap and I couldn't even blog about it. I didn't want to be one of those bloggers who got fired for their indiscretions. Just recently, a temp at Empire Corp. had been fired for posting a picture of Rodney Rolands taking a bong hit at a party. (How the temp had managed to get admission to an event where the likes of Rodney Rolands was partying was never quite explained.) Outside, lightning flashed, and within two seconds, another clap of thunder shook the building.

Something came loose inside me.

Fuck it. If I wasn't going to tell HR what they really should know, I could at least blog about it. What was I being so paranoid about? It wasn't like I was giving away proprietary company information or posting pictures of The Rod. Loser was never going to find this thing, and if he did, so what?

Like the happy couple were going to make an issue about it after what *they* had done? True, I didn't know for a fact that they were fucking, but they'd been *running* together. The evidence spoke for itself. As the storm raged outside—the next day *The Seattle Times* would call it "biblical"—I typed the truth into my computer.

Tuesday, October 29, 2002
9:13 AM Breakup Babe

I knew coming back from vacation would be hard. I just didn't know it would be THIS hard.

That, people, is because my worst paranoid fantasies about Loser have come true. He is f*cking my manager. Not my direct manager, thank God, but my manager's manager's manager—otherwise known as the vice president of our unit. Who, if she wanted, could fire me any old time. And who, judging by the way this woman (let's call her Loserette) reacted to me last time she saw me in the hall—averting her eyes and squirming away from me—would like to do just that.

Well, I'd like to see her do it! Because I'd be at HR's doorstep in no time, pointing out the little conflict of interest that we have here. At which point, her poor underwear-model boyfriend might get wind of this whole thing too.

And you know, I can't help but wonder, was she the one, the one that he cheated on me with back in May? If so, they are even more pathetic, selfish, and unprofessional than I imagined.

I've suspected this putrid little relationship for some time, but was too afraid to mention it here, for fear I'd get fired. Well, f*ck that. I can't be fired for telling the truth, can I? Well, maybe I can. But I just can't keep it from you, my loyal readers, any longer.

E-mail Breakup Babe | Comments 5

POST A COMMENT

You poor thing, it just gets worse and worse! Can you find another job? That is a terrible situation! Want to come be a dental hygienist in Cleveland? Fun, fun! At least there is no Loser and Loserette, only dorky dentists.

Little Princess | Homepage | 10/29/02—3:04 P.M.

•   •   •   •   •

My guess is Loserette would bend over backward not to do anything bad to you, i.e., give you a bad review. It still sucks, though. My advice would be to get out of that situation.

CandyCane | Homepage | 10/29/02—7:38 P.M.

•   •   •   •   •

Why don't you tell her boyfriend?

Anonymous | 10/30/02—12:56—A.M.

•   •   •   •   •

Those two sound like they deserve each other! My ex-boyfriend and my best friend started dating and I had to see them all around town in the same places he and I used to go. I felt so awful I was suicidal. Finally they got married and then divorced after three months, after she cheated on him! Something like that will happen to these two.

Tabitha | Homepage | 10/30/02—10:11 A.M.

•   •   •   •   •

I think all you can do in this situation is try to take the high ground. Don't stoop to their level. Don't try to exact revenge. (In fact, are you sure you want to blog about it?) Just know that eventually their relationship will implode, and if it doesn't, they're at least keeping the world free of their shit by being with each other. You'll be moving on to much bigger and better things. This phase of dealing with it will be the toughest.

Jake | 10/30/02—1:15 P.M.

Chapter Seventeen

At work the next day, shaky from three hours of sleep and three cups of coffee, I blogged from my desk. Though I'd been full of defiance when Arthur broke the news, ready to confront either one of those abominable adulterers, I'd now reverted to postbreakup behavior: keeping my door closed and scurrying around the hallway like a vampire afraid of daylight. I feared the sight of them might cause a meltdown on an epic scale: one to bring the men in the little white coats. General Celexa was hard at work in the trenches, but even he might not be able to handle an enemy incursion on this scale.

I still hadn't decided what, if anything, to do about the situation. I'd changed my mind at least five times: I'd talk to Lyle. I'd talk to HR. I would take a baseball bat to Loser's black BMW. I'd quit. I'd change jobs. I wouldn't do anything.

What I had done thus far, however, was to lose myself in

the oblivion of the Li'l Rockclimbing Spy's copious charms. I was supposed to be finding someone more "suitable," but there was not a suitable boy in sight and I needed comfort, damn it.

Wednesday, October 30, 2002
3:17 PM Breakup Babe

Until the revelations of two days ago, I was determined to stop seeing the Li'l Rockclimbing Spy.

On the plane home from New York, in between episodes of fearing for my life, I mentally rehearsed different variations of my breakup speech:

"Look, you're great, but we're in such different life situations." (Was this really true? He was gainfully employed after all.)

"I'm really attracted to you, but let's face it, I'm looking for someone to get married and have kids with. You're too young for me." (But, wait, wasn't I trying to recover from my last long-term relationship and just have "fun"?)

"I'm still pissed at you for flirting with all those girls at that party, jack-off."

But I didn't get the chance to make any of my little speeches. Because he called last night when I was in a most vulnerable state and said, "Hey, I'm climbing in this little competition at Vertical World, wanna come watch?"

Now, tell me how could I possibly turn that down?

And so the first I saw of the LRS upon my return was not at a dimly lit bar where I would let him down gently over drinks from a position of strength and serenity. It was in a bright climbing gym swarming with shirtless young males where I would watch him display his physical prowess from a position of desperate neediness.

To tell the truth, I was quite apprehensive about this event— and not just because I knew I should be breaking up with him. After the LRS's behavior at our last group function, I assumed he would probably ignore me in favor of all the lithe li'l rock climber girls in attendance. I would skulk in a corner, watching him flirt and climb, meanwhile remembering the glory days when I'd climbed rocks with my old boyfriend, Josh. I would feel rejected and morose, like an earthbound loser.

But no!

I arrived at Vertical World and looked around in confusion at the mass of bodies. Within seconds, the LRS made a beeline toward me, kissed me on the lips, in front of every rock climber girl and boy in the place—not that anyone was paying attention—and said, "Hey! Welcome back!" Then he put his arm around me and led me toward the other end of the high-ceilinged climbing gym. "Come on, I gotta do my first round in a few minutes."

Stunned by this display of boyfriend-like attention, I followed him in a daze. For two hours I watched him scamper up three difficult routes, along with several other scantily clad young studs, and my horniness was at an all-time high. But I got even more excited when he won first place in the speed category.

As I watched the LRS accept his award, Sensible Girl and Needy Girl crowded around me.

"Holy sh*t!" Needy Girl panted. "Can you believe you're dating such a stud?" For the occasion, she had donned a sporty pink tank top that showed off her nonexistent shoulder muscles and a mid-length denim skirt with embroidered flowers on the hem. She stared at the LRS, mesmerized, as he received his little trophy.

"Dating is a strong word for what they're doing," Sensible Girl said through gritted teeth. Her attempts at sportiness tonight included a visor, of the kind housewives from Oklahoma might be spotted wearing at Disneyland. "You were going to break up with him tonight, remember?"

Needy Girl laughed a loud, happy laugh. For once she sounded sure of herself in the face of Sensible Girl's sternness.

"I don't think so," she said, taking her eyes off the LRS long enough to wink at me. "After what she's gone through this week, you need to cut her a little slack. Besides, she's waited a long time to find a guy like this!" Then she nudged me with her elbow and went back to staring at the LRS.

"A guy like *what*?" Sensible Girl spat out the words. "A teenager who looks good in spandex?"

We ignored her.

Two hours after that, the LRS and I were in my bed, a place we'd been numerous times before. But this time, after a mere five minutes, he'd started to peel off his pants. I didn't stop him. Five minutes after that, he took my shirt off, then my pants. Again, no resistance on my part. We'd been this far before, but never this fast. This time, however, the Smart switch in my brain was firmly in the off position.

And because of this flipped switch, I didn't stop the LRS when he started to slide my underwear off (Victoria's Secret, $10). He almost stopped himself, because he was so surprised that I didn't stop him. He paused when they were halfway off, looked at me, started to say something, then thought better of it and pulled them the rest of the way off. Then he lay down gently on top of me.

I stopped typing and looked around my office, which had finally become a little less sterile, and a little more *me*. I'd hung a tapestry from Guatemala, a whimsical poster from France, a silk screen from China. Displaying my travels on the wall reminded me, and everyone who walked in, that this drab office did not define me. But still, it felt jarring to be writing about such *intimate* things in this colorful yet undeniably corporate space.

I stared at the words I'd just written on the screen. I seemed to be getting bolder every day. The first time I'd written about the LRS "kneading my breasts gently with his strong hands" and waited for a thunderbolt to smite me on the head, it did, sort of, in the form of an e-mail from my sister.

FROM: *Sarah Cooper*
TO: *Rachel Cooper*
SUBJECT: *Blog*

> *Hmm, funny blog yesterday, but don't you think you're getting just a little risqué?*

Her comment had bothered me. For about an hour.

Dear Sarah (I wanted to write back),

> *Is there some reason having to do with birth order that you feel you must always be morally superior? Is it simply a way of getting back at me for hitting you one too many times on the head with the Wiffle bat when we were kids?*

Instead, I just didn't respond. Then I mostly got over it, even though her question still rankled. Not because I thought it was bad to be risqué—and God knows, my stuff wasn't really *that* risqué—but because I had my own concerns about why I was writing this stuff. I worried that I was now pandering to my readers, dishing in order to keep them satisfied rather than to satisfy my own creative urges. Funny—for so long I felt like I'd written in a vacuum, and now, all of a sudden, blogging had given me an audience to whom I felt an allegiance. A *responsibility*.

I remembered a job interview I'd had about six years ago. When the dot-coms had just started to boom. I'd applied for a job as an editor at an Empire-sponsored online city guide (now long dead, but popular while it lasted). And the hiring manager asked me a question that I was totally unprepared for. He said, "What do you think is the biggest benefit of the Internet?"

I didn't have a clue. I was not one of the "early adopters" who was communicating via chat rooms and newsgroups.

Even though I'd been the editor of a travel Web site for a year prior to this interview, I still didn't see the appeal of the Internet. I'd rather read a book or a real magazine than go online, except maybe to get directions somewhere or track down long-lost boyfriends. So I gave a lame answer about being able to post new content every day and have "cool multimedia."

He grimaced and I knew I'd given the wrong answer. "It *connects* people in a way that nothing else has before," he said, drumming his fingers on the table, and looking at me intently. "Don't you think?"

"Oh yeah, definitely!" I said in an overenthusiastic way. I didn't get that job. But now I think I would probably do a lot better in the interview. Here I was, typing my self-indulgent brokenhearted musings from Seattle, and now—just three months after I'd launched my blog—people from all over the country (the world, even) were reading it. And not only reading my entries, but leaving comments for me, writing e-mail, and putting links to my site from theirs. And I *loved it*.

Perhaps I was even getting a bit of a movie-star complex about it, but was that so bad? My ego needed all the boosting it could get.

I went back to typing.

> Then, suddenly, I realized what kind of trouble I was in. I felt his smooth, hard body against me. Every inch of his skin pulsated with heat. He breathed raggedly in my ear as he kissed my cheek, my neck. Bit my shoulder.
>
> And, without the shield of stiff denim between my torso and his, well, I felt how big he was. Before this moment, I'd only ever *sensed* the hugeness of his manhood. Because, up until last night, I had not, at any cost, allowed the LRS to remove his undergarments. I had touched his deadly weapon, without looking at it in its entirety. I had made conjectures about its length, its girth—which seemed, to my relatively experienced hand, to be somewhat larger than usual. But I had not seen it. Because until now, the Smart

switch had still been in the on position. Now, however, I realized that the word "Li'l" should never have been part of his name.

Damn!

This realization pulled me out of the moment just long enough that the Smart switch almost flipped back on. I struggled out from under him and sat up straight. I felt longing so intense it made me want to cry. I reached for the water on my nightstand and gulped it.

"What is it?" The LRS looked startled. Startled but gorgeous. The candlelight in my room softened the contours of his face and highlighted his cheekbones. His chest and shoulders seemed to glisten.

"Nothing," I whispered. *It's just that I'm afraid of what might happen to me if I do this. Afraid of how good it will feel now, and how bad it will feel later, when it all falls apart.*

Right then, the evening could have changed course. If he'd done anything else but what he did, I would have pulled my pants back on and called it a night. If he'd reached out to touch my breasts, for example, or sighed in exasperation.

Instead, he touched my face gently with the tips of his fingers. As a scent of jasmine wafted through the room from the candle, he traced my cheekbones with his fingers, brushed them gently through my hair. And watched me. Patiently.

And that was it. The Gesture. I am a slave to that gesture. Touch my face like that and I will do anything you want. It always feels like the most loving gesture in the world to me. Fighting back tears, I turned toward him. Whatever resistance that had briefly, bravely flared was gone.

E-mail Breakup Babe | Comments 3

When I looked up from my computer screen again, I was practically in tears. Of course, my weepiness was probably partly due to sleep deprivation. I'd gotten a whopping three hours of sleep last night before the LRS slipped out of my apartment at 7 A.M. to go to work. He'd attempted to be quiet, but at his first movement, I was wide awake. Listening. Wondering. Waiting. To see if he would say good-bye. To see when this whole thing would crash and burn. He walked quietly over to my side of the bed. Kissed me on the cheek and whispered, "Bye. I'll see you soon." When, I wanted to say? When? But I just whispered back. "Bye." Pretending to be sleepy and nonchalant.

I slumped forward on my desk. Images from last night flitted through my brain. For a twenty-four-year-old, the LRS sure knew his way around the bedroom. I supposed that if one had to be on the rebound, one could do worse than an amply endowed young stud. A mix of happiness, fear, and grief swirled through me. I felt sad, scared, and happy all at once. Then I realized something. I had to go to the bathroom. *Damn it!* I didn't want to leave my office! Especially on the verge of an emotional swoon. What if Loser saw me like this? How I hated it that I had to feel hunted and ashamed in my own workplace! But as I stood up and prepared to brave the dangerous hallways, I had to admit that last night was like a shield that fitted right over my heart. It felt like protection at the moment, even if it would disintegrate under the least pressure.

POST A COMMENT

Oh, jeez, didn't I tell you to ditch this guy already? I swear to God you need to move back in with us where we can keep an eye on you.
I Feel Like Your Mom | 10/30/02—6:04 P.M.

• • • • •

This is your best entry ever!
Delilah | Homepage | 10/30/02—9:09 P.M.

• • • • •

Bad idea to sleep with him. Now he's got what he wanted you won't hear from him again. At least you had fun.
TJ3 | 10/31/02—8:41 A.M.

Chapter Eighteen

Two weeks passed. The trees caught fire as fall progressed. I breathed in the cool air with relief and relished the tang in the air. But sometimes the days went by excruciatingly slowly, especially if I didn't have a date lined up for the evening. My unspoken agreement with the Li'l Rockclimbing Spy was that we saw each other once or twice a week. The other days I found myself anxiously perusing Nervy.com from my office, wondering if I should finally respond to one of my applicants.

If I was out on the town with friends or in bed with the LRS, I didn't think so much about Loser and Loserette: the two of them jogging together into a magenta sunset. Loser telling Loserette she was the "most beautiful woman he'd ever known," just as he'd told me. Loserette preparing his beloved hot dogs for him every single night without a single sarcastic comment. Loserette letting him sleep in on the weekends instead of "forcing" him to go hiking. Loserette being the angelic and accepting Florence Nightingale that I could never be, thus becoming the recipient of even more adulation than I had once received.

But I once again abandoned my Nervy.com hopefuls when the doctor resurfaced. I'd almost forgotten about him in the whirlwind of my first week back from New York, but when he did call, I thought, "Hallelujah, now I won't fall in love with the LRS!" Dating two boys at once, I'd decided, was much more preferable than one. Especially if one was only twenty-four. I could continue to have hot sex with the youngster until the relationship self-destructed (which I was sure it would, even if he had called me the very next day after we'd slept together), meanwhile being chaste and coy with the Jewish doctor, thus paving the way for our eventual marriage.

Ha. Only a grief-choked mind could have come up with such a brilliant plan. My friends, enablers that they were, supported me in it—or it seemed to me that they were supporting me. And the "Breakup Babies," as I'd now started calling them, loved it. Of course. Several men at once? What could be better?! My hits climbed to fifty a day! To an "A-list" blogger, this would be peanuts. To me, it was astronomical!

GalPal #2, for example, had given me advice about the Li'l Rockclimbing Spy one night about a week after I'd started sleeping with him.

"Suggest to him that you can date other people but not sleep with them. If either of you wants to fool around with someone, then you should tell the other one. But until it gets to that stage, you don't have to," she'd said. "Then, after a couple months, you'll know whether you want to get more serious with him or not. Meanwhile you keep your options open."

"If I kissed someone else, would I have to tell him?"

"Well, it would be up to the two of you to decide the particular parameters. Hey, do you think I can borrow that purple Anthropologie blouse of yours for this thing I have to go to next week?" GalPal #2's attention span was often limited, but she gave good advice while it lasted.

I'd been quite nervous to have this discussion with the Li'l Rockclimbing Spy. Though there had been no repeats of the Flirting Incident, I sensed his general restlessness. He always talked about leaving Seattle to go on an "epic adventure." So I worried he might balk at any suggestion of "commitment"— even one as limited as the one I proposed. But instead, when I made my pitch, it was a nondiscussion.

"Sounds good," he said absently, while lightly caressing my stomach with his hand, as if I'd just suggested an acceptable place to go to dinner. I didn't know whether to be happy or offended. I opened my mouth to say something else, then closed it. Because his hand had started moving into other regions, I opted for happy. I figured we could discuss "details," i.e., what happened if we kissed someone else, later. And I succumbed, once again, to his charms.

So, with the cooperation of the LRS, my evil plan worked. For a while anyway. It distracted me from the silent soap opera going on at Empire with Loser and Loserette. I shut my mouth, did my job, and prayed not to see the perpetrators of The Great Unpleasantness in the hallway. They kept themselves pretty scarce, and who could blame them? The pair of them were worms of the lowest sort, subterranean dwellers who couldn't expose themselves to daylight lest the world see how slimy they really were. Of course I had no proof that they were doing anything other than exercising together, but I *knew*.

I also knew we couldn't avoid one another forever, but meanwhile I would fortify myself with the attentions of other men until I had to face them. Who knew? Maybe it would make me strong enough not to care by the time it happened. Because if there was one thing I'd always thrived on, it was excitement, and I was getting that in spades from the Li'l Rockclimbing Sex Machine and the striking yet standoffish doctor. Especially when things finally started to heat up with the doctor, and it looked like my happily-ever-after fantasies might just possibly come true.

By the time the doctor and I went on our third date, I'd successfully ignored a number of red flags. On our strictly G-rated second date, I'd barely been able to get a word in edgewise between all his Robin Williams-like impressions and comic monologues. But there had been a few moments when his "real" personality had shown through, and in those moments he struck me as kind, compassionate, caring. He just needed to relax around me and things would flow more easily. Or maybe not. I tried to adopt a skeptical attitude after receiving this cautionary e-mail from GalPal #1.

> TO: *Rachel Cooper*
> RE: *the Doctor*
>
> *I think you should watch your feelings on this one: People who seem to fit a perfect package sometimes can lead one to close one's eyes to problems. Just because he is handsome and Jewish and went to Harvard means nothing. Loser had all that except for the Harvard part. Do not be seduced by status. The Doctor may be a great guy, but he's going to have to convince you by showing you he's great. You're going to demand nothing less.*

She was right, of course. I'd fallen for Loser in part because of his trappings (handsome! Jewish! rich!), and blinded myself to the faults in his personality (the insecurity, the workaholism, the estrangement from his family, the way he threw a fit if I forgot to put fabric softener in the dryer or tried to sneak vegetables into his Kraft macaroni and cheese). Had my seismographic instruments been working, I would have seen the Big One coming. But, of course, they'd been broken from the beginning. He'd fit my idea of perfection in so many ways. How could I find fault with a rich, gorgeous, and generous man who adored me?

In the post-Loser dating world, however, I had the chance to redeem myself, to keep those instruments fine-tuned and alert for ominous tremors. The doctor, I'd noted on my blog, was only up to three red flags: glib, show-offy, and self-absorbed. According to Juliana's law (five red flags and he's out!), he still had two more to go. If those two popped up, well, I would unceremoniously show him the door.

But my oh-so-sensible attitude evaporated when he asked me out again a mere week after our second date. For a weekend! Thus far, our dates had been sedate midweek affairs. No doubt the doctor would comport himself differently under the spell of alcohol and a Friday night. He would shed his smarmy exterior and reveal himself for what he was: a funny, grounded, and affectionate man just waiting for a girl like me.

To earn that trust, I donned a sexy black sheath dress that showed plenty of cleavage ($8 from the Take 2 consignment store) and figured this date would be it, the night we'd fall into each other's arms. In the four days between the time he asked me out and the actual date, I became more and more convinced that a mighty passion was about to be unleashed upon the Earth. I shivered at the thought.

Monday, November 18, 2002
9:57 AM Breakup Babe

My third and most-anticipated date with The Doctor started out badly. Over dinner at El Camino, a loud, faux-Mexican joint with killer margaritas, he was standoffish. Distracted. Gone was the annoying jokiness that had at least kept his attention focused on me, the pretending-to-be-rapt audience. No, tonight his head was somewhere else. He spoke in monotones and barely looked at me and my artfully revealed cleavage. Instead he stared off into space during the many silences.

Alas, he looked devastatingly handsome. A midnight blue shirt (bold color choice for a man!) clung to his narrow-yet-still-manly shoulders. His face looked exquisite in melancholy mode. I yearned for him more than ever, but his dark mood struck fear into my overly hopeful little heart.

He's going to dump me, I thought. I put my lacy black cardigan on (a steal from Target at $25!) to cover my poor, perky cleavage, which was performing well and yet had not earned even a glance from its ungrateful audience.

Meanwhile, as my heart sank lower, I asked questions and tried to uncover the source of his malaise. *Maybe he'd lost a patient? Maybe something else bad had happened?* But to no avail. His answers were flat, perfunctory. And he asked very few questions in return. Even the margarita I drank in record time did nothing to quell my nerves.

By the time we paid our bill, a sick feeling suffused my stomach. Grim-faced, he drove us to Part II of our date, karaoke at the Rickshaw, a tacky Chinese restaurant in Greenwood where we'd be meeting GuyPal #2. As we drove in near silence in his tricked-out Mazda with the license plate that read "Dr. Bones," I snuck glances at him. He looked as if he were heading for a root canal rather than a fun-filled night on the town.

Why, I wondered, trying to fend off despair, did he hate me all of a sudden? What had happened between the time he asked me out for this date four days ago and now? I dreaded our arrival at the Rickshaw, when, I imagined, he would drop me off in front and then screech off into the night without a word.

Instead he parked (rather abruptly) in front. To my surprise, he even opened the door of the club for me.

And, when we walked into the Rickshaw, my mood shifted. The dim lighting, the happy laughter, the frat boy singing "Play That Funky Music White Boy," all had their effect on me. If The Doctor was going to be a wet blanket, fine. If our wedding was called off, *fine.* But I was wearing a slinky dress, and, damn it, I was going to have fun! The Doctor could f*ck the h*ll off.

I paused and glanced over at the counter despite myself. My mind was firmly on Friday night, but I couldn't help sneaking a peek at the cute barista. It was my first time back in Victrola since the Beret Chick incident. I wasn't going to stop going to my favorite coffee shop just because some pretentious bitch in a beret was flirting with the help.

I looked quickly away from the cute barista before he could see me. We'd already exchanged significant smiles when I walked into Victrola, and I didn't need to be caught looking longingly at him again. I wondered, briefly, how old he was. A whole new world of younger men had recently opened up to me. I thought, suddenly, of the Li'l Rockclimbing Spy. The last time we'd been together, he'd been so attentive. So sweet. Little did he know I had a date the next night with the doctor. I shook the thought off and started typing again.

Two vodka tonics later, I was still waiting to be called for my first song when I realized I was leaning up against The Doctor (who was on his third Manhattan). The alcohol had clearly had a salubrious effect on him, because there was no way I would have gotten into this compromising position without his help. He sat on a bar stool, long legs slightly apart, and I was standing—of all places—right between them, leaning up against one thigh. A ripple of fear and excitement went through me. "Watch it," yelled Sensible Girl over the din of the crowd. She was trying to move toward us from the middle of the room, but had gotten caught up in a karaoke mosh pit of sorts. Needy Girl, on the other hand, was smiling at us from just a little way down the bar, where she'd secured a seat between an Ethan Hawke look-alike and a guy who resembled Latino singing sensation Ricky Martin. Ricky Martin was staring pointedly at Needy Girl's cleavage, also proudly on display tonight in a sequined silver tube top. She gave me a happy little wave.

Just as I noticed my own strategic location, GuyPal #2 leaned over and said, "Hey, R., what are you going to sing?"

"You'll see," I said, looking into GuyPal #2's wide cobalt blue eyes while trying to decide how I felt about being in such thrillingly close contact with The Doctor. Despite my preoccupation with The Doctor's proximity, I noticed yet again how sexy GuyPal #2 had gotten in the last few years. We'd been roommates long ago, and I'd watched him go from chubby, insecure college grad to devilishly flirtatious ladies' man. We were long past the point where anything could happen between us, or I might fall prey to those eyes myself.

I'd invited GuyPal #2 along not only because he was a karaoke master, but to get his objective opinion on The Doctor. So far they'd hit it off swimmingly. The Doctor's mood had immediately improved when GuyPal #2 showed up. Right away they'd started joking around with each other, swapping Johnny Carson and Frank Sinatra impressions. The Doctor warmed up to me then too, and had even said—putting his hand on my bare shoulder, his mouth close to my ear—"Sorry I was so out of it earlier." My body temperature jumped five degrees with that touch. Things had only gotten hotter since then.

I, of course, was going to sing "The Rose." Unlike GuyPal #2, whose repertoire ranged from Foreigner to The Boss, I always sang "The Rose." But it was the very best I had to offer in the karaoke department. If anything could win The Doctor over, it would be me singing "The Rose." It fits perfectly within my limited range, and when I hit the high notes, my voice cracks just a little—but appealingly so, as if tinged with the pressures of a drug-filled life on the road à la Bette Midler.

Given The Doctor's inconsistent behavior, I knew I shouldn't be trying so hard to win him over. But the alcohol and the physical contact had gotten me so giddy there was no going back. Especially because Sensible Girl had been waylaid by a middle-aged guy in a cowboy hat trying to engage her in earnest conversation. She kept shooting worried glances in my direction.

"What about you? What are you going to sing?" I asked GuyPal #2, though I knew he wouldn't tell me either. My arm and right hand were palm down on the bar, and now—I noticed—The Doctor had also put his arm down on the bar right next to mine. It seemed that his fingers—wait, were they really?—were lightly stroking my hand.

My head swam suddenly with the lights, the vodka, those feathery strokes on my skin. For a moment, I thought I might faint. GuyPal #2's face blurred before my eyes.

Just then the M.C. called The Doctor up for his song. My head cleared. I felt a wave of disappointment as he pulled his body away from mine, quickly followed by anticipation as he walked—or, rather, *swaggered*—up to the stage. GuyPal #2 and I exchanged skeptical glances. Longtime Lover Boy had mentioned something about The Doctor's karaoke skills, but I'd been too busy trying to get other kinds of information from him to pay attention.

Within thirty seconds of taking the stage, The Doctor had the audience—me included—firmly under his control. He had everything just right. The poise of a professional singer and the comic timing to parody a rock star. Not to mention a perfect—slightly husky—tenor voice that filled every corner of the room and cut the drunken babble to near silence. His choice of song was bold. In fact, I wasn't sure I'd seen anyone ever do it, much less a nice Jewish boy from Connecticut. "Little Nikki" by Prince. I was shocked at the magnitude of his stage presence. The guy was a born performer.

Halfway through the song, I tore my eyes away from him and looked around the room. More than one woman in the audience was staring at him. A few guys snickered and whispered to each other. Then I looked at GuyPal #2. He watched The Doctor with a mixture of jealousy and awe, his mouth slightly agape. I knew exactly what he would say later: "You gotta marry this guy."

And maybe I would, I thought, as I turned my puppy dog eyes toward the stage again. My imagination suddenly conjured an extravagant Jewish wedding with a karaoke-themed reception, which The Doctor and I would kick off with a cheesily romantic duet. "Endless Love," maybe? It would bring down the house.

Just then, he locked eyes with me. He was now finishing up his song, grinding his hips in an exaggerated yet still sexy way to imitate Little Nikki and her magazine. He kept his eyes on mine for the last fifteen seconds of the song, transforming my whole body to molten lava. The audience burst into cheers and whistles when he finished, and a few people even started banging on their tables. And, if he hadn't secured my undying lust already, the smile he gave at this applause for his blisteringly raunchy song—the modest, sweet, and even slightly embarrassed smile—made me his prisoner for life.

My song went off well too, though The Doctor was a hard act to follow. But I saw the way he watched me. I saw the sultry smile that spread across his face when I sang, in my most soulful, drug-addicted voice, "Some say LOVE, it is a ri-i-i-ver . . ." and knew that whatever cloud hung over him earlier in the evening was gone. He wanted me now.

The feeling of mutual lust was even more palpable when we got back into his car at one in the morning. Now, instead of awkward silence, the car was filled with sexual tension. By the time he pulled up to my house, I could barely restrain myself from tearing my seat belt off and straddling him in the driver's seat.

But it wouldn't have been a date if Sensible Girl and Needy Girl weren't battling it out in the backseat.

"Invite him up!" Needy Girl leaned forward from the backseat and yelled in my ear. She was even louder than GalPal #1. I rubbed my ear.

"NO! Play a little bit hard to get, at *least*." Sensible Girl was directly behind me. She must have escaped the cowboy's clutches. She grabbed my shoulder, startling me. "There's something fishy about this guy and his moody crap. Now he wants you, now he doesn't. What's up with *that*?"

I couldn't see Sensible Girl's face, but I could picture the expression of tension and fear on it. Poor Sensible Girl. She tried so hard, and was always on the losing end. I really needed to listen to her more. I took a deep breath.

"I—really had fun," I said.

"Fun—yes. Fun was definitely had," he said, turning to look at me. Then he turned the car off. My heart tapped an obnoxious rhythm. Miraculously, I kept my mouth shut. Didn't babble. Didn't invite him up. But just let myself enjoy, as much as possible, the electric awkwardness in the car.

He looked at me in the dark and didn't say anything either. Cigarette smoke clung to us both from the bar, mingling with my perfume and a whiff of alcohol. I worried that he might try to fill the awkward silence with jokey banter, like he'd done many times on our dates. He started to say something, then stopped.

Suddenly, I flashed back to that night at Sexy Boy's house, when I sat there waiting for the kiss that never came. I felt sick to my stomach for the second time that night.

Then, without further ado, he leaned over and kissed me.

I stopped and stared off into the distance. I was envisioning that kiss in my head—that long, delicious kiss—and trying to figure out how to describe it. In my recent foray into "risqué" and "romantic" material, I'd discovered how difficult it was to write about sex in a nonclichéd way. I recalled, how, when I first wrote about the Li'l Rockclimbing Spy, I'd actually used the phrase "wet, warm, and hungry" to describe my physical state. When I'd read it over a few minutes later, I'd laughed out loud then immediately deleted it. Had my writing gotten any less hackneyed since then? I wasn't sure. But if I didn't provide details, my readers would feel cheated. I was sure of it. So I dove in.

It was the kind of first kiss you wait for all your life, the kind that melds passion and tenderness with undeniable technique. It was as if, alongside his medical degree, The Doctor had earned an advanced degree in Kissology.

As he held my face in his hands and kissed me—softly at some moments, more insistently at others—his tongue going to just the

right places at just the right times, every other thing in my life
melted away. All there was, for fifteen minutes in that car, were his
lips and mine, his hands in my hair, my hands in his hands, his
breath on my cheek, my tongue on his neck. Our kiss.

Until I finally pulled away and said, in a hoarse voice, "I guess
I should go now." Because something in Sensible Girl's tone got to
me that night. And I knew, if I ever wanted him to come back, that I
needed to leave him wanting more, never mind that I wanted to tear
my clothes off right then and there.

For once, though, I decided to be sensible. Because, lustful as
he made me, I want more than just hot s*x from The Doctor. So, in
the interest of making my dreams come true, I decided to hold out.
Because we'll have plenty of time during our long, happy marriage,
n'est-ce pas?

E-mail Breakup Babe | Comments 4

An "advanced degree in Kissology." Ha! As I packed up
my computer and gathered my numerous items of outerwear
together—hat, scarf, gloves—I chuckled at myself. It was silly,
but sometimes silliness was the only way to keep my attempts at romantic writing from flat-out cheesiness. What I
had failed to tell my readers was exactly how the date had
ended, because the actual ending just hadn't lived up to the
kiss.

"I'll talk to you soon, R.," he'd said, when I finally pulled
myself away and announced that I had to go to bed. I would
have been much happier, of course, had he said, "What are
you doing this week? Want to get together Thursday?" Or,
better yet, "What are you doing for the rest of your life? Want
to get married?"

But I didn't really have to worry. He'd finally kissed me,
after all. Meanwhile, let my readers think the date had ended
with some appropriately sizzling words.

Fully attired and saddled with my laptop case (which, as
always, was loaded down with books, unopened mail,

portable CD player, and a cornucopia of pharmaceuticals), I made my way out of Victrola to 15th Street. A cold, damp wind immediately infiltrated every crack in my scarf and coat. On the trees, gold and red leaves hung bravely, looking heavy and sodden.

Shit! I realized too late that I'd been so preoccupied that I'd forgotten to make predeparture eye contact with the cute barista. I looked inside and saw him at his usual spot behind the espresso machine. But he didn't glance up. *Damn.*

Well, I thought, tightening my scarf against the clammy wind, I could always be extra flirty next time. If I wasn't happily married to the doctor, that is. As I walked to my car, I thought, again, of the Li'l Rockclimbing Spy. I was going to see him later in the week. I had to tell him about that kiss, didn't I? We'd never really worked out that part of the "deal."

Hell, I'd think about it later. There wasn't room in my head for him right now. I just wanted to savor the thought of that kiss. The memory of the doctor's hands in my hair, on my face, and the way his lips had felt so soft against mine. No one had kissed me like that in a long time.

As I drove to work across Lake Washington, my thoughts floated above the traffic, the bridge, the slate gray, wind-slapped water. They hovered somewhere near the cloudy top of Mount Rainier, which was barely visible to the south. The future opened itself up to me once more as Hope-a-noma wrapped its shiny tendrils around my heart.

Oh, my, that kiss sounds divine!
Delilah | Homepage | 11/18/02—12:01 P.M.

•   •   •   •   •

I swear, this site gets more X-rated every day.
Just Call Me a Prude | 11/18/02—2:56 P.M.

•   •   •   •   •

So, are you going to tell the little rock climber boy? From a married woman's point of view, you're living out my fantasy right now. Oh, the grass is always greener, I know, but don't rush into marriage! You've got it pretty good right now.

Ms. G. | Homepage | 11/18/02—5:31 P.M.

•   •   •   •   •

You don't want to date another moody guy! Look how it worked out after dating Loser for two years.

Li'l Sis | 11/18/02—10:16 P.M.

Chapter Nineteen

As the leaves drifted from the trees, I waited for a call from the doctor. Two days passed. Four. A week after our date, my shimmering fantasy lay in pieces around me. Daughters. Pottery Barn. Dark-haired. Crib. Oh, I knew it was too soon to write him off completely, but he should have called by now. Undoubtedly there was some sinister reason why he had not, and I could only suspect the worst. *I had repulsed him.*

It was over. Our kiss, our delightful, delicious kiss, had been, quite literally, the kiss of death. I didn't even want to tell my poor mother. I was her only hope for a good Jewish match now that my sister had married a laid-back blond from the Midwest. If I didn't marry a Jew, all the neuroses might be bred out of our family!

The blog, as usual, gave me some perspective on the situation, but couldn't cheer me up completely.

Monday, November 25, 2002

2:24 PM Breakup Babe

Waiting for a cute boy to call after your first kiss is like waiting for biopsy results. The longer you wait, the more you imagine the worst. And now, six whole days since we passionately locked lips in the front seat of his car, The Doctor has not managed to pick up a phone and reassure me. I can surmise only one thing: MALIGNANT.

But you know what? That's fine. FINE, I tell you! Because the Li'l Rockclimbing Spy—at age twenty-four—is way more of a man than The Doctor. You know why? He called me the night after we met and has called almost every day after that! Whereas Mr. Doctor Man has approached me in a crablike and guarded manner—asking me out once every two weeks for dinner, and now that we've actually kissed (gasp!), scuttling back into his hole.

Oh, I know. The thirtysomething Doctor probably has way more baggage than the youngster. He's probably been "hurt." He probably wants to "take things slow," to make "sure." But f*ck that. You just don't kiss someone like that and not call them unless you're some kind of yellow-bellied loser.

It was a pale gray, cloudy day when I wrote this entry from my office, a day of the sort that plagues Seattle for days on end during our nine-month winter. When those sorts of days piled up around mid-January, I'd find myself begging: "Weather, please do something! Please be stormy! Or please be sunny! But please—stop—doing—THIS!" It was too early in the season for me to be disturbed by the gray, but I was. It mirrored too perfectly the flat, gray future of my love life.

I looked at the phone and resisted the urge to call the Li'l Rockclimbing Spy. I'd seen him once since my kiss with the doctor, but had refrained from telling him anything about it. Instead, I'd tried to savor what was sure to be one of our final trysts before I broke the news to him of my impending happy future with the doctor. Now that the happy future had been canceled, it took all of my willpower not to cling to the LRS.

Meanwhile, I was also tempted, of course, to call the doctor myself. Why sit around and wait like some passive-aggressive princess waiting for her prince to come? I'd never been one of those girls who believed that men should always be the pursuers. I ignored the phone for the moment and kept typing.

As for the Li'l Rockclimbing Spy, our dealings have been mostly businesslike. We stay in; we don't go out. We meet at night, not during the day. We don't engage in bonding activities that might bring us closer, such as romantic trips to the San Juan Islands or sunset walks on the beach. Thanks to this disciplined approach, I've been able to keep my feelings in check. Because, "inappropriate" though he is, he would be easy enough for me to fall in love with if I let myself go. Because how often in the past have I confused lust with love?

Occasionally, he will say things such as "We should take a road trip together" or "We should go on a hike one weekend," to which I reply, "Yeah," or "Sure," in a vague way as I try keep my heart from leaping up and my mouth from saying, "Yes, when?!" Then the conversation trails off and we go back to doing what we do best, f*cking.

Now, of course, my darlings, this is not the kind of relationship I want. You all know that! But on the other hand, it sure beats not f*cking, if you know what I mean.

Now that The Doctor appears to be MIA, though, I wonder if I can keep ahold of that crazy heart that wants nothing more than to fall madly in love. No matter what the consequences.

E-mail Breakup Babe | Comments 0

I felt marginally less blah after posting this entry. I'd especially enjoyed calling the doctor a "yellow-bellied loser." But it was only 2:30. Four more hours of prison time stretched ahead of me, with no meetings to break it up. Jane wasn't logged on to Instant Messenger either, as she usually was at this time of day. Where the hell was she? I felt guilty about what a slacker I was being at work, but how could I possibly work in this kind of emotional limbo?

The phone started whispering to me again. *Call the doctor!* I stared at it. It was beige and innocuous looking. A standard-issue corporate phone that one would not imagine capable of evil. My heart sped up. Would it really be so bad to call him? We'd passionately kissed after all! This enforced silence was so artificial! GalPal #1, an even more impatient person than me, had already advised me to get it over with.

"Just call him already," she'd boomed on the phone the other night (as usual I had to hold the receiver several inches away from my ear). "In the end it's not going to matter who called who. Either he likes you or he doesn't, and it's better to find out sooner rather than later if he's not into you." She'd waited exactly twenty-four hours for the professor to call her after their first kiss (which occurred ten minutes after they met), and then she promptly called him and asked him, "Are you into me or not?" Apparently he was, but had been waiting the requisite three days to call. It had been (mostly) smooth sailing since then.

Playing her words over in my head, I checked my e-mail. There, to my delight, was exactly what I was searching for. Distraction! In the form of an e-mail from Sexy Boy. Sexy Boy, of all people, had become an adviser of sorts over the last month, and he'd responded to an e-mail I'd written him earlier in the day asking for advice about the doctor.

From: *Jack Kilroy*
To: *Rachel Cooper*

R., I'm heading out right now for a three-day trip to Alaska, but I will say this. It's a sad fact but true that people in general—men, especially—always want what they can't get. This doctor fellow is no exception. I'm certain that if you simply act as if you don't care, he

*will be at your feet in no time, since you are such a beautiful and tal-
ented girl. In any case, good luck, and we can talk more when I get
back.*

Ha. I'd gotten used to Sexy Boy's meaningless flirting. I
kind of liked it, of course. But I knew to take everything he
said with a grain of salt. He was a flirt and that was that. The
momentary thrill of seeing his e-mail quickly morphed into
malaise. He was right about the doctor. I couldn't call him.

This day, which had long been teetering on the edge of
a cliff, was about to fall off. I could feel it. Elbow on my
desk, head in my hand, I stared at my computer. If only there
was something interesting in there. Something really, truly
distracting and entertaining instead of boring and anxiety
producing. I'd already obsessively checked my blog for new
comments. Read the few other blogs that I liked, and a few
others that I didn't like that much. So, as I often did when I
was bored, I clicked on my hit counter to see how many hits
I'd gotten today and where they were coming from.

At first, it had always been a thrill to check my hit counter.
My favorite part was finding the new referring Web sites.
These days, I could usually expect to find at least two new
referring Web sites per week—usually other blogs—where
someone had linked to Breakup Babe. The thrill always less-
ened when I read more than a few paragraphs from these
other blogs. The writing was just so *bad.*

On the one hand, I was happy for all these people, who,
like me, had discovered a way to make themselves heard. On
the other hand, couldn't they find something interesting to
write about? Or an interesting way to write about it? Jesus,
people, who cares if you're sick with a fever and have been
vomiting for the last two days? NOT ME! Who cares if you
haven't blogged in two weeks? Don't spend the first half of
your blog entry apologizing profusely for how little you've
blogged recently, because you've been vomiting. The truth is

you've done the world a favor by sparing us your asinine, poorly written musings!

Yet, I was still utterly grateful for every single link, and always added these blogs to my Nice Peeps Who Link to Me list (a categorization that excused me from endorsement). Today, I clicked on to my referring Web pages section without much hope. Right away, I noticed a new referring Web site: *Thirtysomething.blogspot.com*. Promising name, at least. Funny, I remembered watching the show *Thirtysomething* with my parents and thinking thirty was so old.

I clicked on the link to *Thirtysomething.blogspot.com*. Waited for it to load. Stupid, slow Internet. As I waited (wondering how many minutes of how many lives were lost waiting for Web sites to appear), I looked around my office, with its gray carpet, its fluorescent lights, and my own futile attempts at making it colorful and "fun." God, how had I ended up working in a megacorporation? Me! The most promising writer in fourth grade?

Well, the world had clearly been robbed. Because here I was on a gray-nothing day in a gray-nothing office with no one to love me, and nothing to show for my thirty-odd years but a few travel articles and a stupid purple blog.

A feeling of gloom touched me with its clammy tentacles. I knew this drill well enough. Soon enough I would be completely miserable, and the gray afternoon would stretch to infinity. I would be unable to work, yet unable to leave due to my eight-hour quota and the preposterous amount of bridge traffic that made movement impossible before 7 P.M. Where was General Celexa, damn it?!

At last, Thirtysomething loaded on my screen. I noticed the pale pink background and the tasteful green stars that decorated the template. Nice design, but not enough to stop the inexorable advance of despair. Then the words *Breakup Babe* in the middle of the first paragraph drew my eye. Oh! Someone writing about me rather than just adding a link to my blog in their list of links. My dark mood hesitated. And the more I read, the further it retreated. By the time I was done, daffodils bloomed in my heart.

My first, oh-so-articulate thought after reading this paragraph was "Oh my God." My second, even more articulate thought, was *Oh. My. God.* At which point, gloom and doom a distant memory, I grabbed my coat and my cell phone and rushed outside, too happy, even, to fear the sight of Loser/ette. Suddenly my drab, corporate office could no longer contain me and the realization I'd just made.

The next day I blogged about it.

Tuesday, November 26, 2002
12:16 PM Breakup Babe

So, something happened recently that I think you should know about. And, no, I didn't f*ck The Doctor, so please get your mind out of the gutter! No, this event has nothing to do with men—fancy that!—and everything to do with my currently stalled but soon to be star-studded literary career!

Yesterday, as I randomly perused the blogs of those tasteful people who link to me, I found a blog called Thirtysomething. There, smack dab at the top of the page was this paragraph, written by the fabulous "GenieG," author of Thirtysomething.

"Hey, check this out!" said GalPal #2. We were at Victrola together on a Saturday, one of the rare chunks of time I got her to myself, *sans* baby, sans husband. The cute barista was nowhere to be seen.

"Can you hold on for just five minutes?" I looked up at her. In a reversal of my preconceptions about parenthood, GalPal #2 had lost years off her face since her daughter had been born a year ago. She'd recently cut her blond hair into a short pixie do that showed off her high cheekbones and delicate facial structure. Her expression was always alert and ready to smile. Lately, I thought, she was like Tinker Bell, a darting, luminescent presence watching over me, encouraging me. She was even more cheerful now that she'd just started taking Prozac. "I just want to finish up this entry," I said.

"Oh, okay, but this is really cool!" She raised her eyebrows and gestured with her head to her computer screen, which I couldn't see.

"All right, I'll hurry!" GalPal was always getting enthusiastic about something or other, only to be enthusiastic about something else in a day or two. I took her enthusiasms with a grain of salt. To her credit, though, she was just as often enthusiastic about ideas for her friends' lives as for her own.

I turned back to my own computer.

> "So imagine my surprise when I stumbled across Breakup Babe, a blog detailing the aftermath of a failed relationship. Well written, and as funny as it is poignant, the experiences were so relatable, I wished that I could pick them up, like a book, and mark, with a pencil, every entry that seemed familiar. Having dinner with a handsome guy so as to inspire jealousy? That's me! Crying in the office bathroom for an hour? That's me! Feeling your heart split in two because it looks like he has moved on and you have not? Oh, so me!! Revenge fantasies involving fame and fortune for you, poverty and misery for him? Oh, boy!"

This, my friends, was a revelation. Not only did it offer the ultimate praise for a writer—"You are me!"—it helped me to resolve a dilemma I've been struggling with for the last year. My whole life, in fact.

See, ever since my fourth-grade teacher prophesied to our class that I would be a famous writer, I've wanted to write a book. And there was, in my very recent past, a little book I'd slaved away on for nearly two years, a book with great promise and poor followthrough.

But now, thanks to Genie, I know what the problem is and how to solve it. The problem is I didn't have enough passion for that last book. So I'm going to let it die a natural death and start a new book.

And even though she's the genie and I'm just a brokenhearted writer from Seattle, I'm going to make her wish come true. Which means the old book project is retired and I am now officially going to focus on Breakup Babe the Book!

What form it might take I do not know. Yet. But I swear to God, at this moment, I want nothing more than to make it happen. And if there is one thing I learned—and taught myself—with that last book, it was discipline and persistence. That may sound odd, considering I'm giving up on it, but as the great Kenny Rogers said, "You gotta know when to hold 'em, know when to fold 'em." I'm cutting my losses, yes, but I'm not giving up on my dream of being an author. And I want to thank Genie—thank you, thank you, THANK you—for showing me a way to revive that dream! One hundred free auto-graphed copies for you and yours!

Love,
Breakup Babe

E-mail Breakup Babe | Comments 4

"Okay, what's up?" I looked over at GalPal #2, who had stopped working and was reading the most recent issue of *The Stranger*. The cover bore a drawing of a fat, naked elf strad-dling a keg of beer. I felt giddy from caffeine and hope. Though the doctor still hadn't called, this recent turn of events less-ened the sting of his rejection. Who needed a show-offy, self-absorbed Jewish doctor when I was going to be a best-selling writer? GalPal #2 had obviously been waiting impatiently to show me whatever it was. She instantly turned her laptop to face me and said, "Greensleeves Press is accepting submis-sions for their 2005 publishing schedule!"

I stared at her computer, confused, although the word "publishing" made my ears perk up.

"Remember that memoir we read about the woman who did the writing program at U.W.?" Maybe it was that we were both Geminis, but GalPal #2 was more my twin than any of

my other friends. We shared books, clothes, and interests—
and many of the same annoying traits, including impatience,
flightiness, and an inability to navigate. Today, in fact, I was
clothed in a pair of black corduroy low-rider pants that were
on semipermanent loan from her since her pregnancy. "Greensleeves published that book." Impatient, she turned the screen
back toward her and read from it: "We're interested in frag-
mentary writing of literary quality, including journals, diaries, notebooks, and fiction in diary form."

She looked back up at me. Her hazel eyes were open wide.
"This would be perfect for your book!" She looked back down
at her computer and read again. "Greensleeves is currently accepting submissions for its 2005 publishing season. The deadline is December 1." She looked up at me again and waited for
my response.

I had told her, of course, about my discovery on Thirtysomething. She'd been the first one I'd told, in fact. Maybe
that was because she'd been available on IM at the time, but
still she'd reacted in a very satisfying manner.

Lucy says: Wow, it gives me the chills just to read this!

Rachel says: I know. Me, too!

For a moment, I didn't really comprehend what she was
saying. Around me, the regular Victrola noises swirled. Someone ordered a mocha. The espresso machine hissed. A toddler
exclaimed in a high-pitched voice. I looked at GalPal #2 and
wondered what she wanted me to say. Why was she looking
at me so expectantly?

"Don't you think the timing is just too perfect?" she said.
"Finding that blog yesterday, and now this?"

Then someone cheered loudly. Startled, we both looked
over at the counter, where Chuck, the excitable barista, had
raised his arms in a victory salute. "I just won ten dollars in

the lottery. Thank you, thank you!" he said. Several people clapped and whistled.

We looked at each other again. She was right. It *was* perfect. Synchronicity. Wasn't that what they called this? Suddenly everything made sense to me. A smile spread across my face. I thought of the whale from my dream. The whale that had surfaced when Loser and I broke up in a storm-tossed dinghy, rising from the ocean of my tears to tell me *There is a reason for all this heartbreak and pain.*

I'd always believed in that whale.

POST A COMMENT

Wow, great idea! I can't wait till the book comes out! I'll be the first in line to buy it!

Little Princess | Homepage | 11/26/02—4:19 P.M.

•   •   •   •   •

I think we're entitled to a certain amount of the royalties, since the blog started in our house, aren't we?

Greedy | 11/26/02—7:31 P.M.

•   •   •   •   •

I'm honored to be quoted on your blog. You can quote me on your book jacket too!

GenieG | Homepage | 11/27/02—11:51 A.M.

•   •   •   •   •

Ah, yes, revenge will be sweet, won't it? When you're a best-selling author, your ex will be on his way to his fourth divorce, drunk and alone in a single-occupancy hotel.

Jake | 11/27/02—12:11 P.M.

Chapter Twenty

As Thanksgiving flew past, I cranked out a well-written if somewhat vague proposal for how to turn Breakup Babe into a memoir. Now my days at the office were filled with equal parts keeping up my blog and putting together the proposal. The gray walls retreated just a bit and if I was late with a few edits, well, I had a higher cause. I knew this baby could sell. Blogs were in the news all the time these days, so I had a timely hook. Throw in my tales of heartbreak and juicy dating stories, and I had a guaranteed best seller! All my friends and family agreed.

Temporary Insanity had been a promising idea, too, but I didn't have a word of the book written when I made my brilliant pitch, and subsequently failed to produce anything worthwhile. This time around, I had material to back up my promise—four months' worth of blog entries. It wasn't enough to fill a whole book, but it was a start.

A week after I sent my proposal in to Greensleeves Press, it was rejected.

I couldn't believe it. I'd convinced myself that fate was not just knocking on my door, it was barreling in with guns blazing. This was supposed to be it. My big breakthrough! The triumph of the whale!

Ha.

I should have known better. All of the world's most famous authors have gotten rejected—multiple times! So what made me think the first publisher I sent this idea to was going to snap it up? Clearly, in writing, as in romance, I was deluded. My turn in the blogosphere had simply inflated my ego.

To be fair, it was the most encouraging rejection I'd ever received. "Your work is thoroughly entertaining and readable," wrote the publisher, "and I'm sure it will find a home somewhere!" But these words offered no comfort at first. Instead, I could only recall all the times my writing had been rejected in the past: the *Seattle Weekly* editors who'd never bothered to respond to my pitches; the travel magazine editors who sent back form rejection letters; the writing group who had rejected me because they didn't like my excerpt from *Temporary Insanity!*

GalPal #2 was equally disappointed, but more resilient. Over IM one day, she gave me a stern talking-to.

GalPal #2 says: Well, it's ridiculous that they rejected it, but you're going to resubmit it, right? Maybe to one of the big publishers!

Rachel says: Oh, I don't know. I'm not sure I know how to turn this blog into a book anyway. I kind of bullshitted my way through that proposal. You really think I should keep trying?

GalPal #2 says: YES. And don't take too long. Blogging is a hot commodity in the media right now and it's only going to get hotter!

She was right and I knew it. I just needed time to regroup, to think about the best form for my story. I knew, deep down, that my proposal wasn't as strong as it could have been. I'd glossed over the most important thing: how to transform it from a blog into a coherent story. It's just that I didn't really know how to do that yet. In the proposal, I'd talked about using entries from my journal to fill in "narrative gaps." But it was a half-assed solution. I would need to do better if I wanted to sell it.

So, as I tried to slough off the literary disappointments of my past and move forward, I did the same with my love life. Two weeks after the passionate kiss, I stopped obsessing about what had driven the doctor away. In more sensible moments, I reasoned that maybe his disappearance had nothing whatsoever to do with me. Maybe he was an escaped con who'd fled to Nebraska to avoid the FBI! Or maybe I was a horrible kisser with putrid breath. Either way, it didn't matter. He was gone.

I consequently got more emotionally attached to the Li'l Rockclimbing Spy. This was a horrible idea, I knew. But in any case, the original plan—as discussed with GalPal #2—had been to sleep with him for a couple months, then see how I felt about him. From that point, I could make a decision about whether to "take things to the next level" or dump him for a more likely prospect. And now, despite myself, I was starting to wonder if maybe there could be a "next level" with him.

There had been no more repeats of the Flirting Incident, although that was because we hardly ever went anywhere except my bed. Our conversations flowed better now than they had in the past. I could see past his gruff, macho exterior to his tender side, and damn if it wasn't a delectable combination.

I wouldn't have been encouraged in this area if he didn't

show signs of getting attached to me. One night, after the doctor's disappearance, we were lying in bed. A sinuous beat with ethereal keyboards drifted through my room. The bedroom was cold, but our two naked bodies together generated a lot of heat. The Li'l Rockclimbing Spy was talking idly about some jobs he'd applied for lately: outdoor education teacher at a local private school, ranger at Kootenay National Park in Canada.

"What?" I said, turning on my side and leaning on my elbow so I could see him better. "Really? You might go to Canada?" I felt a stab of jealousy. Not only for the cute female rangers he might meet or the grateful damsels in distress he would rescue, but because he might go off and have a grand adventure while I was stuck in my windowless hole. Before I'd gotten hired for my full-time job at Empire, I'd applied to spend the summer of '02 leading bike trips in Europe for high school kids. It had looked like I was going to get hired, too, and then Empire had offered me the job.

I didn't regret taking the job at Empire. For the first time in my life, I'd made economic stability a priority. And, despite The Great Unpleasantness, work had been a stabilizing force, both emotionally and financially (even if lately stability had felt more like boredom and I'd been spending more time on my blog than on editing documentation).

But I hated being limited in how much vacation I could take. Three weeks a year felt like nothing after the freedom of being a temp. Restlessness and wanderlust was bred into me, after all. When my father was thirty-three and had just recovered from his first heart attack, our lives suddenly changed. We stopped sitting around the house and started climbing mountains in Wales, going to sheepdog competitions in England, walking between remote villages in Italy. Summers we backpacked the high-altitude lakes of the Sierra Nevada and winters we skied the forested foothills below. I grew up knowing earlier than most people that you better have fun while you could. So it was no surprise that I already felt myself chafing at the bonds of a staid, full-time job.

"Well, I don't know how likely that is," said the LRS, lying on his back, elbows behind his head. "It wouldn't be till summer anyway."

He looked over at me and said, "Wanna come?"

"I wish," I said, trying to sound equally casual back, as if there weren't a whole mix of feelings swirling in me right now. Did he actually mean it? Or was he just saying it because he knew I couldn't come?

I flashed back to the summer before I graduated from college. Josh, the rock climbing counselor I'd fallen so madly in love with at Snow River Camp (where I was the drama counselor), had invited me to go on a three-week backpacking trip he was leading in September. The Feather, as my dad called him, was an outdoor education major at the University of New Mexico and was slated to lead a group of freshmen on an "orientation" trip in the Sangre de Cristo mountains. He was certain he could get me signed on as an assistant.

I wanted nothing more than to go with him, but I had one semester left to go before I graduated. For the two short months we'd been together, he made everything seem possible. He wrote poetry, painted pictures of the desert, and played guitar. I'd felt creatively blocked all through college, but around him I started drawing and writing poetry—things I hadn't done since I was a kid. He also reignited my love for the outdoors. In college, I'd hung out with a nonoutdoorsy crowd and never once laced up a hiking boot. But Josh took me rock climbing and hiking. I fell back in love with the mountains.

I also fell for the Feather with the wild abandon of someone who's never had their heart truly broken. Twelve years later I was still thinking about him! But even at the height of my infatuation, I was sensible enough not to bail on school to

take this trip with him. Instead we decided that when I graduated, I would move out to Flagstaff and be with him.

Wrong. He came back from his trip a different person.
The same person who a month before had written a letter
that ended, "I love you with all the heart I own," now wrote to
me, "I'm too young to settle down." They were the coldest,
most painful words anyone had ever said to me in my young
life. I went into a yearlong tailspin. The Great Unpleasantness
pales in comparison. Then again, that was before the inven-
tion of Celexa.

I thought about this as I looked at the LRS sprawled on
my bed. He was only two years older than Josh had been
when I'd fallen in love with him. I'd beaten myself up over
that backpacking trip endless times. What if I had gone?
Would he have fallen out of love with me then? It didn't seem
possible. But everyone tried to convince me that Josh would
have flaked on me sooner or later, and better sooner than
later.

I reached out to touch the LRS's smooth chest. What if I
did it? What if I quit my job, went to Canada with him, and
trained to become a ranger? It would be an adventure, that
was for sure, and if there was one thing I craved in life besides love and recognition, it was adventure. As my fingers
brushed his skin, I felt something sad and sharp inside me. I
was not twenty-four anymore. I might be able to pass for it in
dim light, but I wasn't.

"It would be a bad idea for me to quit my job right now,"
I said, as if it were the most obvious thing in the world, as if I
weren't replaying the great romantic tragedy of my youth in
my head and wondering if there were some way, somehow, to
turn back time. My words came out slightly strangled.

He settled his head back on the pillow and faced the ceiling again. "Oh, well," he said; there was only the slightest hint
of regret under his normal tone. "It's tough work fighting off
those grizzlies out there. You gotta carry a gun, you know."

But after that conversation, I couldn't stop thinking about his offer. I knew I was being crazy, but Empire Corp. was not the only place of employment in the world. I could always find another job when I came back, even if it didn't involve the same copious amounts of money. Other employment would have the added benefit of being Loser- and Loserette-free! Even if things didn't work out with the Li'l Rockclimbing Spy, at least I wouldn't be sitting at home living a life of quiet desperation.

The more I thought about it, the better it sounded. The only problem I could see was that I might not be able to plug in a laptop in the remote Canadian wilderness. What if I had a book contract by then? How would I write? Well, hell, I would write my book with a pencil by the light of an oil lamp if I had to, meanwhile fending off the occasional grizzly with a handgun! It would be so . . . *Jack London*.

The night we went out for dinner at Red Mill Burgers, a week later, I was ready to ask him if he'd been serious about his offer. In my mind, I'd almost quit my job already and donned a bearskin cap. But I never got the chance to bring it up.

Monday, December 9, 2002
9:43 AM Breakup Babe

So, last night, the Li'l Rockclimbing Spy and I went out. This is notable because we don't ever go out. But I'd been having fond feelings toward the youngster lately, and had some things to discuss with him. I offered to treat him to dinner at the restaurant of his choice, and he chose Red Mill Burgers.

Not a surprising choice for a growing boy. Although he could have chosen something much more pricey and I would have been game. I'd been hoping for something a little more romantic, but this was his night.

I should never have let him choose.

Because who did we see stuffing burgers in their faces as we approached the restaurant?

That's right. Loser and Loserette.

I slumped over my laptop. Today I'd ended up in the Yuppie Queen Anne neighborhood of all places, at a coffee shop someone had once recommended to me, El Diablo. It was lively and colorful with good coffee and another hot male barista to boot, but I was not in an appreciative mood. I'd driven clear across town just to get away from everything I knew. I couldn't bear to go into Victrola today looking like a downtrodden and desperate loser. I had to go where no one knew my name. I took one furtive glance around me. This was Sexy Boy's neighborhood, but as far as I knew, he never went to coffee shops.

I recognized them from fifty feet away and immediately froze.

The LRS looked at me standing there in shock as if I'd just witnessed a murder. If he said something right then, I didn't hear it. I was too busy looking at my ex-boyfriend eating dinner with another woman. There was a part of me viewing it from a very detached place, thinking, "Oh, how dramatic. I've just run into my ex on a date with my manager! What good blog material!" Then there was the fragile part of me that had been trying to heal for months, that felt like it had just been thrown against a wall and shattered.

"Oh my God," I murmured.

The LRS walked back toward me. "What IS it?" he said.

"In the window," I said. "It's my ex."

"The guy who—"

"Yes." Now we both stood staring. The two of them hadn't seen us yet. They were too busy looking at each other and wadding fries into their mouths.

"Dude. Is that his new girlfriend?"

"Yes," I said, anger toward the two of them appearing as a

wave offshore. If the LRS said anything about her being "hot," I would seriously turn around and kick him in his magnificent crotch.

"I wouldn't date her," he said in a conversational tone. I laughed, but the laugh had no joy in it. The wave of anger was about to swamp me. A few seconds ago, I'd wanted to turn and run away as fast as I could. Now, though, I wanted to do something else.

"Wait here," I said to him, my jaw clenched.

Then I strode up to the window. My cheeks blazed. The closer I got, the more details I could see. He wore his standard black winter turtleneck. His monobrow was back in force above his tiny glasses. Apparently she didn't insist that he shave it! Her curly red hair, I noticed in shock, was in pigtails, a style I often wear my hair in, but had never once seen on her. Instead of looking cute and perky, however, the springy pigtails and the smeared pink lipstick made her look like an older Pippi Longstocking who's been let out of the mental institution on a day pass.

Just as I noticed her abominable pigtails, she noticed me. Loser was still tucking into his French fries. She froze for a second, then quickly looked down.

I had no thought for my job as I walked toward that window. My only thought was *I want them to see me seeing them*. As I continued my march, she must have said something to him, because he did not look up. Instead, he swiveled his stool to face the inside of the restaurant, so all I saw was his back. The back I had curled up against during so many cold nights. Then she turned her back too.

But it didn't stop me. I walked right up to the window. Gave them a second to turn around. They didn't, of course. Then I rapped on the window. Lightly. My heart pounded like crazy. Why was I doing this?

Neither one of them turned around. So I knocked harder. *Damn it*. They needed to SEE me. And if they didn't, I was going to march right in there, and—

She swiveled around on her stool. She looked pale. The unfortunate yellow peasant blouse she wore did nothing for her pale skin. Objectively speaking, she was a semiattractive woman, but not today.

I waved at her, plastering a big, fake smile on my face. *Look at me, boss! I see you f*cking my ex-boyfriend!* And then, to my surprise, she waved back. As if to say, *It's all good. We're just coworkers saying "Hi!"*

Then I turned around and marched back toward the LRS, who had no doubt been watching with great interest. I was shaking. "Let's go," I said.

The only problem with blogging was that you had to relive every damn emotion. I felt myself shaking again at the thought of what I'd seen. I dreaded going into work today. I didn't know what I thought would happen, exactly. It wasn't like the two of them were going to go to HR and report me for waving at them in a restaurant. But, still, she was my vice president. She had power.

At this point, I was too fired up to even think of not blogging about it. *Maybe I won't post this,* I told myself, as I wrote. *Maybe I should be cautious.* But I was too pissed off to be cautious.

After a beer and a half at the 74th Street Ale House a few blocks away, I started to feel better. The presence of the LRS cheered me up too, especially because he kept talking about how "nasty" Loserette was.

"You're way hotter than she is," he said, during the first beer.

"Thanks." I wondered if he was just saying that.

"I have to say, though, I'm way hotter than your ex," he said. I laughed my first real laugh of the evening.

By the time I was halfway through my second beer, I'd almost convinced myself that there would be no bad ramifications from my impulsive actions, and that I had come out quite admirably in the situation.

I also felt even more attached to the LRS, who'd handled the whole situation with grace and aplomb. Not judging me. Being supportive. Saying just the right things. Obviously I wasn't the most shining example of a well-adjusted dumpee, but if he had anything critical to say, he kept it to himself.

I looked at him on the other side of the booth. Today he looked especially good. As his arms rested on the table, I could see his shoulder muscles bulging just enough, but not too much, through his T-shirt. His bleached blond mop of hair was less unruly than usual. His brown eyes looked at me thoughtfully, not jumping around like they sometimes did. I noticed how long his lashes were. He should have had a caption above him: "Young Man in the Prime of Life." And suddenly I ached more than I ever had to be part of that life.

And this was what I was going to do. I was going to apply for a job at Kootenay National Park. F*ck Empire Corp. F*ck Loser/ette. I was not meant to sit in a windowless office all day. I'd already researched the jobs available there. From my years of hiking and backpacking I thought just maybe I had enough backcountry experience to qualify for a ranger job. As long as they didn't expect me to read a map.

I took a deep breath. "So," I said, attempting to sound casual, "have you heard back from the people in Canada yet?"

He looked at me with a confused expression on his face.

"You know, from Kootenay National Park?" My heart sped up.

"Oh, right." He shook his head, then took a sip of his beer. "I guess I forgot to tell you. I got another job."

For a moment, everything in the bar came to a standstill. The waitresses froze in place. The bartender stopped with his cocktail shaker in midair. My heart froze too, and then seemed to burst open.

"Oh yeah?" I tried desperately to hide the emotion in my voice. I took a gulp of my beer to try to stop the tears that, if they didn't come now, would come later that night. *You invited me along and now you changed your mind? I'm thinking about quitting my job and you changed your mind??* "What's that?" I looked down at the half-eaten salad on my plate to avoid his eyes.

"I got an offer to be a guide for the summer for this outfitter in Wyoming. In the Grand Tetons. Well, half the time I'm going to guide, half the time I'm going to videotape the trips."

"Wow." I sounded as unenthusiastic as a person possibly could. But he didn't seem to notice. His eyes had focused on someone in the back of the restaurant.

"When do you leave?"

He took his eyes off whomever he was looking at and looked at me. The tone in his voice became kinder. "Well, actually, next month. I'm going to be working in the office there and doing a bunch of other stuff. It's kind of like a ground floor thing."

"Oh." The tears welled up in my eyes instantly. "So it's over. Just like that?"

He looked startled.

"You're leaving town in a month and you forgot to *tell* me?" I could not, repeat, *not* cry. I was not his girlfriend; I had no right or reason to be upset. For all I knew he had five other girlfriends, including several in Wyoming.

"No, I was going to tell you. It's just—" he looked around for the right words to say. *I didn't think things were serious between us* or *I gotta be free, babe.* Instead he settled for a sheepish, "Well, I just found out, really. Yesterday."

I hated him at that moment. Hated his youth and his freedom. His unencumbered heart. I hated whatever girl got to have him and his magnificent body next, and whatever girl might be lucky enough to get his love, too, there amid the spires of the Tetons.

I could *not* cry here in this restaurant. But I did. I ran off to the bathroom and I cried and cried. Not just for him, but for every love affair I've ever had that didn't work out as planned.

E-mail Breakup Babe | Comments 3

POST A COMMENT

Oh God, you're making me cry too. I know it's hard to see the forest for the trees right now, but one day you'll end up with a great guy and will understand that everything else didn't work out for a reason.

Ms. G. | Homepage | 12/9/02–11:03 A.M.

•   •   •   •   •

You seem kind of manipulative and shallow, playing guys off each other like that. You deserve to end up alone.

Anonymous | 12/9/02–1:36 P.M.

•   •   •   •   •

Oh, don't listen to that guy, B.B. (at least I assume it's a guy). You are still on the rebound and it's natural to go through these kinds of ups and downs even though it would be much nicer to fall madly in love right away and live happily ever after without ever having to worry about dating again. It'll happen, but meanwhile you're getting great material for your book!

GalPal #2 | 12/9/02–8:47 P.M.

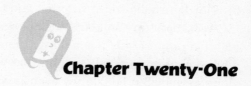

Chapter Twenty-One

Thursday, January 2, 2003

9:56 AM Breakup Babe

Good Lord, what year is it? Oh my God, 2003! What happened on New Year's Eve?! Did I—could I—oh my God. I did. I got drunk on tequila, got high, danced 'til all hours, and, in all the excitement, ended up making out passionately with (mumbles here) at the stroke of midnight.

Who's that, you say? *Who* did you make out with?! What? Girl, you are out of control!

I didn't feel particularly chipper when I wrote this. In fact, I felt downright hellish on this particular January 2 as I downed a triple Americano to rouse myself from my catatonic state. Three short months ago, I would have been giddy at the recent turn of events. But I knew Sexy Boy well enough by this point to realize he was the same charming commitmentphobe he'd always been. It's just that in my drunken New Year's state, I'd fallen prey to his flirtatious ways.

In the last few months I'd heard enough from Sexy Boy about his life's commitment to "freedom and fun" (as well as his recent dalliance with a hot flight attendant) to know that our frenzied all-night make-out session was taking us to the big Nowheresville. Yet it sure felt good while it was happening. We'd built up a solid friendship over the last few months, and that rapport only made things more exciting. Who knew when I first got a crush on him that we would actually get along so well? But I did know, even as we drunkenly, joyously, kissed away the first few hours of 2003, that I would pay for the fun later. Big-time.

Voilà. I'd soared high, now I was sinking low. All through a hungover New Year's Day, my euphoria lingered on. But not today. As work loomed, the events of the last months pressed down on me. The doctor's mysterious disappearance. Loser and Loserette in the window at Red Mill Burgers. Greensleeves Press rejecting my book. The LRS leaving for the Grand Tetons. Stacy or Suzie or whatever the name of that stupid flight attendant was, whom Sexy Boy would be seeing this very morning on his flight to Alaska.

So I was engaging in two quick fixes: drinking caffeine and writing my blog. For the moment, the coffee and the writing held my despair at bay. But I knew that later that day, trapped in my office, I would *really* regret New Year's Eve.

Yes, it's true. I WAS out of control, but no longer. I had a fun-filled flirty night with Sexy Boy, but I have no illusions—NONE—that this is going anywhere. It was a fling and that was all. (Though don't get me wrong. These days, B.B. does not give away the milk for free. At least not to boys she knows will disappear the next day.)

Fine, you say. We don't care if there was actual s*x involved! We want the details anyway! Was it hot? Was it not? Dish!

Sigh. Okay. If you *insist*.

My crush on Sexy Boy never really disappeared. Instead,

it morphed into a friendship wherein he became my dating confidant—at least when he was not jetting off to Alaska and toying with other women. But the sight of him always *did* something to me right where it mattered.

So, when a group of us went to a big party on New Year's Eve, the two of us palled around. Quite innocently at first. But as the evening progressed, alcohol was imbibed and dirty dancing occurred. Our bodies touched in places they had never touched before. He was still playing his role of dating confidant to the hilt when, all of a sudden, the tone shifted, moved into territory we had mostly abandoned three months before, or so I thought.

"Miss R.," he said, "it seems to me that maybe you're taking these men just a little too seriously." He was lounging next to me on a couch in a living room packed with people: drunken, laughing, dancing people. Outside it was a frosty thirty-six degrees; inside it felt like a tropical country. The windows were all steamed up by the revelers.

"Well, what do you recommend?" I said, leaning my head back on the couch, dangerously close to his shoulder.

We had just slow danced to "Open Arms" by Journey—one of many thirtysomething drunk and nostalgic couples who had rushed the dance floor for that one. It brought me back to seventh-grade dances, where I stood on the sidelines in the gym, hoping in vain that some pimply adolescent male would ask me to dance. Who would have imagined I'd one day be dancing with such a gorgeous man! *If only I could see me now,* I thought, encircled by Sexy Boy's strong arms. *I'm living out my junior high school fantasies!*

Now, leaning back on the couch, I had the perfect amount of alcohol in my bloodstream: enough to make me giddy but not out of control. Who in the world had invented alcohol anyway? They deserved some kind of award!

Besides generous amounts of tequila, I'd also indulged in some of Sexy Boy's stash. So now I was high on multiple substances, including the gaze from those sultry, suggestive green eyes of his. A warning bell went off somewhere in my head but the sounds of the party drowned it out. I'd forgotten that those eyes were classified as weapons of mass destruction.

"I think," he said, "and I believe I've told you this before, but this is a time for you to just have fun. You just came out of a serious relationship and frankly you're not ready for another." He shifted positions and his thigh touched mine. "Though I pretty much guarantee you, once you're out there just having fun, all the men you date will be begging for more." An annoying memory passed through my head of Marco's Supper Club. Sexy Boy reaching across the table to touch my arm while advising me to have more "fun." Then the memory floated away.

"Oh, really," I said, pressing my thigh blatantly against his. "Is that what happens with the women you date? They know you're just having fun, so they're begging for more? You're perpetually hard to get?"

"Exactly," he said, smiling. His face was very close to mine. I felt enveloped by his masculinity. By his Drakkar Noir. It caressed me, curled around my body. I closed my eyes to feel it all the better. But I wasn't expecting anything to happen. This was just more of his meaningless flirting. I tried simply to enjoy it and not want more. The pot helped with that. It let me detach, drift above my earthly desires. But then he spoke again.

"Listen," he said, and, despite my altered state, I noticed the lowered voice, the ever-so-slightly more serious tone. "It's almost midnight. And because you are the prettiest girl at this party, I'd like to kiss you then. That's what *I* think would be fun. What do you think of that?"

Bam. I slammed back to reality. I wanted him. I always had! So much for my Zen detachment.

"No," whimpered Sensible Girl, who appeared next to me with a glass of seltzer water in hand. She wore blue flannel pajamas and sheepskin slippers but at least had added a sparkly silver hat for the occasion. "Please don't. You know it would be a mistake." I looked at her in surprise. I had never heard her sound so defeated! But she was staring into her drink and didn't meet my gaze.

"Oh, my GOODNESS!" Needy Girl wobbled up in her most revealing outfit yet, a silver lamé concoction that started just above her breasts and ended just below her butt. She had a drink in each hand. "Go for it!" she said drunkenly. "Don't listen to that old bat. She doesn't know how to have fun, OBVIOUSLY. It's New Year's Eve. HELLO!" She raised a glass to me then drank the entire contents in a single gulp.

I looked back and forth between them. For the first time, I really saw how pathetic Needy Girl was. I also understood that Sensible Girl was on the verge of giving up. If I didn't listen to her this time, would she ever come back?

But Needy Girl was right. It was New Year's Eve! And all the feelings I'd locked up inside me for Sexy Boy had come flooding out. How could I resist them? "I'm sorry," I murmured to Sensible Girl. "I promise I'll be better next year."

"Whoohoo!" yelled Needy Girl.

Then I kissed him at midnight, and on into the morning, so long and so passionately that I forgot about everything else.

But the charmed night is over. The moment of glory has passed, and I feel like complete crap.

We can rejoice, however, because a new year has begun and it's time for me to put this kind of behavior behind me. While it may seem like I'm just a tough-talking, tequila-drinking hottie in a low-cut dress who actually enjoys drinking and dancing and drugging with wild abandon, the truth is I'm just a girl who misses her father and her ex and who wants a man in her life again. ONE man.

So, with the new year comes a new approach to dating. I'm not sure exactly what that approach should be. What I do know is I'm not going to find that one man by being so damn needy.

I need to step back, take my time, and not grasp at pointless relationships with hot but inappropriate boys (HBIBs) just because I'm afraid of dying alone and childless. I also need to listen to my instincts more. Had I been doing that these last six months, of course, I would have gotten no action whatsoever. But I've had enough action for now. The right guy will come along if I'm not busy making out with Mr. Wrong.

My other resolution is to get that nascent book of mine into publishable shape. Thanks to you all, I have confidence in this project despite it being cruelly rejected once already!

So I hereby resolve to get a first draft of my book done. I don't know how I will do that exactly. I have never done such a thing before. To help me along with this task I've signed up for a writing class that will require me to get my first chapter written, because, at this point, I have no f*cking idea how to structure the thing.

So there you have it. New Year's past and future. Happy New Year to you, Breakup Babies. I hope you made more intelligent decisions about who to kiss than I did!

E-mail Breakup Babe | Comments 5

Phew. That was a long entry, but it felt good to get everything out. As I shouldered my backpack, I thought about how, in the old days, something like this would have gone into my diary. Now a diary seemed so damn boring and old-fashioned. There was no Greek chorus to comment on every single little thing!

I knew a day would come when my dating exploits would stop and Breakup Babe would die a natural death. Maybe she would morph into another form, a blog about gardening or cooking or my adorable little children. Or my life as a best-selling author. *Ha.* But it was hard to imagine that day right now. Breakup Babe, in all her heartbroken glory, had become such an important part of my life.

Caffeine coursed through my system as I made my way out of Victrola. Despite my gloom-and-doom mood earlier, I felt almost chipper now. Out of habit, I glanced at the counter, even though the cute barista wasn't working today. Instead there were two female baristas, both wearing skimpy tank tops that revealed upper bodies awash in tattoos. Somehow the cute barista had managed to get a job here despite the job requirement that you be inked over at least 50 percent of your body.

I stepped out into the cold, clammy January day. The sun shone weakly through a high layer of clouds. Maybe work wouldn't be so bad today. Maybe I'd be productive instead of bored, losing myself in my work instead of mooning about Sexy Boy. Lord knows I needed to take my job a little more seriously. This writing class had set me back five hundred dollars, but thanks to my job, I could afford it. The whole reason I'd taken this job, after all, was so that I could have a stable life from which to attempt the perilous task of writing a book.

It sucked, of course, to have to deal with the Loser twins. A person shouldn't *have* to deal with such a thing at work. But, I thought, hurrying toward my car, fortified by my morning writing and coffee-drinking session, they weren't going to get the best of me. This was going to be my year! I would succeed—in my job, with my book, and even in romance—*despite* them.

POST A COMMENT

How do you know SB doesn't want a relationship? Maybe he's ready to have a girlfriend. Don't give up on him so fast. He sounds hot!
Little Princess | 1/02/03–3:19 P.M.

· · · · ·

No, B.B. is right. Guys like SB don't change. The guy I'm dating is just like him. He acts seventeen even though he's thirty, and whenever I want to talk about serious stuff, he says he just wants to have "fun." But I made the mistake of getting hooked early on.
Kissing Geek | Homepage | 1/02/03–5:33 P.M.

· · · · ·

Has anyone told you you're trying too hard? Men can sense that, you know. If you stop looking, that's when you'll meet someone.
George | 1/02/03–8:01 P.M.

•   •   •   •   •

HBIBs—what a great name. I always wondered what to call them!
Delilah | Homepage | 1/02/03–10:51 P.M.

•   •   •   •   •

There's got to be a few Hot but Appropriate Boys (HBABs) out there, don't there?
Jake | 1/03/03–12:09 A.M.

Chapter Twenty-Two

God. I was so bored. And it was only 1:30 P.M. My morning caffeine and blogging therapy had worn off, and I could sense that I was about to plunge into the deep, dark waters of self-pity. I slumped listlessly in front of my computer.

I'd run out of interesting things to do. I'd already checked the comments on my blog several times. I was annoyed by that "you're trying too hard" comment, but gratified that someone had stepped up to my defense. I loved it when my readers got into their own little discussions, or, even better, arguments. The occasional negative comments bothered me, but so far not badly enough to make me dismantle the comments. Most of my readers were enthusiastic and—dare I say it—adoring. And I adored to be adored!

I'd checked my hit counter, which was holding steady at a respectable seventy-five people a day. (I was still jealous of the A-list bloggers and their thousands of hits per day, but at least my hits increased a little every month.) I'd looked at some new referring blogs with the usual mixture of hope and disappointment. I loved my readers (because, after all, they loved me), but none of them could write. I'd e-mailed all my friends, then checked my monthly horoscope for January, which promised "a great deal of excitement and drama around the new moon on January 2." That was today, but what the hell exciting was going to happen today?

Now the only thing left to do was don the editing straitjacket and attempt actual work. But the thought caused me physical pain. It would have helped on a day like today if people in my group actually *talked* to one another instead of hiding behind closed office doors and sending e-mail! They were such an antisocial bunch. There were never any impromptu lunches. No chatty coffee breaks.

In the pre-tech-bubble days of the mid-1990s, work at Empire Corp. had been one big party. Back then, I'd been a temp working in a group full of other young temps to write "cool" multimedia content (which became extinct at Empire when it failed to produce a profit). I'd been surrounded by hot twentysomething guys who were always stopping by my office for a chat. Of course, that created its own set of problems, including one spectacularly failed office romance (you'd think by the time Loser rolled around I would have learned my lesson!), but still I had had plenty of social time. Now that I'd graduated to being a full-time employee in a group of middle-aged, married technical editors, I felt so *old*. There were, however, plenty of other groups at Empire where teammates socialized together. You could see them sitting in the cafeteria in big, chatty groups. But in my group, introversion was the unspoken rule. Arthur, of course, was an exception, but he was still on vacation.

Leaning heavily on one elbow, I clicked over to the University of Washington Web site and read for the zillionth time the description of the evening writing class I would be taking. I really would get to work after this.

The class was called "Crafting a Narrative Arc," and it guaranteed that by the end of the quarter, you would have written an article, short story, or book chapter. The description also said, "We will spend part of the class working on nailing an outline for your story, one of the most important but overlooked aspects of writing a successful piece of nonfiction (or fiction)."

The outlining aspect of the class appealed to me. When I'd tried to write *Temporary Insanity*, I thought I had the story line nailed, but the book constantly meandered off. Scenes started off promisingly, but then went on too long. Or didn't go on long enough. I could quickly spot problems in my own work, but I still didn't have the techniques to fix them. Some people, maybe, could learn those techniques by osmosis. God knows I'd read enough books that if I could simply absorb the tricks of good writing, I would be an expert by now. I could certainly crank out five-hundred-word blog entries that people liked, but a book was a whole different deal.

Suddenly my phone rang. Oh! Maybe it was one of the GalPals or a family member calling to distract me! I looked at my caller ID. *Crap.* It was my boss, Lyle. The sight of his name on my caller ID caused immediate guilt. Could he sense telepathically that I hadn't been working all day? Why was he calling? Usually if he had something to say, he did it in person. He'd learned that in a management class somewhere.

"Rachel," he said, sounding very official and distant, and very unlike Lyle, "I'm wondering if you have time to meet with me this afternoon about some changes in your editing projects."

"Okay," I said. My paranoia increased. Maybe someone had complained about me. One of the technical writers I worked with? What if it was Melanie? She'd been reassigned to me recently after she stormed out of her last editor's office screaming that he was a "technically incompetent idiot who was trying to sabotage" her. Obviously she was crazy, but I still couldn't believe they had then paired her up to work with me, the ultimate in technically incompetent. So far I'd avoided meeting with her, so it was hard to imagine she had anything to complain about.

"Does three work for you?" said Lyle.

"Sure." I tried to sound casual and breezy.

"Okay, then. We'll see you at three."

I hung up and stared at the phone. It was now 1:45. What did he mean by "we" anyway? A frightening thought crossed my mind: *the Red Mill incident.* But how could I get in trouble for that? I couldn't. There was no way. All I'd done was wave at my coworkers. Okay, I'd waved a bit aggressively perhaps, but what could Loser and Loserette possibly say about that incident to indict me? Nothing!

Crap. Okay. Maybe, as Lyle had said, it was actually to talk about my editing assignments. *Deep breath.* If Melanie had complained about me, so what? She'd clashed with more than one editor before. She was a known troublemaker. A "difficult" writer. The other writers I worked with liked me just fine.

For the next hour, I would concentrate. I really would. *Another deep breath.*

I opened up one of my editing projects and told myself I would edit ten pages of it before 3 P.M. I would make the prose sing! I would make the methods and properties dance waltzes around the enumerations and return values. I stared at the document in front of me. There was not a single part of me that felt up to singing and dancing. Then I looked back at the clock.

1:47 P.M.

Concentrate.

When I walked into Lyle's office, my worst fears were confirmed. Because there was Wendii, the plastic HR person who'd welcomed me into the company eight months ago.

I froze just inside the doorway. Back in May, Wendii's white blond hair had been cut into a bouncy bob. Now it was longer and pulled back into a severe bun. She looked at me with a grim expression through black-framed glasses. I didn't remember the glasses. Immediately my heart started to pound. *Was I fired?*

"Rachel," said Lyle, also clearly quite nervous. His eyes darted between Wendii and me. "Please take a seat. Wendii has a few things she'd like to discuss with you."

I flashed back to my first job out of college. I'd been a receptionist in the basement of Sproul Hall, U.C. Berkeley's main administrative building. The other receptionist there called it "Hell's Butthole." My bosses, evil people to begin with, despised me, though in retrospect I couldn't blame them. I usually wore a pink sweatshirt to work that fell off the shoulder *Flashdance* style and called in sick constantly because I'd developed a near ulcer from the stress of realizing I actually had to work for a living.

After a month in the basement, my boss, Joyce, the middle-aged office manager whose complexion and wardrobe looked as if a giant hypodermic needle had sucked all life from them, called me into a conference room with her assistant, Marie. Marie was an obese thirtyish woman with heavy-lidded aqua eyes who looked as if she were perpetually trying to digest a large rat. Joyce told me, smirking, "We're going to give you a review now." At that point in my young life, I had no idea what a review was, but I knew that this one, at least, wasn't going to be good. And it wasn't. They fired me. The reason: "incompetence and a poor attitude."

I had the same ominous feeling now. My throat became extremely dry. I sat down on the empty chair and tried not to shake. I looked at Wendii. Her face was caked with foundation, the skin tinted a perfect peach.

Lyle was looking down at his feet. Wendii cleared her throat. "Rachel, I need to tell you that there has been a complaint lodged against you by two other members of this department."

I didn't say anything. My mind went blank.

"Apparently," she continued, "you have been writing about your coworkers on a website of sorts."

Her words hit me like a slap. At first I sat in stunned silence. Then surprise gave way to humiliation. My face grew hot. My palms began to sweat. Phrases flew back to haunt me: "abominable adulterers," "slutty little VP," "putrid little relationship." Then there were the excruciating details of my own sex life! The Li'l Rockclimbing Spy and his "magnificent crotch." The doctor's "degree in Kissology." Oh my God. What must these people think of me?

I hung my head. Denial was useless. In a barely audible voice that sounded like dry gravel, I said, "Just two of them."

"Just two of them what?" said Wendii sharply. I looked up at her. Cleared my throat. A little bit of defiance crept into me. I wondered what this Borglike bitch would do if her perfectly built blond husband dumped her for the HR bimbo in the next office? Certainly not anything as creative as what I was doing! She would probably just cry until all her foundation came off and mascara ran down her face in rivulets, then throw herself off a bridge.

"I just wrote about two of my coworkers." Though I mumbled it, I looked her in the eye. She averted hers, and looked down at a folder in her hand.

"Well, that's not strictly true, Rachel, but in any case, it's beside the point. I want you to know that right now we are conducting an investigation into your website." She flipped open the folder. "Breakup Babe." She glanced over at Lyle and I did too. Everything about him drooped. He looked mortified. My humiliation deepened. My God, he'd always been so nice to me and I'd let him down. He'd praised me numerous times for what a "good job" I was doing!

But, Jesus, there was not just him to be ashamed for.

There was my whole family, all my friends! If I got fired from this job, would it go on my permanent record? Was it like being a felon? I felt claustrophobic and wanted to run. Anywhere. Perhaps I could hop a plane to Ecuador. Or Mexico. During my carefree pre-Loser days of travel, I'd met many a Latin American man who'd offered to marry me. What a fool I'd been to turn them down. Any one of them: Hector the waiter or Jorge the dive master or Alex the bar owner!

"We'll need you to be available for meetings when we call you. I also want to make it clear to you that this investigation could result in your termination, though we hope it won't go that way." Wendii looked at me, and her eyes were empty, cold. The welcoming persona of eight months ago was gone. "Do you have any questions you want to ask me?"

Yes! I wanted to say. *How the hell did they find out about my blog?* Instead, I said so meekly I could hardly believe it was me, "No."

"Well." Wendii snapped her leather briefcase shut. It was dark, high-quality leather. She looked at Lyle, who was staring at the ground. "Lyle will be in the loop, as will my manager, but except for them and the parties who have placed the complaint, this will be strictly confidential. Do you need me to tell you who filed this claim?"

"No." Again, I was the meek, cringing person I didn't recognize. Maybe this was all a bad dream. Could it be that I was still only five years old and my whole life lay ahead of me, virgin and pure? No broken hearts, no mistakes, only possibilities? If I blinked hard enough, maybe the dream would end and I'd find myself in my old bed, the one with bars to keep me from falling to the floor.

I blinked. Hard.

Fuck.

"We'll be in touch, then." Wendii rose from her chair. So did Lyle. So did I. My legs were rubbery.

I walked out of the office first and wobbled down the hallway as quickly as I could. Because movement was the only thing that felt like it could keep my head from exploding, I kept walking. Out the door and into the parking lot.

I'd been here just this morning, but it looked alien to me now—the gleaming BMWs and Audis; the trees that had flamed with color in the fall but that were now naked and sad. These once-familiar objects looked like relics from another, safer world. Was it possible that just an hour and a half ago, I had been bored? Boredom seemed, suddenly, like the most desirable feeling in the world.

I walked in circles around the parking lot, clutching myself against the cold. The circles I walked with my feet matched the loop in my brain. *How had this happened? Why had I been so stupid? What was going to happen to me?* Round and round. At 3:45, the day was already starting to darken around the edges. The sky was a cold, cruel gray. I wouldn't be able to stay outside much longer without a coat, but still I kept walking, trying to think my way out of this trap I'd set for myself. Round and round.

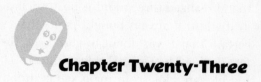

Chapter Twenty-Three

It was 7 A.M. Too fucking early to be awake and on my second cup of coffee. But I hadn't slept well the night before, so when I woke at 6 A.M., I decided it was better to be at Victrola, attempting to write, than lying in bed contemplating my bleak future. As I sat there, bleary-eyed, I remembered a little too clearly the first weeks after the breakup with Loser. I'd briefly, blissfully, forget my grief when I slept, but inevitably wake up much earlier than I wanted to, only to have remembrance slam into me and break my heart all over again.

It had been like that this morning. When my eyes flew open at six, I suddenly remembered everything that had happened the night before. I'd clutched Mr. Pickle to my chest and tried to go back to sleep. But the images that flashed behind my eyelids were too disturbing. Wendii staring at me over her black-framed glasses. Loser and Loserette exulting in each other's arms at the news of my termination.

So I'd gotten out of bed and dragged myself to a half-empty Victrola. The cute barista was there, but I avoided all eye contact. I lacked the confidence to flirt with anyone right now. I looked like hell, with unwashed hair and a pair of jeans that, I realized three months postpurchase, were far too saggy in the butt. I always bought pants that were a size too large, certain that I was about to gain back the twenty pounds I'd lost during The Great Unpleasantness. Then I ended up looking like an adolescent male, pants drooping gangsta style to reveal cotton underwear bought in a five-pack at Target.

Though I had my laptop open in front of me, and a new post started on Breakup Babe, I couldn't think of a thing in hell to say. What, if anything, could I now write in my blog? With Lyle and Wendii and Loser all reading it? That particular question had started circulating feverishly in my brain yesterday, and I hadn't yet answered it.

My mother had given me the following advice after I'd poured out the whole sad story on the phone last night: "You have to stop writing about Loser and Loserette immediately!"

"Well, no duh," I burst out graciously.

Silence on the other end. She was probably contemplating hanging up on me, but I was her firstborn and I was suffering.

"Sorry," I said, in a sulky voice. "I'm just upset." After a second, I said, "Are they going to make me take down my blog?"

This idea, in fact, had been bothering me almost more than the idea that I might lose my job. That had been my first thought when I'd stumbled out of Lyle's office, actually. Not *What about me?* but *What about Breakup Babe?* It was a ridiculous thought, I knew. But this crisis had made me realize, in a way I hadn't before, how much Breakup Babe was now part of me, how much I'd come to rely on her.

"Well," said my mother the lawyer, hesitantly, "Empire HR cannot make you take down your blog."

Relief shot through me.

"*But* they can fire you if they think you're creating a hostile workplace."

"We'll sue them!" I shot back, instantly filled with indignation. I imagined the three of us in a high-ceilinged courtroom furnished with polished wood, just like on the TV shows. I would be dressed impeccably in a stylish yet sexy suit that emphasized my curvy size 6 body (size 4 if I shopped at Banana Republic!), while Loserette would be wearing some dowdy thing she'd bought at Talbots that emphasized the megalithic size of her ass. Loser, who never knew what to wear when he couldn't wear a black turtleneck and black jeans, would be wearing an eight-year-old oversized tie and the too-tight-in-the-chest suit he'd worn at his wedding twelve years ago.

I would have a hot lawyer, à la Robert Downey Jr. in *Ally McBeal*, who would ask incisive yet witty questions that would have the courtroom in stitches while simultaneously making the two of them look like the simpering sycophants they were.

"Mr. Loser," he would say, turning to give me a sexy wink (we would become lovers, of course, after he'd won the case), "are you trying to tell this court that you DON'T wear tightywhities, as Ms. Cooper suggested in her blog? And that you DO have a normal-sized penis?"

"So," continued my mother, interrupting my reverie, "I suggest you just forget the whole thing. Stop blogging and focus on your job. You don't want to get fired!" I'd finally revealed the Breakup Babe URL to my mother a month ago. She'd read it avidly since then with a mixture of "horror and admiration." I knew for a fact, though, that she proudly showed the blog to some of her friends, X-rated content and all, to brag about my writing talent.

"No duh!" I wanted to say again, but this time I restrained myself. "Do you think they'll fire me?" I asked, my voice high and wavering. I was sick of crying. I wasn't going to do it on the phone, I just wasn't.

Silence for a few seconds. "I don't know," she said, finally, her voice weary. I knew what she was thinking: Thank God I have another daughter who has the perfect job, the perfect marriage, and never causes me any trouble.

This conversation replayed itself in my head as I gazed out Victrola's plate glass window and puzzled how to proceed with my blog. The first, and least desirable, option was to get rid of the blog—after saving my archives first, of course. With two clicks of the mouse, I could make Breakup Babe disappear. I suffered no illusions, however, that deleting my inflammatory posts could save me from what was happening. Empire had probably already saved it all to their master server. Still, I could prevent any of my other coworkers from discovering it.

But I couldn't delete Breakup Babe. She was part of me. A troubled, fucked-up part of me, maybe, but I couldn't just abandon her—even if she'd gotten me in trouble. On the other hand, how and what did I write now that I had this unwanted audience? Did I really want my boss to know about my sex life? Not that he would choose to read my blog, but what if morbid curiosity got the best of him one day and he scoured the archives? How would it affect my review when he read about the Li'l Rockclimbing Spy's giant cock?

Rachel does solid editing work, but she seems obsessed with the size of the male member. Not surprisingly, her ability to choose men is spotty at best.

God.

What else was I supposed to write about, though? Funny that just yesterday I'd been musing about the day Breakup Babe died a natural death and turned into a gardening blog or something equally innocuous.

Well, I was *not* ready for that.

I sighed in frustration and watched out the window as people started their day on 15th Avenue. Attired in their

Gore-Tex, fleece, and wool, they looked tired and cranky as they straggled down the street, fighting the cold. It was barely light out now, at 7:30 A.M., and would be dark again by four. With winter clamped down over us like this, it was hard to imagine those July days when daylight lingered until ten. Thank God those demanding days of summer were gone. Brooding felt so much more natural in winter.

I knew, without a doubt, that Loser had already read the entire thing, start to finish. The question was did I want to keep my emotional life on display for him from now on? I wondered, for the hundredth time, how he'd found my blog. Had he stumbled upon it himself? Had some acquaintance of his found it and then told him about it?

Though I'd tried to keep this image at bay for the last eighteen hours, it now came to me vividly: Loser sitting in his office, poring over the blog. Absorbing the insults, the accusations. Feeling, in turn, hurt, outraged, afraid. Some little part of him might have even admired what a good writer I was (unlikely, of course, since he favored serialized science fiction and comic books). But outrage had won out. Outrage and fear. So then he'd gotten together with his contemptible consort and decided—once again!—to ruin my life!

The fucking bastard. There had been moments where I actually felt guilty about what I'd written about him. I knew, deep down, that he'd never meant to hurt me. He'd loved me deeply. He'd cheated on me and lied to me because he was a coward, not because he was cruel.

The stuff that came after that, though, I didn't know how to forgive. There were millions of other women in the world for him to fuck, and, selfish, low-down asshole that he was, he'd chosen my vice president.

And now. NOW. He was trying to get me fired because I'd outed them. Sixteen hours after Wendii broke the news of their "complaint," the injustice of the situation inflamed me.

All lingering hints of guilt disappeared. That selfish coward had proved himself a person of zero integrity, and he didn't deserve one iota of my sympathy.

Damn it! I felt like hurling my half-empty coffee cup across Victrola. I would keep writing Breakup Babe! So what if Loser read it? Or Wendii or Lyle for that matter? So I couldn't write about those two creeps and I couldn't write about the crisis at work, but I could—and I would—continue to write about whatever the hell else I wanted. It was my constitutional right, after all. (Well, I wasn't quite sure about it being a real right, but it felt like it should be!) And I could—and I would—get that book written. Writing a book, I knew, was where the true satisfaction lay.

Satisfaction and revenge. Suddenly, seized by inspiration, I returned to the post I'd started on Blogger, then wrote for forty-five minutes without stopping.

Friday, January 3, 2003
7:33 AM Breakup Babe

One day I'm going to be a famous writer and every boy who's ever wronged me is going to regret it. There I'll be on the back of my book, gazing out at the world with soft yet cynical brown eyes, my long hair just the slightest bit windblown, looking unbearably brilliant, beautiful, and rich.

Trying to escape from their own sordid lives, which will have sadly gone to hell since they dumped me, they will stumble upon my fame and fortune in a variety of painful ways.

There is Josh, for example, the rock climber I met when we both worked as counselors at summer camp when I was twenty-two, who effectively ended my childhood by breaking my heart open like a piñata and leaving the candy to rot in the sun.

Josh will be killing time in his squalid apartment one afternoon, before heading off to his janitorial job, and, quite by accident, will see me appear on *Oprah*. I will be there with my soul mate, Johnny Depp, and we will be sharing our innermost feelings about being madly in love with someone as brilliant, beautiful, and rich as ourselves.

As Josh watches me toss my chestnut mane, charming Oprah and an adoring crowd, he will realize—in one of those life-changing epiphanies—that he's never forgotten me, couldn't forget me if he tried, and that it was the biggest mistake of his life to dump me in such a brutal manner.

Though we haven't talked in more than ten years, and there is no possible way he could have found my unlisted phone number, Josh will call me at two in the morning at the Montana ranch where Johnny and I spend our time when not in Los Angeles or New York, and tell me how he loves me still, and that if I could just forgive him for dumping me like a carton of spoiled milk, he would follow me to the ends of the earth.

There will be silence for a moment, and I will stretch it out, because how many times have I hoped to hear him say this? And then, "Josh," I will say, and my voice won't be trembling at all, despite the fact that until I became a famous writer and met Johnny Depp and became unbearably happy, I could not forget him no matter how hard I tried, "please don't ever call me again."

And then I will hang up. I will go back to sleep with no regrets and Josh will never haunt my dreams again, where he had a habit of showing up to cast a shadow of loss just when everything was going wrong.

My bold proclamation will break Josh's heart so completely that he'll never be able to love again. Instead, he'll spend the rest of his days as a Unabomber-style hermit, venturing into civilization only to buy each of my novels as they come out. Josh will spend the next two years in his dilapidated shack, staring grief-stricken at my smiling photo on the book jacket, until the next novel comes out, with an even more glamorous photo. He will read each book obsessively, over and over again, searching for references to him as the one great love of my life.

But they won't be there, of course.

E-mail Breakup Babe | Comments 5

POST A COMMENT

Wow, poor Josh.

Knut | Homepage | 1/03/03–11:11 A.M.

•   •   •   •   •

This is my favorite Breakup Babe entry of all time. You won't forget the little people when you're famous, will you?

GenieG | Homepage | 1/03/03–1:43 P.M.

•   •   •   •   •

Yes, that would be the ultimate revenge, I agree. I hope to write my own book someday too, but until then I'll have to live vicariously through you. Go, B.B.!

Jake | 1/03/03–6:05 P.M.

•   •   •   •

You seem to have some unresolved bitterness issues about men. No wonder you can't find a boyfriend.

The Pool Boy | Homepage | 1/03/03–9:23 P.M.

•   •   •   •   •

She has a right to be bitter about men! Most of them have their heads up their asses, including you, Pool Boy. Anyway, thank God she is, or she wouldn't have all this entertaining stuff to write. Can't wait to buy your book, B.B.!

Kissing Geek | Homepage | 1/04/03–8:39 A.M.

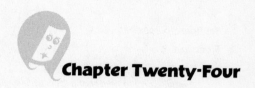

Chapter Twenty-Four

To: *Breakup Babe*
From: *Jake R.*

   *Hey, there, B.B., I'm a neighbor to the south (Portland) and a
longtime fan of your blog. You've probably noticed a few of my comments here and there. I was just writing to say that I've noticed your
posts have been a bit subdued lately. (Although I have to say, I loved
that one a week or so ago about your becoming a best-selling author.) Anyway, just thought I'd drop you a line to see if everything
was okay up there in not-so-sunny Seattle.*

To: *Jake R.*
From: *Breakup Babe*

Hi, Jake,

   *Thanks for the note. Everything is okay, sort of. Well, that's not
true. Things aren't really okay, and the worst part is, I can't *$#%!*

blog about it! Don't worry, I'm not about to die of a horrible disease or anything. It's just a lot of sh*t has gone down. I'm currently pouring my creative energy into developing my book instead of writing the blog—sad as this may be for devoted fans like you. ☺

To: *Breakup Babe*
From: *Jake R.*

Really? Sorry to hear that a lot of sh*t is going down. But you've always got a sympathetic ear here in Portland. Or, rather, a sympathetic computer screen, since I'm pretty much working night and day right now. I promise I won't dish to any of your other fans. But, of course, if you don't want to talk about it, I understand. I'm a complete stranger after all. ☺

To: *Jake R.*
From: *Breakup Babe*

Well, you might be a stranger, but if you love my blog, you're clearly a person of taste and discernment. Let's just say this: Certain people have discovered the blog and I am now in Big Trouble.

The e-mail started on a Saturday afternoon a week and a half after my warning from Wendii. It must have been a combination of boredom and despair that made me open up to Jake so quickly, or maybe it was just that I'd always been in love with the name "Jake." I'd had plenty of e-mail exchanges with male readers before—one of whom had begged me to move to Ohio and marry him—but never had any of them progressed to anything significant. (I'd graciously turned down the guy in Ohio, though I told him to e-mail me again in a few years.)

The particular Saturday when this e-mail exchange started found me, sadly enough, at the office. It was not a place I usually frequented on weekends, but the combination of an upcoming deadline and the suspicion that I should do everything possible to kiss up right now had put me in the windowless hole on a day when I should have been out living my youngish life.

The previous winter, I'd been up in the mountains cross-country skiing or snowshoeing almost every weekend (usually *sans* Loser, since he preferred to spend his weekends fine-tuning his home network). But since The Great Unpleasantness, I'd become a blob. Breakup Blob. I'd been out to the mountains once in the last four months. And my psyche was suffering because of it. I felt restless and pent-up but without the drive to do anything about it.

The advent of The Great Unpleasantness, Part II (aka the HR investigation), should have motivated me. Lord knows I needed the stress relief, the soul-cleansing experience of gliding across fresh snow as I skied through a forest blanketed in white. Yet the weekends flew by without my ever leaving the city limits.

A couple of weeks ago, a flyer in the hallway had caught my eye. "Climb Mount Rainier!" it said. I'd stopped for a minute and looked at it longingly. It was an advertisement for a fund-raising climb that would take place this coming August.

I'd wanted to climb Mount Rainier since 1993. That was the year I'd hiked around the entire mountain with my first Seattle boyfriend, Luke. If Josh (aka the "Feather") was the one responsible for rekindling my childhood love of the outdoors, Luke was the one who got me back into it for good. He resembled John Denver in looks and spirit, and was the kindest, most solid guy I'd ever dated. After three years of outdoor adventures, we were the best of friends, but I didn't feel any "passion" for him. To my mother's deep despair, I dumped him—the one and only guy who ever wanted to marry me.

It had seemed like the right decision at the time, but now I wasn't so sure. Especially as I found myself dating near teenagers or raging commitmentphobes. But Luke had been snapped up by a sensible woman long ago, and was married with kids by now. His wife wouldn't even let him talk to me.

Since that experience on Rainier, I'd been back to the mountain many times, but never on its upper slopes. I'd climbed the other big volcanoes around—Mount Saint Helens, Mount Baker, Mount Adams—with heartier, pre-Loser boyfriends. I loved being high up on glaciers, surrounded by sun and snow and searing blue sky. But Mount Rainier had always scared me. It was bigger and more dangerous than those other mountains. People were always falling off cliffs or into crevasses. Every summer, articles regularly appeared in the papers: "Mount Rainier Takes Another Life."

I'd walked away from that flyer thinking "I can't do it. Not now." Another part of me recognized that climbing Mount Rainier would be a great thing for me to do. The climb was still months away, so I had plenty of time to train. And having that as a goal would force me to get out into the mountains again. If I summited Mount Rainier, I would feel good about myself! My confidence could certainly use a boost.

But then The Great Unpleasantness, Part II, struck, and all thoughts of climbing Mount Rainier became distant and shrouded in clouds, just like the mountain itself. It also explained why I was at work on a Saturday, trying to edit as fast as I could, sending a strategic e-mail here and there to make sure everyone knew I'd been working on a weekend. *See, I really am a good employee, even if I do mock the size of my vice president's ass online!!*

At least I'd written for an hour and a half before I came in today. I'd started my writing class on Thursday, and had already gotten a good start on the first assignment: to outline the first chapter of my book and draft a single, important scene. The writing was going well so far because there was so much detail packed into my blog to draw from.

But now that I was at work, the good feeling that writing gave me had dissipated in the sterile atmosphere. If I found it hard to concentrate on work during the week, it was even harder on a Saturday, when the place was a ghost town. There wasn't even the barrage of boring, work-related e-mails to distract me.

In the void, my thoughts drifted to Sexy Boy. He was in Alaska, thank God, or I might be tempted to call, to flirt, to see if we could reprise our going-nowhere New Year's Eve, even though secretly I would want it to be going somewhere.

So when the e-mail from Jake appeared, no wonder I jumped on it with just a little too much enthusiasm. I'd responded almost immediately after he sent it, and then, to my surprise, there was another e-mail from him ten minutes later.

But, no! I had five hundred files to edit by Tuesday! I was on the verge of getting fired! So I made a heroic effort. I tried to imagine that somewhere, someone's life depended on how quickly I could edit a method page. If I could edit a method page in one minute or less, a starving family in India would have food for a week!

This method returns a non null value.

Hmm. Did "non null" require a hyphen? Yes, maybe. There. I was done with that page! The family now had food on their table, and Rodney Rolands was awarding me a special Medal of Honor in front of the entire company.

Damn it. I really wanted to check my Breakup Babe e-mail account. But, no! I would wait a full ten minutes! If I could only edit for ten minutes more, without stopping, Jake Gyllenhaal would get a starring role in the movie adaptation of my book and we would fall madly in love during the filming! But only if I edited for ten minutes straight! I plunged ahead, into the depths of boredom.

*The Add method appends a Scope **object** to this collection.*

I wondered what Jake looked like. The other Jake. With a name like Jake, he had to be cute. Right?

The Insert method inserts an element into the collection at the specified index.

He was single, right? He had to be single. He wouldn't be writing me two e-mails within twenty minutes if he wasn't single, right? I tried to recollect some of the comments he'd posted on my blog. Oh yes, he was the one who'd advised me to tear up the birthday card from Loser! Someone who'd definitely been through the wringer himself. But what was his status now?

The AddRange method adds an array to the collection.

Not that I should even be thinking about such things. He lived in Portland! Besides, what kind of loser with no life sent two e-mails within twenty minutes to a complete stranger?

The Clear method removes an array from the collection.

On the other hand, Portland was only three hours away. If we did have a steamy romance, I wouldn't have to get on a plane to visit him. Two more minutes and I could check my e-mail! But I couldn't get my hopes up. He wouldn't have sent another e-mail so quickly.

But, in fact, he had.

From: *Jake R.*
To: *Breakup Babe*

Big trouble, eh? I'm sorry to hear that. But you're going to be a famous writer, aren't you, and the blog is going to get you there. So whatever "trouble" you're in right now, I'm sure it's temporary. I don't want to pry, but feel free to unload on me if you want.

Oh God, the temptation was too much. Of course I wanted to unload. Not that I hadn't already unloaded on all of my friends and family. I would spend five minutes on the e-mail, then go back to work for another full hour.

To: *Jake R.*
From: *Breakup Babe*

Yes, well, as it turns out Loser and Loserette found the blog. They have now reported me to HR for various crimes against human-ity. God knows if yours truly will have a job next week. So here I am at the office on a Saturday, trying to prove my worthiness. Not that it will help. What's your excuse for being glued to your computer screen?

We exchanged several more e-mails that day, and contin-ued our e-mail exchange the following week. We wrote each other at least three times a day. He commiserated with me about my work situation and ranted about how unfair it was. He himself worked in the IT department in the Portland of-fice of Nike. He was also starting a small software company with a friend of his, which is what put him in front of the computer for such long hours every day. Jake was also re-cently divorced with a five-year-old daughter whom he saw on weekends. I knew that the phrase "recently divorced" was not exactly the highest recommendation for a guy but, hell, this was probably just a harmless flirtation, right?

Wrong. When he told me he loved to backpack and ski, my interest ratcheted up several notches. When he sent me his picture, it peaked. He was no Jake Gyllenhaal, but he certainly lived up to what my image of a Jake should be: dark-haired, lean, handsome. Add to that his well-written, witty e-mails with nary a spelling or grammar error to activate my innate snob, and we had a romance in the making. But both of us held off that week from making the obvious statement (clearly, we were developing a more than friendly interest in each other) and asking the obvious question, were we going to do anything about it?

The obvious question got answered after the second summons from HR.

Two weeks after my first meeting with Lyle and Wendii, she called me. I'd almost convinced myself by then that nothing bad was going to happen to me. If they were going to fire me, wouldn't they have done it right away? Wouldn't they have hustled me out with an armed security guard to ensure I didn't smash any servers or steal any proprietary information? I heard that's what happened to people who got fired. Maybe the investigation had died a quiet death.

I was in the middle of composing an e-mail to Jake when she called.

"Rachel, this is Wendii Rogers," said the professional, overly polished voice. As if I couldn't see her name on my caller ID: WendiiR. My heart was beating so fast I could barely speak.

"Yeah," I managed to say.

"We've decided to proceed with the investigation, so I need you to be here for a meeting at 3 P.M. next Thursday, in conference room 1783 in the Rolands HR Building. Will that work for you?"

As if she cared whether it worked for me. No, I'm sorry, I can't make it that day, I'm getting a pedicure! Whoops, no can do, I have lunch with Steven Spielberg to discuss Breakup Babe the movie that day! Oh, SORRY, Wendii, I'm scheduled for my regular electroshock treatments that day!

"Yes, okay," I said. The same cringing, simpering employee I'd become during my first meeting with Wendii and Lyle.

"Good," she said. "I'll send you a meeting request."

I hung up the phone and stared at my computer screen, where I'd been going on to Jake about my recent attempts at writing my book and how I'd finally gotten in the habit of writing every day.

I erased everything I'd written. Then wrote, simply, my hands pounding the keyboard, "I just got a call from HR. They want to meet with me next week." Sent it.

Then I quickly threw on my running clothes. One thing about all this stress, it was getting me in shape again. Months after Loser had dumped me while we were running, I'd finally started keeping my running clothes at work again. In the last week, I'd gone running or worked out nearly every day. So far I'd avoided running the route Loser and I had taken that June day, but today I ran it and didn't feel a thing—except to realize how ironic it was that, in some ways, I was getting over him, and in other ways, he was more a part of my life than ever.

Was that my fault? I asked myself, as my feet struck the pavement. For writing the blog and keeping the story alive? Despite all my blog had given me, was it worth it? As I ran past featureless strip malls and Empire buildings, I couldn't find a satisfactory answer to that question. So I ran faster, until all I could think about was how much my legs hurt.

When I got back to my office, I found an e-mail from Jake in response to the one I'd sent just before I left. His note was even more abrupt than mine.

"Call me. 835-675-2190."

I grabbed the phone. Started to dial his number, then

stopped. What was I doing? We'd never talked on the phone before! What if it was awkward in person? Oh, fuck it. If it was awkward, so what? My heart, which had just started to recover from my run, sped up again as I dialed. He picked up after the first ring.

"This is Jake." He sounded businesslike. Bored. The way I did when I answered the phone at work. His voice was lower than I'd expected. But the thing that shocked me was that he had an accent. An English accent. I'd had no fucking idea. Jake seemed like such an American name. How had I possibly missed the fact that he was British? Ever since I was eleven years old and had traveled around England with my parents, I'd been in love with English accents.

"Hi, Jake," I said, even more nervous now. "It's Rachel." My voice cracked strangely. I cleared my throat.

"Oh," he said, and the bored tone vaporized. "*Hi*. How are you doing?" His voice, so male, so British, wormed its way into my torso, creating a warm trail on its way down.

"Oh, I'm doing okay." I tried to sound nonchalant, but it was hard when I was breathing like an emphysema patient. "I just went for a run, so I'm feeling a little better." That was a stupid thing to say, but at least it offered an excuse for the heavy breathing.

"Really? Well, I know the guy who designed the gold-colored Nikes; I can probably get you a good deal if you want a pair."

"Thanks." I laughed. Relaxed a little. "How are *you* doing?" I wished I could travel through the phone line from Seattle to Portland and pop out in his office. He sounded so . . . friendly.

"Oh, you know, work," he said. "At least mine is more harmless than yours these days. I hope they don't fire you, but you know if they do, you'll be famous, right?"

"I *will*?"

"Yeah. It's kind of trendy. Haven't you heard about that

woman who just got fired because of her blog? She worked for Yahoo, wrote stuff about her job on her blog, and then got fired. It just happened last week, and Monday she was on the *Today* show."

This fact, ridiculous as it was, cheered me up. I had a momentary vision of myself on the *Today* show talking about how and why I'd started my blog. The publishing houses would be throwing themselves at my feet!

"Well, that's good to know," I said.

"Anyway, I wanted to talk because I had . . . this idea." He lowered his voice a little.

"Yeah?" There was a slight huskiness to his voice that, combined with his British accent, was irresistible.

"Well, I imagine you're a bit down right now. So I was thinking, well . . . I was wondering if maybe you'd like to meet. I could easily make it up to Seattle this weekend. Help take your mind off things, you know." He trailed off, sounding suddenly shy. Then, before I could respond, he jumped back in. "But I don't have to," he said, "I mean, I don't expect—"

"No!" I interrupted him. "Of course I want you to!"

"I wouldn't have to stay with you," he added. "I think they have hotels in Seattle. Don't they?"

"Yeah, a few." I laughed, relieved that he'd suggested that. Who knew what the chemistry would be like when we saw each other in person? Although with that accent, he could be a toothless troll and I'd probably still want to have sex with him. Then I thought of something.

"Don't you—well, what about your daughter? Don't you have her on weekends?" I felt strange bringing it up. I'd never dated anyone with a kid before. Not that I was against it. In general, I felt more comfortable around kids than adults. Still, it was a little strange.

"Well, yes, normally, but next weekend my ex has her for the whole weekend. They're going off for a bonding weekend at the beach—or some such thing." There was a tone in his voice I couldn't quite decipher.

The few bizarre details he'd supplied about his ex-wife over e-mail had made me very curious about their relationship. He'd written me, in droll detail, the story of how, after a five-year marriage during which she went from 200 to 350 pounds, he divorced her because she had become distant after the birth of their daughter. It didn't help their sex life that she was obese, but, he claimed, he'd been ready to stand by her, "thick and thin." Right after the divorce, though, she'd gotten onto a reality TV show called *Beauty and the Beast,* where a group of overweight women compete and undergo plastic surgery to see who can look the best at the end of six months. She'd won $100,000 and been featured on the cover of *People* magazine. "You might have seen her," he wrote, in his usual witty style. "She wore an expression of vague shock that bingeing on Big Macs and milk shakes could make her a celebrity. Doesn't she know, though, this is America?!"

I couldn't help but wonder that he still held a torch for her, especially now that she was a gorgeous quasi celebrity. But I decided this wasn't the time to worry about the ex-wife. So all I said was, "Sounds like a good plan."

"Listen," said Jake, "I have to run to a meeting right now. I'll be in touch about the details. Probably I'll just drive up tomorrow night, if that's all right with you, and leave on Sunday sometime. I just want to say this, though. You don't deserve what's happening to you right now."

I felt ridiculously grateful to this appealing male voice on the other end of the phone.

"Thanks," I said. "Thanks for being so nice to me." My voice was small. I sounded like a five-year-old suddenly.

"Oh, now *that* you deserve," he said. "What are you going to do tonight?"

"I don't know. Flee the country maybe?"

"All right. Just as long as you're back in time for my arrival."

"Of course."

After I got off the phone, I leaned back in my chair and shook my head a little, as if I needed to wake myself up. But, God, I felt so much *better* than I had an hour and half ago when WendiiR had placed her call. Because there were people out there—*very cute boys, in fact*—who thought I was a good person, and a cool person, and one who totally deserved not to get fired, cute boys who were coming to visit me this weekend.

I flipped the bird to the phone. "Fuck you, Wendii R," I said. Then I got packed up and headed home for the night.

Chapter Twenty-Five

Friday, January 17, 2003
9:23 AM Breakup Babe

Things have been crazy around here, that's for sure. Alas, there is a whole bunch of sh*t going down that I can't tell you about. I know that sounds suspicious coming from the person who reveals the most intimate details of her personal life online. Trust me. I would tell you if I could!

Life is looking up in one regard: Boys! Yes, you'd think that when my life is falling to pieces, I might take it easy when it comes to the male of the species. But what's a girl to do when an online flirtation suddenly heats up at a low point in her life, and a cute boy she's never met proposes a visit?

If you're me, you think about it for one nanosecond, then say, "Okay, sounds great!," conveniently forgetting that you just resolved to take a less impulsive approach to dating.

But what do I have to lose, really? (Except, of course, if he turns out to be a serial killer, in which case I lose my life and a few limbs.)

It's not like I'm accepting a marriage proposal from him sight un-seen or anything! We're just going on a date, albeit an all-weekend date that requires him to drive three hours, but what's the big deal?

There is one little fly in the ointment, however. This boy, who we shall call Long-Distance Boy, reads this blog. Yes, that's how we met, and no, I won't tell you any more!

So I'm sure you've figured out the problem by now. If he reads it, I can't dish about him, now can I? Or *can* I? We'll just have to play that one by ear. Because now that I'm addicted to selling my sex life for entertainment, I'm not sure that I'll be able to stop. But I resolve to try—if he wants me to—and we all know how well I stick to my res-olutions, don't we?

Okay, you're asking yourself, then what *is* this girl going to talk about if not about boys?

I'm trying to figure that one out myself here.

I felt the most cheerful I had in weeks as I took a sip of my Americano and looked around at the 8:35 A.M. Victrola crowd. Maybe because of my own relatively perky mood, everyone else looked a little sharper too. Hottie Dad was dressed in an impeccable Italian suit, outclassing everyone in the place. The guy with the shaved head and the lightning bolt tattooed on his scalp was whispering and holding hands with a relatively normal-looking woman at a corner table. It was the first time I had ever seen him smile.

The cute barista was always a model of adorable funki-ness and today was no exception. He wore a brown T-shirt that said "Hillbilly 5" on it and had a new short haircut that made him look cuter and more clean-cut than ever. When I'd walked in earlier, I'd flashed an alluring smile at him (a solid nine on the Dazzle-O-Meter) as he worked the espresso ma-chine, but felt a pleasing lack of desperate neediness.

Perky as I felt, I worried if my readers felt cheated. I'd de-cided to keep blogging for my own sanity. I just couldn't give it up. But I hadn't been posting nearly as much as usual for fear of who might be reading the blog. I seriously doubted Lyle would have shared the URL with anyone, but how could I be sure? Though he hadn't made eye contact with me at meetings lately, none of my other fellow employees treated me differently. Yet I knew that I had to stop writing about the Loser twins and Empire Corp. if I wanted to keep my job.

I'd tried to hold on to the sense of defiance that swept me the day after my meeting with Lyle and Wendii. But most of the time, I just felt scared. Scared of being judged. Scared of saying the wrong thing and getting fired. The fact that Jake read the blog was just another thing that made me uncertain about how to proceed.

So I'd been putting less energy into the blog and more into the writing class and the book. One of the first thoughts that had crossed my mind when things started to heat up with Jake was *Breakup Babe meets boy via her blog. What a great ending for my book!* At this point, though, the ending of the book seemed impossibly far away. Not quite as far away as it once had, now that I was well into writing the first chapter, but still far enough away that if I thought of the hundreds of thousands of words I'd have to write and revise in order to get to my ending, I got discouraged.

I didn't need to think about that yet. For now, all I had to do was do the assignments for my writing class, and so far I was kicking ass at that.

> How about I discuss writing? Because even if I have been post-ing much less than usual, I've been writing more than ever. That's because I've been taking a writing class for the last two weeks now. This class has been incredibly helpful by requiring me to create an outline for Breakup Babe the book. This is not just any outline, how-ever, but a very specific kind of outline that forces me to plan my story in terms of complications and resolutions—something simple and obvious—but something I've never done before.
>
> Because of this outline, I feel like I'm finally going in the right

direction. And lo and behold, just the other night, the teacher read a scene I'd written out loud as an example of how to do things right.

Now I just have to write about one hundred more great scenes, rewrite them each about ten times, and then—just maybe—I'll have a publishable book.

E-mail Breakup Babe | Comments 7

As I wrapped up this entry, so devoid of the usual juicy details, I wondered how my readers would handle the change in subject matter. Would they stop reading the site in droves if I quit dishing about my love life? I was tempted to say more about Jake, of course, about how hot he looked in his pictures, and how funny he was, and how I liked it that he was so driven and ambitious. Better yet, I wanted to write about how he seemed emotionally available, unlike anyone else I'd dated recently. But I was afraid of displaying my hope so flagrantly on the page. Emotionally available as he might seem to be, I didn't want to scare him off by being too needy.

Needy. As I shut my computer down and steeled myself for another day in white-collar prison, I pondered that word. As I'd written in my blog a couple of weeks ago, I felt like I'd seen Needy Girl clearly for the first time on New Year's Eve. She was frightening! Would I ever be able to get rid of her? A bit of neediness was certainly understandable after a big breakup. But eight months later? The word that scared me even more was "desperate." Was I one of those "desperate" women who scared men off?

Well, I thought, shouldering my backpack, which seemed, as usual, to weigh a hundred pounds, I hadn't scared Jake off. Quite the opposite. While I'd gotten my share of negative comments from male readers about how "manipulative" or "pathetic" I was, Jake clearly didn't think so. He'd read everything in the blog and liked me because of it. "You come across as very human," he'd written to me.

Still, I couldn't help but feel wary. Maybe our rendezvous

was a mistake. I was particularly vulnerable right now with this whole HR mess. What if we met and that electricity we'd built up over e-mail, over the phone, went dead? What if this one hopeful possibility in my life was just another dead end?

A cold panic gripped my stomach as I hurried out of the café into the damp January day without a glance for anyone, even the cute barista. *Damn it!* Was anything in my life ever going to be certain again? I felt a burst of resentment toward Loser. *Everything had been so stable once upon a time.*

"Watch it!" Suddenly there was a squeal of brakes and an angry voice yelling at me. "What the hell are you doing?"

Crossing against a red light, that's what I was doing. "Sorry," I mumbled, not looking at the driver of the black Jetta who was glaring at me. I rushed across the street.

"Those lights are there for a reason," he yelled, then drove off quickly, wheels skidding on the damp pavement.

I watched the car go, shaking. Then I slowly, deliberately put one foot in front of the other as I walked toward my car.

POST A COMMENT

B.B., you can write about anything and we'd like it!
GenieG | Homepage | 1/17/03–1:20 P.M.

•   •   •   •   •

I don't know, I like to hear all the juicy details. You will tell us some juicy details about Long-Distance Boy? Right? RIGHT? After you meet him, of course.
Delilah | Homepage | 1/17/03–4:41 P.M.

•   •   •   •   •

You have a stranger coming to visit you? Are you sure he's not a se-rial killer? Does your mother know about this?
Worried | 1/17/03–6:18 P.M.

•   •   •   •   •

Aw, c'mon, tell us who he is!
Little Princess | Homepage | 1/18/03–9:08 A.M.

•   •   •   •   •

What about not dating for a while and just working on your book?
A Fan | 1/18/03–11:13 A.M.

• • • • •

I think it's a good idea for you to focus less on blogging and more on your book. We readers can live with fewer details about your sex life if we know the book will be out soon.
Knut | Homepage | 1/18/03–12:51 P.M.

• • • • •

I suspect this new guy wouldn't mind you writing about him as long as you gushed about how manly he was, etc.
Jake | 1/18/03–3:39 P.M.

Chapter Twenty-Six

Monday, January 20, 2003
9:46 AM Breakup Babe

Well, that was quite a weekend. I spent several hours lost in the wilderness on Saturday, with a down jacket circa 1973 as my main source of warmth. Okay, maybe you couldn't exactly call it the "wilderness," since we were in the foothills of Puget Sound, a mere five miles from the strip malls and Starbucks of Issaquah. Nonetheless, there were trees and trails and we were freakin' lost, which I think qualifies it as wilderness-y *enough*.

I leaned back in my chair at Victrola. God, I was tired. Jake had gotten up at 4:30 to drive back to Portland and I'd never fallen all the way back asleep. (After his first night in Seattle, he'd ditched the hotel and stayed with me.) There were too many feelings rolling through my brain. Our time together had been so intense, so crazy, it was going to take a few days for me to sort it out.

I hoped that writing the blog, as usual, would help me process my feelings. But I had to be careful. Though Jake had given me carte blanche to write about our weekend—"just use your discretion," he'd said—I knew from our time together that he could be thin-skinned. I would stick with the facts and just the facts. One thing I could say about the long, wet weekend, it had certainly taken my mind off The Great Unpleasantness, Part II!

Yes, that's right. Long-Distance Boy and I got lost while hiking together on our debut weekend. That's because I made the mistake of following him when he boldly proclaimed that he knew which way to go. "It's this way," he said, with confidence, after studying the map, and holding a GPS up to it in a very professional-looking manner. We were at a trail junction with four different trails radiating outward but not a trail sign in sight.

"But," I said, "I've been here before, and I really think I remember going this way!" I didn't say it with much confidence, though, because I am the worst navigator alive. When I attempt to navigate, wrong turns are made. Bad words are uttered. Maps are turned every which way and still I can't read them. I therefore always rely heavily on the navigational skills of my companions, especially in the outdoors.

"Look, though," said Long-Distance Boy, pointing at the map. "The GPS clearly shows that we go this way to get back to the Turtle Ridge Trail, which takes us to the Issaquah River Trail, which gets us back down."

Up until this moment, all had gone swimmingly. From the instant I'd walked in to meet him for dinner at Flying Fish on Friday, we'd hit it off. Within the first five minutes, I wanted to kiss him. Within half an hour, he'd made me laugh so hard water came out my nose. Things had only gotten better from there.

I looked at the map and the GPS. The lines and numbers didn't mean much to me. They did look nice and reassuring, however. Plus, Long-Distance Boy's British accent was so cute. It made him sound like he knew what he was doing.

"Besides," he said, "how lost can we get? We're practically in the middle of civilization. These trails all wind up at the bottom, I'm sure of it."

I was of the same general opinion. They all had to go back to the bottom. This was only Tiger Mountain, the playpen of Northwest hiking. It wasn't like we were climbing Mount Rainier, for crying out loud. Babies and grandmothers hiked here. It couldn't be *too* complicated.

But two hours later, as darkness rapidly approached, we were nowhere near the trailhead. In fact, we seemed to be higher up on the mountain than before. Apparently babies and grandmothers could navigate better than we could.

At the top of a short climb, we arrived at a viewpoint where we could see the lights of the Sammamish plateau start to come on below. This spot looked awfully familiar. I took off my pack, set it with a thud on the ground, then started to dig around for my headlamp and the tattered down jacket I'd inherited from my father. My extensive outdoor experience hadn't ALL been for nothing, at least. I always had emergency gear, even on the most innocent-seeming day hikes.

"I think we ate lunch here," I said, trying not to sound petulant. After all, I couldn't blame our predicament entirely on him. "Doesn't this look like our lunch spot?"

Long-Distance Boy had, in fact, prepared me a lovely lunch. He'd packed his ultralight backpacking stove and a bottle of French wine, and whipped up a delicious pasta dish. He didn't let me do a thing but sit there and sip wine as I watched him cook.

And we'd eaten here, at this viewpoint, I was sure of it. I'd luxuriated in his surprise lunch and admired the views: the one below, of the green valley ringed by the Cascades, and the one right next to me, of Long-Distance Boy's liquid brown eyes and knife-edged cheekbones. I thought to myself how lucky I was to be getting to know such a sweet, adventurous, and thoughtful boy.

I paused here. Did I sound like I was being sarcastic? I wasn't! I'd been thrilled by his whole lunch gesture *and* his suggestion that we go for a hike during his visit. In the two years Loser and I had been together, I couldn't remember a single time he'd voluntarily cooked for me or proposed an outdoor activity on his own. So Jake was busy racking up some major points when things went to hell.

The only thing that had bothered me up to this point was an offhand comment he'd made while preparing his special lunch. "This is the dish that made my ex-wife fall in love with me," he said, while chopping garlic on a lightweight chopping board.

I'd almost gasped out loud at the inappropriateness of this remark. But I didn't want to ruin a romantic event by being petty and jealous. In my experience, men often said inappropriate things like that. It's just that—well, I wondered if some part of him didn't want her back now that she was rich and skinny. In a fit of obsessive curiosity, I'd gone to the library before his arrival and dug up the back issue of *People* magazine whose cover she graced (along with the winners of other extreme makeover TV shows). My stomach had seized up on me when I saw it. She was stunning—in a second-rate celebrity sort of way—her now cellulite-free body pictured in a thong bikini, expertly dyed honey blond hair cascading down over her large new breasts.

Jake, at least, didn't *sound* longing when he talked about her. He sounded angry, mostly, about the custody battle that was shaping up. The two of them were arguing about her wanting to move to Florida with her new real-estate developer boyfriend, and take Jake's daughter, Esme, with her. They'd tried to work things out amicably, but his ex wouldn't budge on the fact that she needed to move.

"She claims that there's this aura of unhappiness that clings to me and that Esme always talks about it," he'd said earlier on the hike. " 'Why is Daddy so sad,' she asks, supposedly. Well, yes, so I'm a little sad that I only get to see my daughter two days out of seven." He'd stopped here and turned to me. "Frankly, I'm a little concerned, too; I mean, what kind of example does my ex-wife set for a little girl when she goes and gets plastic surgery and appears on the cover of a magazine because of it? Not to mention that her boyfriend is a hairy crook who looks like a chimpanzee."

I'd laughed here and the conversation had floated on to other things. I did learn that he'd retained a lawyer to try to stop her from leaving town. Beyond that, I didn't know much. So when he made his inappropriate remark, I opened my mouth to say something, then closed it. I sat in stunned silence for about a minute, with all sorts of questions racing through my head: "Why would you say something like that?" "Are you still in love with her?" "Do you think my thighs are fat compared with hers?" Then I counted to ten, gave him the benefit of the doubt, and let it go. After all, I'd talked plenty about Loser all day and I certainly wasn't in love with him anymore.

Now I debated whether to record this comment for my fans. If I wrote about it, he'd know that I thought it was lame and he'd be hurt. I took a sip of my coffee. Decided to skip it. This whole getting lost episode was damaging enough to his ego, though at least he'd been able to laugh about it afterward. "Go ahead and write about it," he'd said. "I can take it."

"I don't know if this is where we ate lunch," said Long-Distance Boy, setting down his own pack. His voice sounded tense. "I don't think so." The bottle of wine consumed earlier had clearly not enhanced our navigational skills.

He sat down heavily on a rock. I noticed he didn't bother to pull out his GPS again. It made me nervous to see him sitting down. Daylight had almost disappeared. It was getting colder. And while we wouldn't exactly freeze to death out here, at seven hundred feet of elevation, I also didn't fancy spending the night without a tent. I looked up at the sky. Was that a raindrop that had just fallen on me?

"Well, come on," I said, looking at him again. "Get your head-lamp out and let's go." I put on my jacket.

He didn't move. A few more cold drops fell on my head.

"I don't have a headlamp," he said. "I mean, I didn't bring it."

I clamped my mouth shut. A person could be forgiven, I supposed, for not bringing a flashlight on a day hike, though I always did. "Well, just follow me. Mine is pretty bright." I tried to hide the edge of panic in my voice. At least we were on a trail. We weren't THAT lost. We certainly weren't going to DIE. Even if it was the middle of winter and a few drops of rain could ruin my insulation system. Why, oh why, had I brought my *down* jacket of all things? Because I hadn't been able to find my warm fleece jacket this morning, that's why.

"Yes, but which way is it?" He sounded as if he'd entirely given up. Gone was the self-confident, cheerful personality of two hours ago.

"I think if we just keep going, we'll be fine. I'm sure this is where we ate lunch. We've just made a giant loop. We weren't going the WRONG way," I said, trying to cheer him up, though my own voice sounded shaky and high-pitched; "we just went the LONG way." It struck me suddenly that I was now in charge here. That I might have to be the one to lead us to safety. Now *that* was a frightening thought. I noticed that he was starting to shiver.

"So," I said, attempting to sound take-charge and confident, "Put on a warmer jacket and let's go. We'll be back in strip mall city in two hours. Dinner will be on me!"

For all I knew we would still be wandering this maze of trails in two hours. There would be a torrential downpour; my down jacket would be soaked; we'd both be hypothermic; then we would be dead. It would be all over the papers tomorrow. "Local Hikers Freeze to Death on Tiger Mountain, Where Even Babies and Grandmothers Don't Get Lost."

He still didn't move. He started to shiver a little harder. "I'm sorry," he said. He sounded as if he were about to cry. "I really thought we were going the right way."

"You DO have a warmer jacket, right?" I said, starting to move toward his pack. A light rain now fell. I remembered all the brilliant summer days that I'd prayed for rain. This was my karmic payback for not loving every single minute of every single day. It would pour down rain now and soon I would be dead because of it. Okay, okay, I had to get a grip. We would not die! We would get wet and cold but that was it. No one DIED on Tiger—

Just then, a noise made me jump. There was something moving quickly on the trail above us. A bear? No! There were no bears around here. A mountain lion?!

The noise got louder. My body tensed. What the hell were you supposed to do when you saw a mountain lion? Make a run for it? Play dead? Make eye contact? Avoid eye contact? F*CK!

"Oh my God," I yelped as it came careening around the corner. It stopped in its tracks and our eyes locked. The mountain lion looked like a thirtysomething male *Homo sapiens* in running attire. Relief rushed in. I laughed quasi-hysterically. "Oh God," I said again. "You scared me!"

"Likewise," said the guy, who didn't look nearly as startled as me. He was tall and rangy, with broad shoulders tapering to a narrow waist. He looked extremely fit. "How's it going?" he asked, shooting a glance at Long-Distance Boy, who was still sitting on his rock with a hangdog expression on his face. He sounded friendly but reserved. Clearly he was not too thrilled to have his jog down Tiger Mountain interrupted by a couple of lost and hysterical hikers.

I didn't care. I was more grateful to see him than I had been to see anyone in a long time. I wanted to throw myself at his feet, grab his ankles, and say *"Thank you, thank you!"*

"Oh, not too bad," I said, trying to rid my voice of its high-pitched shakiness. "But we seem to have gotten a little bit turned around. We're trying to get back to the parking lot. I think we're going the right way, but I'm not exactly sure."

"Yeah, these trails can be confusing." He had an air of calm self-sufficiency. Everything about him looked lean and efficient, from his cropped dark hair to his compact pack to the single layer of lightweight synthetic clothing he wore. He also looked vaguely familiar, but it was hard to make out his face in the gathering dusk. "But if you keep going this way, you're only about two miles away."

He smiled at me, a slightly lopsided smile that made him seem more human. "Do you guys want to follow me down or will you be okay? Can't get lost if you just keep going this way." He sounded friendlier now. Warmer.

"We'll be fine." Long-Distance Boy jumped in before I could say anything. Then he scrambled up and said, "Thanks very much for your help, though." I was glad he was speaking, though he didn't look Self-Sufficient Guy in the eye. Personally, I was mortified to be caught getting lost on Tiger Mountain, but I was not as embarrassed as he was. After all, I was used to getting lost and asking for help. As Long-Distance Boy put his pack on, he was still shivering. The rain had stopped.

"Yes, thank you!" In my deranged enthusiasm, I sounded like I'd just been released from the mental hospital. I would have preferred to follow him down, but whatever. All that mattered was we weren't going to die out here after all!

"No problem." The guy took off his pack, opened up the top, and fished around for something. He pulled out a headlamp. His pack looked like it weighed only about half a pound. He himself didn't appear to be cold, though he was wearing only a single layer atop a pair of running shorts. In the light of my headlamp, his face looked slightly craggy. He had deep dimples that ran all up and down the side of his face. God, he looked familiar. Where did I know him from? "You guys take care," he said. Then he jogged off down the trail.

Long-Distance Boy and I walked in silence for a while, with me in front so I could shine my headlamp on the trail. I debated a few opening lines. I wanted to poke fun at the situation, but I sensed he wasn't in a lighthearted mood.

Finally he said, "So, that was fun."

I laughed, though I couldn't quite tell if that was the appropriate response. "It was, up until you got us lost."

"Yeah." He snorted a little. "Sorry about that. I feel like a real idiot."

Well, that was a good sign. A man admitting fault! I was about to say something about how I was responsible too when he added, "My wife never even had to read a map to get anywhere. She always knew right where she was. I, on the other hand, am directionally impaired."

HER again! "Your EX-wife, you mean?" I said in a frosty voice before I could stop myself.

Silence. The darkness gathered around us. Luckily, the trail here was wide and easy to follow. My headlamp made a mere prick of light in the middle of the trail.

Trying unsuccessfully to lighten my tone, I said, "I thought she didn't like to hike," though what I felt like saying was, "I thought she was too FAT to hike."

"No, she didn't." He sounded distinctly morose now. "I just meant when we were driving around and all that."

God, what was my problem? I didn't need to get all bent out of shape about the ex-wife just because she looked like a freaking model and he still talked about her all the time.

Suddenly we were at the parking lot. I turned to him. I wanted to make everything better. To remind him how much I liked him and how happy I was to be down here with him instead of freezing somewhere on top of Tiger Mountain.

"You know," he said, his expression sheepish, "I wouldn't be mad if you wanted to run off with that guy. He actually seems to know what he's doing, unlike me. I must seem very unmanly to you now." He looked down at the ground.

"Well," I said, feeling grateful to him for acknowledging his embarrassment, "I think you're very manly for admitting you feel unmanly." I knew it wasn't an easy thing for him to do.

Long-Distance Boy looked up at me and smiled a little. I felt a rush of affection for him. I threw my arms around him. It now seemed like days since I'd hugged him.

"Let's go somewhere and just forget about it," I whispered in his ear.

Then we went back to my place and had s*x five times within twelve hours. So I think we forgot about it!

E-mail Breakup Babe | Comments 5

Phew! That had been a long entry. I looked at the clock on my computer. My God, it was 10:30! I'd been writing for three hours! I wasn't quite satisfied with this ending. There was still more to say, but I had to get to work.

Ugh. Work.

As I scrambled to gather my stuff, I prayed Jake wouldn't get upset at reading my thoughts about his ex-wife. I wasn't saying anything bad about *him,* after all; I was criticizing my own pettiness! By the time we got back to the trailhead on Saturday night, I really was wondering if we'd be able to get past the whole Lost in the Wilderness/Talking About the Ex-Wife episodes. But afterward, over beer, Jake had recovered quickly. His sense of humor had come back and he'd poked endless fun at himself. Not everyone could laugh at themselves that way. I'd relaxed about the whole ex-wife thing, too, especially when he showered me with affection all night long.

In any case, it appeared that our budding new relationship had survived. At least, I thought it had, limping slightly as I headed toward the door, judging from the copious amounts of sex we'd had.

That thought cheered me up as I steeled myself to face work again. I still felt exhausted and rough around the edges, especially when I noticed Beret Chick at a table by the door, looking particularly chic in a dusky pink cashmere sweater set with a silk scarf tied jauntily around her neck. Her long tresses cascaded out from under her stupid gray beret, gleaming and soft. I felt, in comparison, like a coffee-stained oaf in the outfit I'd pulled on at 4:30 this morning—my diaper-

esque thrift store jeans and boring black turtleneck. My hair
was in messy pigtails, the only style in which it looked halfway decent when I didn't have time to spend five hours washing and blow-drying it. Hmmph.

I bet you haven't had sex five times in twelve hours, I said
to myself as I passed her table, and walked outside into the
pale winter sunshine.

POST A COMMENT

Did you get the name of the jogger guy who rescued you? He sounds
hot!

GenieG | Homepage | 1/20/03–12:33 P.M.

•   •   •   •   •

Well, sounds like you guys went through a lot together. I agree that
it's great he was able to admit his mistakes. Of course it's typical for
a guy to think he knows where he's going and get lost!

Little Princess | Homepage | 1/20/03–2:54 P.M.

•   •   •   •   •

I wonder how he'll like to read all this stuff about himself?

Nate | 1/20/03–9:19 P.M.

•   •   •   •   •

Boy, you had me on the edge of my seat with this one. I hope it's
going in the book. I had a boyfriend once who was really reckless.
He almost got us killed whitewater rafting once, because he convinced me he knew what he was doing and he didn't. Both of us fell
off the raft and swam in the freezing cold river for nearly half a mile!
Why do men think they're invincible, anyway? When you hear about
people dying in the wilderness, it's usually men.

Tabitha | 1/21/3—10:44 A.M.

•   •   •   •   •

Someone who's a worse navigator than you? Sounds like a dangerous combination.

Li'l Sis | 1/21/03–12:15 P.M.

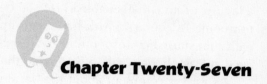 **Chapter Twenty-Seven**

Three days later, I'd received exactly one e-mail from Jake and no phone calls. My meeting with HR was in four hours. It was not as if the one e-mail had been so full of love and support that it could carry me through, either. No. It was one of the most unsatisfying pieces of e-mail ever written. I took a sip of my Americano and reread the maddening little missive, which had come just this morning.

To: *Rachel*
From: *Jake*

Rachel—

 Sorry I've been incommunicado. Work has eaten up all my time and energy these last few days. The legal stuff has been getting nasty, too, and I haven't wanted to bore you with it. I hope you're doing well. Things should clear up in a couple of days or so, and I'll try to give you a call. Good luck with the meeting.

"Good luck with the meeting?" "A couple of days?!" That's all he could fucking manage? I happened to know that Jake's oh-so-busy work schedule kept him glued to his computer screen. If he was away from that, he always had a cell phone, a laptop, or an e-mail-enabled PDA. So he had no excuse for not being in contact. Work had taken up all his time when we'd first started corresponding, too, but back then he'd managed at least three e-mails a day. What the hell was going on?

As for his comment about the "legal stuff," I wasn't sure how to decipher that. Why would he think that it would "bore" me to talk about it? Hadn't I been a good listener when he'd talked about it during our visit? He'd been so supportive of me, through my HR trials and tribulations, so he should know that I wanted to reciprocate. I wasn't exactly thrilled to talk about his ex-wife, but I cared about him and I would do it if he needed me to!

Well, shit. I was worried that maybe I'd offended him by blogging about our misadventures. But he *had* told me I could be honest about everything. I knew, as I was writing it, that some of the details I chose to convey made him sound less than manly. I thought I made up for it by exclaiming about his virility at the end! I'd never gone in and added the part about how well he handled himself afterward. I wished now that I had.

The previous afternoon, Jane had advised me over IM.

Jane says: So tell me, is this guy really a good candidate? I mean, he's hung up on his ex-wife, involved in a custody battle, and lives in Portland!

Rachel says: Well, when you put it like THAT . . . The thing is, he's a really smart, funny, nice guy. Except for the getting lost part, we had a great time. It really felt like there was potential! Being with him was the first real inkling of romance I've had since I broke up with Loser.

Jane says: Uh-huh. But now you've only gotten one e-mail from him in three days.

Rachel says: Right.

Jane says: I dunno. He doesn't sound that emotionally available to me. There's gotta be a guy with less baggage who lives somewhere closer—say, Seattle?

This morning I'd been forced to come to Café Ladro on 15th because Victrola had been full. Full! They really should have reserved tables for patrons like me, who practically kept the place afloat with my Empire cash flow. I could have tried to share a table with another patron, but I really wasn't up to sitting with Lightning Bolt Guy (who was once again alone and looking morose) or Beret Chick. There were always tables at this particular branch of Café Ladro because, despite their superior coffee, the atmosphere was nonexistent.

Even with the HR meeting looming in four hours, I was trying to write this morning. What was I supposed to do, just sit around and worry that I was going to get fired? Now that I was getting into the habit of writing every day, I found that it felt like exercise. Doing it in the morning set a good tone for the entire day, and if I missed it, I felt off. Like a run or a bike ride, a good writing session helped soothe my anxiety.

But I was not having a good writing session this morning. In fact, I was not having much of a writing session at all. For one, the baristas here were too loud. Café Ladro on 15th seemed to employ only cute girl baristas who had a personal relationship with every sentient being who walked in. The one at the cash register was busily greeting every single person, dog, and small child who entered the place with a high, squeaky, "Hiii, how are YOU?" I was certain that no great works of literature had ever been completed here.

Plus, I'd just gotten the e-mail from Jake, and was trying to decide how—or even whether—to respond. One part of

me was relieved that he had finally e-mailed. It had been torture waiting to hear from him for two days. But now that he'd
written, it didn't seem like that big a deal. People in long-
distance relationships probably went much longer without
talking than two damn days. But still. This e-mail was so frus-
trating!

Trying to ignore the squeals of the barista, I decided to answer his e-mail now. I clearly was not going to get any work
done on my writing assignment this morning.

I squirmed in my seat. Stared at his note. Put my fingers
over the keyboard, then put them down again. I didn't know
what to say.

Should I even respond? How? It's not like he had asked
me a single question. It didn't sound like he *wanted* a response. He didn't give a shit how I was doing. It seemed like
he was fulfilling a duty. If I wrote back to him, it would just
give him one more thing to worry and feel guilty about and,
God knows, with his oh-so-important work and legal battles, I
didn't want to do that to him!

I thought back to his visit. I remembered how much
we'd laughed together, even after the Lost in the Wilderness
episode, *especially* after the Lost in the Wilderness episode.
The way he'd listened intently when I talked, as if what I was
saying was the most important thing in the world. How excited I'd been when he suggested we do the Mount Rainier
climb together this summer. Was it possible I'd finally found
a guy (1) I was physically attracted to, (2) I was intellectually
attracted to, and (3) who would push me to be the adventurous person I wanted to be?

It had certainly seemed so when he was here. But now
that he was so *gone*—I had my doubts. Maybe Jane was right
about him. Perhaps he had such serious issues that I should
just back out now, before I got too involved.

No. Not yet. The relationship had too much potential. He
deserved a chance. One chance at least. God, I wished he were

here now. If he were here with me, I knew he'd be the same warm, loving Jake that he'd been before, that he'd hug me and kiss me and help me to feel confident and courageous before this meeting.

The best approach to answering this e-mail, I decided, was to be as straightforward as possible without jumping down his throat.

> Dear Jake,
>
> You do sound busy! I have to admit, it's been a little hard for me that you've been out of touch for so long. It makes me wonder if something is up. Maybe you're having second thoughts? Or maybe what I wrote on my blog upset you? If so, I really apologize and I hope we can discuss it.
>
> I'm also sorry that the legal stuff is getting "nasty," and rest assured, you won't "bore" me if you talk about it. You have been so supportive of me, I'd really like to return the favor.
>
> As for me, I am holding up okay. Today at three I have my meeting with HR, and I have no idea what to expect (as you know). I really wish you were here to talk to and to hold me. You're so good at making me feel stronger.
>
> Anyway, I hope to hear from you soon.
>
> R.

This short e-mail took half an hour to craft. I took out two sentences about how if something was "up," he should tell me and not just keep it to himself, and about how I would "completely understand" if he was rethinking the long-distance thing. I hoped I didn't come off as too guilt-inducing. I *was,* of course, trying to make him feel guilty for not calling me before my meeting, but I didn't want it to seem obvious. I simply wanted to convey that I was not happy with the level of communication I was now experiencing with him, but that I hoped to discuss it in a mature, nonaccusatory way.

Phew. Writing that e-mail had been harder than writing a book. I wondered what my writing teacher would think of it.

"Oh, my gosh, your HAIR!" screamed the blond barista. I looked up and saw a middle-aged woman with a nondescript mousy brown bob walk in. "It looks GREAT!"

"Thanks," said the woman, beaming, and touching the ends of her hair, then walking to the end of the line. I wondered how big her tip would be. It was true that if a food service person offered any endearment to me, or even just smiled at me, I was much more likely to tip. Hell, a compliment like that might set me back a whole fifty cents.

I looked at the clock on my computer: 9:30. Damn. I so did not want to go to work, so did not want to deal with what was about to happen. I felt the tears start to push against my eyes as I got ready to go. A thought struck me. Maybe Jake would call me before the meeting. When he got my e-mail and found out the meeting was at one, he would go, "Oh, RIGHT! Her meeting!" realize how much I needed his support, and give me a quick call.

I tried to quell that thought. But it left a lingering trace of hope. As I headed out the door, into a January day draped with threatening clouds, one of the squeaky baristas cried out, "Oh, my gosh, I LOVE your coat!"

I turned, half-smiling, to acknowledge the compliment, only to see her talking to a woman who'd just gotten to the register. She wore what looked like a pink poodle draped over her, with a tasseled hood that she had on her head. My heart fell just a little. Of course the barista wasn't talking to me. All I had on was a boring black down jacket from Esprit ($60).

I stepped out into the cold, feeling more alone than I had in a long time.

*   *   *

For the next three hours, I attempted to sweat away my fear and loneliness at The Sports Club, Empire's swanky gym. I psyched myself up for this meeting by listening to Green Day and fantasizing fiercely. I ran the treadmill as fast as I could go, imagining the brilliant career that awaited me should I, by chance, get booted out of Empire. I would immediately get asked onto the talk show circuit. There I would charm the world in a variety of stylish outfits as I defended my right to free speech. Random House would pick up my book, though I had only half a chapter written. And Wendii, once I'd exposed her on *Oprah*, would get fired by Rodney Rolands himself, who would roar at her (as he was known to do), "You mentally retarded cyborg bitch, how could you have fired her? She was a fucking genius!"

Then, as I pedaled on the stationary bike, legs burning, I imagined other things: myself at the top of Mount Rainier, sleek and strong, on the summit I'd coveted for so long, all of western Washington spread out behind me and sparkling in the sun. Instead of Jake, who was temporarily banned from my fantasies, there by my side would be a devastatingly hot guide, who would have fallen madly in love with me as he led me up the mountain. He would accompany me to my book launch party in New York, where the two of us would make a splash as we entered the room: a pair of wholesome yet glamorous Northwest deities, whose natural beauty would outshine all the overly made-up celebrities in attendance.

After my workout, I steamed and saunaed and blow-dried my hair to lustrous perfection. By the time I returned to my office, forty-five minutes before the meeting, I barely even cared that Jake hadn't called to wish me good luck. I was a kick-ass goddess after all, and I would prevail. With or without him.

Green Day still playing in my head, I marched across campus toward the HR building, watching nerdy heads turn as I blew by. I wore a pair of cuffed gray pants from Ann Taylor ($55) that made my ass, in the words of the Li'l Rockclimbing Spy, "look totally fine."

Wendii, I thought, was no match for me.

But Wendii, as it turned out, had something going for her: the element of surprise.

When I walked into that conference room, the confidence I'd built up over the last three hours vaporized instantly, because there, sitting next to each other at the conference table, close enough but not too close, were Loser and Loserette.

Not even in my most nightmarish fantasies of this meeting had I imagined they would be here. Those fantasies had spread far and wide, too: In one, Rodney Rolands stalked into the meeting and fired me in person. In another, I was immediately shackled by security guards and hauled away to white-collar prison for giving away proprietary information on my blog. The last people I'd expected to see at this meeting, though, were the two of them.

The Enemy.

I stared at them for a moment, with my mouth open and my heart pounding.

Then I said the stupidest thing imaginable. "Hi." It was reflex, pure and simple. I immediately wished I could take it back.

Only Wendii responded.

"Hello, Rachel. Please have a seat."

I walked over to an empty chair as far from the two of them as I could get. I felt wobbly and prayed I wouldn't pass out. Then I realized that would be an excellent way to get out of this meeting. Maybe I should pretend to faint? No. I wasn't a good enough actress, damn it, even though I'd spent years practicing fake swoons with my best friend, Jessica, when we were growing up.

I reached my chair and sat down with a thud, almost missing it. A whole storm of violent emotions rattled me. Jealousy. Fear. Humiliation. I clenched my jaw to keep my teeth from chattering. Above it all, however, floated a detached feeling that something here was not quite right. I avoided looking at the Loser twins now, but their image had burned itself into my brain during those first few moments that I'd stared at them. There was something different about them since I'd seen them last. Something strange. Then it hit me.

She looked exactly like me.

Maybe it was some sort of optical illusion caused by my shock, but if I wasn't mistaken, Loserette's curly hair was now straightened somewhat, cut in a layered style resembling mine, and dyed a darker color. Where once her hair had been bright red, it was now auburn with blond streaks—just like the blond streaks in my own dark brown hair! She also wore a cleavage-baring T-shirt that looked just like the one I had bought at Banana Republic a month ago!

Things suddenly felt very surreal. Again, I looked over at Wendii, who was shuffling papers. Did she notice, I wondered? Could she SEE that this woman was now a carbon copy of me? But Wendii said nothing. Nor did anyone else. The room vibrated with tension. Out of the corner of my eye, Loser's beanpole body, his sandy brown hair, his tan skin, were a memory from a distant dream. He, unlike Loserette, looked exactly the same as he always had.

Finally, Wendii spoke.

"So, the reason I've brought you all here today is to discuss the complaint that has been brought against Rachel and see if we can come to some kind of agreement about it."

My jaw, which was already clenched, tightened further. I wondered if I'd ever be able to speak again. If I couldn't, I would sue Empire. For A LOT of money.

But wait. She'd used the word "agreement"! Did that mean I wasn't getting fired right away? My jaw loosened ever so slightly.

Wendii nodded at the Loser twins. "Please let Rachel

know the nature of your complaint." Today, Wendii had gone
for a coppery look. Bronze blush streaked her cheeks and she
wore brown lipstick contained by expertly drawn lipliner that
made her lips look just bigger than they were. It looked like
she'd hit the tanning salon in the last couple of weeks.

The two of them looked at each other quickly. Then Loser
spoke. His voice, once so familiar, sounded strange to me
now, and higher than a man's voice should be. Still, it echoed
deep within me. This was the tone he'd used when we'd
argued. The high, nervous, petulant tone. Loser hated con-
frontation. Yet our relationship had been rife with it. I found
myself breathing faster as he talked. I wondered if he would
look at me. But he kept his eyes firmly fixed on Wendii.

"For months now, Rachel has been writing lies about us
on her blog. These are things that could be very damaging
to both our careers and our personal lives. We want her to
stop immediately. We also think that she should take down
her blog, or at the very least, delete everything she's written
about us."

I didn't hear most of what he said. My mind stopped at
the word "lies." Stopped and stumbled.

Wendii chewed her lips slightly. Then she scribbled
something in her notebook and looked over at me. "Is that
something you would agree to Rachel?"

"I—I'm not lying," I said. My throat felt like it was full of
sand. I spoke in a low tone that didn't even sound like me.

"Rachel," said Wendii, looking at me over the top of her
glasses, "that's not really the point here. The point is that
these are your fellow employees, and the things you are saying about them are making them uncomfortable. That needs
to stop."

"Fine," I burst out, and everyone jumped. Now I sounded
like me. "I'll stop writing about them. But what about the fact
that she's my manager and she's dating him and she's HIS

manager too. Is there no PROBLEM with those things? No conflict of interest, no violation of Empire policies?"

Stay in control, I warned myself. I'd planned to say those things, but not so soon, and not in that tone. I kept my eyes on Wendii but with my peripheral vision, I could see the two of them shift uncomfortably. They probably expected that their presence was enough to cow me. Well, they were wrong, weren't they? A loud silence filled the room.

Wendii looked down at the paper in front of her. Then she looked back up at me. Adjusted her glasses, and cleared her throat. "They have told me they have a 'friendly working relationship,' but that is all."

Fury rose in my chest. They were *denying* it. Oh my God. I should have known. I wanted to jump on the table, point at them, and scream, "They are SO dating!" Instead I crossed my arms and said, grimly, "Uh-huh." I stared straight ahead at nothing: My heart slammed against my rib cage. *I would stay in control.*

We all waited for Wendii to speak again.

"Rachel," she said, "I'm going to have to agree with them that what you're writing is potentially damaging. We're going to be issuing a written warning to you, asking that you stop writing about them, and, moreover, that you stop writing your blog on company time."

I opened my mouth slightly, then closed it. *Of course.* Of course, they would have researched that. I looked down at the table, embarrassed.

"Okay," I said, my voice hoarse, "I will stop writing about them. And I'll stop writing at work."

Again, no one spoke for a few seconds.

Then Loser said, in as harsh a tone as he could muster, "We appreciate that but we'd also like you to take your blog down."

I looked directly at him for the first time during this conversation. He returned my gaze for a moment then looked away. Now that I'd gotten accustomed to his presence, I felt less frightened. I remembered what a weak person he was, how he lacked the confidence to face people down even when it was necessary. Our neighbors used to raise a ruckus downstairs late at night when we were trying to sleep and Loser never once went down to deal with them. It was always me.

"Too bad. I'm not taking it down." Adrenaline pumped through me as I said this. I turned back to Wendii, who raised her eyebrows. This was my ace in the hole. I knew from consulting my various legal counsel (i.e., my mother and GalPal #1) that Empire HR could not make me take down the blog. They might fire me for what I'd already written, if they thought it was bad enough, but apparently they were not going to do that. Their job was to monitor what went on in the workplace. If Loser wanted to rid the world of Breakup Babe, he'd have to drag my ass into court to do it.

Loser looked at Wendii for support. Wendii, for the first time, sounded hesitant.

"That is something that the human resources department is not going to ask," she said. She didn't look anyone in the eye when she said it.

Involuntarily, I let out a sigh of relief. Suddenly I liked Wendii much better. I almost wanted to tell her that she had a fleck of mascara resting on her blush-streaked cheek.

"We can sue you for it," said Loser. *Ha.* The royal "we." I wondered if he even realized how that sounded. I snuck a glance at Loserette, who twisted a ring around on her right hand but didn't say anything. I had to hand it to him, he was doing the false bravado thing pretty well today.

"Go ahead," I said. "Sue me." I laughed a little. No one else did, of course. I was feeling more relaxed by the second.

I thought I saw a half smile pass across Wendii's face, but I couldn't be sure. What voyeuristic fun this must be for her! I could imagine her telling her blond husband all about it over dinner at their cookie-cutter suburban house in some newly developed area like the Lake Sammamish plateau, in one of the houses Jake and I might have seen from our lunch spot on Tiger Mountain.

"The thing I want to know," I said, plunging ahead more aggressively than planned, "is what happens now? This woman," I gestured to Loserette, "is the vice president of my group. Now that she's accused me of lying about her and slandering her, what's to say she won't go and give me low review scores to try to get rid of me?"

Wendii started to speak but Loserette interrupted her. "I'm a complete professional and that would never happen," she said. I was shocked by how tremulous her voice was. How like a scared little girl she sounded. "Besides, VPs have very little to do with the review scores of their—the people who are at her level," she finished up. Then she looked at Wendii in a pleading way. Everything about this executive—from the tone of her voice, to her body language, to her expression— said, "Please, don't hurt me."

Then it struck me, suddenly, what was at stake for these two. Especially for her. In a burst of clarity I realized that they were probably almost as scared as I was. I'd made some serious accusations in that blog of mine. I'd written things that, if they were true, could destroy her job. *Me. I'd written them. On a silly blog called Breakup Babe.*

For a moment I felt the power of my words, how they could affect others' lives in a very tangible way. Then my conscience reared its head. And, well, what if I *was* wrong? What if they were just friends? Oh, that wasn't what my instincts told me and the evidence certainly was incriminating, but still . . . I didn't know for sure, did I? Yet I'd gone ahead and posted it, consequences be damned. Maybe I really was just a pathetic dumpee getting revenge in the only way I knew how. Instead of slashing tires, I was spewing lies.

Embarrassment overcame me. Shame. They certainly

weren't the most admirable human beings on the face of the planet, but I'd sunk to their level. A ridiculous phrase—one that I'd seen on a bumper sticker just that morning—passed through my mind. "What would Jesus do?" I was not religious in any way, but still I knew that Jesus would never have started a blog where he gratuitously insulted his ex and made unfounded accusations about her love life.

"I'm sorry," I whispered.

No one said anything.

"I'm sorry I wrote all that stuff. It was not right."

Loser saw his advantage and pushed it. "Do you agree to take the blog down?"

I looked at him. Our eyes met again. I hoped it would be a meaningful look, one where we would acknowledge the tumultuous emotions we'd been through together. With a glance we could forgive each other and mend the rift. To my disappointment, however, I saw only fear and anger in his face. No compassion. To forgive, one needed compassion.

I swallowed. My throat was dry.

Well, then, I could be the compassionate one. I could stop the mudslinging. I could take down the blog, or at least the things I'd written about them. It would probably make me feel better about myself. But then Loser made a fatal error.

"Because it's all lies," he said, turning to Wendii. "It should not be allowed to stay on the Web."

"They are not lies!" I burst out. Loser looked startled. "I didn't make up things maliciously to hurt you! I wrote what I felt and what I saw! Some of it wasn't nice, and I might have guessed wrong about some things, but I wasn't LYING! Are you saying it was a lie I saw you at Red Mill Burgers to-gether?"

Loser didn't say anything. Instead, he looked down at the table with an expression I recognized. Guilt. I had seen it on his face so many times during The Great Unpleasantness, Part I. He was going to lie again. I knew it. He was going to humiliate me to save his own ass and hers. How had I ever, EVER fallen in love with such a slimy worm?

He looked at Wendii and started to speak. "I'm saying—" But I didn't let him finish. There was no way he was going to do this to me.

"Fuck you, Loser! I forgot for a minute that you're the one who is a liar. I have a witness who saw you there!" So much for my brief Jesus-like humility. Then I burst into tears.

He flinched a little but then looked over at Wendii smugly, as if to say, *See, she's hysterical. A hysterical, pathetic, heart-broken bitch.*

"Rachel, please." Wendii raised her voice. But I couldn't help it. I put my face in my hands and sobbed.

"I think we're done here," I heard her say. "You do, of course, have the option to retain a lawyer," she said to the two of them.

"Rachel," she said. Then louder, "Rachel."

I looked up. The tears were still falling down my face and I was gasping for breath. So much for my blow-dried hair, my sexy pants; I looked like a full-blown basket case now. The mascara I'd put on that morning was no doubt running all over my face.

Wendii's tone softened just a little when she looked at me, but there was a tinge of disgust in it too, as if I were a leper. Such drama would never occur in her perfect little world.

"You'll be receiving your written warning in interoffice mail tomorrow."

"R—right," I gasped.

The two of them rose from the table and left the room to-gether. After they'd exited, I got up and wobbled toward the door. I walked slowly, giving them time to disappear before I got outside the conference room. The usual closings didn't seem to apply here. "Thanks," I could have said to Wendii, or "See you later." Instead I swam through the uncomfortable silence, opened the door, and peered out into the hallway. They were gone.

"Bye," I whispered to Wendii, unable to overcome my innate politeness.

She didn't hear me or else chose to make no reply. I stepped out into the hall as if it were a minefield.

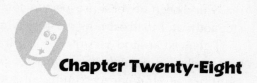

Chapter Twenty-Eight

My God, people, I feel as if I've been hit with a truck. If there is a single thing that's going right in my life right now, I'd like to know what it is.

Work is all f*cked up—though not as badly as it could be—and my love life, as of last night, is nonexistent. All I have now is a great idea for a book, and a horribly written first half of a chapter.

Things aren't looking so good.

I leaned my chin on my hands. Stared at my computer screen. I felt hollow and sad, but also very relieved. For one, I hadn't gotten fired, but I'd also made a wise decision in the romance department for once.

I'd dumped Jake.

Or had he dumped me? I wasn't exactly sure. All I knew was, I'd taken matters into my own hands and now things were over.

I'd expected to feel worse about ending things with him,

and wondered if I was experiencing some sort of delayed re-action to the grief. After all, he'd been my lifeline through this HR mess. And—if you subtracted the quasi-celebrity ex-wife, the custody battle, and the fact that he'd almost killed us—he really *had* been the best prospect to come along since Loser.

But that, I realized now, wasn't saying much.

I glanced around Victrola for inspiration. The art exhibit this week had something to do with primates. There were paintings of chimpanzees doing all sorts of human things: chimpanzees going to McDonalds, chimpanzees washing their cars. Was it supposed to be some sort of political statement? I wondered. Involuntarily, I wished Jake were here. He'd have something witty to say about these paintings, which were, in fact, quite hideous.

A little burst of grief exploded, burned brightly, left a smoky trail. There it was. The grief. I waited for more explo-sions but none came.

Yes, I thought, gazing at a painting of chimpanzees sitting in traffic on the 520 bridge, Jake had his good points. They were just outweighed by the bad. I wanted to be careful, though, how I wrote about him. I could so easily go to town on the blog about him. My readers would love the ex-wife story, for example! They would love, too, to know exactly how our strange, sad conversation had gone down last night.

I wasn't going to tell any of those stories, though. Even though bitter words had been exchanged last night, I wasn't angry. He hadn't been the easiest guy to deal with, but I also didn't blame him for how things had worked out. Hell, part of it was my fault for writing about him the way I had on the blog. So, tempted as I was to divulge the details of our breakup online, I was going to do something different for once. I was going to respect his privacy.

The conversation had not gone particularly well. On the other hand, I had been mature. I hadn't lashed out at him for being unsupportive and distant—which he had been. He didn't get in touch with me for a full twenty-four hours after my HR meeting. And then, all I got was another unsatisfying and somewhat testy e-mail.

R—

Second thoughts about the relationship? Frankly, with my work schedule and the custody stuff, I haven't had time to have any thoughts, much less second thoughts.

As for the blog, well, you wrote about the situation as you saw it. How can I have any complaints with that?

How was the HR meeting?

I'll call you soon.

My God! I felt like I should be wearing a T-shirt that said "I practically got fired and all I got from my boyfriend was a stupid e-mail." This e-mail was even colder than his last one. When I read it, something twisted inside me, and I knew. Jane had been right about him. Whatever was going on with Jake—whether it really was this custody battle, lingering feelings for his ex-wife, or he was pissed off about what I'd written—it was not the warm, friendly Jake I knew. And it was not the Jake I wanted to be with.

If he lived in Seattle and we could see each other on a regular basis, we might be able to work through this, whatever "this" was. I just did not have the time or energy to deal with a difficult, baggage-ridden guy who lived in Portland. Besides, as GalPal #1 had put it on the phone last night (loudly, as usual), if our relationship was this difficult in the early "honeymoon" stage, how likely was it that it would get better?

Not very damn likely.

When I called him, I jumped in immediately so I wouldn't lose my nerve. "I think," I told him, "that we need to cut this off now. It's just not working. I think you're too busy for me. It makes me sad when I don't hear from you, so instead of being one of those nagging girlfriends, I'm just going to say, Okay, that's it. We have different needs. And let you go. Even though I really don't want to."

I had rehearsed that speech many times in my head. I was hoping, of course, that he would leap in and say, "I'm sorry. This is just temporary!" But I knew he wouldn't.

Silence on the other end.

"Jake?"

"Yeah, I'm here."

"Oh." The English accent still made me melt. Suddenly I wanted to take everything back.

Finally he spoke. "What would you like me to say? Sounds like I don't have much of a choice in the matter. Not that I ever did."

"What do you mean?" The cold tone in his voice broke my heart.

"Well, your whole blog is an ode to commitmentphobia, isn't it?"

"What?" This comment shocked me so much, I almost laughed. I imagined, for a second, making it the subtitle of my blog: "Breakup Babe: An Ode to Commitmentphobia."

"Haven't you noticed? You just use guys up and throw them out so you have something to write about."

"Oh my God." How had this suddenly turned into a conversation about what was wrong with *me*? I was the one who had complaints here!

"That's what you did with me, too."

I felt like I should argue. Protest. Slam down the phone. It seemed so unfair that he was using my blog against me. But I was too curious about my intriguing new status as a literary man-eater.

"I did?"

"Yes! You told me one of the reasons you agreed to meet me was that if we got together, it would be a 'great ending' for your book."

I was about to say something, but he kept going. "More-over, you made me look like a fool, didn't you?"

"I didn't mean—"

"But you certainly got a lot of laughs out of your readers, which is all you were looking for, I'm sure. They all think I'm a raging idiot. Well, I tell you what. I feel like one right now, for ever agreeing to be one of your subjects."

I didn't know whether to feel guilty or outraged. He'd given me permission to write about that trip! He'd said, specifically, that he deserved "a little ribbing" for what happened! So I'd given him a little gentle ribbing. I hadn't been that bad, had I?

"If you can, during an argument, try to step outside the situation and put yourself in the other person's head. What are they feeling right now? If they are upset, in their own head, they have a valid reason for it. But often, if a person is angry, they will not be directly addressing this reason. Instead, they'll be casting blame" (Amos White, *Relationships for Dummies*).

He was hurt. I had to understand that. I had hurt his feelings.

"I'm sorry, Jake," I said, "I'm really sorry if I made you feel bad. That was not my intention."

"And now that you've already featured me as the Clown of the Week on your blog, you're ready to back out of the whole thing just because I'm not e-mailing you ten times a day. Because I'm not 'supporting' you, or whatever. As if my own troubles don't count for a damn. No. I'm only about to lose my daughter, that's all! Did it occur to you that maybe I need support too, and the best way you could be supportive is by being patient?" His voice cracked here.

"I'm sorry," I said again. This time it came out as a whisper. There was no point arguing now. I wished we could turn the clock back to that moment when he told me, over e-mail, the whole sordid story of his ex-wife, *People* magazine, the rich new boyfriend, the moment when I could have said "too much baggage," and steered the tone of our e-mail away from the flirtatious and back to the friendly. When I could have heeded my own New Year's resolution not to "grasp at point-less relationships with hot but inappropriate men."

"Don't feel sorry for me," he said. "Save it for the next guy. That's who *I* feel sorry for."

Then he hung up the phone.

I'd cried for half an hour afterward. For hurting him. For being hurt by him. For the potential that had shimmered so brightly for such a short time. Then I picked myself up and, miraculously, got a solid hour of work done on the latest as-signment for my writing class. I noticed, yet again, how the act of writing smoothed the jagged edges of my life.

Now, as I wondered how to blog about it the next day, I felt a sort of admiration for him. The way he'd extricated him-self so quickly from the conversation. What if I'd done that when Loser had first wanted to break up with me? It would have saved me a full month of excruciating heartbreak.

It's true. The daydream that is Long-Distance Boy is over. I'm not going to give the hows and the whys here. Last night it all ended in a brief burst of explosives that hopefully left no permanent dam-age.

And, yes, I'm sad. But I'll survive. It was short, after all. Short, then sweet, then very bitter. I've learned from it, though, and the most important thing I've learned is this:

Don't date a guy who reads my blog!

So if I'm ever tempted to do that again, please stop me, okay?

Meanwhile, my book marches forward at a snail's pace! There are now three full scenes written with plans for a fourth. At this rate,

I will be done in forty years, and you will all have to come to the nursing home to get your autographed copy!

Just imagine, though, the merchandising potential. Action figures, for example! "Nursing Home B.B." with portable oxygen tanks and little pink vial for her meds!

So there you have it. That's what I have to look forward to right now: a book that will be published in forty years and, until then, a life bereft of s*x and companionship, because—you know what?—boys are just a distraction and I don't need them, do you hear me? I DON'T NEED THEM!

I felt a little better after writing my blog. Especially, because, just as I finished, I looked up to see the cute barista gazing at me with what could only be described as a longing look. Where had he come from?

I smiled at him and he smiled back, then quickly looked away, as if he hadn't expected to get caught. My insides fluttered. Maybe today was the day to go strike up a conversation with him. Then I caught myself.

JESUS! Would I never stop?

I snapped my computer shut, trying to put a businesslike expression on my face. I'd been sarcastic, of course, when I said I didn't need boys, but I knew without a doubt by now that the steamroller approach I'd been using post-Loser just wasn't working.

I need to chill out. Cool off. Mellow out. Stop the insanity. Take some me-time.

For at least a day.

Chapter Twenty-Nine

I managed to take some me-time for a full two weeks. Instead of moping around about boys, I focused like a laser beam on the things that had to be done.

One, I had to improve my work performance so that I could get back in Empire's good graces.

Two, I had to work on the first chapter of my book, which was due at the end of the class in March.

Three, I had to start training for Mount Rainier. I'd decided, in a wave of momentum after breaking up with Jake, that I would climb it without him. Who needed a guy to do such things? Certainly not *moi*! The day after we broke up, I signed up on the American Lung Association website before I could lose my nerve.

Merely putting my name down, however, didn't fully commit me. In May, I would have to make a deposit of $200 if I wanted to climb. That gave me two months to decide if I really wanted to do it. By signing up on the site, I could reserve myself a spot and get in touch with other potential climbers so we could train together.

I got into a solid routine. Up at 7:30 A.M., write, and get to work at the very Empire-acceptable time of 10 A.M. When I wrote every day, even just for an hour, I made a lot of progress. The story line of my memoir (girl gets heart broken, girl starts blog, blog helps girl get over broken heart) started to become more than just an outline. It was a living, breathing thing. I realized, as I combed through my blog, that I had tons of material.

While some other blogs were short and pithy, giving only a bird's-eye view of people's lives, mine really delved into the details. I'd worried about it on a number of occasions. Was I going on too much? Did people reading about my life on the Internet want something quicker, snappier? Whether or not they did, at least I now had the details that made for a good book: smells, sounds, feelings, settings.

When I'd written my proposal back in December, I didn't have a good idea about how I'd tie all my blog entries together. Now, as I learned more about structure, I realized that to turn them into a cohesive story would require connective narrative and a good, dramatic shape. The beauty of a blog was partly its randomness, the way it reflected what was going in a person's everyday life. A book couldn't have that arbitrariness. There had to be a sense that everything was leading somewhere.

Which meant, of course, that I had some thinking to do about my life. Where *was* all this dating leading? All this blogging? To true love and a multimillion-dollar book deal, I hoped! A life of endless glamour! *Breakup Babe quits her boring job to become a jet-setting travel journalist and scores an assignment to travel the globe with the Italian men's soccer team, where she must fend off marriage proposals left and right!* But who knew what the real ending would be? I'd have to figure it out when I got there. Meanwhile, I knew now that if I had a good outline in place, a compelling story would emerge. I saw it happening already.

After my daily writing session, I'd head to work. In the past, I'd arrive at the office and wallow in boredom and misery for several hours before doing any actual work. Now I fought these feelings with a variety of successful tactics. Previously, I'd started the day by checking my e-mail, arranging and rearranging my task list, and IMing the GalPals. Now, when I arrived, I would immediately dive into my editing without checking my e-mail. I turned IM on only for brief periods of time (much to GalPal #3's dismay), and made reading my e-mail a "reward" for doing actual work.

Not that there was ever anything scintillating in my in-box. It was the same old work-related technical gobbledygook as always. Messages with subject lines such as: **Missing Parameter in the CreateNullVoid method—can you fix?** But I always looked forward to reading it just in *case* I got that e-mail that changed my life forever. An old flame could miraculously e-mail me and beg me to come back! Some other random, cute boy could have miraculously gotten my e-mail address and decided to contact me! Johnny Depp could have miraculously stumbled upon Breakup Babe and begged for the rights to the movie!

Every other day at 3 P.M., I went running or to the gym. The Mount Rainier climb was still months away, but I was already getting in shape for it. I'd gotten soft and lazy in the months after The Great Unpleasantness! It was very unlike me. I'd always been disciplined about exercise, ever since I first started running with my dad at age twelve. But it helped to have some sort of goal, a race or an event to motivate me to train. In the past, there had been triathlons. Marathons. Even a relay race at Mount Baker called "Ski to Sea" that I'd been drafted into three years ago despite my protests that I was the slowest cross-country skier on the face of the planet. Well, now I had the biggest, baddest goal of them all, one that on sunny days loomed over all of Puget Sound, looking deceptively beautiful and benign.

I'd get home from work at 8 or 9 P.M. and try to find someone to hang out with who wasn't a hot but inappropriate male. This wasn't the easiest thing for me to do, since at that hour, GalPals #2 and #3 were putting their children to bed and GalPal #1 was in bed herself. One night Sexy Boy invited me out for drinks, and I found the New, Improved Rachel™ being put to the test.

"You're looking awfully well these days, Miss R.," said Sexy Boy over beers at Paragon, a meat market for well-groomed denizens of yuppie Queen Anne Hill (so different from the jaded grunge holdovers of my own Capitol Hill neighborhood). Since our New Year's Eve fling, we'd e-mailed and talked on the phone a few times, but had seen each other only once—at a group event right before Jake's arrival. As befitted a dating confidant, Sexy Boy knew all about the rise and fall of Jake. There had been no further discussion of our own midnight escapades.

"Thanks," I said. "I've been working out a lot."

He reached over to squeeze my arm, then let his hand linger. "I can tell!" he said, winking. "Those muscles are feeling very strong." Sexy Boy's flirtation was always over the top but in a self-consciously silly way that made it hard not to be charmed. I smiled then looked down. Last time I'd seen him there had been another prospect in the wings, so my usual lust had been dimmed. But tonight, as soon as I'd seen him sitting in the booth at Paragon, looking slightly tousled and überhot in a sky blue American Apparel shirt, my lust made a vigorous comeback.

"How are the friendly skies?" I mumbled, focusing on Sexy Boy's mouth rather than his eyes. It was his eyes, as usual, that held power over me. If I could avoid looking at them, maybe I could prevent myself from falling back under his spell.

"Oh, they're not quite as friendly these days, if you know what I mean." He laughed a little.

"Hm. Too bad." He must be referring to the demise of his "relationship" with Stacy or Suzie or whatever the name of that flight attendant was. I wanted to ask him about it but took a sip of my beer instead. Let him think I didn't care. He could play my dating confidant all he wanted, but I didn't really want to play his.

"How is your work going?" he asked. I'd told Sexy Boy that work had been difficult lately, but not why. Some days I was tempted to tell him about the blog because he was a good friend and I wanted to confide in him. But he was in so many entries! For all I knew, GuyPal #1 had given him the URL already and he was reading it behind my back, enjoying every minute that I talked about his stupid, sexy eyes and soft kisses. I wouldn't put it past either of them.

"Oh . . . it's okay. It's getting better," I said. "But things are still a bit . . . tense."

"That's too bad," he said. Then he looked up from his drink and trained the deadly weapons on me. "I have a few ideas about how to relieve that tension."

I laughed in surprise.

"Very subtle," I said, trying, at all costs, to avoid those eyes. I looked instead at his right ear, which bore an old piercing that I'd yet to see an earring in. My heart beat faster. I hadn't expected a proposition tonight. I really shouldn't be flattered because what was there to be flattered about in a guy wanting to have no-strings sex with me? Yet I was. Ridiculously flattered.

"Yes, I'm known for my subtlety," he said. He was still looking directly at me, weapons trained on their target. I couldn't do it, of course. I couldn't hook up with him again, unless . . .

I looked in his eyes. Big mistake. I was hoping to see a look that told me maybe this time would be for real, that this time our ongoing attraction could morph into something else. But his eyes didn't tell me anything. Instead, they worked on me as they always had, making every rational thought in my head disappear. I *really* wanted someone to be close to. I looked into those big green eyes, the pupils slightly dilated as usual, and was pulled forward into the night. We would have another drink, we would go back to my apartment, we would . . .

"Can I get you anything else?" The waitress's tired voice broke the spell.

I looked up at her in a daze. On her left hand a wedding ring glittered. Funny how that was now the first thing I looked for—especially on men, but also on women. How did people ever end up getting married? It seemed like such an impossible state to get to—that level of love and commitment.

But a person had to start somewhere. And meaningless flings were not a good starting point. I glanced back at Sexy Boy. He was looking at me with raised eyebrows. He was clearly up for more drinking if I was. For getting this party started and continuing it long into the night.

"No, thanks," I said.

"Me, neither," said Sexy Boy, attempting not to react. But a fleeting expression of disappointment passed over his face. Longing flashed in his eyes, which in turn caused my stomach to twist with desire. I looked down at my beer.

"Got an early morning tomorrow?" he asked, after the waitress had walked away. I thought, right then, about putting it all on the table, asking him why we couldn't just date. For real. But I would only get some slippery answer. We couldn't date because he was a commitmentphobic pothead, that's why! Funny and charming and sweet and great as a friend but completely unsuitable as a boyfriend. "Yeah," I said. "I have to get up early and write."

"Well, then," he said, holding up his beer, "here's to your writing." It reminded me of our toast months ago, in Hattie's

Hat, which was the first time I'd turned him down for mean-ingless sex. We'd toasted to friendship then, and, amazingly, we seemed to have become good friends.

"By the way," said Sexy Boy, "am I in your book?"

"Maybe." He most definitely was in my book but I wasn't going to stoke his ego just then by telling him that.

"Really? Well, if I am, could you could make my character into a race-car driver?"

So, for a full two weeks, it felt as if my life was actually on track, making progress on all fronts, and, especially, making good choices about men! Was it possible I'd actually learned a few things since The Great Unpleasantness, that I was now emerging from the deep emotional trough I'd been swim-ming in to become a high-functioning human being again, that all the therapy—blogging and otherwise—that I'd been going through these last few months had actually yielded re-sults?

No, it wasn't possible, though you couldn't blame a girl for thinking it was! Just how impossible it was didn't become clear to me until March 13, however.

The day the cash register in the Empire cafeteria broke.

Chapter Thirty

I looked out the window of the Globe at the blinding sunshine and wanted to cry. But here I was at my favorite breakfast spot on a sunny Tuesday morning, eating vegan biscuits and gravy, when I would normally have been in a windowless conference room discussing, ad nauseum, the use of "byte" (lowercase *b*) versus "Byte" (capital *B*).

Monday, March 17, 2003
10:03 AM Breakup Babe
So I got fired three days ago for dumping soup on my ex-boyfriend's head.

  How's that for a conversation starter?

This sounded so ludicrous, I had to chuckle. My mood improved for one fraction of a second, then reverted to glum. Around me, art school hipsters with hangovers and green hair gathered in big groups. Perhaps it had been a mistake to come to the Globe alone. But this was my favorite breakfast place in all of Seattle, and their biscuits and gravy were the food I most craved in times of stress!

I looked back at the laptop that sat open on the table in front of me. I wanted, more than anything, to finish the chapter that was due in my writing class in three days, but I was undeniably blocked right now. I still had at least two more scenes to write for that chapter, but I'd been staring at it, paralyzed, for the last hour.

So I'd given in to the temptation to write my blog. After all, I was understandably traumatized by losing my job in such an unceremonious manner. Anyone would be! Perhaps once I got the whole sad story of the soup incident out, I would feel better. Thus cleansed, I would be able to move on to the more important things in life, such as finishing this chapter and turning it into a best-selling book that would then be made into a hit movie starring Johnny Depp and Jake Gyllenhaal! Propelled by this thought, I took a sip of my ultra-strong Globe coffee and kept typing.

> Now, just for the record, the soup wasn't hot and he suffered no permanent damage. Loser will survive to impregnate women (alas).
>
> Before you let out your collective gasp, wait! There is more you don't know. I didn't get fired solely for the soup incident. (A hush falls over the crowd.) Here is the thing I've been keeping from you, my dear readers, for the last month: I was *already* in trouble at work. Because of the blog.
>
> (Crowd rumbles in surprise.)
>
> Yes, Breakup Babe was ferreted out by the enemy! Loser and Loserette discovered it and turned me in to HR. A series of horrible meetings ensued, one in which I had to face the two of them across a table, only to have Loser swear, in cold blood, that every single thing I'd written about them was a *lie*.

Okay, okay, quiet down people. I'm not done here!

Instead of kicking me to the curb, my generous employer gave me a written warning: *Don't blog about them anymore, missy, and don't blog at work.*

Fine, I could handle that! *Thank you, O Mighty Empire Corp., for letting me keep my job!* I tried to straighten up, take my job more seriously. I did in fact stop writing at work and, as I'm sure you noticed, Loser and Loserette have not made an appearance here in quite some time. But all the while anger toward Loser seethed beneath the surface. So when I saw him in the cafeteria two weeks later, I should have worn a sign that said "Contents Under Pressure—Do Not Shake!"

I was standing in the lunch line when I saw him, surrounded, as usual, by fat, balding developers with tie-dyed T-shirts hanging over their fried-food-fed paunches, purchasing their lunches of hamburgers, fries, and chocolate cake. I, on the other hand, had a salad and a cup of low-fat tomato soup.

My mind was on a comment I'd gotten from my writing teacher on my last assignment. "Parts of this are very funny," he'd written. "But the tone is uneven. Try to get it all to snap."

This little bit of criticism destroyed the warm glow that had remained after the triumphal reading of my scene to the class. It wasn't a fatal criticism by any means, but I couldn't help but be discouraged. It made me tired to think of how much work I had to do. If I couldn't even make half a chapter "snap," how could I make a whole book do it?

As the long line inched forward, I happened to glance up at the salad bar and there he was. Spooning up a heaping helping of blue cheese dressing and looking the same as he always did: black T-shirt, khaki pants.

All thoughts of my writing class dropped away. My stomach tightened. I started to tremble.

I looked away quickly when I saw him. Stared off into the middle distance, heart pounding. I was shocked at how angry I felt.

I'd been furious at the HR meeting when he called me a liar, but I'd expressed my anger at the time by oh-so-maturely yelling "F*ck you, Loser!" then bursting into tears.

The line inched forward. What the hell was taking so long? I craned to see around the people in front of me. The woman at the register shook her head. A manager looked at the register with her. People in line shifted their weight around. Rolled their eyes at one another.

I looked at Loser again. He was now getting a piece of pizza. Sh*t! I turned to face in the other direction. I tried to envision a soothing, meditative scene. My "peaceful place." A high Sierra meadow with a babbling brook and butterflies flitting about.

Instead, I visualized me, in a Lara Croft–style black leather outfit, deadly weapon in hand. I would point it at Loser, while the computer geeks around me drooled at my outfit and the sleek, high-tech gun. "Drop the pizza and get the f*ck out," I'd say. "And don't ever, EVER come where I can see you again." The cafeteria would erupt in cheers.

Then he did it. He got in line. I watched him with my peripheral vision. Two seconds after getting in line he saw me for the first time. Flinched. I could see the flight impulse grip him. Then he stood his ground, pretending, as I was, that nothing was awry.

Well, okay, then! All I had to do was stand in this line with him for another five million hours or so! At least there were four people separating us. I turned to face forward. Stared at the bowl cut of the guy in front of me, which dipped down in back to the middle of his fuzzy neck. *Go to the peaceful place! The peaceful place!*

"I don't *know* what's wrong with it!" The high, excited voice of the cashier pierced my attempt at meditation. I peered around the guy with the bowl cut for a glimpse. The manager, a tall, balding guy with white hair at his temples, stood with his hands on his hips, looking sternly at the cashier, a short, stout Mexican woman. She, in turn, glared at the cash register.

"Jesus," muttered someone behind me. "Let's get out of here and go to Azteca or something."

Then, before I knew it, the four people behind me in line had disappeared. The only thing separating me from Loser was a few feet of air. I realized all of this without even turning around. I felt the whoosh of their disappearance and the electric hesitation of Loser. He either had to move up or get booted out of line by the unruly mob of hungry Empire workers now lining up behind him.

I clenched my institutional gray tray so hard that my knuckles turned white. My food trembled a little, the tomato soup sloshing gently in its white Styrofoam container. Though I couldn't see him, I could feel him behind me. He moved up ever so slightly. My back felt as if it were on fire. My head throbbed.

Then, miracle of miracles, the line started to move! As if to make up for lost time, the cashier whipped people through. Thirty seconds later, I was at the register. It would be only another minute before I could get out of this cafeteria and away from him. I held my breath as the cashier rang me up.

I sprang away toward the counter that held the jars of plastic eating utensils. Quickly I grabbed a fork and a spoon, then rushed toward the cooler for a drink.

Why I did that, I do not know. The exact same drink cooler stood in the kitchen of my building. There was not anything better or different in this cooler. It was habit pure and simple. If I'd fled directly to my office after getting my utensils, everything might be different now.

But I didn't. I charged toward the drink cooler and ran smack into Loser, who was making a beeline for the utensils from the cash register. Rather, the edge of my gray tray ran into his side.

"Ow!" he said, before fully realizing it was me. I knew it couldn't have hurt that much, but Loser always was one to exaggerate his aches and pains. A mere sniffle would keep him in bed for an entire weekend, where he would moan about how sick he was.

"Sorry," I muttered, reflexive politeness taking over. Then it sunk in. For both of us. Me jamming him in the side with a gray tray was the first physical contact we'd had in seven months. It had felt good, I realized. Suddenly I wanted to do it again. *Harder.*

For a moment, the rest of the cafeteria fell away. We stood trapped in our own little bubble and stared at each other. Three years earlier, when I'd been a temp and he my cute, across-the-hall coworker, we'd eaten at many an Empire cafeteria together. It seemed like a different life altogether now. Those had been such fun days before we ever started dating. We'd roam the Empire hallways together, all sparkle and sexual tension. No one had come close to making me feel that way again. And no one had ever hurt me the way he'd hurt me.

Now, as I faced him, I felt nothing but anger. We would never be "friends." There was nothing left of our relationship but a bloody stain on Empire's walls. If I said anything to him now, I'd just start yelling and screaming and never stop. So I started to move past him, when he said, quietly, but not quietly enough, "Bitch."

I froze. "What did you say?"

He had already started to walk away and didn't respond.

"*What* did you say?" I said more loudly. A couple people glanced at me. I could see Loser stop, momentarily, as if deciding whether to face me, but then he kept walking toward the utensils.

Then a wave of emotion swamped me. How *dare* he call me a bitch? How *dare* he ignore me, the sniveling little no-balls, lying, cheating, scumbag bastard? That was it. He was going to get what he deserved. Instead of becoming hysterical, however, I became calm. Focused. Furious.

I followed him to the utensil bar. Everything in me was tightly wound but I didn't shake. I had to be precise. At first, he didn't notice me. I watched him get a fork. A knife. Some napkins. I moved in right behind him. I had never been stealthy but the skill descended upon me in my moment of need. I reached for my cup of soup.

When he turned back toward me, I did it. I was so focused that I seemed to move in slow motion. *Lara Croft, paid assassin*. I locked the target in my sights.

"You think I'm a bitch?" I said, and my voice rung out crystal clear, as I positioned my hand over his head. "Well, I guess I am!"

Then I turned the soup cup upside down, dumping its contents over him.

I felt euphoric as I relived this scene. Of course, I had just finished my second cup of ultrastrong Globe coffee. As I glanced around the place, I didn't feel like such a loser anymore. Could these art school poseurs tell how tough I was just from looking at me? Doubtful. I smirked.

In a corner booth, a white guy with many dreadlocks cozied up to his girlfriend, who had black hair with magenta tips and a dog collar tattooed around her neck. Every two minutes or so, they would kiss and whisper to each other in a smiley sort of way. Even the sight of this lovey-dovey couple didn't bother me right now. No doubt they both smelled horrible. Plus, one day, their love, too, would be a distant memory, drowned in tomato soup. I laughed to myself. I was so clever.

"Oh my God," he screeched. "You f*cking bitch!" People were staring. Tittering. I proceeded to move calmly toward the exit as he yelled behind me. "You're not going to get away with this!"

He was right about that much. Twelve hours later, I no longer had a job.

But at least I have my dignity, and that's all that matters, right?

Did I have my dignity, I wondered? A clichéd phrase appeared unbidden in my head: *cutting off your nose to spite your face.* It was the phrase my mother had used when I told her what had happened. She hadn't seemed the least bit proud or impressed by my behavior. Oh, I knew I hadn't acted in the most mature manner, but couldn't she give me any credit for standing up for myself? No. All she did was hurl clichés at me and tell me I needed to grow up.

My friends had been slightly better. At least some of them

had laughed. Said "good-for-you!"-type things. "This will be great for the book!" said GalPal #1, whose general tactic when something bad happened was to tell me how great it would be for the book. GalPal #2, who laughed in a very long and satisfying way when I told her the story, asked in a worried tone, "Are you doing all right with your medications?"

That was, I had to admit, a very good question. The last few days had been tough. I'd been vacillating between anxiety-tinged excitement and a deepening sense of despair. Just as I seemed to be doing again today.

Crap.

I looked longingly over at the coffee urn, wondering if another cup would help. I was approaching the down slope from the first two, and if the last few days were any indication, I would hurtle downward quickly. No. A third cup would only make things worse. I hurried to finish writing my blog before my high crashed completely.

> I guess dignity is not *all* that matters. A person needs to eat. And a person needs to write. If I can keep doing both of those things, I'll be okay.
>
> Unemployment benefits will cover the first for now. But I'm a little worried about #2. Since my termination, I've made no progress on my book. This wouldn't be such a problem except that the first chapter of my book is due tomorrow in that writing class I paid five hundred dollars for, and it's only three-quarters done!
>
> I'm starting to fear that perhaps General Celexa has abandoned me in my time of need. How else to explain the way my demons have wrested control of my brain and I can no longer concentrate on creating Great Art?

I snuck another glance at the couple in the booth. Now that they had their food, Rasta Man no longer had his arm around Dog-Collar Girl but they were sitting smashed up as close to each other as they could possibly get. Even while they ate, they kept giving each other pecks on the cheek.

God, people, give it a break!

I took another sip of my coffee, now cold. Not long now before the daily meltdown. I typed even faster.

> I start out every day intending to write. I go to the coffee shop. Pull out my laptop. I look at that three-quarters of a chapter I've written and prepare to power through the rest. *I can do it,* I tell myself in my brief, caffeine-induced moments of hope. *I can write this. I was doing so well!* Then the demons swoop in and start their chatter.

> **Anxiety:** Your book sucks. Your teacher said the tone was "uneven." Why are you even bothering?

> **Loneliness:** You're going to spend the whole day alone, writing this uneven schlock? That sounds pretty damn lonely. Go have lunch with one of your friends instead.

> **Boredom:** Look at that beautiful day out there. You could be out cross-country skiing or biking! Why would you sit inside and write uneven crap anyway? This is boring.

> **Loneliness:** Her job was boring, too, but at least there were other people around!

> **Anxiety:** You need another job ASAP! Now that you've gotten used to new clothes and designer cocktails, you can't live on unemployment!

> **Loneliness:** Yeah, and that's a long time that you have to spend *alone,* and you know how, when you're *alone* too much, you get sad, and when you're sad you can't write. A boyfriend would sure help, but you're about as good at keeping one of those as you are at holding down a job!

> **Boredom:** Jesus, we are all so screwed. Let's go for a bike ride.

Anxiety: No, we need to look for a job!

Loneliness: Don't you have any unemployed friends who can hang out with us today?

These demons have been dogging me ever since The Great Unpleasantness began. But General C. has always been there to knock their heads together and drag them out screaming. So what I want to know is this—*where the hell did he go? Doesn't he know my writing career is at stake?*

Meanwhile, another day looms ahead of me. My computer sits in front of me. I'm going to get some writing done, I swear to God I am. I am a Writer, therefore I write. I am a Writer, therefore I . . .

Ugh. I don't even know anymore. I'm probably just a big fat loser who can't keep a job or a man. I'll spend my days loveless and jobless until I move into a nursing home where no one will visit me and my only form of entertainment will be to torture the poor old men by yelling, "I was a hottie once! I could have been a famous writer! Wanna get married?"

E-mail Breakup Babe | Comments 4

Even poking fun at myself did not do the trick. The tears dripped down my face as I wrote this last line. I quickly pushed my sunglasses onto my face. Then I turned my computer off. Maybe if I went to Victrola, I could get some work done. Clearly this place was not doing it for me today. I looked at my watch. Only 9:45 A.M. My God was time passing slowly.

A bizarre thought struck me. *I wish I could go to work.* I tried to squash it, but it stuck in my head as I scurried to my car. What was I thinking? My job had always bored the crap out of me!

I got into my car. It was such a beautiful day outside. One of those rare winter days when Seattle was like a crystal goblet, everything inside it sharp and clear and beautiful, including Mount Rainier to the south, the Cascades to the east, and the Olympics to the west. And look at me. This beautiful world was now mine for the taking and I was sitting in my car crying, wishing I could go back to work in my windowless office.

This was not good. Not good at all.

POST A COMMENT

Who knew our beloved B.B. was going through such drama! Good for you for giving Loser what he deserves! Maybe you can get another job as someone's hired gun—you know, someone who gets revenge on other people's exes.
Delilah | Homepage | 3/17/03–2:18 P.M.

•   •   •   •   •

Oh, how I wish I could have seen the look on Loser's face!
Juliana | Homepage | 3/17/03–5:41 P.M.

•   •   •   •   •

B.B., it sounds like maybe you need some new drugs! As a connoisseur of the antidepressants, I can tell you that sometimes you need to take more than one for them to really work.
The She-Devil | Homepage | 3/17/03–9:09 P.M.

•   •   •   •   •

Don't worry, you will not end up old and alone in a nursing home. You'll be a beautiful, talented, much-sought-after best-selling author with many men vying for your attention. If not, you can move into our basement and we'll let you take care of the kids in exchange for room and board.
A Fan | 3/17/03–9:09 P.M.

 **Chapter Thirty-One**

Tuesday, March 18, 2003
11:37 AM Breakup Babe
Darlings, you know I've been in a bit of a crisis lately, what with getting fired and having writer's block and being certain that I'm going to die old and alone and childless. It's a lot for a girl to handle all at once.

So I think you'll forgive me for what I'm about to tell you. I went out with The Doctor last night—you know, the one who swept me up in the most passionate kiss of all time, then disappeared into the night never to be heard from again?

I smiled to myself, took a sip of my latte. Amazing what a date and a little bit of denial could do for my mood. Twenty-four hours earlier I'd been ready to throw myself off the Space Needle. Now I felt almost perky. It also helped my mood immensely that there had been so many supportive comments on my blog from yesterday (the entry was up to fifteen comments now!), and that it was pouring rain outside.

> Yes, that's the one! As you know, I never expected him to reappear. I'd written him off, and even managed to erase our delicious kiss almost (but not quite) from my memory. So imagine my surprise when he called yesterday and asked me out to dinner. Had Sensible Girl been in the vicinity, she would have ripped the phone from my hand and thrown it across the room. But I do believe she was so dismayed by my New Year's Eve antics that she went somewhere tropical for the winter. Florida, perhaps? She did not leave a forwarding address.
>
> So I agreed to the dinner date, making sure to sound appropriately suspicious on the phone.

I watched the rain pour down in satisfying sheets outside. I loved the rain. It made me feel that it was okay to be melancholy. The rainy climate was one of the things that made me feel so much more at home in Seattle than I ever had in California.

I just hoped that the weather was clear on Sunday. I'd be doing my first "official" Mount Rainier training hike with a few other people who'd signed up for the fund-raising climb. We were going to Tiger Mountain, of all places. It was one of the few trails with elevation gain that you could hike this time of year. I just hoped my fellow hikers had better navigational skills than Jake. Or me, for that matter.

Today had started off promisingly. After a week of being completely blocked, and getting dangerously behind on the chapter that was due tonight, I'd worked on it for a full hour this morning. I wouldn't have it completely done by tonight, but we still had one more class after this. My writing teacher would certainly let me turn it in a week late. After all, I'd paid him five hundred dollars!

It did frighten me that my current good mood and ability to write seemed solely dependent on the fact that I'd gone on a date with the doctor last night. I knew I had more going for me than a handsome yet unreliable guy. It's just that my self-esteem had taken a real beating in the last couple of weeks (though all the reader love that poured forth yesterday had certainly restored some of it). Could I be blamed for needing a little male attention to perk me up again?

At least I hadn't capitulated completely to the doctor's desires, Sensible Girl's absence notwithstanding.

"Look," said The Doctor when we were halfway through our first cocktails at a new bar called the Brite Lite Lounge. All the walls were white and the waitresses were extremely pale and blond. "I'm really sorry about what happened. There was just some . . . unfinished business in my life that I was trying to take care of."

I looked at him. Waited for more of an explanation. He was just as handsome as he'd ever been, if not more so. He had a soulful look about him today that I'd not seen before. His chocolate eyes looked bigger. Sadder. This was not the same cocky jokester who'd mesmerized an entire club with his karaoke rendition of "Little Nikki."

Instead of offering an explanation, he took a big sip of his whiskey and looked down at the table, which was made of bright blue plastic. Other tables were blue, yellow, or red. "What do you mean by unfinished business?" I said impatiently. I wanted him to get to the point.

He looked up again. Ran his fingers through his hair. I noticed puffy little circles under his eyes. My heart melted still further. Techno music thrummed in the background.

"I think you're seeing the real him for once," Needy Girl said in a stage whisper. I looked to the right, where she'd seated herself at a small table. She wore a tight white sweater dress that made her boobs look huge. She gave me the thumbs-up sign. I tried to ignore her.

"There was this woman," he said, looking me directly in the eye at last. "I was really hung up on her, and when you and I met, the whole thing was ending, but I was just . . . holding on."

So, I wanted to say? Why the hell are you telling me this? Suddenly I just wanted to be at home, in bed. I didn't know why I'd agreed to be here. I'd been jittery and excited for this meeting, but not because I actually expected romance. It was a distraction, and I was desperate for distraction, but who wanted another woman to be part of it? My mood threatened to take a nosedive.

"Huh. Well, sorry to hear that," I said, not sounding sorry at all. "What are you going to order for dinner?" I gestured at his menu. I wanted to get this night over with now. I was tired of rejection. Tired of losing things: love, jobs, the ability to write.

"Well, now it's over," he said. "For good."

"Oh." My hand stopped halfway on its journey to the bread basket. In my confusion, I retracted it. Put my hand on the table instead.

"R.," he said, putting his hand on mine. I was so surprised by that touch I didn't have time to steel myself against it. Suddenly it felt as if every nerve in my body was located in my right hand.

"What?" I said, looking at him, trying to make my voice cold despite the fact that my body temperature had just jumped up to fever levels. I looked at his lips. Remembered that kiss.

Good God, I had to get a grip.

He looked around. Then at me again. Lowered his voice. "What I want to say is I'm really sorry because I liked you. A lot. I mean, I like you. Still."

I stared at him. Tried to think of something clever and cutting to say. But in my feverish state, the best I could come up with was, in a strangled tone, "Well, you sure didn't act like you liked me." Suddenly the techno music boomed about three times louder. We both jumped.

"I KNOW!" he said, practically yelling to be heard over the music. Then he heaved his shoulders upward dramatically, and rolled his eyes. A hint of the old performer-doctor was coming back.

"I acted like a COMPLETE ASS!" The couple at the next table glanced over at us.

I giggled despite myself.

"I was an IDIOT!" he said even louder.

"Okay, okay," I said, looking around to see who else might be listening in. The couple at the table to the left immediately looked back at their dinners, trying to hide their interested expressions.

"Well," I said, raising my voice to be heard over the music while also trying to be discreet. I leaned toward him. "What about this ex-girlfriend of yours? How do I know she's completely out of the picture?"

He looked briefly around the restaurant, then leaned forward, and said in as low a voice as he could given the sonic chaos around us, "She's been taken care of."

I laughed again, despite myself. Damn it, he was not supposed to be charming me! He could tell that his act was working, though, and he leaned back in his seat, a little more relaxed now. Then he gave me a hopeful smile, and cocked his head like a puppy.

"We could rewind a bit," he said, "start things over. Or maybe just go back to that kiss." He still had his head cocked when he said that, but I saw a softening in his eyes.

And I started. My first thought was, "He's read the blog! He's mocking me." For a second, I felt nothing but complete mortification as I recalled my swooning blog entry about his kissing skills. But, as I looked at him, there was no sign of mockery on his face. Then a second, more sensible thought struck me: "No, that kiss meant something to him, too."

The air was thick between us for a minute. I didn't know what to say. He waited, but now he wasn't looking at me anymore. Instead, he looked down at the table.

"I—"

He looked up.

There's no point going back, I should have said. I would have if Sensible Girl hadn't been on vacation! Instead, Needy Girl was staring at me, eyes wide, her Lemon Drop tilting dangerously as she held it in her right hand.

"Give him another chance!" she whispered. "He's begging! Wait, wait. I have to get a picture of this." She quickly pulled her cell phone out of her purse, placed her Lemon Drop on the table (where some of it sloshed over the side of the glass), and took a picture of The Doctor. "Okay, continue!" she said to me, grabbing hold of her Lemon Drop again.

"Well," I said, "how about this? We can hang out and get to know each other better before we—" I stopped. Smiled in an embarrassed way. "I don't really feel like I know who you are." I plunged forward, surprised by my own honesty. "It seems like you're always hiding behind some . . . persona."

He looked surprised too. Then he shook his head and laughed, with a rueful expression on his face.

"Yeah," he said. "I know. I wasn't—how shall we say—very emotionally available before."

"Hmm." I looked at him, waiting.

"But I'm getting more emotionally available by the second."

"Oh, really?" I couldn't keep the flirtatious tone out of my voice.

"Yes, really."

"Well, then, we'll just have to see how things go, won't we?"

"I guess so," he said. Paused. "Meanwhile, do you think we can ask them to turn this music UP so I have to talk even more LOUDLY?" he said, raising his voice so the whole restaurant could hear and grinning a smile at me that was so sexy it should have been illegal.

Outside the rain was coming down even harder. On the street, people scurried from one place to another. I felt better than I had since the spectacular conclusion of The Great Unpleasantness, Part II. At least on the surface. Underneath I had a vague sense of impending danger.

I pushed it away. So maybe my mood was precarious. Maybe I was taking too much of a chance by even hanging out with the doctor. The important thing was that the episode had temporarily dissolved my loneliness and boredom, and I knew I could continue to be productive today. I would finish up the blog entry and get to work on my book.

After dinner, he walked me to my car. It was warm for March, with a scent of salt in the air. As we walked down Second Avenue, past a string of trendy restaurants filled with thirtysomethings dressed in fashions that were at least a year behind New York's, he draped his arm over my shoulder. "You're a trooper to put up with me, R.," he said.

It was as if Sensible Girl heard that remark from her beach cabana and sent me a telepathic message cross-country. "You're an *idiot* if you put up with him. Don't let yourself backslide!"

Needy Girl, on the other hand, did a little tap dance on the sidewalk next to us. "Oh, yes, The Doctor likes you; he likes you!"

Ignoring them both, I pretended, for a minute, that everything was as it should be in my world. That the handsome man with his arm around me was my Jewish doctor husband, the one I'd been programmed to marry since birth. The one who would support me while I wrote my books and raised our children. The one all of my grandparents—were they alive—would be celebrating! *Oh, yes, my granddaughter R. She's so beautiful and smart. She's writing a novel and she married a nice Jewish doctor!*

I reluctantly let go of the fantasy when we got to my car. Hope-a-noma would not control me this time. It would NOT. I fumbled for my keys for an extra-long time, hoping the sexual tension that hung in the air would magically disappear by the time I'd found them in my purse.

It did not.

"Kiss him." Needy Girl's voice was breathy.

Sensible Girl was silent in her hammock, or wherever she was.

"Well, good night," I said, my voice artificially perky.

"Good night, R.," he said. Why did he have to keep saying my name like that? Every time he said my name, I lost a little bit more of my willpower. Then he leaned over to hug me.

I took a deep breath as his arms went around me. He was so tall, so strong, so—

I pulled out of the hug quickly. "I'll see you soon," I said, trying not to pant. If I'd let myself go for a fraction of a second longer, I would never have escaped.

"Yes, you will, R.," he said.

E-mail Breakup Babe | Comments 5

POST A COMMENT

Noooo! Not The Doctor! He's evil!
The Girl from Maine | Homepage | 3/18/03–3:11 P.M.

• • • • •

Oh, come on, give the girl a break. She needs some distraction! I've been hoping he would come back. I want to find out if he has a big c*ck.
Delilah | Homepage | 3/18/03–6:04 P.M.

• • • • •

As a longtime reader, I have determined you have an addiction to men. You are always looking for that next fix. It's great for us readers, but I am worried about B.B.
A Reader Who Cares | 3/18/03–10:31 P.M.

• • • • •

Okay, that's it. You're definitely moving into our basement where we can keep an eye on you.
Worried Yet Again | 3/19/03–9:00 A.M.

• • • • •

Have any of you considered that maybe this time The Doctor is sincere? I say she should give him a second chance!
Little Princess | Homepage | 3/19/03–11:47 A.M.

Chapter Thirty-Two

Sunday, March 23, 2003
9:38 PM Breakup Babe
Dear Breakup Babe readers,

This morning, I woke up surrounded by my demons. Five days after our glorious reunion, The Doctor still had not called. My euphoric mood (Day 1, postdate) had given way to cautious optimism (Day 3), then to doubt (Day 4), then to utter despair (today).

"Ha!" said Boredom as soon as I opened my eyes. He was dressed from head to toe in ill-fitting beige castoffs and held a rifle pointed straight at me. "This is it for you, girlie. No guy, no job, no *nothing*. You might as well die of boredom right now!" He turned to Loneliness, who stood next to him with another rifle, and they high-fived.

"Yeah!" said Loneliness, who was attired in an oversized Mariners T-shirt and a pair of O.P. shorts circa 1983, "You have no one to hang out with today, do you? You've got no one to hang out with tonight either." His voice got even more shrill and grating. "No one except your own loser self! Why even get out of bed?"

"Just lie there until the state comes to cart you away! It won't be long now," Anxiety chimed in. He wore a green Izod shirt of the type that had been popular when I was in the seventh grade and too-tight jeans. He stood on the side of my bed opposite Boredom and held a revolver to my temple.

Then a loud thump startled everyone. General Celexa burst into the room, trailing a cloud of cigar smoke. He looked suspiciously tan. Had he been off vacationing with Sensible Girl? I didn't have time to ponder this question because as soon as he entered the room, the demons pointed their weapons at him.

"Stop it right there," barked Anxiety in a high, quavery voice. He did not sound the least bit authoritative, but he was wielding a large weapon. General C. stopped abruptly, his bushy eyebrows raised in surprise. I could almost hear the sound of the brakes squealing, as in a Woody Woodpecker cartoon.

"Whoa!" The sound of his gruff voice was reassuring. It had been so long since I'd heard it! Where the hell had he been?

General C. stared at the demons. They pointed their weapons at him. He backed off slowly, hands in the air.

"Crap," he muttered. "Are you okay, sister?" he asked, not taking his eyes off them.

"No," I whimpered. How could I possibly be okay? I was about to die of loneliness and boredom. I hoped they could at least shoot straight so that I would die right away. They didn't look overly capable to me.

"Jesus," said General C., looking at me with pity. "I didn't know things had gotten this bad." He continued his slow backward retreat toward the door. "You have to do something for me," he said. "I can't fight these guys alone anymore. If I do, I'll die trying."

"What?" I said in a weak voice. I didn't know if I *could* do anything. My body felt sapped of all energy.

"Call your f*cking psychiatrist, okay?" General C. said. Loneliness and Anxiety looked at each other. Smirked.

"Can he really help?" I whined. I was already on drugs! What more could he do besides throw me in the loony bin and forget about me?

"Yes! He can help."

Suddenly, Loneliness and Boredom lunged at General C. But he was prepared. He smacked Boredom with the butt of his rifle, knocking him over, then ran out of my bedroom and out the front door. Loneliness and Anxiety ran after him.

"Call him!" he yelled. I heard him tearing down the stairs.

Surprising myself, I jumped out of bed and ran for the phone while Boredom was out cold. Who knew I still had so much life in me? It helped to remember that one of my dear readers—just a few days ago!—had suggested I do this very thing. I speed-dialed Dr. Melville's number, left a desperate message, then threw on some clothes and fled the apartment while I still could.

Then I walked all over town. In the unseasonably warm March weather, I roamed the streets filled with mansions on north Capitol Hill. Longed for the perfect lives that the inhabitants of such beautiful homes undoubtedly had. I walked down "Pill Hill," past the hospitals, and tried not to see visions of myself in the psych ward. I walked all the way downtown and attempted to console myself by walking around Pike Place Market, where I had sold sheepskin slippers when I first moved to Seattle. What an innocent time that had been, when I still had hope that I could "succeed" in life, when I still thought love was possible!

Sensing a meltdown, I walked faster as I headed up the steep hill toward home. Momentarily, the incline reminded me of the training hike I'd been on last weekend. I brightened ever so slightly when I remembered it. Three boys and me on Tiger Mountain and we hadn't gotten lost! We had another training hike planned this weekend on Mount Si.

But who was I kidding? Quickly, the fragment of happiness slid away. I would never make it up Mount Rainier! I was too afraid of heights. What if Anxiety tackled me while I was up there? What if we had to cross a steep section and I froze, caused the entire team to stall, or, even worse, to turn around?

I walked even faster now, nearly running. I was in good shape from all of my recent workouts. But all I could think about were the things I wouldn't be able to do if I didn't get a grip: climb Mount Rainier, finish that damn book chapter that was due in four days and that I'd already gotten an extension on, fall in love with someone who was not a lying, cheating bastard, a flaky, "Little Nikki"–singing egomaniac, or a flight attendant–f*cking commitmentphobe!

Oh God. I hurried up to my door so I wouldn't start bawling on the street. When I got upstairs, fully prepared for the demons to devour me for good, I saw that my answering machine was flashing. Like a starving person falling on a piece of bread, I lunged toward it, pressed the button, and found two messages, both from doctors.

Message #1: Rachel, it sounds like you need to come in for an appointment. I have an opening in my schedule on Friday at 3 P.M. Please let me know if that works for you.

Message #2: Hey, there. Sorry I've been out of touch; I was in California for a few days for a conference. What are you doing Friday night? Want to hang out?

E-mail Breakup Babe | Comments 5

POST A COMMENT

I'm glad you called your shrink. He'll fix you right up.
She-Devil | Homepage | 3/24/03–9:07 A.M.

•   •   •   •   •

You're not going to go out with The Doctor again, are you??
The Girl from Maine | Homepage | 3/24/03–11:53 A.M.

•   •   •   •   •

I have also been feeling like I might perish from loneliness and boredom! My boyfriend dumped me two months ago and I thought

I would be over it by now but the hurt just goes on and on. Maybe it's time for me to get on some antidepressants too!
Sad Sadie | Homepage | 3/24/03–2:10 P.M.

.   .   .   .   .

What has this society come to when, as soon as people have any problems, they go rushing to take drugs to fix them? Have you tried vitamins instead? I also notice there doesn't seem to be much spirituality in your life. I suspect this is a big part of your problem. Just know that there are other answers out there besides dangerous pharmaceuticals.
Scientologist and Proud | 3/24/03–4:37 P.M.

.   .   .   .   .

Even I am now rethinking this Jewish doctor guy. I say give him a taste of his own medicine and wait five days before calling HIM back!
Little Princess | 3/24/03—6:19 P.M.

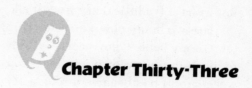

Chapter Thirty-Three

Ouch. My head hurt. Dr. Melville had warned me about this when he'd put me on the new drug, which, he said, would "boost the effectiveness of the Celexa." My stellar Empire benefits would continue for only another couple of weeks; after that I'd probably have to sell off all of my possessions to pay for the medications.

For now, the important thing was that I felt better. And if I felt better, I could write, which was the most important thing of all, considering the e-mail I'd gotten a few days earlier.

I took a sip of my Americano and glanced around the Fremont Coffee Company. Now that I was writing "full-time," I found I had to vary the places I went to hang out even more. So here I was at a funky old house that had been converted to a coffee shop. It had hardwood floors and several different rooms. I leaned back in my chair and stretched.

It was much quieter here than in Victrola. Then again, it

was noon on a Wednesday; not exactly a high time for most people to be hanging out in coffee shops. Or maybe it was just my own head that was quieter. I felt like I'd stepped off the roller coaster I'd been hurtling around on for the last month. But I was still a little dizzy from it all.

For two hours now, I'd been writing a first draft for chapter 2 of my book. I'd managed—barely—to get the first chapter done in time to turn it in for the last writing class. Only a week late! It had been very rough, of course. It still didn't all "snap." But it was nonetheless a complete draft and the structure was in place. That much I could tell.

I winced as I remembered the circumstances under which I'd managed to finish it. After getting that message from the dashing doctor last week, my mood had taken a quick upward swing. Oh yes, his excuse for not calling was pathetic, but I was even more pathetic. I'd called him back immediately and invited him to a party with me on Friday. Then I'd rushed out the door with my laptop to take advantage of the surge in happy hormone.

Ay. I put my aching head in my hands. The doctor. What a joke! At least I'd *known* that I was being deluded. Lonely, sad, depressed little me, I just couldn't help myself!

Well, that seemed to be changing, thanks to the latest in designer antidepressants and a few dramatic events. I would give myself an hour to blog about it, then get back to my real work.

Thursday, April 3, 2003
12:14 PM Breakup Babe

Move along, move along. Nothing to see here except one unemployed, drugged-up writer trying to pick up the pieces of her life and move on.

Oh God, you're saying. What happened this time? Let us guess. The Doctor disappeared again! In your weakened state, you let him sweep you up in his spell, then he turned tail and ran, leaving you even more destitute than before!

That is a very good guess. But, no.

I came close, it's true. I was seconds—mere seconds—away from falling back into his embrace. Then Sensible Girl flew back from Florida to rescue me. Rather, she staged an intervention with a whole cast of characters, including General C., GalPal #1, and Sexy Boy, to save me from the self-destruction I was about to wreak.

Oh, this sounds juicy, you're saying. *Tell us more!*

As I prepared to dish, a conversation flashed through my head. A few days earlier, GalPal #3 and I had been IMing while she was supposed to be analyzing samples of mouse poop for her big E. coli study.

Jane says: So, I have a question. Are you always going to be Breakup Babe?

Rachel says: I hope not! Although I'm living up to that name pretty damn well these days, aren't I?

Jane: Yeah. And I'm just wondering: Do you think the name Breakup Babe might be jinxing you? Just a little?

Rachel says: I don't know. Do you think so?

Jane: Not that I want you to get rid of Breakup Babe! It's the first thing I read every morning. It's just that as your friend, I feel compelled to say that perhaps something like "Bound for the Altar, Babe" might create better karma for you. You know what I mean?

I stared off into the distance for a few moments, remembering this exchange. It gave me an unpleasant feeling now. The truth of it was like a kernel of corn stuck in my teeth. When I'd created the name "Breakup Babe," it had been in reference to The Great Unpleasantness. It wasn't supposed to spawn a cottage industry of breakups.

Then I pushed the thought away. I would think about it later. I'd been to hell and back this weekend! Didn't I deserve to blog about it? To entertain my readers and get love and catharsis back in return?

So here is *le scoop*.

The Doctor accompanied me to a party last Friday night wherein a group of my friends gathered to celebrate the glorious occasion of GuyPal #1's engagement.

In the last few months, as I'd been chasing inappropriate men down dead-end streets, dumping soup on my ex-boyfriend, and getting fired, GuyPal #1 had fallen in love with—surprise—Jenny! Six months after we'd all flown to San Juan Island, and Jenny had held *my* hand, the two of them were tying the knot and jetting off to Tahiti for their honeymoon.

"No, I don't feel jealous at all." Sexy Boy was addressing me, The Doctor, GalPal #1, and her boyfriend, The Professor, while waving a glass of champagne in the air. Someone had asked SB how he felt about the fact that Jenny had been his prospect before GuyPal #1 "stole" her away.

"I like to share my women," continued Sexy Boy, glancing at me with a sly smile. Everyone laughed appreciatively, except me. I was still irrationally annoyed about the whole Jenny–San Juan Island incident. At least my feelings for SB were firmly under control tonight because of The Doctor's presence. The Doctor was looking quite handsome, I thought, except for that Tintin hairdo, which had made an unfortunate reappearance.

"So," said Sexy Boy, giving The Doctor the once-over, "we hear you're a surgeon?"

"Yes, I am," said The Doctor, taking a sip of his drink. He'd had an awful lot to drink in a short time. I wasn't sure, exactly, what number drink he was on, but I thought maybe it was his third. We'd been at the party for forty-five minutes.

I, unfortunately, was not drinking at all. Dr. Melville had put me on a new drug called BuSpar that he said would help the Celexa start to work again. "It's very common for the Celexa to lose its effectiveness over time," he'd said. "The BuSpar will help it, and it has very few side effects."

This was great news. I wasn't thrilled to be such a druggie, but it beat getting thrown into the loony bin! He'd warned me, however, not to drink for the first week. "Give your body some time to get used to this," he'd said, looking sternly at me over his unfashionably large pink-framed glasses. "It would be best if you avoided alcohol for at least a week."

"Of course!" I was so grateful at that moment, I would have sacrificed my firstborn to the God of Pharmaceuticals if Dr. Melville had asked me to. Whatever got the demons under control! Though now that I was at a party, where everyone else was drinking and I was nervous about the impression my date was making, it would have been nice to have a drink. Just a little one.

"What kind of surgery do you do?" said The Professor, who had his arm around GalPal #1. As usual, he had a semidistracted look on his handsome face, as if he were really thinking about the effects of aesthetic and economic trends on German cinema in the period just following the fall of the Berlin Wall. I shot a glance at GalPal #1, wondering what she thought of The Doctor so far. She watched him with intense concentration, as if listening to evidence in one of the murder trials she argued. Her face didn't give anything away.

"Well, I put people back together who've had horrible accidents. The worse the accident, the more likely I am to get them." The Doctor glanced around at the group to see how they reacted to this.

"Is that so?" said Sexy Boy. I glanced at him. Was it possible I detected a slight *tone* in his voice? A jealous tone, perhaps?

"Yep." The Doctor didn't seem to notice the tone. "I just had a patient last week"—he took another sip of his drink—"a climber who fell a thousand feet on Rainier. He broke thirty-three bones in his body. I sewed him up."

Oh God. I was going on my next Mount Rainier training hike tomorrow. What was I thinking? I should cancel. Just forget the whole damn thing.

"Oh yeah," said GalPal #1. "I read about that guy! Is he going to be okay?"

"Well, as okay as you can be when you've suffered major fractures in every part of your body and severed your spinal cord, which is to say, not really that okay. The guy will probably be in a wheelchair for the rest of his life. But he's lucky to be alive at all."

The flip tone in The Doctor's voice surprised me. He'd been so sweet when I last saw him. I'd conveniently forgotten about his arrogant side. The group was silent for a moment. I hoped maybe The Doctor would ask the rest of them what they did for a living. But instead he looked around expectantly.

GalPal #1 played along. "So who was the most messed up patient you've had to put back together?" She was already predisposed not to like The Doctor, I knew.

"I don't trust this guy," she'd said over the phone after The Doctor and I had gone on our date at the Brite Lite Lounge. "Once a guy backs off like that, they'll usually do it again."

"I know, I know." I wasn't exactly sure where she got her information, because it seemed men never backed off from her. They fell madly in love with her and wanted to stay with her forever. "That's why I'm not getting back together with him! We're just going to hang out," I said.

What a liar I was! Of course I wanted to get back together with him. He was a man, wasn't he? My standards—never the highest—had completely disappeared in my post-Empire-firing *crise d'identité*.

"Oh, let's see," said The Doctor, clearly relishing GalPal #1's question. "There was the guy who jumped off the Aurora Bridge, a woman who was in an elevator accident in the Columbia Tower . . ."

Ten minutes later, I snuck off to the kitchen for a drink. Dr. Melville hadn't actually said I *couldn't* drink, he just suggested I *didn't*. Well, I didn't feel a damn thing from the new drug and I needed a drink.

The Doctor was still regaling everyone with his tales of horrible accidents and miraculous surgery. I couldn't tell if they were entertained, repulsed, or bored to tears. I myself didn't know how I felt. That's why I needed a drink. Besides, even though the demons had been absent the last few days, there was an undercurrent of sadness I couldn't shake.

The blissful union of GuyPal #1 and Jenny, for one, wasn't doing much for me. GuyPal #1 had been on a so-called dating hiatus when they met! How unfair was that? To make matters worse, he'd said to me dreamily a couple of weeks back, "It's true what they say, you know. You find love when you're not looking for it." Well, screw that! I poured a glass of tonic water and put a generous serving of vodka in.

Even if I didn't like GuyPal #1's bullsh*t advice, I was still jealous. What a great feeling it must be to love someone and have her love you back enough to want to marry you! But I'd had that feeling once not so long ago, hadn't I? With Loser. *And it all turned out to be a sham!* I added more vodka and took a giant swig of my drink.

Two drinks later, I was standing next to The Doctor watching GuyPal #1 and Jenny give a sappy little speech about how they met. They told the story of the flight to San Juan Island, getting lots of laughs along the way. Even I, feeling giddy and a bit light-headed by now, laughed at their stupid jokes. Then I leaned over and whispered in The Doctor's ear, "The funny thing is, Jenny and GuyPal #1 didn't even know each other then, and when she got scared, she reached over and held MY hand!" I sprayed his ear a little with saliva, but he didn't seem to notice.

He turned to me. The look on his face was familiar, though I couldn't place it. My vision was a bit blurry. "She held your hand?" he said. "Like this?" The Doctor took my hand in his, interlaced his fingers with mine. His hand was so *warm.*

Suddenly, I wasn't listening to what GuyPal #1 and Jenny were saying anymore. My attention zoomed to my right hand, which The Doctor was now holding. His fingers gently massaged mine. He kept his eyes on me but I looked down. I could feel his breathing speed up. My own sped up in response.

I knew, without a doubt, that if I turned my face toward his, he would kiss me. Gently at first, then more passionately. Soon his hands would be in my hair, on my face—just like they had been in the car that time, and—oh my God, it would feel sooo . . .

Awful. I felt awful.

"Excuse me," I mumbled, then ran out of the living room, into the kitchen, then out into the backyard. I had not felt this nauseated in a long time. I knelt on the ground and laid my arms down in front of me. An innocent bystander versed in yoga might have thought I was doing Child's Pose, instead of preparing to vomit.

"Well, this is a fine mess you've gotten yourself into, isn't it?" a familiar voice said. "I take off for a month and you completely lose it."

I didn't have to look up to know it was Sensible Girl. "Leave her alone," came another, more tipsy-sounding voice. Needy Girl. "She's been through a rough time lately!"

"Clearly." Sensible Girl sounded much tougher than she had on New Year's Eve, which was the last time I'd seen her. "That's because you've been in charge around here."

I retched. God, I felt awful.

"Well, guess what?" said Sensible Girl. "Your reign of terror is over."

"Reign of terror!" Needy Girl let out a drunken cackle. "That's a good one! So, what, you expect to take off for however long you please, then come back and just take OVER? Go back to Florida and leave us alone!" Someone took a few steps.

"Don't go near her!" said Sensible Girl. I retched again. I wished something would just come up already. I wondered if The Doctor was going to come out after me and see how I was. Would I confess to him the story of the alcohol and the antidepressants? How would he feel about me then?

"Oh, please, you fat, boring loser, would you just go AWAY?" Suddenly there was running. Shouting. More voices.

"All of you, get out of here! We run the show now!" The demons. Needy Girl screamed. I realized with a start how desperately Needy Girl had tried to protect me from the demons these last few months. In the end, she'd only helped their cause. I retched again.

"Fat chance, you pieces of scum." General C.! I hadn't even heard him approach. He must have been practicing guerrilla warfare techniques.

Then a full-scale battle erupted above me. Punching. Screaming. Yelling.

"Ow! Stop that!"

"I am so sick of you!"

"Take that, you good for nothing—"

"Ouch! Hey, this is a new dress. Would you—"

"Get out of here before I do more damage! If you think we were just getting a tan in Florida, you were wrong." Sensible Girl's voice rang out, unafraid, through GuyPal #1's backyard. "We were learning how to deal with riffraff like you!"

"You think you're so— OUCH!"

"We better get out of here—"

WHAM!

Someone fell to the ground with a thud, then picked themselves up off the ground and ran. More running feet followed behind. Then I vomited for a few minutes. When I was done, it was silent outside. I rolled over onto my back. In the sky, a few stars managed to shine weakly through the cloud cover.

I heard people coming out the back door and sat up quickly. Too quickly. My head started to spin again. I made a halfhearted attempt to get up, then collapsed back onto the ground.

"There you are! Are you okay?" said GalPal #1, rushing over to me. I had never heard such alarm in her voice. She probably thought I was having a heart attack. I wasn't normally one to get drunk, much less get sick from too much alcohol—though the one and only time I had, GalPal #1 had been right there with me. We were at a party our sophomore year of college. I'd been drinking Jim Beam straight from the bottle. GalPal #1 had been doing a beer bong. When I got sick on the balcony of whoever's apartment it was, she rushed to my aid even though a group of long-haired musician boys had been gathered around her while she regaled them with tales of her cousin who was a roadie for Prince. She got sick about half an hour later. As far as I knew, it had been her last bout with alcohol poisoning too.

"I think so," I said, feeling dizzy and humiliated. I got even more embarrassed when I saw that Sexy Boy was with her. I wiped my arm across my face.

"What happened?" she said, kneeling next to me in the wet grass. "Are you sure you're okay?!" The scent of White Linen wafted over me. She'd been wearing that perfume ever since I met her in our freshman-year Peace and Conflict Studies class. A few minutes ago it would have made me sicker, but now I found it comforting.

"I wasn't drinking that much. It's just, well, I wasn't really supposed to be drinking tonight because of those"—here I glanced sheepishly over at Sexy Boy—"new drugs." Sexy Boy knew about my antidepressants but, with him being a fan of "self-medication," I got the feeling he disapproved (the hypocrite).

"I think maybe she just got nauseated from hearing that doctor talk about himself all night long," said Sexy Boy, who walked over to the other side of me. "We should get you inside where it's warm," he said, taking my left arm.

"Oh God," said GalPal #1, taking my other arm. "He is really obnoxious. You know that, right?"

The two of them lifted me off the ground. I felt better, but so tired all of a sudden.

"You can bring that guy to parties or whatever because he's kind of entertaining, but you're not allowed to date him," said GalPal #1. "Plus, I think he's got a drinking problem. I've never seen anyone put back so many drinks." The three of us walked slowly toward the kitchen door. I was wobbly and my head still spun slightly, but at least the nausea was gone.

"If you date him, we'll be forced to kill him, and then you might not like us anymore," said Sexy Boy. GalPal #1 laughed. I laughed too, but a little less enthusiastically. We walked in through the kitchen door and there was The Doctor downing a straight shot of vodka. He put down his glass quickly when he saw us.

"Heeyy," he said, "where ya been? I missed you." His Tintin lock bounced around in front of his head. Then he noticed that Gal-Pal #1 and Sexy Boy both had their hands on my arms. He got a concerned look on his face. "You okay?"

"Um, sort of," I said. The sound of John Coltrane's music mixed with laughing voices filtered into the kitchen from the living room. "I'm not feeling very well, though; I think I have to go home."

"Well, lemme take you home, then," he said.

In my girlhood, I'd always had crushes on TV doctors. Paramedics John Gage and Roy DeSoto from *Emergency 1*. Adam Bricker on the *Love Boat*. Noah Drake (played by handsome rocker Rick Springfield) on *General Hospital*. I knew if they were my husbands I would never have to worry about a thing.

This doctor, however, was far drunker than me and in no shape to take care of anyone.

Before I could say anything, GalPal #1 spoke. "No, that's okay; I'll do it," she said in a tone that made it nearly impossible to argue.

"Oh. Are you sure?" said The Doctor. He looked at me and his big brown eyes widened in a hurt way. If GalPal #1 had not been all business, I might have taken pity on him.

"Yes," she said to The Doctor, not allowing me to speak. "I was going to leave anyway. Just stay and enjoy the party." She smiled a completely fake smile.

"Hey, brother, how about another shot of that vodka?" said Sexy Boy to The Doctor. Then he turned to me. "You take care, Miss R. I'll call you tomorrow to see how you're doing."

I felt a rush of warmth toward Sexy Boy. It was nice to know that in the disaster zone that had been my dating life these last six months, I'd found a friend, at least (no matter what else we might be at times).

The Doctor opened his mouth to say something else but GalPal #1 hustled me out of the room before he could.

"Let's go," she said.

That was the last I saw of The Doctor. With Sensible Girl's tri-
umphant return, I could no longer justify my association with him.

I looked up from my computer. The light had shifted and
was now lying in bars on the hardwood floor of the Fremont
Coffee Company. My God, I'd been writing for an hour without stopping. It had been quite a while since time had flown
this way. I glanced over at the next table, where the twentysomething female occupant appeared absorbed in the book
Good in Bed by Jennifer Weiner. I stared at the cover. I'd seen
that book everywhere lately. It showed a pair of crossed female calves resting on top of a pink blanket. Pink, the color of
chick-lit covers everywhere!

I let my mind wander to my own book cover. What might
it look like? No doubt the publishers would insist on pink
somewhere. I would fight it, of course, but maybe not too
hard, because, after all, I had to admit to myself that I was a
chick-lit writer. Sure it would be nice if I could be the next
James Joyce. But since I hadn't even been able to finish reading *Ulysses* in college, that wasn't likely. An image came into
my head. A pink background. A typewriter. A stylized woman
bursting out of the typewriter as if it were a cake. That stylized woman, of course, being me! Breakup Babe!

Jeez. I'd say those new drugs were working pretty good!
"Euphoria or unusual excitement might be one of the more
pleasant side effects of this drug," Dr. Melville had said as he
wrote out the prescription.

But, I thought to myself as I took a sip of my lukewarm
coffee, didn't I have just a little more cause for such flights of
fantasy now? Two days after the engagement party, when I'd
finally gotten over my hangover, I'd gotten an unexpected
e-mail. I was planning to tell my readers about it but I'd saved
the best for last.

It wasn't exactly easy to let The Doctor go, seeing as he was my only prospect. The day after the party, he even called, all sweet and sober, to see how I was and to apologize for how drunk he'd gotten! But I did let him go. Because even I, apparently, have my limits.

Then a piece of good news came at exactly the right time to make my jobless, sexless existence easier to bear.

Remember four months ago when my book proposal got rejected by Greensleeves Press? Well, at the same time that I'd sent it to them, I also sent it to a family friend who happens to be an editor at one of the big New York publishing houses. I'd waited eagerly for her response, but I never heard back. A month passed. Two months. Then I got embarrassed. Clearly she was ignoring me because I was a talentless hack and she didn't want to be the one to tell me.

But yesterday I heard from her, and here is what she said.

Hi, R.,

I am so sorry for the long delay in getting back to you! It has been crazy around here. But I want you to know that I read your proposal and sample all the way through and was very impressed! So impressed, in fact, that yesterday I plopped myself down in the office of our senior editor and told him all about your project. He really liked the sound of it and wanted me to communicate to you that if you could get him three sample chapters (or 50 pages) by July 1 at the latest, then he would consider it for a new series of books he's doing called "Love and Work in the Information Age." There's no guarantee, of course, that he would buy it, but I can tell you that getting this far is quite an accomplishment. I'm not sure how far along you are in your writing. Do you think you can have three chapters done by then?

I was beside myself when I got this e-mail, of course. My first reaction had been to burst into tears (slightly embarrassing because I'd been in a coffee shop at the time), then to call everyone I knew.

Now the celebrating is done and it's time to do this thing.

Plenty of time on my hands? *Check.*

Demons under control via pharmaceuticals? *Check.*

Hot But Inappropriate Boys (HBIBs) banished to the sidelines for now? *Check.*

Desire to write a book more than anything else in the world? *Check.*

So here I go.

Ready. Set. *Write.*

E-mail Breakup Babe | Comments 4

POST A COMMENT

Go, B.B. That completely rocks! I knew you had it in you to write a book!

GenieG | Homepage | 4/03/03–5:10 P.M.

•   •   •   •   •

Good job for dumping The Doctor, getting loaded on good drugs, and getting a potential book deal. Not bad for a week's work.

Knut | Homepage | 4/03/03–5:10 P.M.

•   •   •   •   •

Loser and Empire will rue the day they dumped you.

El Politico | Homepage | 4/03/03–10:48 P.M.

•   •   •   •   •

Well, I have to say I'm disappointed we never found out the size of The Doctor's c*ck. Just be sure there's lots of hot s*x in the book, okay?

Delilah | Homepage | 4/04/03–10:23 A.M.

Chapter Thirty-Four

I stared at the ledge in front of me. It was about two feet wide and ten feet long. On one side of it was a crevasse, on the other a cliff that dropped off at ninety degrees. Spread out below it was a wonderland of ice, snow, and crevasses.

Holy. Mother. Of. God.

I stared at it, trying to will my body forward. I'd crossed this section on the way up. Why hadn't it looked quite so scary then?

Oh, *right*.

I hadn't been looking down.

Well, I told myself, as I stared at the airy view, at least I'd already made it to the top. When they found my body at the bottom of this valley (along with the bodies of my hapless teammates whom I would pull down with me when I fell) my family would at least have the comfort of knowing I'd seen the summit.

This thought did not help.

The other thing about this spot was that there was a fixed line set up specifically for people to hold on to. And although I'd held on to it on the way up, our Northwest Mountaineering guide Noah had instructed me not to use it this time. He himself had already crossed the ledge without a moment's hesitation and was now waiting for me on the other side. "Use your ice ax here instead of the fixed line," he'd called back to me. Noah was first on the rope, I was second, and my teammates were behind me.

"Why?" I called back, knowing that I was stalling for time. You didn't really question an N.M. guide; you just did what they said.

"I just think you're better off using your ice ax." Noah sounded irritated. Last night, as we'd eaten dinner at base camp, he'd been chatty and charming and friendly. Ever since we started the summit climb at 1 A.M., he'd sounded like a drill sergeant. No doubt he just wanted to get us down, even though the climb had gone very smoothly so far. We'd summited at 7 A.M. and enjoyed a sunny hour on the top, exhausted and elated as we posed for pictures with all of Washington state below us. Except for a headache that had disappeared after ten thousand feet, my body had done me proud. I'd certainly had my Moments o' Terror, especially as we approached the spot where eleven climbers had been swept away by a giant block of falling ice in 1981 (as I knew from my obsessive Internet research), but I'd kept it together pretty well mentally. Until now.

"Are you coming, Rachel?" said Noah. He was getting impatient. I could tell he was about to get angry. He wanted us off this mountain before the day got too hot and the avalanche danger increased.

"Yes, I'm coming," I said, not moving. I stood staring at the ledge. I thought about ignoring his advice. Every instinct I had told me to hold on to that rope for dear life. (Actually, every instinct I had told me to lie down, pound my arms into the ground and yell, "I don't waaannnt to!" as had been a frequent tactic of mine at age three to avoid onerous tasks such as eating green beans or taking a bath.) But his instincts were probably a little better than mine in this situation. And if I didn't move soon, he would yell at me. Despite the fact that I was wearing giant bug-eyed glacier glasses, I still had my pride. I did not want to be yelled at by a hot young mountain guide, especially one who had already rescued me once from an embarrassing situation.

I took a deep breath. I had a Russian great-uncle whom I saw only sporadically but who was famous in our family for his hard-drinking ways and risky international business ventures. His favorite saying was, "We all gonna die anyway." I'd whispered that phrase to myself several times today already. Now I repeated it to myself again. Then, legs trembling, I took a tiny step forward. My crampons crunched in the snow.

A few days before the climb, I'd been at Victrola writing my blog. I wanted to be sure I said good-bye to everyone, including my readers, in case I never returned from the mountain.

Sunday, June 29, 2003

2:16 PM Breakup Babe

Well! That was a long three months! I have just sent chapters 1–3 off to their uncertain fate.

As empires were built, babies were born, wars were fought, marriages dissolved, I obsessed about just the right way to describe my first date with The Doctor and how to portray my ambivalence over the Li'l Rockclimbing Spy. Remember those oldies but goodies?

Yes! That is my life. It's not a bad life, really. Because when I get lonely in the morning, as I often do these days, I just plunge back into the world of my book and there are all my old friends—and enemies! Sexy Boy, the pilot who is just a little more dashing in the book than he is in real life! GalPal #1 in all her wavy-haired, White-

Linen-smelling glory! And certain other people, who I can make as badly dressed, overweight, and psychotic as I choose!

As you know, for these past few months I have—gasp!—not had a boyfriend! Instead, as I mull over my recent misadventures in love, and try to feel lonely without feeling afraid, I have had books. Books have been my friends since I was little and will be my friends until such time as I no longer have eyes that can see (or, if worse comes to worst, ears that can hear).

If I get lonely in the evening, as I often do, it disappears when I crawl into bed with a book. Fictional worlds that it took other authors years to create, I tear through in weeks or days. I mingle with transvestites in the 70s, alcoholics in the 90s, Dutch servant girls in the 1800s. The better the writing, the more I feel the texture of the worlds, and the less lonely I am.

Of course, books (and little pink pills) are not always enough. I rely heavily on my friends, with their open arms, full refrigerators, and spare beds. Going to the mountains every weekend has helped too. It's so hard to hold on to petty worries among ancient trees and sparkling lakes (or when you can hardly breathe because the incline is so steep).

Back at sea level, I still have my bad moments. They usually happen in the morning when loneliness hits me the hardest. In a sudden fit of desperation, I'll draft an e-mail to Long-Distance Boy or The Doctor. I'll dial six digits of Sexy Boy's number and hang up. Or I'll feverishly review the available men on Nervy.com like an addict looking to score drugs.

But I've learned something about impulse control in the last few months. If I can ignore an impulse for just a couple of hours, it will go away. I might sob and wail during those two hours and feel oh so sorry for myself because clearly I am the most unlovable pariah who ever lived, but once the meltdown is over, I can usually get back to doing whatever it is that needs doing.

Which, of course, is writing. The most important thing is that through it all, I've managed to write almost every single day—

through the kinds of feelings that previously sent me careening through the streets of Seattle grasping at hot but inappropriate boys (HBIBs).

I realized, after The Doctor debacle, that ever since The Great Unpleasantness I'd been dating out of fear. Out of a natural desire to love and be loved, yes, but *so* compulsively! Each guy would soothe that fear for a nanosecond, but when it would end, the fear and loneliness were worse than before.

So I've decided to just live with loneliness for a while. If I can live with it, I will be less afraid of it, and if I'm less afraid, I can make better decisions about my love life. (Or so I think in my more lucid moments. In my less lucid moments, I crank all the saddest country songs I know and soak the carpet with my tears.)

This dating-free period hasn't made for the best blogging, but it has helped to clear my head. And I've started to wonder if perhaps it isn't time to retire Breakup Babe. Because if I ever want to find a man who can commit for more than a week, maybe I need to stop looking for *material*, if you know what I mean.

It's just a nascent thought, so don't fret quite yet! It will take some time for me to send Breakup Babe to the great beyond, given that she (and you) saved my life this last year, *and* grew my confidence as a writer, *and* gave me the book idea that will rocket me to best-sellerdom (or at least the remainder table).

Meanwhile, all this plotting might be moot, because in three days I will be climbing a big-a*s mountain called Rainier. I might not make it down alive (and yes, GalPal #3, the red couch will be yours). If we do not meet again, please know that I ♥ you all.

E-mail Breakup Babe | Comments 0

A minute after I'd finished this entry, GalPal #2 walked into Victrola and sat down across from me. Her year-old daughter, Celia, was asleep in a sling. "They're going to love it!" she said, putting my manuscript down on the table. "I was reading it at work today; I couldn't stop! The third chapter is great. I have only a few comments." She had thoroughly read my chapters and critiqued them, as had my sister and my writing teacher, Byron, whom I'd hired as a private coach to help me get these chapters ready for Myra.

I'd learned from hard experience that it was important to get feedback early on in a project. Back when I'd tried to write *Temporary Insanity*, I'd slaved away for a year and a half without showing it to anyone. When I finally did, the negative comments I got destroyed all my forward momentum. Breakup Babe the book, on the other hand, had been born in a community of people. So I wasn't nearly as scared to let people critique it. Plus, I knew it was good. Or at least better than anything I'd written before. In his final comments on my third chapter, Byron had written:

> You're a very talented writer and this is great stuff; it needs to be published, and not just on a blog!

"So," said GalPal #2, after getting her coffee, "if they like it, what does that mean? Will you get a big advance?" She leaned on her elbows on the table and looked at me, childlike in her anticipation and excitement. Her yoga-sculpted shoulder muscles peeked out from under a short-sleeved blouse that she'd borrowed from me a month ago and refused to give back.

"Oh, I doubt it," I said. I thought, a bit sadly, how GalPal #2 would always have that blouse to remember me by should I disappear forever into a crevasse the next weekend. Celia, of course, would not remember me at all despite the good times we'd had together in her short life.

"But you would get an advance, right?" GalPal #2 seemed more than unusually pumped up, despite the decaf soy latte she was drinking.

"I think so."

The truth was that even if my wildest dreams came true and Myra's boss bought the book and gave me an advance, I would still (1) have to get a job and (2) spend at least another year writing the book.

At the thought of getting another job, I felt a stab of dejection. I was still traumatized by getting fired from Empire. Though I'd been sending out the requisite three resumes a week so the state wouldn't cut off my unemployment money, I really had no idea what kind of job I would get next.

"What's wrong?" said GalPal #2, who saw my expression change.

"I don't know . . . ," I said. "I guess I just don't know what I'm going to do for a living. I'm obviously not fit to hold down a job."

"Oh, come on!" GalPal #2 rolled her eyes. Out of all my friends, GalPal #2 was the least likely to let me indulge in self-pity.

I sighed heavily. Suddenly I felt transported back to age twenty-two, when I'd just graduated from college, when it seemed so unfair that all I wanted to do in life was be an *artiste,* but I would instead have to work for a living.

"I thought you actually missed working," she said. "Missed the structure and stuff?"

"I do, sort of. I just can't go back to a job like that; it was so boring." I glanced over at the cute barista. Wondered if he liked his job or was just doing it until he got his big break as an actor or a writer or something. He was as cute as ever, but in my current dating hiatus, I could actually look at him without getting all nervous or excited or desperate to talk to him. It was so very Zen of me.

"So don't! This is your chance to do something else! Like teaching writing to kids. Isn't that something you want to do? Or being a full-time freelance writer.

"Hey, look at that painting," said GalPal #2, her attention

span now stretched to the limit. She pointed to a piece from Victrola's most current art display. It was cartoonlike, depicting a bright blue whale joyously jumping out of a vivid green ocean. An orange sun smiled down on the whale. "Wouldn't that look good in Celia's room?"

"Yeah," I said, gazing at the picture, but my heart wasn't in it. I was too busy telling myself what I couldn't do. I couldn't go back to Empire, even as a contractor. I couldn't teach writing to kids—not enough money. I couldn't be a full-time freelancer—too hard. So what was I supposed to do with myself now?

Funny how such all-consuming worries could disappear when one misstep meant falling to your death and bringing four other people with you.

All my earthly concerns were now forgotten. The void spread out below me as I walked farther onto the ledge. *Don't look down.* I tried to dig my ice ax in as I walked, to secure myself in case I fell, but the ice ax barely penetrated the surface of the hard snow. So much for that plan.

"Rachel!"

God, what did he *want*?! "You're walking too fast and creating slack in the rope. Come on, now!" The harsh tone in Noah's voice stung me, even as I teetered thousands of feet above the ground. But he was right. In my terror, I'd been walking faster than him, and now the length of rope between us lay on the ground, limp and coiled in the middle. If I were to fall, the chances that he could arrest my fall were drastically decreased if the rope had slack in it. "You need to stop for a second so I can tighten up the rope. Then I want you to slow down!"

Are you fucking kidding! I wanted to say. *I'm not going to stop!* But I did. As if watching a movie, I saw myself—clad in black fleece pants, a black polypropylene top, a white climb-ing helmet and giant bug-eyed glacier glasses—pause on this sunny ledge straddling the abyss.

Then something strange happened. My mind became crystal clear.

This—right here—represented my ultimate fear, the thing I'd had nightmares about, the reason I'd never climbed Mount Rainier before.

But I stopped thinking about that.

The whole team would self-arrest with their ice axes if I fell. Still, it wouldn't do much good on this section. Gravity would take over. We'd all go down.

But I stopped thinking about that, too.

There were times in life when it was good to think about the big picture. This was not one of them.

So I stopped thinking. Except about what I was going to do next. Which for the moment was stand here until Noah told me to start moving again. Standing was easy enough, right? I'd been doing it since age one.

"All right!" said Noah. "Let's go!"

I took a step forward. That wasn't too hard. I took an-other. Walking was another skill I'd acquired a long time ago. Around me, the Emmons Glacier gleamed in the sun. Distant crevasses glowed blue. But I didn't notice any of that right now. I was focused only on the next step. And the next.

Then, almost as soon as it had started, it was over.

"Good job, Rachel," said Noah, under his breath, but now he was moving forward as the teammate behind me stepped onto the ledge.

"Thank you!!" I wanted to say. I resisted the urge to fling myself at him and say "I survived, I survived!" *Most accidents happen on the way down,* I reminded myself sternly. One of my fellow climbers could go plunging off that ledge. Or we could get caught in an avalanche on the way down. Or—I found my mind racing ahead again—I could fall and slip on the rocky Disappointment Cleaver, where there was no snow to self-arrest in. I couldn't stop paying attention yet.

So I didn't. Instead I followed behind Noah, trying to focus only on the next step.

An hour and a half later, we made it down Disappointment Cleaver and descended the lower part of the Ingraham Glacier.

We'd last been here at three this morning, which now seemed like a lifetime ago. I'd been too terrified then to appreciate the immense sky, the multitude of stars, the ghostly grandeur of the mountain. I could barely even enjoy the sight of the northern lights that Noah had pointed out to us, flashing white like a lighthouse beacon.

Now tears came to my eyes as the panorama of the Ingraham flats unfolded. The hardest part of the climb was over. I'd done it!

A celebratory mood overtook the group as we sat down for our last rest stop. People were laughing and chatting in a way they hadn't been before. At the previous stops, everyone had been too busy stuffing food into their mouths, catching their breath, and worrying about the next part of the climb.

I sat down next to Noah. Now that I suspected I would survive, I felt self-conscious about how I looked. I wished to God I could take my helmet and my glacier glasses off. I remembered my gym-fueled fantasy, suddenly, about going to my book launch party in New York City with my hot mountaineering guide boyfriend by my side.

God.

I quickly opened the top of my pack and dug around for snacks. At least the sunglasses hid my embarrassed expression.

"So, Rachel," said Noah. "What's next?"

"Hmm?" I said, my mouth full of half-frozen Oreo crumbs.

"Well," he said, turning to me, and I could see the summit of Rainier reflected in his glasses, "you said you'd been wanting to climb Rainier for years. So I'm just wondering what your next big challenge is."

I paused. Debating. Should I tell him?

"I'm—um—writing a book." I prayed he wouldn't ask me what it was about.

"Oh, really? What's it about?"

Right then.

"It's about . . ." Blogging? Dating? All the lame men I've dated in the last year? Heartbreak? Writing? Giant cocks? "It's a memoir," I said, "about how grief can inspire us to do things we thought we could never do." Not bad for the spur of the moment. I mentally patted myself on the back.

"Huh," he said, smiling. "Will the Rainier climb be in your book?" He had a beautiful smile. His teeth were almost as white as the glacier.

"I don't know. I hadn't thought about that." I smiled back. I hoped I didn't have Oreo crumbs stuck in my teeth.

"Cool. Well, if it is, you have to tell me when it comes out. I'd like an autographed copy."

The night before, Noah had ambled over and sat down next to me while I was eating dinner. Or trying to eat, anyway. Nerves had taken away my appetite. It was 4:30 in the afternoon. We'd have to get in bed by 6 P.M. and be up again by midnight to start the climb.

But his relaxed manner immediately had a soothing effect on me. As soon as he plopped himself down next to me, he said, "So did your friend recover okay from that trip? He seemed pretty stressed out." Noah stretched out his long legs and leaned back on his elbows on the ground—the complete opposite of someone who was stressed out.

I, of course, had recognized Noah instantly when he'd been introduced to me two days before. A few weeks ago, I'd been surfing the Web, compulsively looking up horrible accidents on Mount Rainier, and had stumbled across his picture. No wonder he'd looked so familiar when Jake and I had run into him on the trail! About a year and a half ago, he'd been involved in a high-profile rescue on Rainier in which he'd single-handedly rescued four climbers who'd fallen into a crevasse on a winter climb.

When I ran across this article, a memory suddenly came back to me. I recalled watching him on the news while sitting on the couch next to Loser, thinking longingly about how handsome and windblown he looked as the news crews interrogated him about the accident. He was rugged and independent in a way that Loser would never be. Loser refused to put his Kenneth Cole–clad feet anywhere near a crevasse. No wonder we had always fought so much about outdoor activities.

When I found the article online and put the pieces together, I'd been thrilled and slightly embarrassed to realize I'd been "rescued" from Tiger Mountain by a quasi-celebrity mountain climber. (I toyed with the idea of e-mailing the article to Jake, then thought better of it.) I wondered, briefly, if he would be my guide for the upcoming trip, then dismissed that idea. Northwest Mountaineering was a huge guide service and that would be far too much of a coincidence.

So imagine my surprise when, voilà, who should be introduced to me as my head guide but Noah, aka Mr. Self-Sufficiency. He didn't recognize me right away when we met, but he did say, "You look really familiar. Have we met before?"

Mortification took over and I almost didn't tell him who I was. But in the end I did and he laughed out loud. "Oh, that's right!" he said. "How could I forget? My daring Tiger Mountain rescue." Had I been a blusher, I would have been beet red, but his tone was warm and I didn't feel as if I were being mocked—not too much, anyway. "I'll have to keep a close eye on you," he'd said, then winked at me.

We hadn't talked about it again until the next night at base camp, when he sat down next to me and asked about whether Jake had "recovered" from the trip.

"Well, I'm not sure," I said. "We had a bit of a falling out after that and I haven't talked to him in a while." Might as well make sure Noah knew we weren't a couple. In the distance, Mount Saint Helens blew the faintest bit of steam.

"Oh, that's too bad."

"Not really," I said. He laughed a little, drawing squiggly lines in the dirt with a stick. It reminded me of the many hours my sister and I had passed on family backpacking trips doing the exact same thing.

"It was good thing you showed up," I said. "If you hadn't, we'd still be there!"

"Yeah, I've heard there are whole hordes of lost Seattleites dwelling under rocks and in caves in the Tiger Mountain vicinity." Then we both laughed. He seemed so much friendlier now than he had that day; friendlier, too, than he had been on the five-hour slog up to base camp, or all through today's climb.

Now as I looked at that heart-stopping grin again, I knew not to take it personally that Noah had transformed himself into a drill sergeant during the climb. That was his professional persona. I liked this flirty, friendly one better.

"Of course you can have an autographed copy," I said. "As long as you get me down off this thing alive."

"It's a deal."

I looked away from Noah and back at the equally stunning scenery. Nearby, Little Tahoma, Washington's third-highest peak, shimmered like a mirage. Next to me was a beautiful man, all around me were mountains, and I'd just climbed the biggest one of them all. I couldn't remember feeling this happy in a long time.

Then a pang of sadness penetrated my euphoria. I wished I could tell my dad about this. He would have been so proud of me! Better yet, I wished he were *here*. But, I reminded myself, as I drank the dregs of my Cytomax, he was always with me when I was in the mountains. It was his legacy to me. He had taught me to love the mountains. If it weren't for him, I wouldn't even be here.

I plucked another piece of Oreo from my bag. I wished I could stay in this spot forever, this place of empowerment, with the hardest part just behind me and the triumph still to savor, with a hot guy by my side, who had not yet revealed any of the unsuitable qualities he undoubtedly possessed (i.e., commitmentphobia, alcoholism, inability to hold down a job. Oops, wait, that was me!).

I knew, when I went back down, that there would be more struggle. That my book might or might not sell. I knew that even if it did, I would struggle with the writing of it, and that I would fight with loneliness and boredom, just as I always had. I knew that I might fall in love soon, that I might not, that I would probably get my heart broken again. That I would have to find a job, and the process would make me feel like a worthless speck of dirt.

But, I thought, casting a sideways glance at Noah, who was now devouring a chicken thigh, happiness would come again. I was finally learning that it was not something that you could hold on to, but that it always came back sooner or later—sometimes for a short stay, sometimes for a longer stay.

I'd counted on Loser to bring me happiness, and he had—for a while. Then he made me very unhappy for a while, and now I was happy again.

A light wind blew across the glacier. By now we weren't putting on the heavy parkas when we took a break. Most people just wore a single layer. We were baking in the bright sun, even brighter because it was reflecting off the snow. It was strange to imagine this place in bad weather, when the wind came howling through and a whiteout turned everything into a featureless mass of gray. The bad weather would come, though, that was certain. Then, after that, the sun would return.

"Everyone ready to head out?" said Noah. "It should be a quick trip back to base camp. We'll spend about an hour there packing up our stuff, then we'll take off."

No one, of course, wanted to head down. But there were books to write, jobs to find, friends to celebrate with. We put our heavy packs back on and headed down the mountain.

PHOTO: © BRADLEY HANSON

REBECCA AGIEWICH lives in Seattle, where she has dated some of the city's most eligible bachelors and almost all of the ineligible ones. She also plays keyboards in a country rock band, roughs it in the mountains, and writes her blog, Breakup Babe (http://breakupbabe.blogspot.com), at assorted Seattle coffeehouses. Her travel writing has appeared in the *Seattle Post-Intelligencer* and *Lonely Planet Seattle*. This is her first novel.